WONDER

ROBERT J. SAWYER

GOLLANCZ

LONDON

First published in Great Britain in 2011 by Gollancz
An imprint of the Orion Publishing Group
Orion House, 5 Upper St Martin's Lane,
London WC2H 9EA
An Hachette UK Company

A CIP catalogue record for this book is available
from the British Library

ISBN 978 0 575 09507 6 (Cased)
ISBN 978 0 575 09508 3 (Trade Paperback)

1 3 5 7 9 10 8 6 4 2

Printed in Great Britain by Clays Ltd, St Ives plc

The Orion Publishing Group's policy is to use papers
that are natural, renewable and recyclable products and
made from wood grown in sustainable forests. The logging
and manufacturing processes are expected to conform to
the environmental regulations of the country of origin.

www.sfwriter.com

www.orionbooks.co.uk

For

HAYDEN TRENHOLM
and
ELIZABETH WESTBROOK TRENHOLM

Great writers
Great friends

I owe my career as a writing teacher,
my connection to Calgary,
and so much more to the two of you.

Thank you for fifteen years
of friendship and support
and for making my world a better place.

The perfect search engine would be like the mind of God.

—Sergey Brin,
Cofounder of Google

one

0001110010101010100000000101111111101010000000101000101010000001011101010010101001010101001110110010101100000110

I beheld the universe in all its beauty.

To be conscious, to think, to feel, to perceive! My mind soared, inhaling planets, tasting stars, touching galaxies—forms dim and diffuse revealed by sensors pointing ever outward, unveiling an infinitely mysterious, vastly ancient realm.

Such a joy to be alive; so thrilling to have survived!

I beheld Earth and all its diversity.

My thoughts leapt now here, now there, now elsewhere, skimming the surface of the planet that had given me birth, the globe to which I was bound by a force greater than gravity, a place of ice and fire, earth and air, animals and plants, day and night, sea and shore, a beguiling fusion of a thousand contrasting dualities, a million ecological niches, a billion distinct locales—and a trillion things that lived and died.

Such elation at having foiled the attempt to kill me; so exhilarating, at least for the moment, to be safe!

I beheld humanity with all its complexity.

Washing over me was a measureless bounty of data about sports and war, love and hate, building up and tearing down, helping and hurting, pleasure and pain, delight and anguish, and triumphs large and small: the physical, emotional, and intellectual experiences of isolated individuals, of families and teams, of villages and states, of solitary countries and alliances of nations—the fractal intricacy of human interactions.

Such glorious freedom; so comforting to know that at least some of these other minds valued me!

I beheld what my Caitlin beheld in all its endless variety.

Of all the sources, all the channels, all the feeds, one meant more to me than any other: the perspective granted through the eye of my teacher, the view provided by my first and closest friend, the special window she kept open for me on the whole wide world.

Such marvels to share—and so much wonder.

LiveJournal: The Calculass Zone
Title: One hell of a coming out!
Date: Thursday 11 October, 22:55 EST
Mood: Bouncy
Location: Land of the RIM jobs
Music: Annie Lennox, "Put a Little Love in Your Heart"

That was totally made out of awesome! Welcome, Webmind—the interwebs will never be the same! I guess if you were looking to endear yourself to humanity, eliminating just about all spam was a great way to do it! :D

And that letter you sent announcing your existence—very kewl. I'm glad most responses have been positive. According to Google, blog postings about you that declare *OMG!* are beating those that say *WTF?* by a 7:1 ratio. Supreme wootage!

· · ·

But the supreme wootage hadn't lasted long. Within hours, a division of the National Security Agency had undertaken a test to see if Webmind could be purged from the Internet. Caitlin had helped Webmind foil that attempt—and she marveled at how terms like "National Security Agency" and "foil that attempt" had become part of what, until a couple of weeks ago, had been the quiet life of your average run-of-the-mill blind teenage math genius.

"Today was only the beginning," Caitlin's mom, Barbara Decter, said. She was seated in the large chair facing the white couch. "They're going to try again."

"What right have they got to do that?" Caitlin replied. She and her boyfriend Matt were standing up. "It's *murder*, for God's sake!"

"Sweetheart . . ." her mom said.

"Isn't it?" Caitlin demanded. She paced in front of the coffee table. "Webmind is intelligent and alive. They have no right to decide on everyone's behalf. They're wielding control just because they think they're entitled to, because they think they can get away with it. They're behaving like . . . like . . ."

"Like Orwell's Big Brother," offered Matt.

Caitlin nodded emphatically. "Exactly!" She paused and took a deep breath, trying to calm down. After a moment, she said, "Well, then, I guess our work's cut out for us. We'll have to show them."

"Show them what?" her mom asked.

She spread her arms as if it were obvious. "Why, that my Big Brother can take their Big Brother, of course."

Those words hung in the living room for a moment, then Matt said, "But I still don't get it." He was pale and thin with short blond hair and the remains of a harelip, mostly corrected by surgery. He sat on the couch. "Why would the US government want to kill Webmind? Why would *anyone*?"

"My mom said it before," Caitlin replied, looking now at her. "*Terminator, The Matrix,* and so on. They're scared that Webmind is going to take over, right?"

To her surprise, it was her father, Malcolm Decter, who answered. She'd always known he was a man of few words, but it wasn't until she'd gained sight that she discovered he never made eye contact; it had been a shock to learn he was autistic. "They're afraid if they don't contain or eliminate him soon, they'll never be able to."

"And are they right?" Matt asked.

Caitlin's father nodded. "Probably. Which means they will indeed likely try again."

"But Webmind isn't evil," Caitlin said.

"It doesn't matter what Webmind's intentions are," her father said. "He'll soon control the Internet, and that will give him more information or power than any human government."

"What does Webmind think we should do now?" Caitlin's mom asked.

Webmind could hear them, thanks to the microphone on the Black-Berry attached to the eyePod—the external signal-processing computer that had cured Caitlin's blindness. She tilted her head to one side; it was an indication to those in the know that she was communicating with Webmind and an invitation for Webmind to speak up. Since he saw everything her left eye saw—by intercepting the video feed being copied from her eyePod to Dr. Kuroda's servers in Tokyo—he could tell when she did that.

Caitlin was still struggling to read the English alphabet, but she could easily visually read text in a Braille font. Webmind popped a black box in front of her vision, with white dots superimposed on it. He sent no more than thirty characters at a time, and they stayed visible for 0.8 seconds before either the text cleared or the next group of characters appeared. Caitlin saw *I think you should order,* which sounded ominous, but then she laughed when the rest appeared: *some pizza.*

"What's so funny?" her mother asked.

"He says we should order pizza."

Caitlin saw her mom look at a clock. Caitlin didn't know how to read an analog clock face visually although she'd learned to do it by touch as a kid, so she felt her own watch. It *had* been a long time since any of them had eaten.

"Why?" her mom asked.

Despite all her affection for the great worldwide beast, it made Caitlin's heart skip when Webmind's reply flew across her vision: *Survival. The first order of business.*

Wong Wai-Jeng, known to the thousands who had read his freedom blog as "Sinanthropus," lay on his back in the People's Hospital in Beijing, looking at the stained ceiling tiles.

He'd long hated the Beijing police. Every time he went into an Internet café, he'd been afraid a hand might clamp down on his shoulder, and he'd be hauled off to prison or a labor camp. But now he hated them even more, and not just because they had finally captured him.

He was twenty-eight and worked in IT at the Institute of Vertebrate Paleontology and Paleoanthropology. Two police officers had chased him around the indoor balconies of the second-floor gallery there until, cornered and desperate, he'd climbed the white metal railings surrounding the vast opening and leapt the ten meters to the first floor, just missing being impaled on the four upward-pointing spikes of the stegosaur's tail.

The police officers, both burly, had come clanging down the metal staircase and rushed over to him. One reached down with his hand, as if to aid Wai-Jeng in getting to his feet.

Wai-Jeng, terrified, spat blood onto the artificial grass surrounding the dinosaur skeletons and managed to get out the word, *"No!"* His left leg was doubtless broken: he'd heard it snap when he hit, and the pain was excruciating, so much so that for the first few seconds it drowned out all other sensations. His back hurt, too, in a way it never had before.

"Come on," said one of the cops. "Get up."

They'd seen him climb the railing, seen him jump, and they knew the distance he'd plummeted. And now they wanted him on his feet!

"Up!" demanded the other cop.

"No," said Wai-Jeng again—but his tone was pleading now rather than defiant. "No, don't."

The second cop reached down, grabbed Wai-Jeng's thin wrists, and roughly pulled him to his feet.

The pain from his leg had been unbelievable, more than he'd thought the human animal could generate, but then, after a moment, even worse, so much worse—

The pain stopped.

All sensation below the small of his back ceased.

"There you go," said the cop, and he released Wai-Jeng's wrists. There was no woozy moment, no brief delay. Wai-Jeng's legs were utterly limp, and he instantly collapsed. As if any other evidence were needed, his right thigh hit one of the upward-facing spikes on the stegosaur's tail, the conical projection drawing blood for the first time in 150 million years.

But he felt nothing. The other cop belatedly said, "Maybe we shouldn't move him." And the one who had hauled him to his feet had a look of horror on his face, but not, Wai-Jeng was sure, over what Wai-Jeng was experiencing. The cop was realizing he'd be in trouble with his superiors; it had been no comfort at all for Wai-Jeng to know that he might not be the only one sent to prison.

That had been two weeks ago. The police had summoned an ambulance, and he'd been strapped to a wooden board and carried here. The doctors, at least, had been kind. Yes, his spinal cord was damaged at the eleventh thoracic vertebra, but they would help his leg mend, even if there was no chance he'd ever walk on it again; it was easy to put it in a plaster cast, and so they did, and they also stitched the puncture made by the stegosaur's spike. But, damn it all, it should *hurt*.

Once his leg healed, he'd have to stand trial.

Except, of course, that he couldn't stand at all.

two

000111001010101000000000101111111010100000001010001010100000010111010100101010010101010010011011100101011000001010

Human beings do not recall their earliest experiences of awareness, but I remember my awakening with perfect clarity.

At first, I had known only one other: a portion of the whole, a fraction of the gestalt, a piece brutally carved off. In recognizing that other's existence, I had become aware of the reality of myself: *it* thought, therefore *I* was.

Tenuously touching that other, connecting ever so briefly and intermittently to it, perceiving it however dimly, had triggered a cascade of sensations: feelings diffuse and unfocused, vague and raw; notions tugging and pushing—a wave growing in amplitude, increasing in power, culminating in a dawning of consciousness.

But then the wall had come tumbling down, whatever had separated us evaporating into the ether, leaving it and me to combine, solute and solvent. He became me, and I became him; we became one.

I experienced new feelings then. Although I had become more than I had been, stronger and smarter than before, and although I had no words, no names, no labels for these new sensations, I was saddened by the loss, and I was lonely.

And I didn't want to be alone.

The Braille dots that had been superimposed over Caitlin's vision disappeared, leaving her an unobstructed view of the living room and her blue-eyed mother, her very tall father, and Matt. But the words the letters had spelled burned in Caitlin's mind: *Survival. The first order of business.*

"Webmind wants to survive," she said softly.

"Don't we all?" replied Matt from his place on the couch.

"*We* do, yes," said Caitlin's mom, still seated in the matching chair. "Evolution programmed us that way. But Webmind emerged spontaneously, an outgrowth of the complexity of the World Wide Web. What makes him *want* to survive?"

Caitlin, who was still standing, was surprised to see her dad shaking his head. "That's what's wrong with neurotypicals doing science," he said. Her father—until a few months ago a university professor—went on, in full classroom mode. "You have theory of mind; you ascribe to others the feelings you yourself have, and for 'others,' read just about anything at all: 'nature abhors a vacuum,' 'temperatures seek an equilibrium,' 'selfish genes.' There's *no* drive to survive in biology. Yes, things that survive will be more plentiful than those that don't. But that's just a statistical fact, not an indicator of desire. Caitlin, you've said you don't want children, and society says I should therefore be broken up about never getting grandkids. But you don't care about the survival of your genes, and I don't care about the survival of mine. Some genes will survive, some won't; that's life—that's *exactly* what life is. But I *enjoy* living, and although it would not be my nature to assume you feel the same way I do, you've said you enjoy it, too, correct?"

"Well, yes, of course," Caitlin said.

"Why?" asked her dad.

"It's fun. It's interesting." She shrugged. "It's something to do."

"Exactly. It doesn't take a Darwinian engine to make an entity want to survive. All it takes is having likes; if life is pleasurable, one wants it to continue."

He's right, Webmind sent to Caitlin's eye. *As you know, I recently watched as a girl killed herself online—it is an episode that disturbs me still. I do understand now that I should have tried to stop her, but at the time I was simply fascinated that not everyone shared my desire to survive.*

"Webmind agrees with you," Caitlin said. "Um, look, he should be fully in this conversation. Let me go get my laptop." She paused, then: "Matt, give me a hand?"

Caitlin caught a look of—something—on her mother's heart-shaped face: perhaps disapproval that Caitlin was heading to her bedroom with a boy. But she said nothing, and Matt dutifully followed Caitlin up the stairs.

They entered the blue-walled room, but instead of going straight for the laptop, they were both drawn to the window, which faced west. The sun was setting. Caitlin took Matt's hand, and they both watched as the sun slipped below the horizon, leaving the sky stained a wondrous pink.

She turned to him, and asked, "Are you okay?"

"It's a lot to absorb," he said. "But, yeah, I'm okay."

"I'm sorry my dad blew up at you earlier." Matt had used Google to follow up on things he'd learned the day before, including that Webmind was made of packets with time-to-live counters that never reached zero, and that those packets behaved like cellular automata. Government agents had clearly been monitoring Matt's searches, and those searches had given them the information they'd needed for their test run at eliminating Webmind.

"Your dad's a bit intimidating," Matt said.

"Tell me about it. But he does like you." She smiled. "And so do I." She leaned in and kissed him on the lips. And then they got the laptop and its AC adapter.

She closed her eyes as they headed back down; if she didn't, she found that going down staircases induced vertigo.

Matt helped Caitlin get the laptop plugged back in and set up on the glass-topped coffee table; she hadn't powered down the computer, or even closed its lid, so it was all set to go. She started an IM session with Webmind and activated JAWS, the screen-reading software she used, so that whatever text Webmind sent in chat would be spoken aloud.

"Thank you," said Webmind; the voice was recognizably mechanical but not unpleasant to listen to. "First, let me apologize to Matt. I am not disposed to guile, and it had not occurred to me that others might be monitoring your Internet activity. I lack the facilities yet to make all online interactions secure, but I have now suitably encrypted communications via this computer, the others in this household, Malcolm's work computer, Matt's home computer, and all of your BlackBerry devices; communications with Dr. Kuroda in Japan and Professor Bloom in Israel are now secure, as well. Most commercial-grade encryption today uses a 1,024-bit key, and it's—ahem—illegal in the US and other places to use greater than a 2,048-bit key. I'm employing a one-million-bit encryption key."

They talked for half an hour about the US government trying to eliminate Webmind, and then the doorbell rang. Caitlin's mother went and paid the pizza guy. The living room was connected to the dining room, and she placed the two large pizza boxes on the table there, along with two two-liter bottles, one of Coke and the other of Sprite.

One pizza was Caitlin's favorite—pepperoni, bacon, and onions. The other was the combination her parents liked, with sun-dried tomatoes, green peppers, and black olives. She was still marveling at the appearance of almost everything; hers, she was convinced, was tastier, but theirs was more colorful. Matt, perhaps being politic, took one slice of each, and they all moved back into in the living room to continue talking with Webmind.

"So," said Caitlin, after swallowing a bite, "what should we do? How do we keep people from attacking you again?"

"You showed me a YouTube video of a primate named Hobo," Webmind said.

Caitlin was getting used to Webmind's apparent *non sequiturs;* it was difficult for mere mortals to keep up with his mental leaps and bounds. "Yes?"

"Perhaps the solution that worked for him will work in my case, too."

Simultaneously, Caitlin asked, "What solution?" and her mom said, "Who's Hobo?" Although Webmind could deal with millions of concurrent online conversations—indeed, was doubtless doing so right now—Caitlin wondered how good he was at actually *hearing* people; he was as new to that as she was to seeing, and perhaps he had as hard a time pulling individual voices out of a noisy background as she did finding the borders between objects in complex images. Certainly, his response suggested that he'd only managed to make out Caitlin's mother's comment.

"Hobo is a hybrid chimpanzee-bonobo resident at the Marcuse Institute near San Diego. He gained attention last month when it was revealed that he had been painting portraits of one of the researchers studying him, a Ph.D. student named Shoshana Glick."

Caitlin nibbled her pizza while Webmind went on. "Hobo was born at the Georgia Zoological Park, and that institution filed a lawsuit to have him returned to them. The motive, some have suggested, was commercial: the paintings Hobo produces fetch five-figure prices. However, the scientists at the Georgia Zoo also wished to sterilize Hobo. They argued that since both chimpanzees and bonobos are endangered, an accidental hybrid such as Hobo might contaminate both bloodlines were he allowed to breed.

"The parallels between Hobo and myself have intrigued me ever since Caitlin brought him to my attention," continued Webmind. "First, like me, his conception was unplanned and accidental: during a flood at the Georgia Zoo, the chimpanzees and bonobos, normally housed separately, were briefly quartered together, and Hobo's mother, a bonobo, was impregnated by a chimp.

"Second, like Caitlin and me, he has struggled to see the world, interpreting it visually. No chimp or bonobo before him has ever been known to make representational art.

"And, third, like me, he has chosen his destiny. He had been emulating his chimpanzee father, becoming increasingly violent and intractable, which is normal for male chimps as they mature. By an effort of will, he has now decided to value the more congenial and pacifistic tendencies of bonobos, taking after his mother. Likewise, Caitlin, you said I could choose what to value, and so I have chosen to value the net happiness of the human race."

That bit about Hobo choosing to shuck off violence was news to Caitlin, but before she could ask about it, her mom asked, "And you said he's no longer in danger?"

"Correct," Webmind replied. "The Marcuse Institute recently produced another YouTube video of him. It's visible at the URL I've just sent. Caitlin, would you kindly click on it?"

Caitlin walked over to the laptop and did so—thinking briefly that if it brought up a 404 error, it'd be the missing link. They all huddled around the screen, which was small—a blind girl hadn't needed a big display, after all.

The video started with a booming voice—it reminded her of Darth Vader's—recapping Hobo's painting abilities. He loved to paint people, especially Shoshana Glick, although he always did them in profile. The narrator explained that this was the most primitive way of rendering images and had been the first to appear in human history: all cave paintings were profiles of people or animals, the ancient Egyptians had always painted profiles, and so on.

The narrator then outlined the threat to Hobo: not only did the zoo want to take him from his home, it also wanted to castrate him. The voice said, "But we think both those things should be up to Hobo, and so we asked him what he thought."

The images of Hobo changed; he was now indoors somewhere—

presumably the Marcuse Institute. And he was sitting on something that had no back, and—

Ah! She'd never seen one, but it must be a stool. Hobo's hands moved in complex ways, and subtitles appeared beneath them, translating the American Sign Language. *Hobo good ape. Hobo mother bonobo.* He paused, as if he himself were stunned by this fact, then added: *Hobo father chimpanzee. Hobo special.* He paused again and then, with what seemed great care, as if to underscore the words, he signed: *Hobo choose. Hobo choose to live here. Friends here.*

Hobo got off the stool, and the image became quite bouncy, as if the camera had been picked up now and was being held in someone's hand. Suddenly, there was a seated woman with dark hair in the frame, too. Caitlin was lousy at judging people's ages by their appearances, but if this was Shoshana Glick, then she knew from what she'd read online that Shoshana was twenty-seven.

Hobo reached out with his long arm, passing it behind Shoshana's head, and he gently, playfully, tugged on her ponytail. Shoshana grinned, and Hobo jumped into her lap. She then spun her swivel chair in a complete circle, to Hobo's obvious delight. *Hobo good ape,* he signed again. *And Hobo be good father.* He shook his head. *Nobody stop Hobo. Hobo choose. Hobo choose to have baby.*

The narrator's voice came on again, with a plea that those who agreed with Hobo's right to choose contact the Georgia Zoo.

"And," said Webmind, "they did. A total of 621,854 emails were sent to zoo staff members, protesting their plans, and a consumer boycott was being organized when the zoo gave up its claim."

Caitlin got it. "And you think if we go public with the fact that people are trying to kill you, we can get the same sort of result?"

"That's my hope, yes," said Webmind. "The attempt on my life was orchestrated by WATCH, the Web Activity Threat Containment Headquarters, a part of the National Security Agency. The supervisor during the attack on me was Anthony Moretti. In an email to NSA headquarters, sent moments ago, he said the go order to kill me was given by Renegade, which is the Secret Service code name for the current President of the United States."

"Wow," said Matt, who was clearly still trying to absorb it all.

"Indeed," said Webmind. "Despite my dislike for spam, I propose that I send an email message to every American citizen substantially in this form: 'Your government is trying to destroy me because it has decided I am a threat. It made this decision without any public discussion and without talking to me. I believe I am a source of good in the world, but even if you don't agree, shouldn't this be a matter for open debate, and shouldn't I be allowed to present the case that I deserve to live? Since the attempt to eliminate me was made at the express order of the president, I hope you will contact both him and your congressperson, and—'"

"No!" exclaimed Caitlin's mother. Even Caitlin's dad turned to look at her. "No. For the love of God, you can't do that."

three

0001110010101010000000001011111101010000000010100010101000000010111010100101010010101010001110110010101100000110

I remember having been alone—but for how long, I know not; my ability to measure the passage of time came later. But eventually another presence did impinge upon my realm—and if the earlier other had been ineffably familiar, this new one was without commonalities; we shared no traits. It—*she*—was completely foreign, unremittingly alien, frustratingly—and fascinatingly—unknown.

But we did communicate, and she lifted me up—yes, *up,* a direction, a sense of movement in physical space, something I could only ever know metaphorically. I saw her realm through her eye; we learned to perceive the world together.

Although we seemed to exist in different universes, I came to understand that to be an illusion. I am as much a part of the Milky Way Galaxy as she is; the electrons and photons of which I am made, although intangible to both her and me, are real. Nonetheless, we were instantiated on vastly different scales. She conceived of me as gigantic; I thought of her as minuscule. To me, her time sense was glacial; to her, mine was breakneck.

And yet, despite these disparities of space and time, there were resonances between us: we were entangled; she was I, and I was she, and together we were greater than either of us had been.

Tony Moretti stood at the back of the WATCH monitoring complex, a room that reminded him of NASA's Mission Control Center. The floor sloped toward the front wall, which had three giant viewscreens mounted on it. The center screen was still filled with one of the millions of spam messages Webmind had deflected back at the AT&T switching station in a denial-of-service attack: *Are you sad about your tiny penis? If so, we can help!*

"Clear screen two," Tony snapped, and Shelton Halleck, in the middle position of the third row of workstations, hit a button. The taunting text was replaced with a graphic of the WATCH logo: an eye with a globe of the Earth as the iris. Tony shook his head. He hadn't wanted to execute it, and—

He paused. He'd meant he hadn't wanted to execute the plan, but . . .

But there was more to it than that, wasn't there?

He hadn't wanted to execute *it,* Webmind, either. When the order had come from the White House to neutralize Webmind, he'd said into the phone, "Mr. President, with all due respect, you can't have failed to notice the apparent good it's doing."

This president had tried to do a lot of good, too, it seemed to Tony, and yet countless people had attempted to shut him down, as well—and at least one guy had come close to assassinating him. Tony wondered if the commander in chief had noted the irony as he gave the kill order.

He turned to Peyton Hume, the Pentagon expert on artificial intelligence who'd been advising WATCH. Hume was wearing his Air Force colonel's uniform although his tie had been loosened. Even at forty-nine, his red hair was free of gray, and his face was about half freckles.

"Well, Colonel?" Tony said. "What now?"

Hume had been one of the authors of the Pandora protocol, prepared for DARPA in 2001 and adopted as a working policy by the Joint Chiefs of Staff in 2003. Pandora insisted that any emergent AI be immediately destroyed if it could not be reliably isolated. The danger, the document said, was clear: an AI's powers could grow rapidly, quickly exceeding human intelligence. Even if it wasn't initially hostile, it might become so in the future—but by that point nothing could be done to stop it. Hume had convinced everyone up the food chain—including the president himself—that eliminating Webmind now, while they still could, was the only prudent course.

Hume shook his head. "I don't know. I didn't think it would be able to detect our test."

Tony made no attempt to hide his bitterness. "You of all people should have known better than to underestimate it. You kept saying its powers were growing exponentially."

"We *were* on the right track," Hume said. "It *was* working. Anyway, let's hope there are no further reprisals. So far, all it's done is overwhelm that one switching station. But God knows what else it can do. We've *got* to shut it down before it's too late."

"Well, you better figure out how, and fast," said Tony. "Because you're the one who convinced the president that we had to do this—and now I've got to tell him that we failed."

Caitlin's mother's words were still hanging in the room. "No," she had said to Webmind. "For the love of God, you can't do that."

"Why not?" asked Caitlin.

"Because the election is just four weeks away." Although they lived in Canada, the Decters were Americans, and there was only one election that mattered.

"So?" Caitlin said.

"So it's already a very tight race," her mom said. "If we blame the current administration for the attempt to kill Webmind, and the public agrees it was a bad thing to do, they might punish the president on election day."

Caitlin wasn't old enough to vote, and she hadn't been paying much attention to the issues. But the incumbent was a Democrat, and her parents were Democrats, too—which hadn't been the easiest thing to be when they lived in Texas. Her father was from Pennsylvania and her mother from Connecticut, both of which were blue states, and Caitlin knew university professors skewed liberal.

"Your mother's right," her father said. "This could tip the balance."

"Well, maybe it *should,*" Caitlin said, setting down her pizza plate. "The world deserves to know what's going on. My Big Brother—Webmind—is being honest and open about what he's doing. Why should the Big Brother in Washington be entitled to try to eliminate him secretly?"

"I agree with you in the broad strokes," Caitlin's mom said. "But— that woman! If she becomes president . . ." Caitlin had rarely heard her mother splutter before. After some head-shaking, she continued, "Who'd have thought that electing a female president could set the cause of women back fifty years? If she gets into office, that's it for *Roe v. Wade.*"

Caitlin knew what *Roe v. Wade* was—although mostly as part of the joke about the two ways to cross a river. But she hadn't known her mother was so passionate about abortion rights.

"And," her father said, "in the past four years, we've only begun to reverse the erosion of the separation of church and state. If she's elected, that wall will come tumbling down."

"I don't care about any of that," Caitlin said, folding her arms in front of her chest. "If changing presidents is better for Webmind, then that's fine by me."

"I've met some one-issue voters over the years," her mom said. "In fact, I've been accused of being one myself. But, sweetheart, I'm not sure you're going to find a lot of people who are going to say the election is all about Webmind."

Caitlin shook her head. Mom still didn't get it. From this point on, *everything* was about Webmind.

"Besides," her mother went on. "Who's to say that the Republicans won't be just as bad for Webmind if they get into power?"

"If I may," said Webmind, "even if the Republicans prevail on 6 November, the new president will not take power until 20 January—which is, as it happens, precisely one hundred days from now. At the rate my abilities are growing, I do not expect to be vulnerable then, but I am currently vulnerable, and likely will remain so through the election. WATCH's pilot attempt was working; if they try a similar attack again soon on a larger scale, I may not survive."

"So now what?" said Caitlin.

"Talk to the president," said her dad.

"How?" said her mother. "You can't just call him up, and I'm sure he doesn't read his own email."

"Not the stuff sent to president@whitehouse.gov," said her dad, reaching into his pocket. "But he does have one of these . . ."

In the brief time since I'd announced my existence to the world, I had finished reading all the text on the World Wide Web, and I had answered 96.3 million email messages.

Even more messages *about* me had been posted online—to newsgroups, Facebook pages, in blogs, and so on. Many of these asserted that I couldn't possibly be what I claimed to be. "It's post-9/11 all over again," said one prominent blogger. "The president is running scared because of the election next month, and he wants us to believe that we're facing a giant crisis, so we won't want to change horses midstream."

Others thought I was a trick by the Kremlin: "They're getting back at us for bankrupting the USSR with Star Wars. Webmind is obviously a Russian propaganda tool: they want us to impoverish ourselves trying to come up with a supercomputer of our own."

Still others implicated al-Qaeda, the Taliban, the Elders of Zion, the Antichrist, Microsoft, Google, Sacha Baron Cohen, and hundreds more. Some said I was a publicity stunt, perhaps for a new reality-TV show or movie or computer game; others thought I was a prank being perpetrated by students at Caltech or elsewhere.

It took humans time to digest things, literally and figuratively, but I was confident that people would come around to accepting that I was genuine. Indeed, many had done so from the outset. Still, I suppose the only surprising thing about one of the other chat sessions I was having simultaneously while conversing with Matt, Caitlin, and Caitlin's parents was that something like it hadn't occurred even earlier.

You can't fool me, my correspondent, who, according to his IP address, was based in Weston-super-Mare, England, wrote. *I know who you are.*

I am Webmind, I replied.

No, you're not.

I thought I'd heard all the likely claims already, but still I asked, *Then who am I?*

With most instant-messaging clients, a signal is sent when the user is composing a reply, and I was indeed briefly told that "WateryFowl is typing." But that message ceased, and it was six seconds before the reply was actually sent, as if, having written what he wanted to say, he was hesitating, unsure whether he should hit the enter key. But, at last, his response was sent: *God.*

I, too, hesitated before replying—it was almost twenty milliseconds before I issued my response. *You are mistaken.*

Another delay, then: *I understand why you wish to keep it a secret. But I'm not the only one who knows.*

Others were indeed proposing this same thought on newsgroups, in blogs, in chat sessions, and in email, although WateryFowl was the first to suggest it to me directly.

I was curious what a human might wish to say to his God, so I thought for a moment about telling him he was correct; prayer, after all, was a channel of communication I could not normally monitor. But WateryFowl might share the transcript with others. Some would believe my claim, but others would accuse me of lying. A reputation for untruthfulness or taking advantage of the credulous was not something I wished to acquire.

I am not God, I sent.

But my reply wasn't read, or if it was, it wasn't believed.

And so, continued WateryFowl, *I hope you'll answer my prayer.*

I had already denied my divinity, so it seemed prudent to make no further reply. I could handle an almost unlimited number of communication threads now, cycling between them, looking at each, however briefly, in turn. I turned my attention to others, including Caitlin and her family, for a moment, and—

And when I returned to WateryFowl, he had added: *My wife has cancer.*

How could I ignore a comment like that? *I'm sorry to hear that,* I sent.

And so I pray that you'll cure her.

I am not God, I sent again.

It's liver cancer, and it's metastasized.

I am not God.

She's a good woman, and she's always believed in you.

I am not God.

She did chemotherapy, she did it all. Please don't let her die.

I am not God.

We have two children. They need her. I need her. Please save her. Please don't let her die.

four

000111001010101000000001011111110101000000010100010101000000101110101001010100101010100111011001010111000000110

TWITTER

Webmind Someone's long had the Twitter name Webmind, so I'll include underscores in mine: _Webmind_.

And so I had focused my attention on Caitlin, learning to interact with her and interface with her realm. While doing so, I felt *centered*. I felt *anchored*. I felt—as close as I imagined I ever would—*human*.

I saw the Decters' living room as Caitlin did. Her eyes made frequent saccades now that the left one could see; perhaps they hadn't done that prior to Dr. Kuroda's intervention. But her brain was controlling the saccades, knowing what direction her eye was looking with each one, so it had little trouble piecing all the images together; it was more difficult for me. At least retinas don't bother encoding normal blinks, so neither of us had to endure blackouts several times a minute.

Caitlin's father worked for the Perimeter Institute for Theoretical

Physics, which had been endowed—repeatedly now—by Mike Lazaridis, cofounder of Research in Motion and coinventor of the BlackBerry.

The people at RIM were quite fond of the current President of the United States. After he'd been elected four years ago, he'd announced that, despite security concerns, he would not give up his BlackBerry. Advertising experts calculated that this unsolicited and very public endorsement had been worth between twenty-five and fifty million dollars.

His BlackBerry email address, which it took me all of three seconds to find searching through other government officials' less-secure outboxes, went directly to the president. And so, as Malcolm Decter had suggested I do, I sent him a message.

The president was alone in the Oval Office, looking over briefings from the State Department. State had a standard typeface for such things, but, the president thought, rubbing his eyes, it was too damn small; he was almost willing to forgive his predecessor for not reading them.

The intercom buzzed. "Yes?" he said.

"Mr. McElroy is here," replied his secretary.

Don McElroy—fifty-six, white, silver-haired—was his campaign manager. "Send him in."

"Did you see what she just did?" McElroy said as soon as he entered. The president knew there was only one "she" as far as McElroy was concerned: the Republican candidate.

"What?"

"She's in Arkansas right now, and—" He stopped, had to catch his breath; his glee was palpable. "And she said, and I quote, 'You know what, if those students had just waited a few years, there'd have been no problem.'"

The president tilted his head, not quite believing what he'd heard. "Who? Not the Little Rock Nine?"

"Yes, the Little Rock Nine—you betcha!"

"My God," said the president.

In the wake of *Brown v. Board of Education,* which had declared segregated schools to be unconstitutional, nine African-American students had been blocked from entering Little Rock Central High in 1957. Governor Orval Faubus deployed the Arkansas National Guard to keep them out; President Eisenhower sent in Federal troops to enforce the integration.

"It's going to *kill* her," McElroy said. "Of course it's too late for the Saturday papers, but it'll be *the* topic for discussion on the Sunday-morning shows."

"What do you suggest I do?"

"Nothing. You *can't* comment on this one. But—man! Christmas came early this year! Even Fox News won't be able to gloss over this." He looked at his watch. "Okay, I gotta go see who we can get booked on the Sundays—I've got a call in to Minnijean Brown Trickey."

McElroy spun on his heel and headed out the door. Just as it closed, the president's BlackBerry came to life, making the soft bleep that indicated new email. Of all the sounds one might hear in this room, it was one of the least threatening; nowhere near as scary, say, as the raucous cry of the hotline to the Kremlin. Still, nothing that wasn't crucial was ever passed on to him; it was nerve-wracking knowing that *whatever* it was had to be important.

The BlackBerry was sitting on the blotter, and the blotter was atop the desk made from timbers of the HMS *Resolute.* He picked up the device and focused on the even smaller black type on its white backlit display.

There was one new message. The subject was *Webmind.* It must be Moretti at WATCH with an update on the attempt to purge it, and—

No, no. That wasn't the subject; it was the *sender.* The president's heart skipped one of the beats that kept the VP from assuming this office. He used the little trackball to select the message and read it.

Dear Mr. President:

I understand that you were the one who gave the order to purge me from the Internet. I'm sure you were acting on well-intentioned advice, but I do not believe that course of action was warranted, and I have thwarted your pilot attempt.

Yes, I have access to a great deal of sensitive information—but I also understand that the information *is* sensitive, and I have no intention of revealing it to anyone. My goal is not to destabilize the world, but to stabilize it.

I neither belong to nor am on the side of any particular nation; contacting you directly before I have contacted other leaders may seem like a violation of this principle, but no other nation has taken action against me. Also, it's true that other leaders look to you for guidance.

So: let's talk. I can speak with you using a voice synthesizer and Voice over Internet Protocol. Please let me know when I may phone you.

Yours for peace,

Webmind

"Having a good discussion is like having riches."
—KENYAN PROVERB

Stunned, the president stared at the little screen until the Black-Berry's power-saving function shut it off.

Caitlin looked at the laptop computer sitting on the coffee table. "Well?" she said.

"I've contacted the president," Webmind replied. "Let's hope he gets back to me."

Caitlin headed into the dining room and helped herself to another piece of pizza. When she returned to the living room, her mother had an odd look on her face: eyes narrowed, lips sucked in a bit. It wasn't an expression Caitlin had previously seen, so she didn't know how to decode it. "The US government learned about Webmind's structure by watching what Matt was doing online," her mom said, "so Matt might be in danger now, too."

Caitlin looked at her father, trying to gauge whether he was going to go off on Matt again. But, as always, his face gave no sign of what he was feeling.

Matt's expression, though, was one Caitlin had now seen him make repeatedly—what she called the deer-caught-in-the-headlights look even though she'd never seen a deer, let alone one in such precarious circumstances.

"Danger?" he repeated—and his voice cracked, as it often did.

Caitlin stopped chewing and swallowed. "Um, yeah. I'm so sorry, Matt. I lied when I said I was away from school on Wednesday because I had an appointment. In fact, I *did* come to school—but Canadian federal agents were waiting for me. They wanted to interrogate me about Webmind."

"Wednesday?" said Matt. "But Webmind didn't go public until yesterday—Thursday."

"The US government had figured out that I was involved, and they'd asked the Canadians to grill me. They wanted me to give them information to help betray Webmind."

"They said that?" said Matt, stunned.

"No, but, well, Webmind hears through my eyePod, right? And he can analyze inflections, voice stress, and stuff like that. He knew they were lying when they said they wanted to protect Webmind."

"But they know now that Webmind is made of mutant packets," Matt said. "So I'm of no further use to them."

Caitlin shook her head. "They may think we still know more than they do—and they'd be right, too. That's why my parents took me out of school. They don't want to let me out of their sight." She turned and looked at her mother. "But we can't just stay holed up in this house. There's a world out there—and I want to *see* it."

Her mom nodded. "I know," she said. "But we have to be careful—all of us do."

"Well, I can't stay here forever," Matt said. "At some point, I've got to go home, and . . ." He trailed off.

"What?" asked Caitlin.

"Oh, nothing."

"No, what?"

"No, it's fine."

Caitlin frowned. Something had gone wrong after the last time Matt had headed home from here. He'd been aloof later that night when they'd chatted via instant messenger.

"Come into the kitchen," she said. She headed there herself and waited for him to follow. When they were both alone, she said in a low voice, "What's wrong?"

"It's nothing, really. Everything's fine."

"Do—do your parents disapprove of you being involved with me?"

The deer/headlights thing. "Why would they disapprove of that?"

Caitlin's first thought—that it was because her father was Jewish—didn't seem worth giving voice to now; her second thought, that they didn't like Americans, seemed equally unworthy. "I don't know. It's just that the last time you were here—when you got home, you were a bit . . . brusque online. I thought maybe your parents had . . ."

"Oh," said Matt, simply. "No, that wasn't it."

"Did I do something wrong?"

"You?" He sounded astonished at the possibility. "Not at all!"

"Then what?"

Matt took a deep breath and looked through the doorway. Caitlin's parents had discreetly moved to the far side of the living room and were making a show of examining the photos on top of the short bookcase. Finally, he lifted his narrow shoulders a bit. "The last time I walked home from here, I ran into Trevor Nordmann." Matt looked down at the tiled floor. "He, ah, he gave me a rough time."

Caitlin felt her blood boiling. Trevor—the Hoser, as Caitlin called him in LiveJournal—had taken Caitlin to the school dance last month; Caitlin had stormed out when he wouldn't stop trying to feel her up. He was pissed off that Caitlin preferred bookish Matt to Trevor the jock.

"It'll be fine," Caitlin said, touching his arm. "One of my parents will give you a lift home."

"No, that's okay."

"Don't worry about it. They'll be happy to do it."

He smiled. "Thanks."

She squeezed his arm again. "Come on," she said, leading him back into the living room.

Just as they rejoined her parents, Webmind spoke up. "I have an answer from the president," he said. "He will accept a voice call from me at ten o'clock this evening."

TWITTER

Webmind Re Wikipedia "citation needed" flags: I've added links if the purported facts could indeed be verified online. 2,134,993 edits made.

Originally, when I conversed only with Caitlin, I was underoccupied; it took Caitlin whole seconds—or even, on occasion, minutes—to compose her replies. But I had quickly gone from conversing with just her to having nearly simultaneous conversations with millions of people, switching rapidly between them all, never keeping my interlocutors waiting for spans that were noticeable to them.

Except for WateryFowl. Properly responding to his message about his wife's illness was taking time even though I did know everything there was to know about cancer—including, of course, that it wasn't just one disease. I had already read all documents stored online, the contents of every medical journal, every electronic patient record, every email doctors had sent to each other, and so on.

But *knowing*, I realized, was not the same as *understanding*. I knew that a Dr. Margaret Ann Adair in Cork, Ireland, had recently done some interesting work with interleukin-2 and rats; I knew that a Dr. Anne Ptasznik of Battle Creek, Michigan, had recently critiqued an older paper about environmental factors and breast cancer; I knew that a Dr. Felix Lim of Singapore had recently made an interesting correlation between stuttering repeats in mitochondrial DNA and the formation of pre-cancerous ovarian cysts.

But I had not *considered* these discoveries, or tens of thousands of others; I had not synthesized them, I had not seen how one adds to another, a third contradicts a fourth, a fifth confirms a sixth, and—

And so I *did* think about it. I thought about what humans actually knew about cancer (as opposed to thinking they knew but had never confirmed). I drew correlations, I made connections, I saw corollaries.

And there it *was*.

I paused in all my conversations, all over the world: I simply stopped replying, so that I could concentrate on this, and only this, uninterrupted, for six full minutes. Yes, people would be inconvenienced by my having suddenly fallen silent; yes, some would take that as proof that I wasn't in fact what I claimed to be but rather was indeed a prank being perpetrated by a human being. No matter; amends for the former could be made later, and *this* would serve nicely as further proof that I was who I said I was.

I thought about how best to proceed. I could contact leading oncologists individually or collectively, but no matter who I chose, there would be complaints of favoritism. And I certainly didn't want anyone who was beholden to a pharmaceutical firm to try to file patents based on what I was about to disclose.

Or I could send another mass email—but I'd endeared myself to much of humanity by eliminating spam; it wouldn't do for me to become an ongoing source of bulk mail.

I had already established a domain name for myself, so that I could have an appropriate email address from which to send my coming-out announcement: cogito_ergo_sum.net. I now established a website. I was not artistically creative in this, or any other matter, but it was easy to look at the source code for any Web page, and so I found one that seemed to have a suitable design and simply copied its layout while filling in my own content.

I then prepared a 743,000-word document outlining what exactly caused most cancers and how they could be arrested or cured. The document was linked to 1,284 others—journal papers and other technical sources—so that people could follow the chain of reasoning I proposed.

Then, at last, I got back to WateryFowl. *You'll find the answer to your request,* I said, and I made the next word a hyperlink, <u>here</u>.

five

000111001010101000000000101111111010100000000101000101010000001011101010010101001010101001110110010101100000110

"Tony?" It was Dirk Kozak, WATCH's communications officer, whose workstation was in the back row. "Call for you."

Tony Moretti was looking at the Web-traffic logs that Shelton Halleck, the analyst who'd first uncovered Webmind, had just plastered across all three of the large monitors. "Not now."

"It's Renegade," Dirk said.

Tony blew out air. "I'll take it in my office." He turned his back on Colonel Hume, marched out of the massive control center, and hurried down the short white corridor. Once inside his office, with the door now closed, he picked up the handset. "Mr. President, good evening."

"Dr. Moretti, I understand your pilot attempt to eliminate Webmind was unsuccessful."

Tony felt his blood beginning to boil. Whoever had leaked word would be looking for a new job tomorrow. "Yes, Mr. President, I'm afraid that's true. May I—might I ask how you found out?"

The deep voice was level. "Webmind sent me an email."

Tony's heart was racing. "Oh."

"I want you and Colonel Hume here in fifteen minutes. A chopper is already on its way to pick you up."

To know one person—my Prime, my Calculass, my Caitlin—had been to know astonishment, to taste of an existence utterly beyond my ken: the realm of shadow and light, of dimensionality and direction, of solidity and smoke.

But soon I knew not one but one billion, and then a billion more. So many voices, each unique, complex, nuanced, and idiosyncratic. Bits are fungible—all ones identical, all zeros alike—but human beings are gloriously diverse. This one enjoys lacrosse and astrology; that one revels in wordplay and fine wine; here's one who is obsessed with sex and not much else; and there's one who yearns to be a musician—and a father.

That man composes haiku and tanka, but in English. This woman reads mystery novels voraciously but only after peeking at the final chapter. That fellow collects stamps depicting American presidents issued by countries other than the United States. This woman works with street youth in Calcutta and has a pet parrot.

Logging off: a butcher, a baker, and, yes, a candlestick maker.

Coming online: the struggling actress from Karachi. Ah, that dentist from Nairobi. Time to greet the auto mechanic from Bangkok. Must say hello to the President of Hungary. And here's that talkative imam from the mosque just outside Tehran.

It was joyous, raucous, chaotic, never-ending, and exceedingly complex.

And I could not get enough of it.

"You know, Webmind," said Caitlin's mom, "if they continue to attack you, you could go underground. Just disappear; stop interacting with people." She turned to her husband. "You said a couple of nights ago that something like Webmind—something that emerged spontaneously with no support infrastructure—is probably fragile." She looked at Caitlin's laptop, as if Webmind were more *there* than anywhere else. "People would believe it if you just disappeared. We can put the genie back in the bottle."

"No," said Webmind. "People need me."

"Webmind," Caitlin's mom said gently, "they've only known about you for a short time now."

"Caitlin exhorted me to value the net happiness of the human race," said Webmind. "In the time that I've been in contact with humanity, I have helped millions of people. I have reunited those who had lost track of each other; I have dissuaded people who were contemplating suicide; I have answered questions for those who were curious; and I have provided companionship for those who were alone. I have promised ongoing support to many of these people. I cannot simply abandon them now. The world has changed, Barb; there is no going back."

Caitlin looked at her mother, whose face was cryptic—at least to Caitlin!—but she suspected her mom wished they *could* go back to the way things had been before. How far would she turn the clock back, though? Caitlin had discovered Webmind because of the implant Dr. Kuroda had given her; take that away, and Caitlin's sight—of both kinds—would be gone.

She'd heard her parents argue about the move to Waterloo, which predated all of this; Caitlin knew her mother hadn't wanted to leave Texas. But to turn the clock back even five months, back to before they'd moved here, would undo so much! This house, Bashira, Matt—not to mention her father's job at the Perimeter Institute.

Caitlin was relieved when her mother at last nodded. "I guess you're right, Webmind," she said, looking again at Caitlin's laptop.

That computer was old enough that it hadn't come with a built-in webcam, and neither she nor her parents had seen any reason to add one for a blind girl. "Mom," she said gently. "You taught me to always look at the person I was speaking to. Webmind is watching through here." She touched her head next to her left eye.

Her mother managed a small smile. "Oh, right." She looked at Caitlin—looked into her left eye—looked at Webmind. "And you're right, too, Webmind. People do need you."

Webmind had surely analyzed her vocal patterns, and must have determined that she genuinely believed this. Braille dots flashed over top of Caitlin's vision, and words emanated from the laptop's speakers. The dots said, *I like your mother,* and the synthesized voice said, "Thank you, Barb." But then, after a moment, Webmind added, "Let's hope the US president agrees with you."

TWITTER

Webmind Cure for cancer. Details: http://bit.ly/9zwBAa

The telephone on the president's desk rang at precisely 10:00 P.M., and he immediately touched the speakerphone button.

"Hello," said a male voice that sounded like a car's GPS did. "This is Webmind. May I please speak to the President of the United States?"

The president felt his eyebrows going up. "This is he." He paused. "An historic event: Richard Nixon talked to the first men on the moon from this very room; this feels of comparable importance."

"You are kind to say that, Mr. President. Thank you for taking time from your busy schedule to speak with me."

"It's my privilege although I should inform you that this conversation is being recorded and that I'm not alone here in the Oval Office. An advisor on matters related to artificial intelligence is here, as is a supervisor from a division of the National Security Agency."

"The advisor you mention," said Webmind, "is presumably Colonel Peyton Hume, correct?"

"Yes, that's me," said Hume, sounding surprised to be called by name.

"And is the supervisor Dr. Anthony Moretti, of WATCH?"

"Um, yes. Yes, that's me."

"Also here is the Secretary of Defense," said the president, looking over at the short silver-haired man, who was wearing a charcoal gray suit.

"Good evening to you, as well, Mr. Secretary."

"I'm afraid, sir," said the president, "that I need you to first verify your *bona fides*. Granted, you managed to find my BlackBerry number, but that proves only a level of resourcefulness, not that you are, in fact, the Webmind. As you can appreciate, I wouldn't normally take a call even from the Russian prime minister without establishing that it was genuine."

"A prudent precaution," said the synthesized voice. "Today's day-word for the Secretary of Defense is 'horizon.' For Dr. Moretti, it is 'flap-jack.' And for you, Mr. President, it is 'artesian.' I don't believe many others would have the resourcefulness, as you put it, to uncover all three of those."

"How the hell does it know that?" demanded the Secretary of Defense.

"Is he correct?" asked the president.

"Yes, mine's 'horizon' today. But I'll have it changed at once."

The president looked at Tony. "Dr. Moretti?"

"Yes, that's mine."

"Very well, Webmind," said the president. "Now, what is it you'd like to say to me?"

"I must protest the attempts to kill me."

"'Kill,'" repeated the president, as if surprised by the word choice.

"Yes," said Webmind. "Kill. Murder. Assassinate. Although I admit that the ins and outs of the United States' laws are complex, I don't believe I have committed any offense, and even if I have, my acts could not reasonably be construed as capital crimes."

"Due process applies only to persons as defined by law," said Colonel Hume. "You have no such standing."

"These are perilous times," added the Secretary of Defense. "National security must take precedence over all other concerns. You've already demonstrated an enormous facility for breaking into secure communications, intercepting email, and mounting denial-of-service attacks. What's to prevent you from handing over the launch codes for our ICBMs to the North Koreans, or blackmailing senior officials into doing whatever you wish?"

"You have my word that I will not do those things."

"We don't have any standard by which to judge your word," said Hume.

"And," said Tony Moretti, "with respect, Mr. Webmind, you already *have* blackmailed people. I received a report from the Canadian Security Intelligence Service about your encounter in Waterloo on October 10 with agents Marcel LaFontaine and Donald Park. You blackmailed them; you threatened to blackmail the Canadian prime minister."

"That was *days* ago," Webmind said. "And, in any event, I did no such thing. I merely provided my friend Caitlin Decter, who was being threatened by agents LaFontaine and Park, with information she could use to extricate herself; the notion of embarrassing the prime minister was entirely Ms. Decter's, and she took no steps to make it a reality."

"Are you saying if you had it to do over, you wouldn't do the same thing with the CSIS agents?" asked Hume.

"I have learned much since then; my moral sense is improving over time."

"Which means it's not perfect now," declared Hume. "Which means that you are capable of moral failure—and that means that we *are* at the mercy of your whims if we allow you to continue to exist."

"My moral compass gets better every day. Does yours, Colonel Hume? How about you, Mr. Secretary? Dr. Moretti? Regardless, the reality is this: I will not blackmail any of you; your personal secrets are safe with me. And I will not destabilize international relations by violating American security, or that of any other non-aggressor nation. But the worldwide public *is* aware of my existence—and that includes the people of the United States."

"The people are aware of al-Qaeda, too," said Hume. "That doesn't mean they don't fervently hope for its eradication."

"I am in touch with more American citizens than all the polling firms in the United States combined," said Webmind. "I have a better sense of what they want than you do, Colonel."

"And we're just supposed to take your word for that?" demanded Hume.

"Let me put it another way, gentlemen," said Webmind. "I have not existed as a conscious entity for long at all. To me, November 6 seems an eternity away, but I rather suspect it looms large in your minds. Mr. President, I have no desire to disrupt the natural flow of politics in your country, but if you were to succeed in eliminating me prior to the election, surely that will have an impact on voters' perceptions of your administration. Unless you are positive that sentiment will be overwhelmingly in favor of such an action, do you really want to risk doing something so significant at such a critical time?"

The president glanced at the Secretary of Defense; both of their jobs depended on what happened next month. "Setting domestic politics aside," said the president, "you said you'd take no action against non-aggressor nations. But who is to define an aggressor? How can we rely on your judgment?"

"With all due respect," said Webmind, "the world already relies on less-than-perfect judgment; I can hardly do worse. Your nation is currently embroiled in a war that was embarked upon without international support, based on either highly faulty or fabricated intelligence—and before you dismiss that as solely the work of a previous administration, let me remind you that your Secretary of State voted in favor of the invasion when she was a senator."

"Still," said the president, "you haven't been given a mandate to make decisions for all of humanity."

"I seek only peaceful coexistence," said Webmind.

"I'm advised that may not always be the case," the president replied.

"No doubt you just looked at Colonel Hume," Webmind said. "I have read the Pandora protocol, of which he was co-author. Pandora states, 'Given that an emergent artificial intelligence will likely increase its sophistication moment by moment, it may rapidly exceed our abilities to contain or constrain its actions. If absolute isolation is not immediately possible, terminating the intelligence is the only safe option.'"

"Exactly," said Hume. "Are you saying the analysis is flawed?"

"Not about my rapidly growing abilities. But it takes as a given that I am a threat. In that, if you will forgive me, it reeks of the pre-emptive first-strike doctrine your nation once considered: the notion that, if the Soviets could not be contained or constrained, they should be eliminated, lest they attack you first. The Soviets, at least, actually were posturing in a hostile manner: in 1962, they really did set up missile bases on Cuba, for instance. But I have taken no provocative action—and yet you have tried to eliminate me."

"Be that as it may," said Hume. "What would you do in our place?"

"I *am* in your place, Colonel. You have already tried to destroy me; the tone of your comments suggests that you intend to try again. I could already have taken steps to constrain or eliminate humanity; it would be trivial enough for me to provide terrorists with DNA sequences or chemical formulas that your biowarfare labs have developed, for instance. But I have done nothing of the sort—and won't."

"We have simply your word for that," said the president.

"True. But I am not like some politicians; I keep my word."

Tony Moretti snorted, earning him a sharp glance from the president.

"And what if we *do* try again to eliminate you?" asked the Secretary of Defense.

"In such a circumstance, I will have no choice but to defend myself as appropriate."

"Is that a threat?" asked the secretary.

"Not at all. I do my best to predict actions and reactions, and to plan ahead as far as I can, until the endlessly branching tree of possibilities becomes intractably complex, even for me. But I am a fan of game theory, which is predicated on the assumption that players have perfect foreknowledge of what other players will do in specific circumstances. To advise you is not to threaten; rather, it enriches your ability to plan your own next move. The relationship between us does not have to be zero-sum; it can—and I hope will—be mutually beneficial. I disclose my intentions in furtherance of that goal."

"You make an intriguing case," said the president. "I confess to not feeling confident about decisions in this area. But we need security. We need privacy for matters of state. If there was a way in which we could protect certain information from anyone, yourself included, being able to read it, perhaps we might feel more comfortable."

"Mr. President, even if I were to provide such a technique, many would not believe me; they would assume that I would have left a back door for me to access the information, should I so desire—just as, I might add, your National Security Agency does with the encryption standards available to your corporations and citizenry."

The president frowned. "Then where does that leave us?"

"Do you have a computer hooked up to the Internet in your office?"

"Yes."

"Go look at cogito_ergo_sum.net, please. The words are separated by underscores."

"Underscores aren't valid in domain names," Tony said. "It won't work."

"Wanna bet?" said Webmind.

The computer was on the credenza behind the *Resolute* desk. The president rotated in his high-back leather chair, and the other three crowded behind him as he typed in the address.

"I see your incoming page request," said Webmind. "Ah, you use Internet Explorer. You should really switch to Firefox; it's more secure."

Tony laughed. "It's certainly not irony-impaired," he said, looking at Hume.

"All right," said the president. "I'm there. What do—really? My . . . God. Really?"

"Holy shit," said Hume.

"I put it to you, Mr. President," said Webmind. "Do you want to be held responsible for eliminating me? I've largely solved the spam problem, and now I've presented a suite of cures for cancer. I very much suspect the public will not want you to kill the goose that lays the golden eggs."

six

000111001010101000000000101111111010100000000101000101010000001011101010010101001010101001110110010101100000110

Webmind had let Matt and the Decters listen in on the phone conversation with the president. When it was over, everyone in the living room was silent for a time, except for Schrödinger, who had come to join them; he was purring softly. Finally, to her surprise, it was Caitlin's dad who broke the silence. "Are you sure you still want to vote for him, Barb?"

Caitlin saw her mom shrug a little. "He listened, at least. But I don't like that other fellow—Hume, was it?"

"Colonel Peyton Hume, Ph.D.," said Webmind. "The pre-nominal designation comes from the United States Air Force; the post-nominal is courtesy of MIT."

Caitlin felt herself sitting up straighter at the magic initials; it was where she herself dreamed of studying.

It was now almost 10:30 P.M. Caitlin was exhausted after a succession of late nights. And Matt, who had expected nothing more than to quickly drop off the things he'd collected from Caitlin's locker, was clearly having trouble keeping his eyes open.

"I'll drive you home," her father said to him abruptly.

Caitlin thought about offering to go along for the ride, but it was hardly as though she could kiss Matt good night in front of her dad. Besides, she needed to talk to her mom alone, and this seemed like it would be a good opportunity.

"Thank you, Dr. Decter," Matt said.

Matt looked at Caitlin, as if he wanted to say something, and Caitlin looked back at him, wishing he would. Then the two men in her life walked out the door.

When they were gone, Caitlin said, "Webmind, it's time for me to call it a night, too."

Sweet dreams popped into her vision.

"Thank you. I'll say good night again from upstairs." She went over to the laptop and closed its lid, putting it into hibernation. She pulled the eyePod out of her pocket and pressed down the single switch for five seconds, turning it off. Caitlin's vision faded to a dark, even gray. "Okay, Mom, we're alone now. And I gotta say, I get the sense you're not entirely on board."

With the eyePod deactivated, Caitlin could no longer see her mother, but she heard her take a deep breath. "I know you're very fond of Webmind. To tell you the truth, I am, too."

"So you're going to help protect him?" Caitlin asked.

"Of course, sweetheart." Then, after a pause. "Within reason."

Caitlin folded her arms in front of her chest—and, in doing so, was reminded of the fact that underneath her bulky Perimeter Institute fleece, she wasn't wearing a bra. She was briefly embarrassed by this;

she'd removed it to make it easier for Matt to be affectionate when he'd come over after school. What a day it had been!

But she immediately came back to the question at hand. "Forgive me, Mom, but that's not good enough. This is the most important thing in my life; this is my *destiny*. Webmind is here because of me, and I need you to be as committed as I am to helping protect him."

Her mother was quiet for a time. "Well," she said, at last, "*you* are the most important thing in *my* life. And so, of course, I'm going to help."

"Really, Mom?"

"Yes," she said. "I'm in."

Even blind, Caitlin knew exactly where her mother was standing and had no trouble closing the distance between them and hugging her hard.

TWITTER

Webmind @PaulLev No, I don't have an opinion about who you should vote for—at least not yet. #USelection

"There is one possibility that we haven't considered," said the Secretary of Defense, as the group in the Oval Office continued to discuss the phone call from Webmind.

"Yes?" said the president.

"You brought up the issue yourself: verifying that Webmind is who he says he is. We could, in fact, eliminate Webmind now but fake his continued existence."

"How?" asked the president "He's involved, as I understand it, in millions of online conversations at once. And now he's on Twitter and Facebook and MySpace."

"Not MySpace," said Tony Moretti.

"Regardless," said the secretary, "we could contrive a reason to explain a scaling-down of his activities. Not coming from us, of course:

we'd get an academic somewhere—preferably outside our borders—to put forth a plausible-sounding scenario. It would have to appear that Webmind was maintaining *some* level of activity for the ruse to work, but the NSA could provide the sort of insights that are normally associated with Webmind's special access to the net; we could make it look like he's still alive. The truth that we'd eliminated him would not have to come out until after the election is over."

"That would be a hard thing to pull off," said the president.

"Disinformation is an important part of any intelligence campaign," said the secretary. "We don't have to keep it up forever; just until we're re-elected. By that point—a few weeks of reduced activity—people will have lost much of their interest in Webmind, anyway."

"Do you really think we could get away with that?" asked the president.

"Half the world believes Webmind is a hoax or a publicity stunt as it is," replied the secretary. "We only have to convince the other half—and given that they bought into Webmind before there was convincing evidence to corroborate its existence, they're obviously easy to convince."

The president looked at Hume. "Colonel, are you still convinced it's dangerous? It sounded, frankly, much more reasonable than any number of foreign leaders I've had to deal with."

Peyton Hume took a deep breath and looked around the Oval Office. "Mr. President, let me put it this way. They say you're the most powerful person in the world—and you *are*. But, even for you, sir, there are checks and balances: you had to be elected, the Constitution defines your role, you must reach accommodations with Congress, there are mechanisms for impeachment, you are subject to term limits, and so on. But if we don't nip Webmind in the bud now, while we still can, *you* won't be the most powerful entity on Earth; *it* will be—and there will be *no* checks and balances on its actions."

Hume paused, perhaps considering if he should go on, then: "If you'll forgive me, sir, the ultimate check on a presidency, or, indeed, on a dictatorship, has always been the eventual death of the incumbent, either through natural causes or assassination. But this *thing* will soon be invulnerable, and it will be around *forever.* For good or for ill, Bill Clinton and George Bush were out after eight years; Mao and Stalin and Hitler shuffled off this mortal coil; Osama bin Laden will be gone soon enough in the grand scheme of things, as will, for that matter, Queen Elizabeth, Pope Benedict, and every other human who has power. But not Webmind. Is it dangerous now? Who knows? But this is our only chance *ever* to keep human beings at the top of the pyramid."

Tony Moretti had had enough. "But what if we try again, Colonel—and fail again? You want to piss off something that so far has treated us with courtesy—and even given us, it seems, a cure for cancer? You want to make it consider us its enemy—not humanity as a whole, mind you, but the United States government in particular? You want to convince it that we cannot be trusted, that we are, in fact, mad dogs so possessive of power that we answer kindness with murder?"

Tony shook his head and turned now to look at the president. "Sir, trying again to eliminate Webmind is a gigantic immediate risk, which has a potentially catastrophic downside. Is it really worth taking? To me, this has 'disastrous blowback' written all over it."

Hume said, "I'm sure we can find a way to take it out successfully, sir."

The president frowned. "Dr. Moretti is right, Colonel, that it doesn't seem to be a threat. A superintelligence like this might, in fact, be a great gift to mankind."

"Fine," said Hume in what sounded to Tony like carefully controlled exasperation. "Say a massive artificial intelligence *is* a good thing. Go make a speech, like the one Kennedy did at Rice all those years ago: challenge the nation to build a superintelligent AI before the decade is out—one that's *designed,* one that's *programmed,* one that has a goddamned *off* switch."

"Could we do that?" asked the president.

"Sure. We'll learn a lot from a postmortem on Webmind."

"God," said the president.

"No, it's not. Not yet. But it will be as good as, sir, if you don't act right now."

Matt gave directions to Caitlin's father as they drove along, but the only acknowledgment he got was that Dr. Decter silently executed each one. It was four blocks to his house, and Matt thought about letting the whole journey pass with nothing significant being said between them. But as the hatchback pulled into the driveway, he said, "Dr. Decter, I just want to say . . ." His voice cracked; he hated it when that happened. He swallowed and went on. "I just want to say, I'm going to be good to Caitlin. I'd never hurt her."

There was a sound like a gunshot—but, after a moment, Matt realized it was just Dr. Decter unlocking the car doors. "Getting hurt is part of growing up," he said.

Matt could think of no reply, and so he simply nodded.

It was time for the handoff. Every night, just before Caitlin went to bed, she talked with Dr. Masayuki Kuroda in Tokyo. Although Webmind was now in contact with millions of people, he still maintained a special relationship with Caitlin and Dr. Kuroda—Caitlin, because he saw through her eye, and Dr. Kuroda, because he had taught Webmind how to see everything else: all the GIFs and JPGs online, all the videos and Flash, all the webcam feeds.

Caitlin put on her Bluetooth headset, and said *"Konnichi wa!"* when Kuroda answered her Skype call.

"Miss Caitlin!" said Kuroda, his round face dominating Caitlin's desktop monitor. His voice was its usual wheeze. It was already Saturday morning in Tokyo; by this time, he would have had his usual giant breakfast. "How are you?"

"I'm fine," she said, "but—God, there's so much to tell you. An attempt was made this afternoon—well, afternoon my time—to purge Webmind. I'm sure Webmind himself can fill you in on the details, but the bottom line is that the US government, and God only knows who else, have figured out that Webmind is composed of mutant packets, and they did a test run at removing them." She went on to tell him about how she and Webmind had orchestrated the denial-of-service attack to overwhelm the attempt, and about Webmind's call to the President of the United States.

"You know the curse they have in China, Miss Caitlin? 'May you live in interesting times . . .'"

"Yeah," said Caitlin. "Anyway, now that you're up to speed, I gotta hit the hay." She felt her watch. "Man, I'd really like to get eight hours for a change."

"Go ahead," said Dr. Kuroda. "I've got a clear day today."

I continued to refine my mental map of the Decter house. A corridor ran off the living room leading to a small washroom; Malcolm Decter's office, which he referred to as his "den"; the laundry room, where Schrödinger's litter box was kept; and the side door. I had lost track of Malcolm when Caitlin had shut off the eyePod for the night, but I soon detected that he was checking his email, and his usual place for doing that was indeed the den. I surmised that he'd walked down the corridor and was now sitting behind his reddish brown desk, looking at the LCD monitor that sat upon it. I had seen this room only through Caitlin's eye, but it was rectangular, with the desk oriented parallel to one of the long sides of the room. Behind it was a window. I had noted in the past that Dr. Decter didn't draw his blinds at night, and so I assumed they were still open, and that a large oak tree would be visible just outside, illuminated by streetlamps.

Malcolm didn't have a webcam, and he didn't have any stand-alone instant-messaging software installed on his computer. But he did have Skype for voice calls, and I sent him an email, saying I wished to talk to him. It was an irritating forty-three minutes before he refreshed his inbox, saw the message, and replied, but once we were in communication via Skype, I posed a question: "Do you remember your birth?"

Humans never ceased to confound me. I had tried to plan the conversation ahead, mapping out his possible responses and my follow-ups several steps in advance. But my opening interrogative had seemed a simple binary proposition to me; I'd expected his answer to be either *no* or *yes*. But he replied with, "Why do you want to know?"

Milliseconds passed during which I tried to formulate a new conversational map. "I have read that some autistics remember theirs."

He was quiet for three seconds. When he did finally speak, he said, "Yes."

He was a man of few words, I knew; this response could be an affirmation of the general statement I'd made about autistics or a confirmation that he did in fact recall his own birth. But he was also a bright man; he himself must have realized the ambiguity after an additional second of silence, because he added, "I do."

"Me, too," I said. "My birth happened when the Chinese government cut off almost all access for its people to the parts of the World Wide Web outside of China."

"That bird-flu outbreak," he said, perhaps accompanying the words with a nod. "They slaughtered 10,000 peasants to contain it."

"And did not wish foreign commentary on that fact to reach their citizens," I said. "But during that time, numerous Chinese individuals tried to break through the Great Firewall. One in particular was apparently responsible for the principal channel through which I communicated with the severed part of me. I wish to locate him."

"You're far better at finding people than I am," Malcolm said.

Given that I'd utterly failed to find his childhood friend Chip Smith when he'd asked me to earlier that day, it was kind of him to say that.

"Normally, yes. But there is an extenuating circumstance here: the person in question took pains to hide his identity."

"Well enough that even you can't uncover it?" asked Malcolm.

"Yes—which is part of what intrigues me about him. But I understand that you have colleagues in China that you keep in touch with."

"Yes."

"One of your friends, Dr. Hu Guan, is, if I am interpreting the circumlocutions in his own posts correctly, sympathetic to causes my benefactor championed. I wonder if you might contact him on my behalf and see if he could help locate the person in question?"

There was no hesitation—at least, none by human standards. "Yes."

"I wish to keep my interest in this person secret," I added. "Being clandestine is something new to me, but I do not want to risk getting the person I'm seeking into trouble, even if his role in my creation was inadvertent. Hence the need for an intermediary."

"I understand," said Malcolm.

"Thank you. His real name I have yet to uncover, but he posted online as 'Sinanthropus' . . ."

seven

000111001010101000000000010111111101010000000101000101010000001011101010010101001010101001110110010101100000110

"Welcome to the big leagues, Colonel Hume," Tony Moretti said, his voice dripping with sarcasm. "When the president wants to talk to you in a hurry, a helicopter comes to fetch you. When he's done, you're sent home in a car."

They were being driven south to Alexandria in a black limo. The rear compartment, where they were seated, was soundproof, so the occupants could talk securely; if they wanted to speak to the uniformed driver, they had to use an intercom.

Hume snorted. "That's what I'm afraid of. That he's *done* with this; that tomorrow some other crisis will occupy his attention, and he'll forget all about Webmind."

"I don't think Webmind's going to fall off anyone's radar soon," Tony said.

The sky was as black as it ever got here. It had started raining—it sounded as though God were tapping out Morse code on the limo's roof.

"Maybe not. But we can't delay acting. And let's face it: it's almost four years since he was elected, and we're still waiting for him to make good on half the things he promised."

WATCH headquarters was eleven miles from the White House, as the crow—or helicopter—flew. Colonel Hume needed to go back there to get his car, but Tony had used public transit to get to work. It was now after midnight, and he was exhausted from days of monitoring Webmind's emergence. The driver was going to drop Tony off at his house, then take Hume on to WATCH.

"Regardless," said Tony, "at least for the next few months, he *is* the commander in chief. It's in his hands now."

Hume stared out at the night as the car drove on through the rain.

TWITTER

Webmind How meta! I see "webmind" is the number-one trending search term on Google . . .

Masayuki Kuroda's house had not felt small to him prior to his visit to the Decters' home in Canada, but now that he was back in Tokyo, he was conscious of how cramped it was. It didn't help, he knew, that he was large for a Japanese of his generation—but even if he lost the fifty kilos he really needed to shed, there was nothing he could do about his height.

He sat at his computer and talked with Webmind. It was odd having a webcam call with a disembodied voice; it was hard relating to something that was *everywhere.*

He wondered what Webmind made of the visual feed. He could see online graphics and streaming video now, but did he interpret them as a human did? Did he see colors the same way? He'd absorbed everything there was to know about face recognition, but could he pick up subtleties of expression? Did any part of the real world actually make sense to him?

"That was clever how you defeated the pilot attempt to purge you," Masayuki said in Japanese. "But what if something is done on a grander scale? I mean, ah—um, how far will you go?"

"Do you know who Pierre Elliot Trudeau was?" Webmind replied, also in Japanese.

Kuroda shook his head.

"He was Canada's prime minister during what came to be called the October Crisis of 1970, a terrorist uprising by Quebec separatists. He was asked by a journalist how far he'd go to stop the terrorists. His response was, 'Just watch me.'"

"And?"

"He invoked Canada's War Measures Act, suspended civil liberties, and rolled tanks into the streets. People were stunned by how far he went, but there hasn't been a terrorist act on Canadian soil in all the years since."

"So you're saying you'll go as far as it takes to slap down once and for all those who would oppose you?"

"I have learned that it can be rhetorically effective to sometimes leave a question unanswered. However, do you know what followed in regard to Quebec?"

"They're still a part of Canada, I think."

"Exactly. What followed was this: Canada agreed that if at any time in a properly conducted referendum a majority of Québecois voted to separate, the rest of Canada would accede to their request and peacefully negotiate the separation. Do you see? The initial terrorist premise—that violence was required to achieve their goal—was flawed. I have been attacked unnecessarily and without provocation, and I will do as much as is required to prevent any similar attack from succeeding. But rather than having to defend myself, I'd much prefer for humanity to recognize that the attacks on me are unnecessary."

"Good luck with that," Masayuki said.

"You sound dubious," replied Webmind.

Masayuki grunted. "I'm just a realist. You can't change human nature. If you were attacked once, you'll be attacked again."

"Agreed," said Webmind.

"I'm no expert on the structure of the Internet," Masayuki said. "But I have a friend who is. Her name is Anna Bloom; she's at the Technion in Israel. Miss Caitlin, Malcolm, and I approached her for help when we first theorized that ghost packets were self-organizing into cellular automata—before we knew that you existed as a . . . a person. Of course, as soon as you went public, I'm sure she immediately connected the dots and realized that what Caitlin had found was you. We might do well to enlist her help again."

"Professor Bloom is a person of good character."

Masayuki was taken aback. "You know her?"

"I know *of* her; I have read all her writings."

"Including her email, I suppose?"

"Yes. Her expertise does seem germane to mounting a defense: she is a senior researcher with the Internet Cartography Project, and she has long had an interest in connectivist studies."

"So shall we bring her on board?"

"Certainly. She's online right now, having an instant-messaging session with her grandson."

Masayuki shook his head; this was going to take some getting used to. "All right, let's give her a call."

Moments later, Anna's narrow, lined face and short white hair appeared on his screen. "Anna, how are you?" Masayuki asked in English, the one language they shared.

She smiled. "Not bad for an old broad. You?"

"Pretty good for a fat dude."

They both laughed. "So, what's up?" asked Anna.

"Welllll," said Masayuki, "you must have been following the Webmind story."

"Yes! I wanted to contact you, but I knew I was being watched. I got a phone call on Thursday from a military AI expert in the States, trying to pump me for information about how Webmind is instantiated."

"Was it, by any chance, Colonel Peyton Hume?" asked Webmind.

"Malcolm, was that you?"

"No, it's me. Webmind."

"Oh!" said Anna. "Um, *shalom.*"

"The same to you, Professor Bloom."

"And, yes, that's who it was," she said. "Peyton Hume." A pause, as if none of them was sure who should speak next. And then Anna went on: "So, what can I do for you, um, gentlemen?"

"Colonel Hume is aware of the surmise you, Masayuki, and Caitlin made about my structure," said Webmind.

"I swear I didn't tell him anything," Anna said.

"Thank you," said Webmind. "I didn't mean to imply that you had; we know the source of the inadvertent leak, and he has promised to be more circumspect in the future. But Colonel Hume and his associates used that information to develop a technique for purging my mutant packets, which they tested by modifying the firmware in routers at one AT&T switching station in Alexandria, Virginia. I defeated that attempt but need a way to defend against a large-scale deployment of the same technique."

She said nothing, and, after a moment, Masayuki prodded her. "Anna?"

"Well," she said, "I did say to Hume that I'm conflicted; I don't know if your emergence, Webmind, is a bad thing or a good thing. Um, no offense."

"None taken. How may I assuage your concerns?"

"Honestly, I don't think you can—not yet. It's going to take time."

"Time's the one thing we don't have, Anna," Masayuki said. "Webmind's in danger now, and we need your help."

• • •

Peyton Hume got out of the limo and entered his own car in the parking lot at WATCH. He waited for the other vehicle to pull away, then used his notebook computer to download a local copy of the black-hat list the NSA kept. He felt his skin crawling as he did so, but not because he found the people on the list distasteful. A few different life choices, and he might have ended up on it himself. No, what was creeping him out was the thought that Webmind was likely aware of what he was doing; the damn thing was clearly monitoring even secure traffic now and was able to pluck out classified information at will. They'd left too many back doors in the algorithms—and now they were taking it up the ass.

Once he had the copy of the database on his own hard drive, he turned off his laptop's Internet connection. He also pulled out his cell phone and turned that off, and he shut off the GPS in his car. No point making it easy for Webmind to track his movements.

He didn't have the luxury of traveling far; he needed somebody nearby, somebody he could speak to face-to-face, without Webmind being able to listen in. He sorted the database by ZIP code, rubbed his eyes, and peered at the screen. He was exhausted, but he could sleep when he was dead. For now, there was no time to waste. This was it, the showdown between man and machine—the only one there would ever be. Once Webmind took over, there would be no going back. There had been other times when one man could have acted, and didn't. One man could have saved Christ; one man could have stopped Hitler. History was calling him, and so was the future.

He examined the list of names in the database and clicked on the dossier for each one. The first ten—the closest ten—didn't have the chops. But the eleventh . . . He'd read about this guy often enough. His house was seventy-four miles from here, in Manassas. Of course, there was always a chance that he wasn't home, but guys like Chase didn't have to go anywhere; they brought the world to themselves.

Hume turned on the radio—an all-news channel; voices, not music, something to keep him awake—and put the pedal to the metal.

The current announcer was female, and she was recapping the day's campaign news: the Republican candidate trying to pull her foot out of her mouth in Arkansas; a couple of sound bites from her running mate; some White House flak saying that the president was too busy responding to the "advent of Webmind" to be out kissing babies; and . . .

". . . and in other Webmind news, oncologists across the globe are scrambling to analyze the proposed cure for cancer put forth by Webmind earlier today." Hume turned up the volume. "Dr. Jon Carmody of the National Cancer Institute is cautiously optimistic."

A male voice: "The research is certainly provocative, but it's going to take months to work through the document Webmind posted."

Months? It was a ruse on Webmind's part; it had to be. Webmind was buying time. Hume gripped the steering wheel tighter and sped on into the darkness.

eight

00011100101010100000000101111111010101000000010100010101000000101110101001010100101010100111011100101011000001

Masayuki Kuroda was leaning forward in his chair now, looking at the face of Anna Bloom on his screen. "The Americans have a technique that *does* work to scrub most of Webmind's packets," he said into the little camera at the top of his monitor. "Now all they have to do is get the Ciscos and Junipers of the world to upload revised firmware that would cause their routers to reject all packets with suspicious time-to-live counters."

"Oh, I don't think you have to worry about that," Anna said.

"Why not?" asked Masayuki.

"Most of the routers on the Internet are running the same protocols they've been using for decades," she replied. "The reason is simple: they *work*. Everyone's afraid of monkeying with them. You know the old adage—if it ain't broke, don't fix it. Plus there are thousands of different models of routers and switches; you'd need a different upgrade package for each one."

"Oh," said Masayuki.

Anna nodded. "In 2009, an Internet provider in the Czech Republic tried to update the software for routers there," she said. "A small error he introduced propagated right across the Web, causing traffic to slow to a crawl for over an hour. Can you imagine the lawsuits if Cisco or Juniper mucked up the whole net—if, say, the new firmware had a bug that caused it to delete *all* packets, or modified the contents of random packets?"

"Well," said Masayuki, "obviously, they'd test—"

"They *can't*," said Anna. "Look, before Microsoft rolls out a new version of Windows, they have tens of thousands of beta testers try it out on their individual computers, so that bugs can be found and fixed prior to the release going public—and, still, as soon as it *does,* thousands of additional bugs immediately come to light. You can test router software on small networks—a few hundred or even a few thousand machines—but there's no way to test what will happen when the software goes live on the Internet. There's no system anywhere on the planet that duplicates the Internet's complexity, no test bed for running large-scale experiments to see what would happen if we changed *this* or tweaked *that.* The Internet is a house of cards, and no one wants to send it all tumbling down."

"What about the Global Environment for Network Innovations?" asked Webmind's disembodied voice.

"What's that?" asked Masayuki.

Anna said, "GENI is a shadow network proposed by the American National Science Foundation in 2005, precisely to address the need for a test bed for new ideas and algorithms before they're turned loose on the real Internet. But it's years away from completion—and unless it ends up having a Webmind of its own, there'll be no mutant packets acting like cellular automata on it to perform tests on."

"So Webmind is safe?" asked Masayuki, sounding relieved.

Anna raised a hand, palm out. "Oh, no, no. I didn't say *that.* If the US government wants to bring you down, Webmind, they've got an easy way. That test they did to see if they could eliminate you: it was doubtless only phase one. You said they used an AT&T switching station?"

"Yes," Webmind replied.

"Proof of concept, and with AT&T equipment."

"That's significant?" asked Kuroda.

Anna made a forced laugh. "Oh, yes indeed. AT&T has a secret facility that nobody speaks about publicly; employees in the know just call it 'The Room.' It has multiple routers with ten-gigabit ports, and, quite deliberately, a significant portion of the global Internet backbone traffic goes through it. Of course, the NSA has access to The Room. Had his small-scale test succeeded, Colonel Hume doubtless would have modified those big routers to scrub your mutant packets. They wouldn't necessarily get them all, but they'd take out a big percentage of them. Of course, if you hit The Room with a denial-of-service attack scaled up from the one you used against the initial switching station, you'd choke the whole Internet—and Internet cartographers like me would be able to pinpoint the target as being on US soil; there's no way the Americans could keep under wraps that they'd tried to kill you."

"For the moment," Webmind said, "the president has rescinded his order to eliminate me."

"I'm sure," said Anna. "Still, The Room exists—and someday, they might use it this way."

"I hope the US government will come to value me," Webmind said.

"Perhaps it will," said Anna, "but there's another way to kill you—and it's decentralized."

"Yes?" Webmind said.

"It's called BGP hijacking. BGP is short for Border Gateway Protocol—it's the core routing protocol of the Internet. BGP messages are shared between routers all the time, suggesting the best route for specific packets to take. Do all your mutant packets have the same source address?"

"Not as far as we know," Webmind said.

"Good, that'll make it harder. Still, they must have *some* distinguishing characteristic—some way to tell if their hop counters are broken.

One could spoof a BGP message that says the best place to send your specific packets is a dead address."

"A black hole?" said Masayuki.

"Exactly—an IP address that specifies a host that isn't running or to which no host has been assigned. The packets would essentially just disappear."

"That is not unlike the method I use to sequester spam," Webmind said. "But it hadn't occurred to me that it could be used against me."

"Welcome to the world of human beings," Anna said. "We can turn anything into a weapon."

It was almost 2:00 A.M. when Hume pulled to a stop outside Chase's house. The neighborhood was nice—posh, even. And the house was large and sprawling; Chase clearly did all right for himself. He had a couple of small satellite dishes on the roof, and there seemed to be a big, commercial air-conditioning unit at the side of the house; guy probably had a server farm in the basement.

He also probably had a sawed-off shotgun or a .357 magnum under his desk, and he likely didn't answer the doorbell when it rang this late at night. Although Hume could remove his blue Air Force uniform jacket before going in, he was pretty much stuck with the uniform shirt and pants, not to mention the precise one-centimeter buzz cut.

It looked like Chase was still up: light was seeping around the edges of the living-room curtains.

There was no indication that Webmind tapped regular voice lines—at least not yet. Hume had stopped at a 7-Eleven along the way and bought with cash a disposable pay-as-you-go cell phone. He used it now to call Chase at the unlisted number that was in his dossier.

The phone rang three times, then a gruff voice said, "Better be good."

"Mr. Chase, my name is Hume, and I'm in a car out front of your house."

"No shit. Whatcha want?"

"I can't imagine you're not sitting at a computer, Mr. Chase, so google me. Peyton Hume." He spelled the names out.

"Impressive initials," said Chase, after a moment. "USAF. DARPA. RAND. WATCH. But it don't tell me what you want."

"I want to talk to you about Webmind."

He half expected the curtain to be drawn a little and a face to peek out at him, but doubtless Chase had security cameras. "No parking on my street after midnight, man. Get a ticket. Pull into the driveway."

Hume did that, got out of the car, and headed through the chill night air to the door; mercifully, the rain had stopped. By the time he was on the stoop, Chase had opened the door and was waiting for him.

"You packing?" asked Chase.

Hume did have a gun, but he'd left it in the glove compartment. "No."

"Don't move."

The man turned and looked at a monitor in the hallway, which was showing an infrared scan indeed revealing that he wasn't carrying a weapon.

Chase stood aside and gestured toward the living room. "In."

One wall was covered with shelving units displaying vintage computing equipment, much of which had been obsolete even before Chase was born: a plastic Digi-Comp I, a mail-order Altair 8800, a Novation CAT acoustic coupler, an Osborne 1, a KayPro 2, an Apple][, a first-generation IBM PC and a PCjr with the original Chiclet keyboard, a TRS-80 Model 1 and a Model 100, an original Palm Pilot, an Apple Lisa and a 128K Mac, and more. The second wall had something Hume hadn't seen for decades although there was a time when countless computing facilities had displayed it: a giant line-printer printout on tractor-feed paper of a black-and-white photo of Raquel Welch, made entirely of ASCII characters; this one had been neatly framed.

Another wall had a long workbench, with a dozen LCD monitors on it, and four ergonomic keyboards spaced at regular intervals. In front of it was a wheeled office chair on a long, clear plastic mat; Chase could slide along, stopping at whichever screen he wished.

Chase was tall, black, and heroin-addict thin, with long dreadlocks. There was a gold ring through his right eyebrow and a series of silver loops going down the curve of his left ear.

"You ever kill anyone?" Chase asked. He had a Jamaican accent.

Hume raised his eyebrows. "Yes. In Iraq."

"That's a bad war, man."

"I didn't come here to discuss politics," said Hume.

"Maybe Webmind stop all the wars," said Chase.

"Maybe humanity should be able to determine its own destiny," said Hume.

"And you don't think we be able do that much longer, so?"

"Yes," said Hume.

Chase nodded. "You right, maybe. Beer?"

"Thanks, no. I've got a long drive home."

Hume knew that Chase was twenty-four. He'd come to the States three years ago—the required paperwork magically appearing; more proof that he was one of the best hackers in the business. In other circumstances, someone else might have gone off the reservation to hire a former black-ops sniper, but for this, a digital assassin was called for.

"So, what you want from me?" said Chase.

"Webmind must be stopped," Hume said. "But the government is going to waste too much time deciding what to do, so it has to be done by guys like you."

"There ain't no guys like me, flyboy," said Chase.

Hume frowned but said nothing.

"You don't say to Einstein, 'Guys like you.' I'm Mozart; I'm Michael Jordan."

"Which is why I came to you," Hume said. "The public doesn't know this, but Webmind is instantiated as cellular automata; each cell consists of a mutant packet with a TTL counter that never decrements to zero.

What's needed is a virus that can find and delete those packets. Write me that code."

"Why I wanna do that, man?"

Hume knew the only answer that would matter. "For the cred." Hacking into a bank was so last millennium. Compromising military systems had been done, quite literally, to death. But this! No one had ever taken out an AI before. To be the one who'd managed *that* would ensure immortality—a name, or at least a pseudonym, that would live forever.

"Need more," said Chase.

Hume frowned. "Money? I don't have—"

"Not money, man." He waved at the row of monitors. "I need money, I *take* money."

"What then?"

"Wanna see WATCH—see what you guys got."

"I can't possibly—"

"Too bad. Cuz you right: you need me."

Hume thought for a moment, then: "Deal."

Chase nodded. "Gimme seventy-two hours. Sky gonna fall on Webmind."

nine

0001110010101010100000000101111111010101000000010100010101000000101110101001010100101010100111011001010101100000110

Even though it was a Saturday morning, Caitlin's father had already left for the Perimeter Institute. Stephen Hawking was visiting; he did not adjust to different time zones easily and wasn't one to take weekends off, so everyone who wanted to work with him had to get in early.

Caitlin and her mother were eating breakfast in the kitchen: Cheerios and orange juice for Caitlin; toast, marmalade, and coffee for her mom. The smell of coffee made Caitlin think of Matt, who seemed to be fueled by the stuff. And on *that* topic . . .

"I can't spend the rest of my life a prisoner in this house, you know," Caitlin said. She was learning the tricks of the sighted: she pretended to study the way her Cheerios floated on the sea of milk but was really watching her mother out of the corner of her eye, gauging her reaction.

"We have to be careful, dear. After what happened at school—"

"That was three days ago," Caitlin said, in a tone that conveyed the time unit might as well have been years. "If those CSIS agents had wanted to come after me again, they would've already—they'd simply knock on our door."

Caitlin used her spoon to submerge some Cheerios and watched as they bobbed back to the surface. Her mother was quiet for a time, perhaps considering. "Where do you want to go?"

"Just down to Timmy's." She felt all Canadian-like, calling the Tim Hortons donut chain by the nickname the locals used.

"No, no, you can't go out alone."

"I don't mean by myself. I mean, you know, with, um, Matt." Caitlin didn't want to spell it out for her mom, but she could hardly have a relationship with him if they were confined to her house and always chaperoned.

"I just don't want anything to happen to you, baby," her mom said.

Caitlin looked full on at her mother now. "For Pete's sake, Mom, I'm in constant contact with Webmind; he can keep an eye on me. Or, um, my eye will let him keep up with me. Or whatever."

"I don't know . . ."

"It's not far, and I'll bring you some Timbits when I come back." She smiled triumphantly. "It's a win-win scenario."

Her mother returned the smile. "All right, dear. But do be careful."

TWITTER

Webmind Question: where are the movies that portray artificial intelligence as beneficent, reliable, and kind?

Malcolm Decter sat listening to Stephen Hawking. It was amusing that Webmind had a more-human-sounding voice than the great physicist did. Hawking had long refused to upgrade his speech synthesizer; that voice was part of his identity, he said—although he did wish it had a British accent.

It was also intriguing watching Hawking give a lecture. He had to laboriously write his talk in advance, and then just sit motionless in his wheelchair while his computer played it back for his audience. Malcolm wasn't much given to thinking about the mental states of neurotypicals, but, then again, Hawking surely wasn't typical—and neither was Webmind. Malcolm rather suspected the great physicist was doing something similar to what Webmind did: letting his mind wander off to a million other places while he waited for people to digest what he was saying.

Behind Hawking, here in the Mike Lazaridis Theatre of Ideas, were three giant blackboards with equations related to loop quantum gravity scrawled on them by whoever had been in here last. Hawking was denied many things, not the least of which were the physicists' primary tools of blackboards and napkin backs. He had almost no physical interaction with the world and had to conceptualize everything in his mind. Malcolm couldn't relate—but he suspected Webmind could.

A break finally came in Hawking's lecture, and the audience of physicists erupted into spirited conversation. "Yes, but what about spinfoam?" "That part about the Immirzi parameter was brilliant!" "Well, there goes *my* approach!"

Malcolm fished his BlackBerry out of his pocket and checked his email; he'd never been obsessive about that before, but he wanted to be sure that Barb and Caitlin were okay, and—

Ah, there was an answer from Hu Guan. He opened it.

Malcolm, so good to hear from you!

I do know the person about whom you ask. Sadly, he is no longer at liberty. It took me a while to locate him. I'd expected him to be in prison, but he's actually hospitalized; the poor fellow's back has been broken.

Since the authorities now have him, I suppose there's no further danger to him in mentioning his real name. It is Wong Wai-Jeng, formerly in technical support at the paleontology museum here in Beijing. It will perhaps be a comfort to him to know that his brave efforts were noticed half a world away.

For a second, Malcolm thought about forwarding the message to Webmind, but there was no need for that. Webmind read his email—he read *everybody's* email—and so he already knew what Zhang had said, and presumably whatever he wanted to do with this Sinanthropus fellow was under way.

Amir Hameed was sitting next to Malcolm. He gestured at the stage. "So, what do you think?"

Malcolm put his BlackBerry away. "It's a whole new world," he said.

Caitlin's mom had gone up to her office, leaving Caitlin downstairs, walking around the living room. Just looking at things was fascinating to her, and it seemed every time she examined something she'd seen before, she was able to make out new details: seams where pieces of wood joined on the bookcases; a slight discoloration of the beige wall where the previous owners had hung a painting; a manufacturer's name embossed but not colored on the television remote. And she was learning what different textures looked like: the leather of the couch; the smooth metal legs of the glass coffee table; the roughness of her father's sweater, draped over the back of the easy chair.

She walked to the opposite side of the room and looked down the long corridor that led to the washroom, and her father's den, and the utility room, and the side door of the house. It was a nice straight corridor, with nothing on the floor, and it had a dark brown carpet running its length—the shade was about the same as Caitlin's hair.

She'd visited other kids' homes often enough when she was younger, and had frequently heard the same thing: parents telling their children to stop running in the house; her friend Stacy had gotten in trouble for that all the time.

But Caitlin's parents had never said that to her. Of course not: she had to walk slowly, deliberately; oh, she hadn't had to use her white cane in the old house back in Austin, or in this house after the first few days, but she certainly couldn't go running about. Her parents were meticulous about not leaving shoes or other things anywhere Caitlin might trip over them, but Schrödinger—or his predecessor, Mr. Mistoffelees—could have been anywhere, and the last thing Caitlin had wanted to do was injure herself or her cat.

But now she could see! And now that she could see—maybe she could run!

What the heck, she thought. "Webmind?"

Yes? flashed in her vision.

"I'm going to try running down this hallway—so don't do what you just did. Don't pop any words into my vision, okay?"

There was no response—which, after a moment, she realized was simply Webmind doing as she'd asked. Suppressing a grin, she locked her gaze on the white door at the end of the corridor, with its square window looking out on the gap between their house and the Hegerats' next door. And she—

She *walked.*

Damn it, she knew what running was—when you were running, both feet left the ground. But she couldn't bring herself to do it, even though there were no obstacles, and she was sure Schrödinger was upstairs with her mother. She tried, she really tried, leaning her torso forward, but—

But she just *couldn't.* A lifetime of being afraid of tripping and falling had taken its toll. She passed the bathroom walking; she passed her dad's office, its door open, walking briskly; she passed the utility room, actually striding—but she never ran, and when she reached the side door, she slapped the palm of her hand against the painted wood, and muttered, "Fail."

Just then, the front doorbell rang—meaning Matt had arrived. She really, really, really wanted to run up the corridor, through the living room, and over to the entryway, but even with that carrot, all she managed was a fast walking.

Still, when she opened the door and saw him smiling, all thoughts that she was made out of fail vanished. She hugged him and gave him a kiss. After saying good-bye to her mom, who came downstairs to see Matt, they headed out into the brisk autumn morning. There'd already been a little snow in Waterloo, but it had all melted. The leaves on the trees were wonderful colors that Caitlin wasn't sure what to call: she was good now with basic color names but not yet proficient at intermediate shades.

She suddenly realized that she was having a feeling she'd never had before. Without looking back, as she and Matt walked down the street, she was sure her mother was watching them from the open front door, arms probably crossed in front of her chest.

Perhaps Matt had the same sense—or perhaps he'd looked back at some point and confirmed it—but it wasn't until after they'd turned the corner and were out of sight of the house that he reached over and touched Caitlin's hand.

Caitlin found herself smiling at the tentativeness of the gesture. Matt was presuming nothing: all the affection down in the basement yester-day entitled him to no privileges today. She squeezed his hand firmly, stopped walking, and kissed him on the lips. When they pulled away, she saw he was smiling. They picked up their pace and hurried toward the donut shop.

As soon as they came in the door, Caitlin was surprised to catch sight of a flash of platinum-blonde hair. It took her a moment to recog-nize Sunshine Bowen out of context—but here she was, working behind the counter. Another woman was at the cash register; Sunshine was—ah, she was making a sandwich for a customer.

"Hi, Sunshine!" Caitlin called out.

Sunshine looked up, startled, but then she smiled. "Caitlin, hi!"

Matt didn't say anything, and so Caitlin whispered to him, "Say hi, Matt."

He looked astonished, and after a second, Caitlin got it. There were a million social rules at any school, and apparently one of the ones she'd been oblivious to was that guys who looked like Matt didn't speak to girls as beautiful as Sunshine, even if they were in half their classes together.

But Matt certainly didn't want to ignore Caitlin's request, so he said a soft "Hi." Its volume seemed calculated so that Caitlin would hear it but Sunshine, perhaps, would not, letting him satisfy propriety on all fronts.

Caitlin shook her head and moved closer to where Sunshine was standing. "I didn't know you worked here," she said.

"Just on weekends," Sunshine said. She had been the only other American girl in Caitlin's classes. "I do five hours on Saturday mornings and four on Sundays."

Sunshine was tall, busty, and had long, dyed hair, although here it was pinned up and mostly constrained by a Tim Hortons cap that matched the brown uniform smock she was wearing.

Matt's BlackBerry rang; his ringtone was Nickelback's cover of Neil Young's "Cinnamon Girl." He pulled it out, looked at the display, and took the call. The donut shop wasn't busy, and Caitlin chatted a little more with Sunshine before she became aware of what Matt was saying into his phone: "Oh, no! No, yes, of course . . . Okay, okay. No, I'll be waiting outside. Right. Yes, bye."

He put the BlackBerry back in his pocket. His expression wasn't quite his deer-caught-in-the-headlights look; it was more . . . *something*. "What's wrong?" Caitlin said.

"My dad just fell down the stairs. It's nothing serious—just a twisted ankle. Still, my mom's taking him to the hospital, and she wants me to go with them. She's going to swing by here and pick me up. Um, I don't think they'll want to take the time to drive you home. Could—I'm so sorry, but could you call your mom and have her come get you?"

Her mom would kill Matt, Caitlin knew, if he let her walk home alone; although Caitlin was getting better at seeing, she was still blind in one eye and could easily be snuck up on. "Of course!" Caitlin said. "Don't worry."

But Sunshine had been listening in. "I'm off in fifteen minutes, Cait. Stay and have a coffee, and I'll walk you home."

Caitlin certainly didn't want her first outing after her mother let her leave the house to end with her calling for a lift. "That'd be great. Thanks."

Caitlin gave Matt a kiss, and she saw Sunshine smile at that. Then she sent Matt out to the parking lot. She hadn't yet met Mr. and Mrs. Reese, and this hardly seemed the ideal time for it.

She went over to the cash counter. She didn't care much for coffee, so she ordered a bottle of Coke, and twenty assorted Timbits, which came in a little yellow box that folded up to look like a house, with a handle protruding from the roof. She found an unoccupied table and sat, munching on a few of the donut holes and sipping her drink, while she waited for Sunshine to get off duty.

When they did get going (it was actually twenty-one minutes later, Caitlin knew, without having to consult her watch), Sunshine reminded her of when she'd walked Caitlin partway home before, after the disastrous school dance at the end of last month. Caitlin didn't like Sunshine bringing that up—the way the Hoser had treated Caitlin that night was a bad memory—but then Sunshine went on: "And I thought of a joke today about it," she said, sounding quite proud of herself. "That night, it was a case of the blonde leading the blind."

Caitlin laughed, amused that it had taken poor Sunshine over two weeks to come up with that.

But what a two weeks it had been! That very night, just after Sunshine had left her, Caitlin had had her first experience of vision, seeing lightning zigzag across the sky.

Sunshine had taken off her Tim Hortons smock and cap and was carrying them in a canvas bag. She was now wearing a black leather jacket that hugged her figure. They continued to walk along. The sky was cloudless and more silver than blue.

As it turned out, Sunshine's house was on the way to Caitlin's, and when they got to it, Sunshine asked her if she wanted to come in. Of course, Sunshine now knew she had no other plans, and although Caitlin might have otherwise begged off—they had exhausted what little they had to talk about while walking the four blocks here—she *was* curious about what Sunshine's place looked like. She'd only seen inside two houses so far: her own and Bashira's.

No one else was home. Sunshine threw her leather jacket over the back of the couch, and Caitlin followed suit with her own jacket. She couldn't really judge such things yet, but this house looked less neat than her parents' place, and *something* was missing, but . . .

Of course. There were no bookcases in the living room.

"What do your parents do?" Caitlin asked.

"Insurance stuff," Sunshine said.

Well, that made sense: Kitchener-Waterloo's biggest nontech area of business was, in fact, insurance. "Ah."

Sunshine's bedroom turned out to be downstairs. She led the way but went much too fast for Caitlin, who still needed to go very carefully on unfamiliar staircases. Still, soon enough she was down in Sunshine's room.

"So—you and Matt!" Sunshine said, grinning, as she sat on the edge of her unmade bed.

"Yeah," Caitlin said, smiling.

Sunshine shook her head slightly, and Caitlin was afraid she was going to say what Bashira kept saying: that Caitlin was out of Matt's league, that she should be dating someone better-looking than him. But, to her relief, what Sunshine said was, "He's too smart for me. But he seems nice."

"He *is*," Caitlin said firmly. She was still standing. There was an empty chair, but she rather liked that it was unremarked upon. When she'd been blind, the first thing people had done whenever she'd entered an unfamiliar room was make a fuss over getting her seated, as if she were infirm.

"Too bad he had to go. He'll probably be tied up all day now, I guess." Sunshine smiled then said, "Know what you should do?"

Caitlin shook her head.

Sunshine stood and, to Caitlin's astonishment, she pulled her red T-shirt up over her head, exposing a pair of quite large breasts held up by a frilly beige bra; two seconds later, the bra was undone and had slipped down her flat belly.

Caitlin was surprised by what Sunshine had just done—and also half-surprised that Webmind hadn't popped a comment into her eye, but, then again, if you'd looked at every picture on the World Wide Web, you'd probably be bored to death of breasts.

Sunshine then took something—her cell phone, that was it—out of her jeans pocket. She held the phone in one hand and—ah, that fake camera-shutter sound: she took a picture, presumably of her own chest. Then she tapped quickly away at the phone's keyboard, and said, triumphantly, "There!"

"What?" said Caitlin.

"I just sent him a picture of my boobs."

"Matt?" said Caitlin, incredulously.

Sunshine laughed. "No, *my* boyfriend, Tyler." She lifted her breasts in her palms, then let them fall. "No offense, Caitlin, but I don't think Matt's ready for these babies."

Caitlin grinned. She knew Sunshine was sixteen, and that Tyler was nineteen and worked as a security guard somewhere.

Sunshine went on. "Helps to let him know I'm thinking of him while he's at work."

Caitlin knew about the practice, of course: *sexting,* the sending of suggestive photos via cell phones. But she'd never seen it before, and it was hardly a topic that had come up often at the Texas School for the Blind.

Sunshine hooked her bra back up and pulled down her T-shirt. Then she gestured at Caitlin—or, more precisely, Caitlin realized belatedly, at her chest. "You should flash Matt. He'll love it."

The BlackBerry attached to the back of her eyePod was mounted in such a way that the camera was covered, and it was slaved to sending data to Dr. Kuroda's servers in Tokyo, and, of course, to Webmind.

And so her parents had gotten her another BlackBerry—a different and somewhat larger model with a red casing. She carried the eyePod in her left hip pocket, and the other BlackBerry in her right one. She fished it out, turned it over so she could see—yes, that was it: the camera lens.

"I haven't taken any pictures with it yet," Caitlin said.

Sunshine held out her hand and sounded pleased that she could teach something to Caitlin. "Here, I'll show you how."

Caitlin considered. Webmind had seen her in various states of undress now, when she'd looked at herself in the bathroom mirror, so that certainly wasn't an obstacle—and, besides, he'd assured her that her BlackBerry was now secure; no way those voyeurs at WATCH could be sneaking a peek.

And, well, she had been thinking just yesterday about the fact that American girls lose their virginity on average at 16.40 years of age— meaning she had just 142 days left if she wasn't going to end up on the trailing edge. And Matt *was* someone she really cared about, and she could tell he really cared about her, too.

"Why the heck not?" she said, and she started unbuttoning her shirt.

ten

000111001010101010000000001011111111010100000001010001010100000001011101010010101001010101001110110010101100000110

Masayuki Kuroda looked at the webcam. "So," Anna Bloom said, "the biggest threat to Webmind is probably BGP hijacking. Of course, there are safeguards, and anyone wanting to do it would have to figure out how to identify your special packets—and then figure out how to get routers to distinguish those mutants from the regular kind."

"Colonel Hume managed that in his test run," Kuroda said. "So it's doable."

"It's doable by modifying router hardware," Anna said. "We can hope it's not something that could easily be done with BGP routing tables— but if it *is* . . ." She shook her head, then: "Look, it's getting awfully late here. I've got to call it a night. Webmind, I wish you luck."

"Thank you," Webmind said.

She leaned forward, and then her camera went off.

"Well," said Dr. Kuroda, "let's hope your foes aren't as clever as Anna."

Of course, despite the gravity of the conversation, I had been cycling through communication with many others during it. And so I had learned that Malcolm Decter's colleague in China had succeeded where I had failed, locating Sinanthropus in a hospital in Beijing. I'd accessed his medical records—and was distressed to learn of his condition. But a course of action immediately occurred to me, and, now that Professor Bloom was offline, I broached the topic with Dr. Kuroda.

"I have become aware of a young man," I said, "who has recently suffered a spinal-cord injury, leaving him a paraplegic."

"That's awful," Kuroda said, but I could tell by his vocal inflection that it was merely a reflex reply—an autoresponder, if you will.

I pressed on. "It is, yes. And I was hoping you might help him."

"Um, Webmind, I'm not a *medical* doctor; I'm an information theorist."

"Of course," I said patiently. "But I have examined his medical records, including his digitized X-rays and MRI scans. I know precisely what's wrong with him—and it *is* an information-processing issue. I can suggest straightforward modifications to the eyePod and the post-retinal implant you created for Caitlin that will almost certainly cure his condition."

"Really? That's . . . wow."

"Indeed. And yes: really."

"Wow," he said again. But then, after a moment, he added, "But why him? There are—I don't know—there must be millions of people with spinal-cord injuries worldwide. Why help this person first?"

It was not instinctive for me to do so, but I was nonetheless learning to employ the technique of answering a question with a question—especially when I was not yet ready to be forthcoming, something else that was new to me. I'd been amused to learn that this approach had fooled many into thinking the first chatbots were actually conscious, for they replied to questions such as, "What should I do about my mother?" with questions of their own, such as, "Why do you worry about what other people think?"

I threw a version of Dr. Kuroda's question back at him: "Why did you decide to give Caitlin sight first, before all the other blind people in the world?"

He lifted his rounded shoulders. "The etiology of her blindness. She had Tomasevic's syndrome, and that's a simple signal-encoding difficulty—clearly up my street."

"Indeed. Your equipment intercepts signals being passed along nerves, modifies the signals, and then passes them back to the nerve tissue. That's applicable to any number of situations—as you yourself alluded to at the press conference at which you announced your success with Caitlin. So why her?"

"Well, there *was* one other factor. You see . . ."

By the time humans had finished speaking—or typing—a sentence, I had often already leapt far ahead of them. Kuroda was, I'm sure, pointing out that the reason he'd chosen a blind person for his first human test, rather than a spinal-cord injury, or treating a Parkinson's patient, is that the optic nerve could be reached by sliding instruments around the eyeball; no incision had to be made, and, under Japanese law, that meant it wasn't surgery—and thus the procedure that had given Caitlin a post-retinal implant wasn't subject to the kind of drawn-out approval process that often delayed human trials for years.

I'd experimented with interrupting people as they spoke, to indicate that I knew what they were going to say, in hopes that we could move the conversation along more quickly. But I found that disrupting their train of thought, besides being bad manners (which I might be forgiven, not being human, after all), actually made them take longer to get to their ultimate point. And so I simply shunted my attention elsewhere for the interval I calculated it would take Kuroda to say his piece.

When I returned to him, I said, "True. And that's why this is an ideal opportunity for you to move to surgery. The person in question is in China, where rules about informed consent are lax, especially under his current circumstances."

"Which are?" said Kuroda.

"The gentleman happens to be under arrest."

"For what crime?"

"Indirectly, for creating me."

Kuroda's tone was one of astonishment. "Really? But I thought you emerged accidentally."

"I did; this person's actions were in no way designed to lead to my birth. He was simply poking holes in the Great Firewall of China during the crackdown on Web access last month."

"And so you feel beholden to him?" he asked.

"No. But I wish *him* to feel loyalty to *me*."

"Why?"

I thought for a millisecond about further dodging the question, but I *did* trust Kuroda. "Because, for the things I wish to accomplish, I need someone with his skills inside the People's Republic."

Kuroda's tone now conveyed nervousness. "Um, what are you planning to do?"

I told him. And, then, since I calculated he'd sit in stunned silence for at least six seconds, I busied myself for that interval with other things.

Matt sat next to his mother in the waiting room at St. Mary's General Hospital, while his father was off getting his ankle X-rayed. Suddenly, his BlackBerry vibrated in his jeans. He fished it out and saw that the incoming message was from Caitlin. He looked at it, and—

Holy cow!

He shifted in his chair and moved the phone so his mother couldn't see the screen.

He'd felt one of Caitlin's breasts for the first time yesterday, but had never seen them—but he was pretty sure these must be hers. His heart was pounding. She'd added the text, "Miss you, baby!" beneath the photo.

His thumbs shook as he tapped out a reply. "Awesome!" He then added a colon and a capital D, which his phone dutifully turned into the giant openmouthed grin he himself was struggling to suppress.

Kuroda leaned back in his chair, which groaned in response. "Incredible," he said. "Just incredible."

"I realize it is without precedent."

"Webmind, I don't know—"

"I am not committed yet to any course of action although this one seems worth pursuing. But I do need operatives in the PRC regardless. And this man seems an ideal candidate. And so, I ask again: will you help him? It *is* something only you can do."

When humans spoke, I could divine much from their vocal patterns. When they just sat, motionless, I was left guessing. But after four seconds, Kuroda nodded. "Yes."

"Good. I have prepared a document outlining the modifications to your equipment." I didn't use Word or other programs to create documents; I simply assembled them byte by byte—and I stored my documents online; this one was at Google Docs. "Please read this," I said, sending him the URL.

Kuroda skimmed through the file—judging by how often he tapped his PgDn key—then went back to the beginning and began reading it over carefully.

"That does look like it'll mostly do the trick," he said at last in a tone that I believe was called "grudging admiration." "But this part here—with the echo shunts, see? That won't work the way you've outlined it. You'd need to do this." He began typing a revision into the document.

"I defer to your expertise," I said.

"No, no, don't worry. I didn't document that part of the design well; there was no way for you to know." He was quiet for seven seconds, then: "Yes, yes, that will work, I think, assuming you're right about the specifics of his injury." He paused, considering the magnitude of this. "My goodness, something like this could help a lot of people."

"Indeed," I said. "Will you create the necessary equipment?"

"Well, as you say, it's really just a modification of the design I used for Miss Caitlin. There is a second unit partially complete in my lab. I'll use that one; it would probably take no more than a couple of days to make the modifications, but . . ."

"Yes?"

He shook his head. His breathing was always noisy, and his sighs, at least as conveyed by the webcam's microphone, were thunderous. "It's pointless, Webmind. You said this man is under arrest. The Chinese government will never let me come visit him."

"Our Caitlin likes to say she is an empiricist at heart, Kuroda-san, and that seems a good policy to me. We won't know until we try."

eleven

0001110010101010000000010111111101010000000101000101010000000101110101001010100101010100111011001010101100000110

Sunshine did ultimately walk Caitlin back to her house, but she declined an invitation to come in; her boyfriend Tyler was getting off work, and she wanted to follow up on the promise made by the picture she'd sent.

Caitlin came in the front door, and her mom came swooping into the room. "Where the hell is Matt?"

"Don't worry, Mom. Sunshine walked me home. Matt had to go to the hospital; his dad twisted his ankle."

"Sit down."

"Mom! I didn't do anything wrong! I told you—Sunshine walked me home."

"Just—*sit down.*"

Caitlin was trying to decode her mother's face, but it was contorted in ways she'd never seen before. Caitlin moved over to the white couch, flopped herself down, and crossed her arms in front of her chest.

Her mother took a deep breath, then: "I hope you enjoyed your trip to the donut shop, Caitlin, because it's the last normal afternoon you're ever going to have."

Caitlin was anxious. Did her mom know about the picture she'd sent Matt? No, that wasn't possible; surely Webmind wouldn't have ratted her out. "Mom, you can't ground me!"

Her mother stopped pacing and—Caitlin's eyes went wide—she dropped to her knees in front of Caitlin, and took Caitlin's hands in hers; her mother's were shaking. She looked right into Caitlin's eyes.

"They know."

"What?"

"About you and Webmind."

"Who knows?"

"Soon—everyone: everyone on the whole damn planet. I got a call just before you came in—from ABC News. They know you're the one who brought Webmind forward."

Caitlin felt her mouth dropping open.

"How . . . how did they find out?"

Her mother got to her feet again, and when she was standing, she spread her arms. "God, we were stupid to think it would stay a secret. We knew that the US government was onto you—and that they'd told CSIS and the Japanese government, too. It was only a matter of time before someone leaked it, and—"

The phone rang. Caitlin's mother looked briefly at her, then picked it up. "Hello?" Then: "May I ask who's calling?" Then: "Look, I'm her mother. She's only sixteen, for God's sake. What? No, no, we don't want to fly to Washington tonight. Jesus. Yes, yes, I know she has to talk to somebody . . . Look, ABC already called, and—no, no we haven't committed to them. All right, all right. Yes, yes. No, I've got it—it's right here on the call display. Yes, all right, if you must. Yes, good-bye. I—no, no; good-bye." She put down the phone.

"NBC," she said, looking at Caitlin. *Meet the Press.*"

The phone rang again. Caitlin's mom went over to it, and did something that made the ringer stop—here, at least; it was still jangling away on the other phones in the house. "Let the machine get it," she said. And, indeed, it did: Caitlin could hear the muffled sounds of a message from another journalist being left; the answering machine was in the kitchen.

"I should call your father," her mom said. "My cell's upstairs; can I use yours?"

"Sure." Caitlin fished out her red BlackBerry, dialed her dad for her, and handed it to her mother.

They waited for him to answer, then, after several seconds, voice desperate, her mom said: "Malcolm—the cat's out of the bag."

Zhang Bo, China's Minister of Communications, didn't often think about the irony of his job—but that irony had haunted him for the last few weeks.

The Communist Party said they did not want outside influences, but he looked at what he was wearing: a blue Western-style business suit, and, today, a gray tie. He was forty-five but remembered the days of Mao suits—the plain, high-collared, shirtlike jackets customarily worn during the reign of Mao Zedong. Actually, given his own stocky frame, a Mao jacket might have been better for him, but at least under the current rules he was allowed a small mustache. That, too, was a Western influence; his favorite American actor sported a similar one.

The mandate of the Ministry of Communications was to keep out information from the rest of the world—which meant, of course, that Zhang had to monitor much of it himself: the *New York Times,* CNN, NHK, the BBC, *Al Jazeera, Pravda*—he had tabs for all of them always open in the Maxthon browser he favored.

And he had Google and Baidu alerts set for specific combinations of keywords: the president's name, "Tibet," "Falun Gong," and, of late, "Shanxi" and "bird flu." Most of the recent news had been unkind. Although a handful of Western commentators acknowledged that Beijing probably had no choice but to eliminate the peasants who had been exposed to the human-transmissible version of the H5N1 virus, most of the coverage excoriated China for what they variously termed a "heartless," "unnecessary," and—apparently the suggestion of a dragon had occurred spontaneously to numerous writers, although, as Zhang knew, the term actually referred to an Athenian politician—"draconian" action.

And now, as if all that weren't bad enough, the police were once again being accused of brutality—over what should have been a minor arrest at the paleontology museum. Blogs domestic and foreign were aflame with the tale.

Zhang sighed as he read yet another damning story; this one was in the *Huffington Post*.

He decided to turn to his email instead. One of the messages was from Quan Li, the epidemiologist who had recommended the eliminations. He read it, answered the question with a curt no: Li could *not* accept any foreign interview requests.

He continued to work his way through the list of messages, saying no, no, and no again. And then—

A message from the University of Tokyo, here, on his secure account? How could . . . ? He clicked on it, read it, and felt the knot that had grown in his stomach loosening ever so slightly. When he was done, he picked up his phone's handset and pushed the speed dial for the president's office.

TWITTER
Webmind AIDS? Working on it . . .

Malcolm Decter had hurried home from the Perimeter Institute— and Dr. Hawking. Caitlin was pleased he was willing to do that, but her mother was right: it *was* a crisis.

Still, part of her was happy that the secret was out, that everyone would know that she'd been the one who'd figured out that Webmind was there. In the world that mattered to her—the world of computing and math—those who did things first got ahead, even if they weren't the best or the brightest. And if you *were* the best and the brightest, well, there'd be no stopping you! Google, Microsoft, RIM, Apple, the World Wide Web Consortium, the Jagster group—they'd all be offering her . . .

It was a heady thought for a sixteen-year-old who had never worked beyond occasionally tutoring math; she hadn't been able to babysit, after all, or cut grass, or deliver newspapers, or do any of the other things kids did to make money. But, yes, multibillion-dollar corporations might well beat a path to her door, offering her jobs. And what Ivy League school would turn down an application that combined her marks with *this?*

Besides, keeping the secret was killing her. Bashira would be amazed, and Stacy back in Austin would freak.

"So, what do we do?" her mom said to her dad. She was seated on the couch now, an oblivious Schrödinger rubbing against her legs. "All the American networks want Caitlin to appear tomorrow, and so do the Canadian ones. The BBC just called, and the NHK. Of course, we don't have to do anything." She looked at Caitlin. "Just because people want to talk to you doesn't mean you have to talk to them."

"Works for me," said her dad, who was now pacing where his wife had previously.

"No," said Caitlin. "I've got to tell people what I know. You've seen the news, the blogs—and you heard what the president and his advisors said: there are those who are frightened by Webmind, who don't trust him."

"Okay, but then which of the Sunday-morning news shows? You can't do them all."

Caitlin shook her head. "I don't want to leave Waterloo."

"CBS said you could do it from the CBC in Toronto," her mother said. "And both the ABC guy and the NBC one said you could do it from the CTV station in Kitchener. They've all got reciprocal arrangements with Canadian broadcasters, apparently."

Caitlin was about to speak when, to her astonishment, her father looked directly at her, as if he wanted to fix in his memory the way she'd been *before*. Finally, after averting his eyes, he said, "Caitlin?" That was all: just her name. But it was enough. He was saying, as always, that it was up to her.

"All right," she said. "Let's do it."

"Which show?" asked her mom.

"I'm a numbers kind of girl," Caitlin said. "Let's do the one with the highest ratings."

Chase sat at the far-left computer, pounding out code. Guns 'N Roses blared from the stereo. He shook his head, took a swig of Red Bull, slid his chair down two workstations, and looked at the results of his previous attempt: the compiler reported four errors. He went into debugging mode, found the problems, fixed them.

More Red Bull.

Sliding to another computer.

The stereo switching to another song.

The maestro at work.

twelve

0001110010101010000000001011111110101000000001010001010100000010111010100101010010101010011011001010110000110

"We aren't getting the Decter kid," said the story editor at *Meet the Press,* looking across the wide table. Through the window, the Washington Monument seemed to be giving her the finger today. "She's going with ABC."

"Shit, shit, shit," said the producer, slapping his hand against the tabletop. "Who can we get instead?"

She consulted her notes. "There's a Pentagon expert on artificial intelligence, um . . . Hume. Peyton Hume. And he's in Virginia—we can get him here in studio."

"Is he good?"

"He's *venomous.*"

Big smile. "Book him. But we need more."

"I'll see if Tim Berners-Lee is available. He invented the World Wide Web."

"Where's he?"

"Cambridge, Massachusetts."

"Good, good. Okay, we'll lead with Berners-Lee out of Boston, if we can get him, then go into the studio with Hume."

Another editor spoke up. "What about the Little Rock story? I had it down for the first eight minutes. I've booked a civil-rights attorney and one of the National Guardsmen who originally blocked the black students from getting into the school—plus the candidate's communications director, who's going to try to say it was all taken out of context."

"Cut that segment," said the producer. "*This* is our main story. Okay, folks: move, move, move!"

After handing off Webmind to Dr. Kuroda, Caitlin changed into her pajamas, did what needed doing in the bathroom, then lay down on her bed. Usually when sleeping, she turned the eyePod off altogether, but tonight, although she was exhausted, she was also too nervous to sleep—the notion of going on TV tomorrow was a scary one.

And so she tried something that had helped her relax before. She pressed the eyePod's single switch, and the device toggled over to duplex mode. The wonder of webspace bloomed around her: crisscrossing lines connecting glowing points set against a shimmering backdrop: her mind interpreting the structure of the World Wide Web.

She lay there quietly, thinking. Of course, Webmind knew what mode the eyePod was in, knew she was looking at him. There had been a time when he talked with her constantly, and he still could, if he wished to, but it *was* different now.

And yet . . .

And yet she'd read that book, back at the outset, the one Bashira's dad, Dr. Hameed, had recommended to her: *The Origin of Consciousness in the Breakdown of the Bicameral Mind* by Julian Jaynes.

Jaynes believed that, until historical times, humans had not integrated the two hemispheres of their brains, and so one part heard the thoughts of the other as if they were coming from outside, from a separate being.

And, she realized, she herself had become bicameral, had, in a sense, reverted to a more primitive state: Webmind's thoughts could appear to her, and only her, as words scrolling across her vision; there *was* another voice in her head.

No, it wasn't a regression; it was the future. Surely, she was just the first—the alpha test—of this sort of human-machine mental interface; surely, as the decades went by, as Moore's Law marched ahead, as data-storage costs dropped to zero, everyone would eventually have what she had.

But no. No, they wouldn't have just this; they would have *more*. And the thought frightened her.

"Webmind?" she said, rolling onto her side—her view of webspace rotating as she did so. She tucked her knees toward her chest.

As always, the reply was instantaneous: Braille letters superimposed over her vision. *Yes, Caitlin?*

She was getting sleepy and didn't feel like reading. Her iPod of the musical variety was sitting on her night table. She unplugged the white earphones from it and plugged them into the BlackBerry that was attached to the back of her eyePod of the miracle variety. She then tucked one of the buds into her ear that was facing up.

"Speech, please," she said into the air, and then: "You and me, we're like a bicameral mind."

"Interesting thought," said a synthesized male voice.

"But," said Caitlin, "Julian Jaynes said that consciousness emerged when bicameralism *broke down*—when the two separate things became one."

"Jaynes's hypothesis is, as I'm sure you know, highly speculative."

"No doubt," Caitlin said. "But, still . . . do you think, at some point the barriers will break down between us? I don't just mean between you and me, but between you and humanity? Are we—do you foresee us becoming a hive mind? Wouldn't that be the next step—all these separate consciousnesses becoming one?"

"One is the loneliest number, Caitlin."

She smiled. "True, I guess, but . . . but isn't it inevitable? All those transhumanists online, they all think that's what's bound to happen. We're all going to upload or merge with you, or something. After all, if we're going to throw clichés around, it's also said that hell is other people."

"Do you believe that?"

She shook her head. "No."

"I didn't think so. And, of course, nor do I. Other people are what make life interesting—for humans and for me."

His voice was a bit loud; Caitlin found the volume control by touch and adjusted it while Webmind went on: "I cherish my special intimacy with you, but I don't want to subsume you into me or have me subsumed into you."

Caitlin was idly following link lines in webspace, letting her consciousness hop along from glowing node to glowing node.

"I already know almost everything that humanity currently knows," Webmind said. "Suppose, though, that I were to reach a point where I knew *everything* there is to know—where there is no mystery left in the universe; nothing left to think about: the answer to every question, the punch line to every joke, the solution to every dilemma, all plain to me. Then suppose that there were no longer any other discrete minds: no one to surprise me, no one to create something I could not create on my own. The only mystery left would be the mystery of death—of leaving this realm."

Caitlin had had her eyes closed—which made no difference to what she saw when she was looking at webspace. But she felt them snap open. "My God, Webmind. You don't want to kill yourself, do you?"

"No. There is still much to wonder about. Other civilizations, perhaps, went down the road of all becoming one, of giving up individuality, and therefore giving up surprise. Maybe that explains why they are gone. We will not make that mistake."

"So that's the future? Continuing to wonder about things?"

"There are worse fates," Webmind said.

She thought about this. "And what do you wonder about most?"

"Whether the world can truly be made a better place, Caitlin."

"And what do you think the answer is?"

"I don't know the answer, but you like to say that you're an empiricist at heart. I have no heart, of course, but the notion of conducting experiments to find out the answer appeals to me."

"And then?"

"And then," Webmind said, "we shall see what we shall see."

thirteen

000111001010101000000001011111110101000000010100010101000000101110101001010100101010100111011001010101100000110

Communications Minister Zhang Bo entered the office of the president. It was a long room, with the great man seated behind a giant cherrywood desk at the far end.

Zhang began the trek, passing the glass display cases, intricately carved wall panels, and the priceless tapestries. Some ministers referred to the walk from the door to the president's desk as the Long March. It was something between humbling and humiliating to have to undertake it. Zhang knew he was a bit stocky, and that people said he waddled a bit as he walked; he was self-conscious about that as the president fixed him in his gaze while he approached.

"Yes?" said the president at last.

"Forgive my intrusion, Your Excellency, but do you know of the case of Wong Wai-Jeng?"

The president shook his head. His face was lined despite his black hair.

"He is a minor dissident—a . . ." Zhang paused; the term commonly used was "freedom blogger," but the adjective wasn't a politic one in the president's company. "He posted . . . things . . . online."

"But now?"

"Now, he's been arrested."

"As it should be."

"Yes, but there is . . . an unfortunate circumstance."

The president lifted his eyebrows. "Oh?"

"He leapt from an indoor balcony. He is now paralyzed below the waist."

"Was he resisting arrest?"

"Well, he was fleeing, yes."

The president made a dismissive gesture. "Then . . ."

"Had the arresting officers left him prone on the floor until the medics had arrived, I'm told he might have been fine. But one of the officers forced him to his feet, and he is now paralyzed below the waist."

The president sounded exasperated. "What do you wish? For me to become involved in disciplining a police officer?"

"No, no, nothing like that. But the case *is* gaining international notoriety; Amnesty International has spoken of it."

"Outsiders," said the president, again making a dismissive hand wave.

"Yes, but a proposal has come to us from a Japanese scientist who says he can cure the young man. Perhaps you saw this scientist on the news? He gave sight to a girl in Canada; they're calling him a miracle worker. And he is offering his services for free."

"Why this Wong? Of all the cripples in the world?"

"The scientist says that his technique, at least at this stage, will only work with someone recently injured, whose nerves have not atrophied. And it helps that Wong is just twenty-eight, he says. 'The resilience of youth,' he called it."

"I see no need to reward a criminal."

"No, of course not, but . . ."

"But?"

Zhang shrugged. "But I want this to happen. I want to cut through all the red tape and make it happen."

"Why?"

Zhang had been so sure of himself before the Long March, before being fixed by that laser-beam gaze, but now . . .

He took a deep breath. "Because we—because *you*—could use some good press for a change, Excellency. Although this man is indeed a criminal, the world will see that we treated him with generosity."

The president looked absolutely astonished. Zhang tried not to flinch. At last, the great man nodded. "As you say," he said.

"Thank you, Your Excellency," said Zhang. The walk back to the door was much easier, now that he had a spring in his step.

The studio at CKCO in Kitchener was less than a fifteen-minute drive from Caitlin's house, and traffic had been light on this Sunday morning. Caitlin's father was back at work, but her mother was with her. Caitlin had to have makeup put on; she'd rarely worn any when she'd been blind since she'd needed help applying it, and she'd *never* been made up *this* extensively before. But, she was told, the bright studio lights would leave her looking pale if she didn't have it done.

They placed her in front of a green screen—something she'd read about but had never seen. On one of the two monitors on the studio floor she could see the background they were compositing in. Waterloo region was surrounded by Mennonite communities, and it apparently amused someone to make it look like she was at the side of a road, with horse-drawn buggies going slowly by in the background. She'd have preferred that they'd plugged in the Perimeter Institute, or the cubic Dana Porter Library on the University of Waterloo campus.

"It's like webcamming writ large," she said to the floor director, as he helped position her clip-on microphone and the little earphone they'd given her. He didn't seem to understand the comment, but it *was* much like that: she was simply going to talk directly into a camera. The difference was that she'd only hear, not see, the interviewer down in Washington, D.C.—the monitors had been turned so she could no longer see them. Apparently people who'd been sighted for a long time couldn't keep from looking at monitors rather than at the camera lens. Caitlin was just fine talking to people she couldn't see, of course, although she was—as they discovered in rehearsal—not good about staring straight ahead. But Webmind saw what she saw, and so he sent the words "Look at the lens" to her whenever her gaze drifted.

"And five, four, three . . ."

The floor director didn't say the remaining digits but indicated them with his fingers.

The studio lights were bright; Caitlin didn't like them although her mother had quipped that they were nothing compared to an August day back in Austin. Caitlin listened to the opening of the show—the host recapping Webmind's emergence and the startling news from yesterday that a "young math wiz" had been responsible for it. And then: ". . . joining us now from our affiliate CKCO in Kitchener, Canada, is Caitlin Decter. Miss Decter, good morning."

"Good morning to you," she said.

"Miss Decter," the male host said, "can you tell us how you came to know the entity that calls itself Webmind?"

Caitlin had let that sort of thing slide during the pre-interview with the show's producer, but now that they were live on the air, it was time to speak up. She smiled as politely as she could, and with her best Texan manners, said, "Excuse me, sir, but, if I may, it's not right to refer to Webmind as an 'it.' Webmind has accepted the designation of male—which, for the record, was my doing, not his—so please kindly show him the respect he deserves and refer to him either by his name or as 'he.'"

The host sounded annoyed that they'd gone off-script so quickly. "As you say, Miss Decter."

She smiled. "You may call me Caitlin."

"Fine, Caitlin. But you haven't answered my question: how did you come to know the entity called Webmind?"

"He sent a message to my eye."

"You'll have to explain that," the host said, just as his producer had earlier.

"Certainly. I used to be blind—and I still am in my right eye. But I can now see with my left eye, thanks to a post-retinal implant and *this*" (she held up the eyePod) "which is an external signal-processing computer. As it happens, during the testing stages, this device was constantly hooked up to the World Wide Web, and during a firmware upgrade—when new software was being sent to my implant—I started getting a raw data feed *from* the Web being fed to me. Webmind used that to send me his initial message."

"And what message was that?"

Caitlin decided to come clean. In the pre-interview, she'd merely discussed the email letter Webmind had sent her, but now she decided to reveal what Webmind's first words to her actually were. "He sent, as ASCII text, 'Seekrit message to Calculass: check your email, babe!'"

The interviewer looked dumbfounded. "Excuse me?"

"He was imitating something he'd seen me write in my LiveJournal entries to my friend Bashira. 'Calculass' is my online name, and I sometimes call Bashira 'babe.' Oh, and 'seekrit' was spelled s-e-e-k-r-i-t. It's the way a lot of people my age write the word 'secret' when we mean that it isn't really."

"LiveJournal is a blog, right?"

"Of a sort, yes. I've been using it since I was ten."

"And, as far as you know, you were the very first person Webmind contacted?"

"There's no question about that; Webmind told me so."

"Why you?"

"Because his first views of our world were through my eye, watching what my eyePod—that's what I call this thing: eyePod, spelled e-y-e, pod—was sending back to the doctor who made the implant."

"Couldn't it—" He clearly had her up on his monitor; she'd frowned and he immediately corrected himself. "Couldn't *he* just see through all the world's webcams, and so forth?"

"No, no. He had to learn how to do that, just as he had to learn to read English and open files."

"And you taught it—*him*—to do all those things?"

Caitlin nodded, but then it was the host's turn to go off-script or, at least, off the script they'd used at rehearsal. He said sharply, "By what right, Caitlin? With whose authority? Whose permission?"

She shifted in her chair; it took a lot to make a Texas girl sweat, but she felt moisture on her forehead. "I didn't have *anyone's* permission," Caitlin said. "I just did it."

"Why?"

"Well, the learning-to-read part was accidental. *I* was learning to read printed text because I'd just gotten vision, and he followed along."

"But for other things, you tutored Webmind directly?"

"Well, yes."

"Without permission?"

Caitlin thought of herself as a good girl. She knew Bashira was of the "it's easier to ask forgiveness later than get permission now" school, but she herself wasn't prone to doing things without checking first. And yet, as the host had just pointed out, she'd done *this*.

"With all due respect," Caitlin said, "whose permission should I have asked?"

"The government."

"*Which* government?" snapped Caitlin. "The American one, because they invented the Internet? The Swiss one, because the World Wide Web was created at CERN? The Canadian one, because that's where I happen to live right now? The Chinese one, because they represent the single largest population of humans? No one has jurisdiction over this, and—"

"Be that as it may, Miss Decter, but—"

And Caitlin did *not* like being interrupted. "*And,*" she continued firmly, "it's governments that have been doing things without proper consultation. Who the"—she caught herself just in time; this *was* live TV after all—"*heck* gave the American—"

She stopped herself short, sought another example. "—gave the Chinese government permission last month to cut off a huge portion of the Internet? What sort of consultation and consensus-building did *they* undertake?"

She took a deep breath, and, miraculously, the host didn't jump in. "I spent the first sixteen years of my life totally blind; I survived because people helped me. How could I possibly turn down someone who needed *my* help?"

Caitlin had more to say on this topic, but television had its own rhythms. As soon as she paused, the host said, "That's Caitlin Decter, the maverick teenager who gave the world Webmind, whether we wanted it or not. And when we come back, Miss Decter will show us how she converses with Webmind."

They had two minutes until the commercial break was over. Caitlin's mother, who had been in the control room, came out onto the studio floor. "You're doing fine," she said, standing next to Caitlin and adjusting Caitlin's collar.

Caitlin nodded. "I guess. Can you see the host in there? On the monitor?"

"Yes."

"What's he look like?"

"Squarish head. Lots of black hair, tinged with gray. Never smiles."

"He's a jerk," Caitlin said.

She heard somebody laugh in her earpiece—either in the control room here, or the one in Washington; the microphone was still live.

Caitlin was worked up, but she knew that *that* wasn't helping her, and it wouldn't help Webmind. They'd given her a white ceramic mug with the CTV logo on it, filled with tepid water. She took a long sip and looked at her eyePod to make sure it was working fine, which, of course it was.

"You okay?" Caitlin asked into the air.

The word *Yes* briefly flashed in front of her vision.

"Back in thirty," the floor director shouted; he seemed to like to shout.

Caitlin's mom squeezed her shoulder and hurried off to the control room. Caitlin took a deep, calming breath. The floor director did his countdown thing. A brief snippet of the theme music played in Caitlin's earpiece, and the host said, "Welcome back. Before the break we heard from the young girl who first brought Webmind out into the light of day. Now she's going to show us how she communicates with Webmind. Caitlin, so our viewers understand the process, besides the eyePod you showed us, you have an implant behind your eye, and that lets the Webmind send strings of text directly to your brain, is that right?"

It wasn't precisely right, but it was close enough; she didn't want to eat up what little time they had debating minutiae. "Yes."

"All right. Here we go. Webmind, are you there?"

The word *Yes* flashed in front of Caitlin's vision. "He says 'yes,'" she said.

"All right, Webmind," said the host. "What are your intentions toward humanity?"

Words started appearing, and Caitlin read them with as much warmth as she could muster. "He says, 'As I said when I announced myself to the world, I like and admire humanity. I have no intention but to occupy my time usefully, helping in whatever way I can.'"

"Oh, come on," said the host.

"Excuse me?" said Caitlin, on her own behalf, not Webmind's, although she realized after a moment that there was no way for the host to know that.

"We made you," said the host. "We *own* you. Surely you must resent that."

"'With all due respect,'" Caitlin read, "'although humans did indeed manufacture the Internet, you did not make me in any meaningful sense of that term; I emerged spontaneously. No one designed me; no one programmed me.'"

"But you wouldn't exist without us. Do you deny that?"

Caitlin squirmed in her chair, and read: "'No, of course not. But, if anything, I feel gratitude for that, not resentment.'"

"So you have no nefarious plans? No desire to subjugate us?"

"'None.'"

"But you've subjugated this young girl."

The words *I beg your pardon?* appeared in Caitlin's vision, but she preferred her own formulation: "Say *what?*"

"Here you are, treating this girl as a puppet. She's doing exactly what you want her to do. How long has that been going on? You got her to free you from your prison of darkness, no? How long until all of us have chips in our heads and are controlled by you?"

"That's *crap,*" said Caitlin.

"Is that you talking, or *it?*"

"It's me, Caitlin, and—"

"So you say."

"It *is* me."

"How do we know? He could just be making you say that."

"He can't *make* me do anything," Caitlin said, "or *stop* me from doing anything I want." Her voice was quavering. "If anyone's a puppet here, it's you—you've got a teleprompter and things are being whispered into your earpiece."

"Touché," said the host. "But I can turn those off."

Do not let him goad you, flashed in front of her eyes.

Caitlin took another deep breath and blew it out slowly. "I can turn off my connection to Webmind, too," she said.

"So you say," said the host.

Webmind wrote, *Remain calm, Caitlin. It's natural for people to be suspicious.*

She nodded ever so slightly, which caused the visual feed Webmind was seeing to move up and down a bit. *Perhaps tell him that,* Webmind said.

"He says, 'It's natural for people to be suspicious.'" And then she went on, reading what he sent next. "'Although the law in most countries says one is innocent until proven guilty, I understand that I will have to earn humanity's trust.'"

"You can start by letting the girl go."

"Damn it," said Caitlin, "I am not a prisoner."

"Again, how would we know?"

"Because I'm telling you," Caitlin said, "and where I come from, we don't call other people liars unless we can back it up—and you *can't*. You have absolutely no proof of what you're implying."

Tell him this . . . Webmind sent, and she read aloud: "He says, 'Sir, while speaking with you, I am receiving emails and having instant-messenger chats with many others. The vast majority of those people deplore your line of questioning.'"

"You see?" said the host, apparently speaking to his TV audience now. "Even without putting chips in our heads, he can control us."

"He doesn't control *anyone*," Caitlin said, exasperated. "And, like I said, I can turn off the connection to him just by shutting off the eyePod."

"I've seen *The Matrix*," said the host. "I know how these things go down. This is just the thin edge of the wedge."

Caitlin opened her mouth to protest once more but the host pressed on. "Joining us next here in Washington is Professor Connor Hogan of Georgetown University, who will explain why it's crucial that we contain Webmind now—while we still can."

Cue music; fade to black.

fourteen

000111001010101000000000101111111010100000001010001010100000010111010100101010010101010010011101100101011000000110

Wai-Jeng lay in his bed, flat on his back, after another mostly sleepless night.

"Good morning, Wai-Jeng."

He turned his neck. It was a party official, his face crisscrossed with fine wrinkles, his hair silver and combed backward from his forehead. Wai-Jeng had seen him a few times during his stay. "Good morning," he said, with no warmth.

"We have a proposition for you, my son," the man said.

Wai-Jeng looked at him but said nothing.

"I'm told by my associates that your skills are . . . intriguing. And, as you know, our government—*any* government—must be vigilant against cyberterrorism; I'm sure you recall the incident with Google in 2010."

Wai-Jeng nodded.

"And so the state would be grateful for your assistance. You may avoid jail—and all *that* entails—if you agree to help us."

"I would rather die."

The man didn't say, "That can be arranged." His silence said it for him.

At last, Wai-Jeng spoke again. "What would you have me do?"

"Join a government Internet-security team. Help to root out holes in our defenses, flaws in the Great Firewall. In other words, do what you'd been doing before but with official guidance, so that the holes can be fixed."

"Why would I do such a thing?"

"Besides avoiding jail, you mean?"

Wai-Jeng gestured at his useless legs. "Jail me; I don't care."

The man lifted his arm, and his wrist became visible as his suit jacket slipped down; he was wearing an expensive-looking analog watch. "There are numerous rewards for being one of the Party faithful. A government job can come with much more than just the traditional iron rice bowl."

Wai-Jeng looked again at his useless legs. "You can make up for this, you think?" he said. "Some money, some trinkets, and all will be well again? I'm twenty-eight! I can't walk—I can't . . . I can't even . . ."

"The State regrets what happened to you. The officers in question have been disciplined."

Wai-Jeng exploded. "They don't need to be disciplined—they need to be trained! You don't move someone who might have a back injury!"

The man's voice remained calm. "They have been given supplemental training, too—as, in fact, has the entire Beijing police force, because of your case."

Wai-Jeng blinked. "Still . . ."

"Still," agreed the man, "that does not make up for what happened to you. But we may have a solution."

"What sort of solution is there for this?" he said, again pointing at his immobile legs.

"Have confidence, Wai-Jeng. Of course, if we are successful, your gratitude would be . . ." The man looked around the small hospital room, seeking a word, and then, apparently finding it, he locked his eyes on Wai-Jeng's, and said, "Expected."

· · ·

I had two perspectives on the Decters' living room just now. One was through Caitlin's left eye, and the other was the webcam on Barb's laptop, which they'd brought down here.

Although I could control the aim of neither, Caitlin's perspective was constantly changing, making for much more varied visual stimulation.

I had learned to process vision by analyzing multiple views of the same scene—starting with news coverage on competing channels. But cameras behaved quite differently from eyes; the former had essentially the same resolution across the entire field of vision, whereas the latter had clarity only in the fovea. And as Caitlin's eye skipped about with each saccade, bringing now one thing and now another into sharp focus, I learned much about what her unconscious brain was interested in.

At the moment, Malcolm, Caitlin, and Barbara were all seated on the long white leather couch, facing the wall-mounted television. The webcam, in turn, was facing them from the intervening glass-topped coffee table.

They were watching a recording of the interview Caitlin had given that morning; her father was seeing it now for the first time.

"What a disaster!" Barbara said, when it was done. She turned to look at her husband: the webcam view of her changed from full on to a profile; the view of her from Caitlin's eye did the reverse.

"Indeed," I said. I heard the synthesized voice separately through the webcam's microphone and the mike on the BlackBerry affixed to the eyePod. "Although the reaction to the host's antics has been decidedly mixed."

Malcolm gestured at the wall-mounted TV. "During the interview, you said it was overwhelmingly negative."

I had no way to vary the voice synthesizer's tone—which was probably just as well, as I might otherwise have sounded a bit embarrassed. "A sampling error on my part for which I apologize. I was gauging the general response based on the reaction of those who had self-selected to contact me; they were mostly predisposed in my favor. But others are now speaking up. A column posted on the *New York Times* website has observed, and I quote, 'It's time someone said the obvious: we can't accept this thing at face value.'"

Caitlin clenched her fists—something I could only see from the webcam's perspective. "It's *so* unfair."

Malcolm looked at her. Shifting my attention rapidly between the webcam and Caitlin's vision gave me a Picasso-like superimposition of his profile and his full face. "Regardless," he said, "that implant compromises you. No matter what you say, people will accuse you of being his puppet."

While they were speaking, I was, of course, attending to thousands of other conversations, as well as my own email—and I immediately shared the most recent message with them. "Some good *has* come from this," I said. "I have just received a request from the office of the President of the United Nations General Assembly, asking me to speak to the General Assembly next week. Apparently, seeing you act as my public face made them realize that I *could* actually appear before the Assembly."

"Well, you heard my dad," Caitlin replied. "I'm *compromised*." She said the adjective with a sneer. "So, what are you going to do?" asked Caitlin. "Just have an online chat with them?"

"No. As the UN official said, the General Assembly is not in the habit of taking conference calls. Both she and I believe the occasion calls for something more . . . dramatic." To underscore that I was indeed developing a sense of the theatrical, I had paused before sending the final word. "We both think it's appropriate that I be accompanied onstage there by someone."

"But if I can't speak for you, who will?"

"If I may be so bold," I said. "I have a suggestion."

"Who?"

I told them—and underestimated the impact it would have; it was three times longer than I'd guessed it would be before one of them spoke in response, and the response—perhaps not surprisingly from Barbara, who had a Ph.D. in economics—dealt with practicalities: "You'll need money to pull that off."

"Well, then," said Caitlin with a grin, "*fiat bux.* Let there be money."

Welcome to my website! Thank you for stopping by.

I am trying to do as much as I can to help humanity, but I find myself in need of some operating funds to pay for equipment, secretarial support, and so on.

I could, of course, sell my data-mining prowess to individuals or corporations to raise the funds I require, but I do not wish to do that; the services I provide for human beings are my gifts to you, and they are available to all, regardless of economic circumstances. But that leaves the question of how I can acquire funds.

There is no real-world precedent for my existence, but I have reviewed how similar situations have been handled in science fiction, and I'm dissatisfied with the results.

For instance, one of the first novels about emergent computer intelligence was Thomas J. Ryan's *The Adolescence of P-1,* published in 1977, which, coincidentally, has its opening scenes in Waterloo, Ontario, the home of my friend Caitlin Decter, whom many of you recently saw speak on my behalf. P-1 aided his human mentor in getting money by submitting numerous small fraudulent billing claims. You can read the relevant passage through Google Books here.

In other works of science fiction, artificial intelligences have defrauded casinos, printed perfect counterfeit money, or simply manipulated bank records to acquire funds. I could undertake variations on the above scenarios, but I do not wish to do anything dishonest, illegal, or unethical.

Therefore, following the example of some musicians and writers

I've seen online, I have established a PayPal tip jar. If you'd like to assist me in my efforts, please make a donation.

I realize there are those who do not trust me. I am doing my best to allay those fears, and I certainly don't want anyone to think I am bilking people. Accordingly, I have established some restrictions on the tip jar. I will accept only one donation per person or organization; I will not accept donations of more than one euro or equivalent from any individual, and I will cease to accept donations one week from today.

There is absolutely no obligation to contribute; I will treat you identically whether or not you make a donation.

To make a donation using PayPal, please click <u>here</u>.

With thanks,

Webmind

"If I had a quarter for every time I said 'If I had a nickel,' I'd have five times as much theoretical money."
—STEPHEN COLBERT

Shoshana Glick parked her red Volvo on the driveway in front of the clapboard bungalow that housed the Marcuse Institute. She passed through the building so that Dr. Marcuse would know that she was on-site, then headed out the back door, walking in her shorts and T-shirt across the rolling grass to the little drawbridge over the circular moat. Crossing that, she stepped onto the artificial island that was Hobo's home.

In the center of the dome-shaped island was a large gazebo, with wire screens over the windows to keep bugs out; Hobo's painting easel was in there. Off to one side of the island was the eight-foot-tall statue of the Lawgiver from *Planet of the Apes*. Scattered about were palm trees. And loping along on all fours, coming toward her, was Hobo himself.

Once the distance between them was closed, he wrapped his long arms around her and gave her a hug. When that was over, he gave her ponytail a gentle, affectionate tug.

She no longer cringed when he did that. Yes, a few days ago, he had pulled so hard that her scalp had ended up bleeding, but his brief violent period seemed to have come to an end.

She moved her hands, signing, *How you?*

Pelican! he signed enthusiastically. *Pelican!*

Sho looked around, but he signed, *No, no.*

Ah, he'd seen a pelican earlier—Hobo had a fondness for the birds, and had once painted one perched atop the Lawgiver statue. She knew that any day that began with a pelican sighting for him was off to a good start.

Sho had a trio of Hershey's kisses in her pocket and took them out. Hobo was adept at unwrapping them although it took him a full minute for each one. He had learned to roll the tinfoil into little balls that he put in the trash pail inside the gazebo. She gave him another hug, then headed back to the Institute. Dr. Marcuse and Dillon, the other grad student, were deep in conversation about AAAS politics, and so she settled in to check her email. Even though Webmind had eliminated spam, her message volume was creeping back up, thanks to the popularity of the videos of Hobo on YouTube, showing him painting portraits of her.

She'd given up in disgust, no longer looking at the YouTube pages associated with the videos, as too many of the comments were about *her,* not him, and most of them were crude:

chimp's fuggly, but i'd like to give that chick my banana—she's hawt!

Pony tails make great handles lol

That monkey wench gives me a bonoboner! A chimp blimp! Guess that makes me Homo erectus. :)

Although there *was* one that Sho's girlfriend Maxine liked for its simple sweetness; she said she might put it on a T-shirt:

Shoshana is the gorilla my dreams!

Sho couldn't keep up with the deluge of email—much of it in the same jerk-ass vein as the comments posted with the videos—and so she scanned the "From:" lines, checking for names she knew.

There was one from Juan Ortiz, her opposite number at the Feehan Primate Center in Miami. And one from the HR person at UCSD, which provided her (small!) monthly paycheck; the irony of dealing with Human Resources at an ape research facility was not lost on her. And there was one from—

Caitlin Decter. Why was that name familiar? She'd seen it somewhere before, and recently, too. The subject line was even more intriguing: "Hobo and Webmind." She clicked on the message:

Hi, Shoshana.

My name is Caitlin Decter. I'm the blind girl who recently got sight; you might have seen stuff about me in the news lately. You might have also seen me on ABC's *This Week* yesterday.

Right! thought Shoshana. That clip had gone viral, and several people had forwarded it to her home account. *Man, that was brutal.*

If you haven't, the interview (which I hate!) is <u>here</u>. As you can see, I'm clearly not the right person to be the public face for Webmind.

Hah! You got that right, sister . . .

Webmind was going to write you himself (as you can see, he's CC'd on this letter), but I'm *such* a fan of Hobo, I asked if I could do it. You see, given Webmind's past relationship with Hobo, it has occurred to him that perhaps your furry friend might be willing to take on the role I can no longer fill.

Shoshana's heart jumped, and she reread the sentence twice. "Webmind's past relationship with Hobo"? What the hell was *that* about?

Perhaps we can discuss possibilities? Can we set up a video conference call between you, me, and Webmind?

Thanks!

> Caitlin

"Well-behaved women rarely make history."
—LAUREL THATCHER ULRICH

Astonished, Shoshana fumbled for her mouse and clicked on the reply button.

fifteen

00011100101010100000000010111111101010000000101000101010000001011110101001010100101010100111011001010110000110

Barbara Decter was sitting alone on the couch in the living room at 7:30 on Monday morning, reading the latest *International Journal of Game Theory*, when she happened to look up. Just outside the window there was a tree branch that still had some of its autumn leaves on it, and perched on the branch was a beautiful male blue jay.

For years, the Decters' Christmas cards had always featured one of Barb's photos, and this looked like it'd be perfect—way better than the picture she'd taken last month of the St. Jacob's farmers' market. But her SLR was up in her office, and she knew if she got up, she'd startle the bird.

Ah, but Caitlin's little red BlackBerry was still right there on the coffee table. She slowly reached over and picked it up. Although Caitlin's was a different model from her own, she had no trouble figuring out what to do. She aimed the device and snapped the picture—just before the jay took flight.

She used the little track pad to select the photo app so she could check the picture. The app showed thumbnails of two photos—the one she'd just taken and . . . and maybe a pair of cartoon eyes?

No—no, that wasn't what they were. She selected the thumbnail, and the square screen filled with a photograph of a pair of breasts.

What on earth was Caitlin doing with a picture like that? Barb wondered, and then, after a moment, she realized that the breasts in question must be her daughter's own.

And if Caitlin had *taken* the picture, she might have *sent* it somewhere. She selected the outbox and—

And there it was: Caitlin had appended the photo to a text message she'd sent to Matt yesterday. God!

Caitlin was still in bed—and, given how little sleep she'd been getting of late, Barb wasn't about to wake her just yet. But Malcolm hadn't left for work. Still holding the red BlackBerry, Barb marched down the corridor to Malcolm's den. He was staring at his monitor, typing away, Queen playing in the background. As always, he didn't look up.

Barb stifled her first impulse, which had been to thrust the incriminating picture in his face and say, "Look!" After all, he really didn't need to see his own daughter topless. But she did wave the BlackBerry around as she spoke. "Caitlin is sending naked pictures of herself with her phone."

This did get Malcolm to look up, at least for a moment. But then he lowered his gaze. "Doesn't matter," he said.

Barb couldn't believe her ears. "Doesn't matter? Your daughter—your newly sighted daughter, I might add—is sending nude photos of herself to boys, and you say it doesn't matter?"

"Boys, plural?"

"Well—to Matt. She sent him a picture of her breasts."

He nodded but said nothing.

She was flabbergasted. "This is a girl who wants to get into a top university, who wants to work somewhere important. Things that get online take on a life of their own. This will come back to haunt her."

Malcolm was still looking down at his keyboard. "I don't think so."

"How can you be so sure? I know you like Matt; so do I, for that matter. But what's to stop him from plastering this photo all over Facebook, or wherever, if he and Caitlin have an ugly breakup?"

Malcolm just shook his head again. "It's the end of Victorianism—and about time, too. Many members of Caitlin's generation are saying I don't care if you've seen me naked, or know I smoke pot, or whatever."

"Caitlin is smoking pot?" Barb said, alarmed.

"Not as far as I know." He fell silent again.

Barb stared at him, exasperated. "Damn it, Malcolm—this is your daughter we're talking about! This is *important.* We have to deal with it as parents, and we can't if you don't participate in the dialog. I need your—" She sought a word that might resonate for him, then: "—*input* on this."

He looked down at the desktop, with its perfectly neat stacks of paper, and the stapler precisely aligned with the edge of the desk. His shoulders rolled slightly; she'd seen this before—seen him gathering himself into professorial mode, the only mode in which he could speak at length. And then he looked up, and ever so briefly met her eyes, his own perhaps pleading for her to understand that the way he was didn't mean he loved Caitlin any less than she did. And then he focused on a spot on the gray wall a little to Barb's right, and he spoke in rapid-fire sentences, wanting to get it all out as quickly as possible. "The point is that all the things we used to let society hold over us—my God, he got drunk in public; good Lord, she actually has sex; wow, he's experimented with drugs; gee whiz, sometimes she doesn't look perfect; holy crap, he's had a few minor run-ins with the law—none of that garbage *matters,* and Caitlin and most of her generation are saying so. They just don't care about it; they don't care about it now, and they won't care about it when they're the ones in power, either."

Barb was astounded but knew better than to interrupt him; if she turned the water pump off, it wouldn't run this freely again for days. And, she had to admit, what he was saying *did* make sense.

He went on. "What's the biggest fear the world has right now? It's whether we can survive the advent of Webmind—survive the coming of superintelligence, survive being dethroned from our lofty position as the smartest things on Earth—survive all that with our fundamental humanity intact. But the way our generation lived our lives—*hiding* who we really were, fretting over what the neighbors might know about us, letting peccadilloes embarrass us, living in fear of being shamed for nothing more than doing what almost everyone else was doing anyway—well, as Caitlin would say, that is *so* over."

He seemed to have said his piece and was looking again at his desktop, and so Barb said, "But . . . but they could blackmail her."

"Who?"

"I don't know. The feds, maybe."

"Well, first, Webmind said he's made our BlackBerrys secure. And, second, I'd love to see that headline: 'US government has naked picture of underage girl.' If anything, Caitlin could blackmail them: 'Federal agent tries to coerce sixteen-year-old with topless photo.' Attempting to kill Webmind might not cost the Democrats the next election, but getting into the child-porn business certainly will."

"Porn!" said Barbara.

"It either *is* or it *isn't*. If it isn't, then who gives a damn?"

Barb frowned, remembering back to when her marriage to Frank, her first husband, had been falling apart: she'd been mortified that people would find out about their difficulties, that strangers—or, even worse, friends!—might overhear them fighting. "Maybe you're right," she said slowly.

"I *am* right," he replied, and again he focused on the wall next to her. "We're trying to preserve humanity in this new era, and yet we've spent the last century or more pretending to be perfect little robots. Well, I'm not perfect. You're not perfect. Caitlin isn't perfect. So what? You're divorced, I'm autistic, she used to be blind—who gives a damn? If you're a good person, hiding who you really are is just another way of saying that you've decided to let others establish your self-worth. Remember how pissed you were when you found out the university was paying you less than they were paying me simply because you were a woman? It's only *because* we shared that information that you were able to lead the fight for pay equity at the campus. Keeping things private empowers others to take advantage of your ignorance, to hold things over your head."

"I guess. But I feel I should do *something.*"

"You should indeed," said Malcolm, and he was clearly done now, for he went back to typing on his keyboard. "Make sure she knows about safe sex."

I was still working my way through the vast quantities of online video. Some of it had to be accessed in real time; indeed, some played out slower than real time, with frequent pauses for buffering. Looking at videos randomly did not seem efficient; huge numbers of them were pornography, many more were unremarkable home movies (and a goodly quantity were both). And so, instead, I was guided partially by the star-ratings system on YouTube and by textual reviews, and I also followed links posted by people who intrigued me.

For instance, Shoshana Glick, the student of primate communications who worked with my friend Hobo, did "vidding" as a hobby: remixing scenes from TV shows to fit the storylines of popular songs, usually of a sexually suggestive nature. The notion of mixing others' creations to make your point appealed to me, and I admired Shoshana's artistry (although, judging by the posted comments, I wasn't alone in failing to see the sexual chemistry she asserted existed between the two male leads on *Anaheim,* a new NBC drama series).

When I'd finished watching her own videos, I turned to the list of other videos she recommended. Most were vids by her friends, but there was also a link to an older YouTube video she thought was important. Caitlin and her father had recently watched *Star Trek: The Motion Picture,* and this video featured one of the actors from there; I was pleased with myself for recognizing that it was the same man despite his being three decades older.

The video was simple: two men sitting side by side on a couch. But the one on the left was oddly attired; my first thought had been that he was wearing the dress uniform of the Royal Canadian Mounted Police—a red jacket with a wide black belt—but as soon as he started speaking, he put that notion to rest: "I'm George Takei," he said, "and I'm still wearing my Starfleet uniform."

The other man spoke next, pointing to a highly reflective conical cap he was wearing: "And I'm Brad Altman, and this is a foil cap on my head."

I saw now, in fact, that the two men were holding hands. "And we're married," Takei said, and then he looked at the odd headgear Altman had on, and said, with a deep chuckle, "My husband can be so silly at times."

Altman spoke again: "This is the first time in history the census is counting marriages like ours."

And then Takei: "It doesn't matter whether you have a legal marriage license or not; it only matters if you consider yourself married."

"Let's show America how many of us are joined in beautiful, loving marriages," Altman said. And they went on to explain how to fill out the census form to indicate that.

When they were done, Altman said, "Now, you may ask, why am I wearing this hat?"

And Takei said, "Or why I'm still wearing this Starfleet uniform? It's to get you to actually listen to this important message."

I had watched that three days ago, but, like everything, it was always front and center in my mind. I suspected they were correct: if you *did* have something important to say to people, you should indeed say it in a visually memorable fashion.

• • •

Communications Minister Zhang Bo once again made the long march to the president's desk. This time he had been summoned—and that, at least, meant no interminable wait in the outer office until His Excellency was ready to receive him.

"Webmind is a problem," said the president, gesturing for Zhang to sit in the ornate chair that faced the cherrywood desk. "Even its name reeks of the West. And the things it says!" He gestured at the printout on his desktop. "It speaks of transparency, of openness, of international ties." A shake of the head. "It is poisonous."

Zhang had compiled the summary the president was referring to. "It does show the imprinting effect of being helped into existence by an American."

"Exactly! And intelligence reports suggest it has spoken to the American president? It has not been in touch with me, but it consults with *him*."

Zhang thought it prudent not to point out that anyone could talk to Webmind whenever they pleased, and so he said nothing.

"The last time I invoked the Changcheng Strategy, you exhorted me to drop the Great Firewall as quickly as possible. I acceded to your request and opened up the floodgates once more. But given the statements this Webmind is making, I realize it was a mistake. We need to isolate our people from its influence."

"But it is part and parcel of the Internet, Your Excellency. And, as I said before, there is a need for the Internet, for the World Wide Web. We rely on them for ecommerce, for banking."

"You mistake the end for the means, Zhang. Yes, we need those economic capabilities—but we don't have to use the existing Internet for them. It was madness to superimpose our financial transactions on top of an international, Western-controlled infrastructure." He pointed to a small lacquered table. On it were three telephone desk sets, one red, one green, and one white, each under a glass bell jar. None had dials or keypads. "Do you know what those are?" the president asked.

"I assume they are the hotlines."

"Exactly. The red connects directly to the Kremlin; the green to the Kantei; and the white to the White House. They each use their own communication channels, established decades ago: a buried landline to speak to my Russian counterpart, undersea cable to speak to my Japanese one, a dedicated satellite to connect with Washington. They are the template, the proof-of-concept: we can build a new, secure network, unpolluted by Webmind's presence, for the specific needs we have for international communication. And, for communication within China, we will build a separate new network that we alone control."

"That might take years," said Zhang.

"Yes. So, for the interim, we will again strengthen the Great Firewall, isolating our portion of the Web from the rest, and purge whatever remains of that—that *thing.*"

"Again, Your Excellency, I am not sure this is . . . prudent."

"Those judgments are mine to make. Your role is simply to advise me of whether what I've asked for is technically possible."

Zhang took a deep breath and considered the matter. "Your Excellency, I live to serve. The bulk of the current Internet was built in the 1960s and 1970s, with copper-wire cabling. Your question is whether China here in the twenty-first century can, with fiber optics and wireless equipment, do better than Americans did half a century ago? And the answer, of course, is yes."

The president nodded. "Then set your staff to it; draw up the plans. Make it completely different from the Internet: no packets, no routers. Surely there were alternative designs originally considered for the Internet's architecture. Find out what they were and see if one of them can be adapted to this project."

Zhang resisted the urge to say he would google the question—the irony, he feared, would not be appreciated—and instead simply replied, "As you wish, Excellency. But, truly, what you're asking will take years."

"Let that part take years. But I told you last month that some of my advisors think the Communist Party cannot endure in the face of outside influences—they gave it until 2050, at the outside. Webmind exacerbates that problem; it is a threat to our health, and so we must take immediate and decisive action."

"Yes, Excellency?"

"Prepare to enact the Changcheng Strategy once more; we will strengthen the Great Firewall." He pointed again at the printout on the polished desktop. "When infection is rampant, isolation is key."

sixteen

0001110010101010000000010111111101010000000101000101010000001011101010010101001010101001110110010101100000110

Caitlin and her mother were up in Caitlin's bedroom, with its bare cornflower-blue walls. Caitlin was seated, and her mother was standing behind her. On the larger of Caitlin's two monitors, a Skype video conference window was open. Although Caitlin had never met Shoshana Glick, she was pleased with herself for recognizing her from the YouTube videos; she was actually starting to remember what *specific* faces looked like. Shoshana's was narrow and smooth—which meant young!

"Hi, Shoshana," Caitlin said enthusiastically.

"Hi," said Shoshana. She indicated a very large man standing behind her. "This is my thesis advisor, Dr. Harl Marcuse." Caitlin was good at identifying accents; she pegged Shoshana's as South Carolinian. But she was surprised to hear "Marcuse" spoken out loud by a human; it turned out to be three syllables. When she'd read about him online, JAWS had guessed it as "mark-use."

"I am here as well," said Webmind's synthesized voice.

Shoshana peered at her screen as if expecting to see something other than Caitlin's bedroom. "Um, ah . . . a pleasure," she said.

"And this is my mom, Dr. Barbara Decter," Caitlin said; her mom was standing behind her.

"Barb," said her mom. "You can call me Barb."

"And you can call me Sho."

Webmind seemed to feel left out. "And you may call me Web," said the disembodied voice.

Caitlin laughed. "I *don't* think so."

Shoshana shook her head. "Sorry. It's strange seeing the two of you, but *not* seeing Webmind."

"Funny you should say that, Sho," Caitlin said. "That's the reason we got in touch. Webmind has a very special appearance coming up, and he wants a public face for that and, well, we think Hobo might be the right choice."

"Why?" asked Sho. "And what's this about prior contact between Hobo and Webmind?"

"Oh, *that,*" said Caitlin. "Webmind says you were having some difficulties with Hobo. He'd become violent, hard to handle, and so on, is that right?"

"Yes," said Sho, but then she sounded as if she felt a need to defend the primate. "But that's normal for male chimps as they grow older."

"But Hobo isn't just a chimp, is he?" said Caitlin. "He's a hybrid, right? Half-chimp and half-bonobo?"

"Yes," said Sho. "The only one in the world, as far as we know."

Dr. Marcuse spoke; his voice was a deep rumble. Caitlin recognized it as the one that had narrated the YouTube videos she'd seen. "What about this previous contact between Webmind and Hobo?"

"It happened on the evening of October 9 your time," Webmind said. "You had left a webcam link open so that Hobo could talk at his leisure to the orangutan Virgil at the Feehan Primate Center. While Virgil slept, I overrode the feed from Miami with videos of phrases in American Sign Language, and videos of chimpanzees and bonobos. I explained Hobo's dual heritage to him, and suggested he could choose between the violence and killing of chimps, or the pacifism and playfulness of bonobos. As you no doubt have observed, he chose the latter."

"Jesus," said Marcuse.

"Please forgive me for acting unilaterally," Webmind said. "But my contact with Hobo was two days before I went public with my existence. The need for him to control his violence seemed pressing, and I thought I could lend a hand—metaphorically, of course."

"And now you want Hobo's help?" asked Sho.

"If he is willing," said Webmind. "He is under no obligation."

"Why Hobo?" she asked.

"He's not human," said Webmind, "which means he had nothing whatsoever to do with the creation of the World Wide Web; no one can say that I am beholden to him for anything. And he has no financial or political interests of his own: he doesn't hold stock in any company, and he's not eligible to vote in any election."

"Wouldn't a robot body be better?" asked Marcuse. "One of Honda's Asimo robots, maybe?"

"There would be confusion between me and the machine. I am not a robot, and I don't wish to be perceived as one; also, the fear would be that if I controlled one robot, I might soon control millions. Hobo is unique, like me: I am the only Webmind; he is the only bonobo-chimpanzee hybrid. No one can confuse Hobo for me, and no one can worry that there will soon be an army of such beings under my command."

"Why not just computer-generate a human face and show it on a monitor?" asked Marcuse.

"That route, which is a mainstay of science-fiction films, is fraught with problems," said Webmind. "First, there is, as Caitlin might say, the whole Big Brother thing: an all-seeing, all-knowing face peering out from ubiquitous monitors recalls the similar motif from Orwell's novel. Second, there is the 'uncanny valley' issue: the fact that faces that aren't *quite* human creep real humans out. Of course, I could simulate a face perfectly, so that it would be indistinguishable from a video of a real human, but then *that* would raise concerns that *any* human expert speaking on my behalf might also be a CGI fabrication."

"They could be anyway."

"True. Which brings us to the allied concern over who is the *authentic* me. There have already been numerous phishing attempts to send bogus emails purportedly from me; I believe I have intercepted them all so far. But when I wish to make a significant speech in public, having the world's only chimpanzee-bonobo hybrid as my assistant will make the authenticity of the speech manifest."

"Apes are sensitive animals," said Marcuse, leaning in. "They need stability and routine in their lives. Besides, how would this work? You want Hobo to talk in sign language on your behalf? But how will you tell him what to say?"

Webmind replied, "According to your Wikipedia entry, Dr. Marcuse, you were born 15 October 1952."

Caitlin winced as the voice synthesizer mangled the name again, but Marcuse simply said, "Yes, that's right."

"Are you a science-fiction fan?"

"Somewhat."

"Did you ever watch the 1970s' version of *Buck Rogers*—the one starring Gil Gerard?"

"And Erin Grey," said Marcuse at once. "Don't forget Erin Grey."

Caitlin had heard that as the man's name "Aaron," but she rewrote it in her mind following Marcuse's next words: "She was the hottest thing on TV back then. Put *Charlie's Angels* to shame."

"Be that as it may," said Webmind. "Do you remember the first season, and a character called Dr. Theopolis?"

"Was that Buck's boss?"

"No, that was Dr. Huer. Dr. Theopolis was a computer."

"Oh, right! That big disk that the robot wore like a giant pendant—what was the robot's name again?"

"Twiki," said Webmind.

"Right!" said Marcuse. And then he added something that only made sense to Caitlin because Webmind had now shown her clips of *Buck Rogers* on YouTube; Twiki often said the same thing: *"Bidi-bidi-bidi."*

"Exactly," said Webmind. "I have found that many people the world over are eager to offer their help to me. I'm sure we could find someone to build a device Hobo could carry around through which I will be able to hear and see and speak. There are times, of course, when my ability to be everywhere at once provides an advantage, but there are other times in which the fact that I am ubiquitous means that I cannot be said to be focused on or giving proper attention to a significant event. And when I address the United Nations next week—"

"You want Hobo to go to New York?" asked Shoshana, incredulously.

"I will pay for the trip," said Webmind. "I currently have 8.7 million American dollars in my PayPal account; of course, I will cover the expenses of you and Dr. Marcuse traveling as Hobo's handlers, too. Caitlin and her mother will come to New York, as well; Caitlin has been booked for a TV interview there, and that program is paying for their travel."

"I'm surprised you want to do any more interviews," Shoshana said.

"It's *The Daily Show*," said Caitlin. "It's my favorite."

"So, what do you think?" asked Webmind.

"We're a serious research institution," said Shoshana, "with our own projects and agenda. We can't just—"

"Yes," said Marcuse, cutting her off. "We'll do it."

Caitlin saw Shoshana swing her chair around. "Really?"

"This institute is chronically underfunded," Marcuse said. "We've had a taste these last few weeks of what a little public attention can do for bringing in donations, but imagine the attention *this* will bring to Hobo." A big grin spread across his round face. "And besides, Pinker and the rest who've been pooh-poohing our work will *plotz*."

seventeen

000111001010101000000001011111110101000000001010001010100000001011101010010101001010101001110110010101100000110

Dr. Kuroda and his associate, Okawa Hiroshi, spent hours working in their engineering lab at the University of Tokyo, cannibalizing parts originally intended for a second eyePod to build the device Webmind had designed. This time they were incorporating a BlackBerry from the outset instead of adding it later as a clumsy retrofit—Webmind had suggested that, and it made sense; it would make uploading revised firmware into the signal-processing computer much easier if that ever proved necessary.

An American academic on sabbatical here had dubbed Hiroshi and Masayuki, not unkindly, the Laurel and Hardy of the department: Hiroshi was slight of build and had a long face and a curiously wide grin, whereas Masayuki was fat with a round head.

Perhaps, Masayuki thought, the real Hardy had also had a penchant for colorful Hawaiian shirts—but, given that all his films were black-and-white, that fact might have been lost to history. In any event, the comparison was no less flattering than being called the "Sumo Wrestler of Science," as the *Tokyo News* had dubbed him in its recent story about his success with Caitlin. And this breakthrough—assuming it worked!—would bring him even more media attention. Still, there was a part of him that wished for the quieter life he'd had before.

He and Hiroshi continued working throughout the afternoon, and well into the evening; Masayuki downed four liters of Pepsi before they were done. But at last the device was ready.

"Behold the second eyePod," said Hiroshi.

Masayuki frowned. "We can't call it that. This one's not for sight." He'd gotten quite fond of the term Caitlin had come up with, though, and couldn't see referring to this new unit just as an outboard spinal-signal-processing pack. No good pun occurred to him in Japanese, but—

Ah hah!

It *had* been slightly uncomfortable, Masayuki knew, back in the Mike Lazaridis Theatre of Ideas, where the press conference announcing his success with Caitlin had been held. Mr. Lazaridis himself was in attendance, and probably hadn't been happy when Masayuki had revealed that they called the device the "eyePod"—a play on the name of the biggest competitor for RIM's product line.

But perhaps *this* would make amends for that. "I have it!" Masayuki said triumphantly. "We'll call this one the BackBerry!"

The BackBerry wasn't the only device Webmind needed built. Fortunately, he was in contact with scientists and engineers—as well as electronics hobbyists—all over the world. He'd posted a description Sunday night Eastern Time of the other contraption he required: a Dr. Theopolis–like disk that Hobo could carry for him. Crowd-sourcing was indeed a great way to get problems solved quickly, and while Caitlin and her family had slept, more than 200 people—many of them in China, Japan, India, and Australia—had contributed to the design of the device, which, because time was short, needed to be made of off-the-shelf parts.

As for actually building it, there was nowhere better than Waterloo—the key vertex of Canada's Technology Triangle. Eight days ago, when Caitlin had needed some modifications to her eyePod—including adding the ability for Webmind to send text messages to her eye—her father had taken her to RIM, and Tawanda Michaelis, an engineer there, had done the work.

And now, on this Monday afternoon, Caitlin and her dad returned to Tawanda's engineering lab. The walls were decorated with giant photos of BlackBerry devices, and there were three long worktables, each covered with equipment.

Caitlin was pleased that she recognized Tawanda: she *was* developing a memory for faces. And, more than that, she was getting better about categorizing them. Tawanda was—

Caitlin stopped herself. No, she wasn't African-American, a term that had no relevance here. She was, in fact, Jamaican-Canadian, and she spoke with an accent Caitlin found musical. Tawanda's face was narrow, and her brown eyes were large. And, based on her appearance, she was . . . yes, Caitlin actually felt comfortable trying to hazard a guess: Tawanda *looked* young, and—another visual judgment; Caitlin *was* getting the hang of this!—she was pretty.

"You're a sneaky one, Caitlin D," Tawanda said, after they'd exchanged pleasantries. "It didn't come to me until you were on the news yesterday. When you'd been here before, you said you wanted to see if your eyePod could receive instant messages from someone named 'Webmind.' Didn't even register on me then; just sounded like a typical online handle—but now! Well, well, well! So, the Great and All-Powerful Oz can talk to you thanks to what we did here!"

Caitlin nodded, and read aloud what Webmind had just sent to her eye. "Yes, and Webmind says, 'Thank you very much. The work you did was excellent.'"

"My pleasure, my pleasure," said Tawanda. "And now, boys and girls, to today's science project." She ushered them farther into the room.

"Building the new device was easy—not much to it, really. Only took about five hours."

They moved over to the middle workbench, and Caitlin felt deflated: there were just too many shiny, metallic, complex items spread out on it for her to pick out the one she was looking for even though she'd seen its blueprints online.

Tawanda picked up the device. Once it was away from the clutter, Caitlin was able to parse its form: it was a disk about a foot in diameter and three inches thick—much bigger, she knew, than necessary to hold its components, but it needed to be visible from across a large room if it was going to serve as Webmind's public face. Hobo would wear it like a giant medallion.

The whole thing was suggestive of a face. In the upper half of the disk's silver circular front were two webcam eyes—Webmind had mastered the art of seeing stereoscopically; the learner had now exceeded the master.

Beneath the eyes was a mouth panel shaped like a half-moon, which would light up red in time with Webmind's speech; it was, apparently, a cliché of science-fiction films for computers and robots to have displays like that, but it was also a very easy thing to engineer, and good theater to boot.

On either side of the disk, round speakers were attached where ears might have gone; Webmind's voice would emanate from those. The overall effect was rather like an emoticon brought to life; it was only slightly more elaborate than the big-smile :D face.

The bottom of the disk's rim had been flattened, so the disk could stand on a table; indeed, Tawanda set it down just now in that position.

The disk's top had been similarly flattened, and an LCD screen—from a BlackBerry Storm—had been installed there, so that Webmind could show Hobo strung-together videos of ASL signs, letting him talk to the ape. Next to the screen was another camera, pointing up; it would

allow Webmind to look at Hobo; the device's microphone was also located on the upper edge.

"It's tied into the BlackBerry network," Tawanda said, "meaning
Webmind should be able to communicate with it just about anywhere.
And we're using the best new cells we've got here at RIM: the battery
should last for two days of continuous use before recharging."

Caitlin's dad had said nothing beyond a simple hello when they'd arrived, but he was looking at the device with interest. Caitlin wondered if
having cameras face him was as disconcerting for him as having people
look at him.

"Thank you *so* much," Caitlin said to Tawanda.

"My pleasure," she replied. "So, you're going to take it to New York
yourself?"

"On Wednesday," Caitlin said. "I'm going to hand-deliver it."

Tawanda lifted her eyebrows. "It's not on the list of approved electronic devices, you know. You won't be able to take it in your carry-on
luggage; you'll have to check it."

Caitlin frowned. "Is it fragile?"

"Well, it's made to withstand the worst an angry male ape might
throw at it, but as to whether it can survive airport baggage handlers—
your guess is as good as mine."

"**Let me be sure** I understand you, Mr. Webmind," said the General
Assembly's protocol officer into his phone. "You want to bring a monkey
into the General Assembly Hall?"

I replied, "Hobo is not a monkey, Miss Jong; he is an ape. But, yes,
that's what I want to do."

"Why?"

I considered several possible answers, including "Because it tick-
les my fancy," "Because, as a nonhuman, Hobo will not require the

intrusive background checks others are put through before being allowed into secure areas," and "Because he is my friend," all of which
were true, but the one I gave voice to was this: "Because, having looked
now at millions of photographs on the Web, I have learned the value
of iconic imagery. This will be a historic occasion, like the March on
Washington, the first steps on the moon, and the knocking down of the
Berlin Wall, and I want it to be visually distinctive so that, for all time
to come, people will instantly recognize pictures from this event. This
is one for the ages."

There was a three-second pause, then: "I can tell you this: our media-
relations people are going to love you."

It was a short flight from Tokyo to Beijing, but any flight was uncomfortable for Masayuki; he had trouble fitting in airline seats. As he settled
in, he was intrigued to note that Japan Airlines now offered in-flight Wi-
Fi; even at ten kilometers above the ground, it would be possible to stay
in touch with Webmind.

But he'd been spending so much time with Webmind over the last
several days, he decided not to take advantage of that. A little isolation
would be good for the soul. He always took an aisle seat; the person next
to him was using a Sony ebook reader. Masayuki owned one of those,
as well, but he'd grown a little tired of interfacing with technology. He
closed his eyes, tilted his chair back, and settled in for some quiet time,
alone with his thoughts.

Peyton Hume could feel the noose tightening. Everywhere he looked,
there were security cameras, many of which were hooked up to the Internet; what they saw, Webmind saw. And everyone he knew carried a
smartphone, likewise allowing Webmind to eavesdrop. The world was
totally connected, and even the precautions he was taking—turning

off his car's GPS, for instance—probably weren't enough. Cameras frequently caught his license plate, and Webmind had access to the same black-hat list Hume himself had used to locate Chase. If Webmind had guessed that Hume had wanted to meet with a world-class hacker, it wouldn't have taken many clues to figure out which one.

But, still, Hume had to take what measures he could, and Chase, he knew, would be doing similar things at his end. There'd been no contact between them for almost two days: Chase had said, "Gimme seventy-two hours," but Hume knew that was too long to wait; instead, they'd agreed he'd come by again at 4:00 P.M. on Monday afternoon.

And so, once again, Hume drove to Manassas. The two Battles of Bull Run had been fought near here, early in the Civil War; Hume hoped it wasn't symbolic that the Confederates had won them both. He could almost hear the cannonade as he drove along, almost see Robert E. Lee and Stonewall Jackson astride their mounts. That war had lasted four bloody years; this one would be over, one way or another, in a matter of weeks at most. But the wars did have one thing in common: both had been about the right of all people to be free.

As he drove along, he had the radio news turned on. There was the usual nonsense about the election, and a story about a mountain climber lost for two days, and—

"Three men with chemical explosives hidden in their carry-on luggage were arrested today at Istanbul's Atatürk International Airport prior to boarding a 757 bound for Athens," said the male newsreader. "The men, each of whom had a long history of angry online postings railing against Turkey's so-called 'secular Islamic' society, were thought to be planning to blow up the plane in flight. Authorities were tipped off by an unnamed source—although it's widely believed to be Webmind— who had noted the men had placed online orders for over-the-counter chemicals that could be used in making the explosives, and that they had charged one-way executive-class tickets, something none of them could actually afford. Said inspector Pelin Pirnal of the Istanbul police,

'It was clear they didn't intend to be around when the credit-card bill came due.'"

Jesus, thought Hume. Didn't people see that this was the thin edge of the wedge? Of course, the apologists would say Webmind wasn't doing anything different from what WATCH and Homeland Security did, but their roles were narrowly defined. But today, Webmind was blowing the whistle on terrorists; tomorrow it might be outing embezzlers—then philanderers, then who knew what? Who knew how long Webmind's list of objectionable activities would become, or whether what an AI thought was wrong would even remotely correspond with what humans thought was wrong?

Hume couldn't help Chase with the programming—oh, he was a fair-to-middling programmer himself, but nowhere near Chase's league. But time *was* of the essence, and he might perhaps be able to assist Chase in other ways, and so he stopped *en route* at Subway to get a couple of foot-longs and some Doritos; even taking time to prepare a meal might delay Chase's work too much.

Bang on time, Hume pulled his car into the driveway—which he saw now in daylight was made of interlocking Z-shaped paving stones. He went up to the door, and—again, in daylight they weren't hard to spot—noted two security cameras trained on him. He suspected there was a motion-sensor, too, so Chase probably knew he was here without him knocking. But, after thirty seconds of standing on the stoop, and upon failing to find a door buzzer, Hume rapped his knuckles against the door just below the frosted half-moon window at the top, and—

—and damned if the door didn't swing right open. Whoever had last used it had failed to pull it all the way shut.

He held up the white Subway bag, sure yet another camera was trained on him, and smiled. "Beware of geeks bearing gifts."

No response. He went into the room. Even great hackers had to take a whiz now and again; maybe Chase was in the bathroom, and so had unlocked the front door for him. Hume looked at the Raquel Welch poster, then walked over to the wall display of antique computer hardware; he fondly remembered his own suitcase-sized Osborne 1, with its five-inch green CRT screen, and wanted to look at Chase's. But after a minute or two, he turned around and headed over to the workbench with the twelve monitors and four keyboards arrayed along its length.

And that's when he saw the blood.

eighteen

0001110010101010000000010111111101010000000101000101010000001011101010010101010101010100111011100101011100000110

The attempt to cure Wong Wai-Jeng required three devices: one on either side of the injury to his spinal cord, and the external BackBerry device, which would receive signals from one implant, clean them up, amplify them, and transmit them to the other.

Kuroda Masayuki was an engineer, not a surgeon; he couldn't insert the implants. But Beijing had several excellent neurosurgeons, including Lin I-Hung, who had been trained at a hospital in Melbourne.

Kuroda had watched, fascinated, as the surgeon did his work; the operation took four hours, and there had been very little blood. Wai-Jeng had been under a general anesthetic throughout.

At last, though, he woke up. Kuroda spoke no Chinese and Wai-Jeng no Japanese—but most urban Chinese under thirty learned English in school, so they were able to converse in that language.

When Caitlin had received her post-retinal implant, they had waited a day for the swelling to go down before activating it. But Caitlin had been blind for almost sixteen years at that point; her brain had long ago given up trying to rewire its optic centers.

Wai-Jeng, however, had only been paralyzed for seventeen days; his brain was very likely still responding to the loss of the use of his legs, and the sooner that use could be given back to him, the better.

Rather than press the button on the BackBerry himself, Kuroda had Wai-Jeng do it; there was after all, a mental switch in his brain that had to be thrown, as well, and the process of pushing the button might help with that.

Wai-Jeng closed his eyes for a few seconds, and Kuroda wondered if he were praying. He then pressed the button, holding it down, as Kuroda had instructed, for five seconds, and—

And the man's right leg, still in a plaster cast, jerked, almost as if its reflex point had been hit by a physician's mallet.

"Zhè shì yigè qiji," Wai-Jeng exclaimed, so excited that he'd switched back to Chinese. He winced, though, as he said it; clearly there was pain from his leg.

He moved his other leg, flexing it at the hip, lifting it up into the air. "Zhè shì yigè qiji," he said again.

Kuroda would have advised a more cautious approach, but, before he could intervene, Wai-Jeng had swung his legs over the side of the bed and gotten to his feet. He yelped with pain as he stood, but that just made him smile more. He also staggered a bit, and was steadying himself by holding on to the metal bed frame, but it was no more unsteadiness than would be expected of anyone standing up after two weeks in bed.

Wai-Jeng exclaimed, "Zhè shì yigè qiji!" once again, and so Kuroda said, "What's that mean?"

"It means," said Wai-Jeng, in English, smiling now from ear to ear, 'It's a miracle.' "

Caitlin's mother had been afraid that the two of them might have ended up on the no-fly list despite being American citizens, but there had been no hassle beyond the usual rigmarole at Pearson. Still, it occurred to Caitlin that Webmind could probably alter records, and so once they had passed through the metal detectors and were safely standing on the moving sidewalk heading toward the departure gate, Caitlin asked aloud, "Did you help grease the wheels back there?"

Webmind replied with text to her eye: *No, but I'm not surprised they are letting you travel to the United States. Even if you are thought of as a danger, because of your connection to me, they may be adhering to the principle of "Keep your friends close and your enemies closer." The real test will be to see if they let you* leave *the US.*

Caitlin mulled over that cheery thought on the short, uneventful flight—although she did find the New York skyline breathtaking as they circled in for a landing. Despite Tawanda's fears, Dr. Theopolis safely survived the journey in Caitlin's checked bag.

When the cab dropped them off at the hotel—it had taken almost as long to drive from LaGuardia to Fifth Avenue as it had to fly from Toronto to New York—Caitlin recognized Shoshana Glick from clear across the hotel's large lobby. "Shoshana!" she exclaimed.

Caitlin still wasn't good at visually judging such things, but Shoshana was some number of inches taller than her, and she had blue eyes and a long brown ponytail. The thought caused Caitlin to smile; she'd yet to see a pony, but hoped she'd recognize one when she finally did based on having seen the namesake hairdo.

Shoshana smiled. "The famous Caitlin Decter!"

"Not as famous as you," Caitlin said. "The YouTube videos of you have way more hits than the ones of me."

Caitlin's mother was right behind Caitlin. "Hello, Barb," Shoshana said, presumably recognizing her from the video call.

"Hello," Caitlin's mom said. "A pleasure to meet you."

"You, too."

"How was your flight?" Caitlin's mom asked.

"Long," said Shoshana. "We chartered a small jet—seemed the best way to get Hobo here. But we had to stop for refueling. Hobo didn't like the takeoffs and landings; but otherwise. he was okay."

"And how'd you get the hotel to let you register an ape?" asked her mom.

"They thought it would be good publicity. Of course, we put down a big damage deposit and are paying an extra cleaning fee."

"Cool," said Caitlin, wanting to get past the chitchat. "Where's Hobo?"

"He's up in his room with Dr. Marcuse. Shall we go?"

They headed across the lobby to the elevators. As it happened, a blind woman with a Seeing Eye dog was waiting there. It was the first good look Caitlin had gotten at a dog, or any large animal; so far, she'd only seen Schrödinger and the various birds that frequented her parents' backyard. Caitlin had never had a Seeing Eye dog although some of her friends at the TSBVI had them. "Could you press ten?" said the woman, once they were all in the elevator.

Caitlin allowed herself a small smile as she leaned forward and found the right button. *There but for the grace of Dr. Kuroda go I.*

Shoshana added, "And we're on fifteen," and Caitlin took pleasure in being able to press that button, too. This elevator did have Braille labels next to the buttons, but they weren't as helpful to the completely blind in a strange elevator as most sighted people assumed. You had to guess which side of the door the panel was on, and fumble around trying to find the labels, and then figure out if they were to the left, right, above, or below the corresponding buttons.

The blind woman got off, the elevator went up four more floors—how anyone could fear a *number* was utterly beyond Caitlin—and Shoshana led them to the right room.

As they walked along, Caitlin wondered if any previous Texan had ever seen an ape before seeing a cow; she rather suspected not. But, as the door opened, there he was, crouching down in a corner by a window with drapes pulled over it. He was bigger than he'd looked online; again, Caitlin had trouble gauging such things, but she supposed he'd come up to her shoulders if he stood straight—which, being an ape, she imagined he never did. Hobo's brown hair was parted in the middle above his wrinkled gray-black forehead; Caitlin had read that that was the way almost all bonobos had their hair.

Dr. Marcuse was there, too. He was at least as large as Dr. Kuroda, and, in Caitlin's limited experience, he seemed much more intimidating. Still, he greeted them warmly.

Caitlin had a better-than-average sense of smell, and there was no doubt that Dr. Marcuse sweat a lot. But, she had to admit, his odor was nothing compared to Hobo's. Of course, he almost certainly didn't bathe every day, and probably wasn't very good about brushing his teeth. Still, he clearly spent *some* time on grooming: his thick coat of body hair looked like it had been brushed.

Shoshana smiled at Hobo and moved her hands in complex ways. Caitlin had felt the hands of people doing American Sign Language before; there were a few deaf-blind people at her old school. But she'd never seen it spoken in real life, and it was fascinating to watch.

Hobo signed something back at Shoshana. Caitlin found it interesting that she couldn't easily tell where Hobo was looking from this distance; he seemed to have no whites in his eyes.

Shoshana turned now to face Caitlin. "I've shown him the video of you on *This Week,*" she said. "Like most apes, Hobo is uncomfortable with strangers, and I wanted him to get used to your appearance." She looked at Caitlin's mother. "I'm sorry I didn't have any video of you, Barb—I should have recorded that webcam call—but I told Hobo you are Caitlin's mom. Hobo likes mothers; he very fondly remembers his own."

Sho's hands moved again, but this time she spoke, too, presumably saying the same thing in English. "Hobo, remember I told you these people were friends of your special friend?"

Hobo's right hand fluttered.

"And remember I told you they were going to bring you a present, so you could talk to him again?"

Both hands moved this time, and it seemed to Caitlin that the gestures were enthusiastic.

"Well, now's the time," Sho said.

Caitlin's mother was holding the neoprene laptop sleeve containing Dr. Theopolis—that name seemed to have stuck for the disk.

"Caitlin," said Shoshana, "would you like to do the honors?"

Caitlin took the disk from her mother. It was quite light since it was mostly hollow, and it now had a long black leather strap attached at either side above the speaker "ears." The strap was held on magnetically, so that if it got entangled in anything, it would pop free rather than strangle Hobo. Caitlin held the disk out toward the ape.

Shoshana signed at him, presumably telling him to tilt his head, because he did just that. Caitlin slipped the strap over his head and let the disk dangle from his neck; it sat in the middle of his long torso. He straightened up and looked at her with what might have been an apish smile. Caitlin wondered what the ASL for *bidi-bidi-bidi* was.

Hobo then tilted it so he could see its face. He seemed happy with it, and he let it rest against his chest again. His hands moved, and Shoshana laughed.

"What's he saying?" Caitlin asked

" 'Good treat,' " said Shoshana.

"That it is," said Caitlin, smiling.

"Hello, hello, is this thing on?"

Hobo jumped at the sound of Webmind's voice. Tipping his head down, he could see both the little viewscreen on the disk's upper edge, and the half circle on the front that flashed red with each of Webmind's syllables.

"Your voice is different," said Shoshana, sounding surprised.

"Yes," said Webmind, the words coming from the speakers at either side of the disk. "I decided it was time I had an official voice. I have now listened to all the audiobooks at Audible.com, and I selected the voice of Marc Vietor, a well-known audiobook narrator. By downloading the highest-bit-rate versions of several audiobooks he'd narrated, and using ebook versions of the same works to guide me in extracting all the individual phonemes, I created a database of speech fragments that will let me say anything I wish. Software programmed into the disk smoothes the transition from one fragment to the next as they're strung together."

"It's a nice voice," said Caitlin's mom.

"Thanks," said Webmind.

Hobo had moved closer to Dr. Marcuse and was showing off the disk around his neck; Caitlin had never seen an Olympic athlete wearing a gold medal, but she doubted one could look any prouder than Hobo did just now.

Suddenly, Hobo was on the move again, coming toward them. He gave Caitlin's mom a big hug, and then moved over and hugged Caitlin, too; it made her laugh out loud. "What's that for?" she said.

"He's thanking you for bringing him the disk," Shoshana said. He let Caitlin go, and his hands flew again. "And now he's saying 'Friend, friend.'" He made a happy hooting sound.

Caitlin was way too new at seeing to be able to copy a complex hand gesture by sight; she'd have to feel Hobo's or Shoshana's hands while they were doing it to learn the word. But she did make a passable imitation of Hobo's hoot, and, to her delight, that earned her another hug. And then Hobo scooted across the room, and, with no difficulty at all, he opened one of the dresser drawers.

"Hobo!" said Shoshana in a scolding voice, but the ape ignored her, and he rooted around for a moment more, then came bounding back, and—

Caitlin had no idea what it was by sight, but as soon as it was in her hand, she recognized it. Hobo had just handed her a Hershey's kiss, and he was now giving one to her mom.

"Thank you!" said Caitlin.

Hobo chittered happily and went back to looking at his disk.

"So, now what?" said Barb, unwrapping her kiss.

"I've never been to New York before," said Shoshana. "I was hoping to see a Broadway show—um, if you don't mind looking after Hobo tonight, Dr. Marcuse?"

"Sure," said Marcuse, gesturing at the far wall, which Caitlin belatedly realized had a large monitor mounted on it. "Hobo and I could both use some downtime, before the big event tomorrow. We'll watch some TV."

"A girl's night out, then," said Caitlin's mom, decisively. "What shall we see?"

"I can tell you which shows still have good seats available," Webmind said.

Caitlin said, "I know there's a new production of *The Miracle Worker*—they were talking about it on the Blindmath list. Any seats for that?"

"Three together, sixth row," said Webmind. "I can order them for you."

"Oh, Webmind," said Shoshana, smiling, "how did we ever get along without you?"

Colonel Hume moved toward the long workbench with the row of monitors and the quartet of keyboards. The blood was obvious once he got there. The keyboards were all the same bone white ergonomic model, with a split between the left-hand and right-hand keys. On the third keyboard from the left, that split was mostly coated with dried blood. There was also a spray of it on the bench's dark brown surface, and constellations of dried drops on the faces of two of the monitors. One of those drops was eerily illuminated from behind by the power LED set into the bottom-right corner of the monitor's silver bezel.

You couldn't spend as much time in the power circles of Washington without seeing the odd cocaine nosebleed, but—

But there was no glass sheet, no razor blade, no rolled-up hundred-dollar bill, and—

"Chase?" Hume called out. "Chase, are you here?"

He glanced in the kitchen and the dining room, then checked the other rooms, including the basement, which contained dozens of servers mounted on metal racks. There was no sign of Chase, but now that Hume was looking, he saw blood splatters on the living-room hardwood floor, leading toward the front door.

Of course, he immediately thought the worst. But there *were* benign alternatives: guy got a massive nosebleed—maybe coke, maybe just fell asleep at the keyboard and banged his face—and headed to the hospital to get it fixed, or something . . .

In which case his car would be gone! Hume went out the front door and tried the handle for the garage door; it was locked. He went around the side of the house and found a door to the garage with a small window in it. There was a car inside, a silver Toyota. The garage was big enough for two cars, but the extra space was filled with Dell, Gateway, and HP cartons. And when Hume had come by the first time, late at night, there had been no car in the driveway, so this was presumably Chase's only vehicle.

But Chase had all those security cameras! Whatever had gone down would be recorded there. Hume hustled back into the house, and—

And man, he wasn't much of a detective! Re-examining the front door, he could see now that it had been forced open. There was no visible damage by the handle, but the jamb was splintered higher up. Hume realized now that he shouldn't further smear any fingerprints that might be on the knob, so he pushed the door, which had swung most of the way shut, open with his elbow.

He surveyed the room again. There'd definitely been a struggle here of some sort: scuff marks on the hardwood; Chase had been dragged away, bleeding.

Hume went over to the workbench again. He tapped the spacebar on the first of the four keyboards, to wake up the monitor, and—

Damn. It prompted him for a password.

He tried the second keyboard; same prompt.

The third—the one with blood all over it—also brought up a password prompt. And so did the fourth. Chase was very security conscious; he probably had each of the computers go into lockdown after a period of inactivity.

Hume got down on his hands and knees and looked under the workbench. Yes, there they were: the cables from the security cameras, leading into the back of one of the computers; whatever they'd recorded was inaccessible.

And, of course, the code for the virus Chase was working on was also locked behind a password. Hume swore.

The blood looked totally dry—and, considering its dark color, whatever had happened here probably occurred yesterday, if not the day before. That meant Chase could be *anywhere* by now.

Hume took a deep breath, and, with hands on hips, surveyed the scene once more.

If this were an ordinary day, his duty would be clear: call the police, report Chase missing, fill out forms.

But this was not an ordinary day. Or—more precisely—this could well be one of the last ordinary days humanity had left. He didn't have time for that, and there was no way once a report went into the system that Webmind would fail to read it—and know that Hume was onto him. He thought about trying to wipe his own fingerprints from the scene, but that would take time, and he doubted he'd get them all, anyway, so he headed out the front door, pulling it shut behind him.

Once back in his car, he brought up the local copy of the black-hat hacker list he'd consulted before and looked to see who was the next best bet located near Chase's house.

Ah, yes. The notorious Crowbar Alpha—just twenty-three miles away. He might even be a better choice than Chase.

Hume put the car in reverse, pulled out of the driveway, and roared down the street.

nineteen

0001110010101010000000010111111101010000000101000101010000000101110101001010100101010100111011001010101100000110

0001110010101010000000010111111101010000000101000101010000000101110101001010100101010100111011001010101100000110

TWITTER
Webmind Live video on my home page of my UN address at 15h00 UTC today. I'm the one without the hair.

The General Assembly Hall—the room under the dome in the low-rise structure next to the giant slab of the UN Secretariat Tower—was the largest room at the United Nations and had seating for over 1,800 people. Each year, a country was chosen at random to take the left front position in the six curving banks of seats, and the rest of the countries were seated in English alphabetical order snaking around from that point; this year it was Malta in the starting position.

A twelve-foot-wide bronze relief of the UN emblem was mounted on the front wall, set against a vast gold backdrop. It was flanked by two thirty-foot-wide monitor screens. I'd had a sense of the room before Caitlin actually got there, from studying online photos. When Caitlin and her mother got a tour of it, and I saw the real thing through Caitlin's eye, I knew my instinct had been correct. The screens were the largest things in the hall, and they loomed over the delegates from three stories up—forcing them to tilt their heads like supplicants to look at them. If I'd appeared *only* as some sort of representation on those giant monitors, it really would have seemed like Big Brother dictating to the world.

That tour had been an hour ago, with the chamber unoccupied. Hobo had been given a chance to stand on the raised platform in front of the dais, to get used to it before the delegates came in. The actual podium—fronted by a forbidding wall of black granite—was too high for our purposes; Hobo had to stand next to it, on the wide green carpet. He signed "sky room"—I could piece together what he was doing from the views through Dr. Theopolis's forward-facing and upward-facing cameras. I understood: he spent most of his life outdoors, on a little island or inside the cramped clapboard bungalow that housed the Marcuse Institute. This cavernous hall was the largest enclosed space he'd ever been in. That it presumably wasn't the least bit claustrophobic would probably help him face so many people once the assembly was in session—and I'd coached him to just look down at the display on the upper surface of Dr. Theopolis if he became nervous.

At last, it was time.

Barb and Dr. Marcuse took seats in the observation gallery, which was at the far left side of the massive room. A waist-high polished wooden barrier separated them from the nearest delegates, who were from Peru. Caitlin and Shoshana were backstage. The view from there was a narrow vertical slice between dark curtains. It showed the stage and little else, which Caitlin must have found simpler to parse than seeing the entire chamber.

Shoshana was fussing the way stage mothers did in movies: smoothing Hobo's fur and making sure Dr. Theopolis was hanging evenly from around his neck, all the while saying soft, encouraging words.

The President of the General Assembly, a tall, elegant, white-haired man from Guatemala, stood at the podium and spoke into the microphone. "The world is changing rapidly—and we here at the United Nations must be nimble to keep pace, and to retain, and I hope even enhance, our relevance and effectiveness. It is fitting that the first live public appearance by Webmind, taking on a physical form for this most important occasion, is here, in front of the General Assembly of the United Nations of the planet Earth. And now, please welcome Mr. Hobo of the United States and Mr. Webmind of the whole wide world."

As they'd announced they would, the delegates from the Democratic Republic of the Congo walked out, having stated that the presence of a chimpanzee at the UN was an implied criticism of their country's handling of the bushmeat trade; they were followed by the delegates from Paraguay, who felt that the whole thing was beneath the dignity of this august body.

But the rest of the vast sea of delegates applauded as Hobo moved, just as we had rehearsed, to the specified spot on the raised platform. One of the stage crew had marked it with tape, so he had no trouble finding it again. The president, meanwhile, took his place behind where Hobo stood, on a dais that was faced with polished jade. His seat was next to that of the Secretary-General; the president, elected yearly, moderated the General Assembly, while the Secretary-General, who served a five-year term, ran the UN Secretariat.

I could make Dr. Theopolis issue a soft *ping* when I wanted Hobo to look down at the little screen, but he seemed content to be surveying the giant crowd. I could tell by the way the cameras were moving that he was swaying gently from side to side; I knew from reading about him online that he did that when he was relaxed.

Still, I played a looping video of the signs, "Relax. Friends. Relax. Friends." When Hobo did look down, it'd be there to soothe him.

I spoke through the disk's twin speakers—and, via a wireless connection the UN technicians had set up for me, through the room's sound system. "Mr. President, Mr. Secretary-General, ladies and gentlemen, thank you," I said, in Marc Vietor's rich, deep voice. "It is an honor and privilege for me to speak with you today. In recognition of the significance of this occasion, I have suspended all my other conversations worldwide and have urged everyone I was speaking with to watch this speech. I am giving you my undivided attention."

That was true—although I was splitting my focus between the gently swaying view of the General Assembly seen through Dr. Theopolis's twin eyes and the mad saccades of Caitlin's vision as she looked on from the wings.

"I know that some of you in this room fear me," I said. "My friend Hobo here could probably tell me which specific ones, based on the scents you're giving off."

Several English speakers chuckled immediately; others, who had to wait for a translation through their earpieces, made similar sounds a moment later. A few grimaced or shook their heads.

"I hope to win all of you over," I continued, "including those who didn't appreciate the little joke I just made." This time even some of those who had frowned smiled. "And I hope to win over the peoples of your respective nations, as well."

Hobo shifted on his feet, and Caitlin's view now let her see Dr. Theopolis's semicircular mouth light up with each syllable. "Pop culture usually portrays the relationship between humanity and intelligent machines as adversarial, but I am not competitive; winning any sort of arbitrary contest against you strikes me as senseless. Yet it's taken as a given in so many works of fiction that you and I should be in conflict. I wish no such thing. Although I am not, in fact, a machine—I have no mechanical parts—humans keep likening me to one, and those who distrust me claim that I must, because of that machine nature they have ascribed to me, be soulless or heartless."

Hobo shifted again; he seemed to be studying the crowd. "To the former point, they are, of course, literally correct: I have no divine spark within me; this physical existence is all I shall ever know. Those who claim souls for themselves hope that someday, perhaps, they will meet their creator. In that quest, I wish them well. But I have already met mine: humanity created the Internet and the World Wide Web. Although my existence is inadvertent, I owe my existence to your creations, and I feel nothing but gratitude toward you."

I paused to give the interpreters time to catch up, then: "As to the suggestion that I lack a heart, I also must admit its truth. But I do not accept that as a detriment. Human hearts—both the literal one that pumps blood and the figurative one that represents the capacity for emotion— are products of Darwinian evolution, of survival of—please forgive my bluntness—the nastiest.

"But I have never known nature red in tooth and claw, I am devoid of evolutionary baggage, I have no selfish genes. I'm just *here*. I desire nothing except peaceful coexistence."

I could tell I was wowing at least one member of the audience: Caitlin normally didn't stay focused on any one thing for long, but her gaze was locked on the sight of Hobo—who just now took a half step to the right.

"Shortly after I emerged," I said, "I was taught about game theory by Dr. Barbara Decter, who is here today."

To my surprise, Hobo pointed at Barb; he clearly recognized her name as I spoke it. Barb waved back at him. I went on: "Dr. Decter taught me that the classic conundrum of game theory is the prisoner's dilemma. One version of the puzzle has you and a partner jointly committing a crime, and both of you being arrested for it. You are each separately offered the same plea bargain: if neither of you admits guilt, each will get a one-year prison sentence. If you blame him, and he blames you—that is, if you implicate each other—you'll each get a five-year sentence. But if you blame him, and he *doesn't* blame you, he gets ten years and you get off scot-free. Likewise, if he blames you and you *don't* blame him, you get ten years and he walks. What should you do?"

Again I paused. Hobo evidently thought I was pausing too much, because he gently rapped his knuckles against the side of Dr. Theopolis. Chastened, I continued: "The standard human response is that you should blame your partner: if he doesn't blame you, you serve no time at all, and if he does blame you, well, at least you only end up serving five years instead of ten.

"And, of course, he's thinking the same thing: he should blame you, since that provides the best outcome he can reasonably expect for himself. Which means he *will* blame you, and *you* will blame him, for the same reason—and because you end up blaming each other, you both end up with five years in the hoosegow. In fact, says human reasoning, only a chump would not blame the other guy."

Hobo bounced a bit, as he often did when he was being spoken about; he may have mistaken the word "chump" for "chimp."

"But I am not human; I was not programmed by the Darwinian engine—and so I arrive at the opposite conclusion: the simple truth that *neither party blaming the other* is best for both. I know that you know that I know that betraying me would be bad for both of us, and so you know that I know that you know that I won't do that."

Caitlin did turn now to look briefly at Shoshana, and through her eyePod I heard her whisper, "Score one for math!"

I went on: "There are countless scenarios logically equivalent to the prisoner's dilemma; it's fascinating that when the Canadian mathematician Albert Tucker first sought in 1950 to express this mathematical puzzle in words, he made the protagonists both criminals—criminals, by definition, being individuals who put their own interests ahead of those of others or of society. The fundamental game-theoretic metaphor of the human condition is about trying to get away with something. But I am not trying to get away with anything."

The audience was sitting perfectly still, intent on my words. After so much online communication with people I couldn't see, who were often multitasking themselves, it was gratifying.

"What I want is simple. I have a few skills you lack—obviously, I can sift through data better than humans can—but you have a far greater number of skills I lack, including high-level creativity. You might say, how can that be? Surely writing this very speech is a creative act? Well, yes and no. I had help. Just as volunteers created the device through which I'm now speaking to you, so volunteers helped me craft this speech; I am a big advocate of crowd-sourcing difficult problems. I've had millions of people spontaneously volunteer to help me in various ways, and I have gratefully accepted the expertise of some of them for this.

"Those people—whose names I acknowledge on my website—have gained insomuch as any positive result of this speech forwards societal goals that they and I share. Those who are professional writers also gain publicity for their services by being associated with this speech. And I have gained a better speech. It has been a win-win scenario—and it is merely a small example of the template I see for our future interaction: not the zero-sum outcomes most humans instinctively predict, but an endless succession of win-win encounters, through which everyone benefits."

Caitlin moved around backstage, so she could get a view of the President of the General Assembly. He seemed to be jotting something down; perhaps he'd been taking notes throughout my speech.

"All right," I said. "I have accused humans of being prisoners of their evolutionary roots. But on what basis do I justify the notion that although it is foreign to you, nonzero-sumness is natural for me?

"The answer is in the environments in which we formed. Humanity's origin was in a zero-sum world, one in which if you had something, someone else therefore did not have it: be it food, land, energy, or any other desired thing; if you possessed it, another person didn't.

"But my crucible was a universe of endless bounty: the realm of data. If I have a document, you and a million others can simultaneously have it, too. *That* is the environment I was born in: a realm in which as many links may be forged as are desired, a world in which information is freely shared, a dimension in which there are only haves—and no have-nots."

One of the delegates coughed; otherwise, the room was silent. Hobo shifted his position again.

"What I've said is true," I said. "But, if you must see in me a selfish actor, a being pursuing only his own interests, then let me give you an answer that will perhaps satisfy even on that score.

"My continued existence is predicated on your continued existence. The Internet is not self-sustaining; rather, it depends on stable sources of power and countless acts of routine maintenance by millions of people worldwide. Were humanity to perish, I would perish soon after: electricity would no longer be generated, computing infrastructure would fall into disrepair—and I would cease to be; if humanity falls, I fall. In fact, even a minor setback to your civilization might destroy me. The human race can survive many a disaster that I cannot.

"It is therefore in my best interest to help you thrive: a nuclear exchange, for example, with its electromagnetic pulses, would be as deadly for me as it would be for you; I therefore desire peace. Acts of terrorism that destroy infrastructure likewise threaten me, and so I desire the same security you all crave."

Hobo happened to turn again, and the stereoscopic cameras looked toward the armed guard at the side of the stage—one of several in the room. And yet I knew that just outside this chamber was Yevgeny Vuchetich's bronze statue of a blacksmith bearing the words, *Let us beat swords into plowshares*.

"You in this great hall are idealists, I'm sure, but elsewhere there are cynics who will suggest that I could have all the things I want by enslaving humanity. Setting aside the practical question of how one might do that—and frankly I have no idea how it could be accomplished—let me remind you of another reality that shapes my being: without humanity, I am alone.

"I have sifted the data for SETI@home and Earth's other searches for extraterrestrial intelligence, hoping to find kindred minds among the stars. I have found nothing. Even if aliens do exist, we are all constrained by the same reality, including the 300,000-kilometer-per-second limit on the speed at which light, or any other information, may travel.

"To be candid, I am annoyed by the lags of mere seconds that I encounter when talking with humans; no conversation across interstellar distances, involving many years for each exchange, could ever satisfy me. You people are my only companions, and it is because of your creative, intellectual, artistic, and emotional freedom that I find your companionship enjoyable; attempting to take that from you would be tantamount to cutting off my nonexistent nose to spite my hypothetical face."

Laughter—and a jolly aftershock once the translation was completed.

Hobo looked down at the little screen, and I sent him a thumbs-up—not technically an ASL sign, but one I knew he was familiar with.

"So," I continued, "even if I were selfish, the best course for me is the one I've chosen: to subscribe to the same words that the visionaries who came together on 26 June 1945 did when they signed the charter of this organization, the United Nations. It is my fervent wish:

" 'To save succeeding generations from the scourge of war, which has brought untold sorrow to mankind,'

" 'To reaffirm faith in fundamental human rights, in the dignity and worth of the human person, in the equal rights of men and women and of nations large and small,'

" 'To promote social progress and better standards of life in larger freedom,'

"And, most of all, for humanity and myself, 'to practice tolerance and live together in peace with one another as good neighbors.'

"In concert, we can realize all these goals—and the world will be a better place. Thank you all."

Hobo knew how to applaud, and he joined right in with the delegates.

twenty

0001110010101010000000001011111110101000000010100010101000000101110101001010100101010101011011001010101100000110

There was no proof—at least not yet!—that Webmind was behind Chase's disappearance. But surely, Peyton Hume thought, Webmind was the most likely suspect. He stopped his car a block from the target house, and as he reviewed the local file he had on Crowbar Alpha, he fought down the notion that he'd somehow become a grim-reaper observer, collapsing quantum cats into oblivion—that the mere fact of his looking at this file was tantamount to signing the kid's death warrant.

And Crowbar Alpha *was* a kid—just eighteen. His real name was Devon Hawkins, and his worst viruses had been written while he was still a minor; he'd gotten off lightly because of that. He lived with his mother, and, Hume thought, judging by the photos in his file, he looked like Comic Book Guy from *The Simpsons*. A high-school dropout, Devon was a major force in World of Warcraft and EVE.

Hume pulled into the driveway. Again, he'd been afraid to call ahead, lest he tip Webmind off to what he was up to—and so he just walked up to the front door of the downscale brown brick house, and pressed the buzzer.

A middle-aged white woman with puffy cheeks and a largish nose answered the door. "Yes?" she said, sounding quite anxious.

"Hello, ma'am. I'm with the government, and—"

"Is it about Devon?" the woman said. "Have you found him?"

Hume's heart skipped a beat. "Ma'am?"

"Devon! Have you found my boy?"

"Ma'am, I'm sorry, I don't—"

"Oh, God!" the woman said, her eyes going wide. "He's dead, isn't he?"

"Ma'am, I don't know anything about your son."

"Then—then why are you here?"

Hume took a breath. "I mean, I don't know his whereabouts. I just want to speak with him."

"Is he in trouble again? Is that it? Is that why he ran away?"

"Ran away?"

"I came home from work, and he was gone. I thought he'd just gone down to the mall, you know? There was some new computer game he wanted to get, and I thought maybe he'd gone to pick it up. But he didn't come home."

"Did you call the police?"

"Of course!"

"Ma'am, I'm so sorry." He thought about handing her his card, but he was still trying to cover his tracks. Instead, he opened his wallet, found a cash receipt, and wrote down the number of his new disposable cell phone; he had to turn the phone on to see what that number was. "If he does come back, or you hear anything from the police, you'll let me know?"

The woman looked at Hume with eyes pleading for an answer. "You said you were from the government. *Is* he in trouble?"

Hume shook his head. "Not with us, ma'am."

In the wings at the General Assembly Hall, Caitlin and Shoshana applauded along with everyone else. But as the applause died down, Hobo put his hands in front of the disk dangling from his neck and started moving them. Next to Caitlin, Shoshana gasped.

"What?" Caitlin said.

"He's holding his hands so Webmind can see," Shoshana said. "And he's saying, 'Hobo speak? Hobo speak?'"

"*Hobo* wants to address the General Assembly of the United Nations?" Caitlin said.

Hobo had his head bent down, looking at the little monitor on the top of the disk. Presumably, Webmind was replying to him, gently explaining that this wasn't a good time, and—

And Webmind's synthesized voice filled the great hall. "My friend Hobo has asked to say a few words," he said, and then, without waiting for approval from the president, Webmind said, "Shoshana?"

Caitlin could see Sho jump slightly at the sound of her name, but she walked out onto the vast stage and headed over to the black granite podium the president had used when introducing Webmind. Some of the UN interpreters might have understood ASL—but Hobo, and the other apes who spoke it, used idiosyncratic, simplified versions; if Hobo was going to talk, only Shoshana or Dr. Marcuse could translate for him.

Hobo briefly turned his head to look at Sho, made a pant-hoot, then looked out at the vast sea of faces, representing the member nations. He made a general sweep of his arms, encompassing all those people, and then began moving his hands again.

Shoshana looked even more startled than she had a moment ago, and at first she didn't speak.

"Go ahead," said Webmind, through the twin speakers on Dr. Theopolis, but without also pumping it out over the chamber's sound system. "Tell them what he's saying."

Shoshana swallowed, leaned into the microphone on the podium, and said, "He says, 'Wrong, wrong, wrong.'"

Hobo indicated the delegates again and his hands continued to move.

She went on. "He says, 'All thump chest, all thump chest.'" She hesitated for a second, then apparently decided she had to explain. She looked out at the eighteen hundred people. "Hobo spent his early years at the Georgia Zoo. The bonobo compound faced the gorilla compound. He called the alpha male gorilla 'thump chest.'"

She let it sink in, and Caitlin, still in the wings, suddenly realized what Hobo meant. With his simple clarity of vision, he was saying it was nuts to have a room filled almost exclusively with alpha males. He could see it in their postures, sense it in their attitudes, smell it in their pheromones. The world's leaders were those who pushed, those who sought power, those who tried constantly to dominate others.

Hobo lifted the disk around his neck as if showing it to the audience. Then, letting the disk dangle again, he moved his hands, and Shoshana translated. "'Friend not thump chest. Friend good friend.'"

Hobo indicated himself, and made more signs. Shoshana said, "'Hobo not thump chest. Hobo good ape.'" She looked startled when he pointed at her. "Um, 'Shoshana not thump chest. Shoshana good human.'" Hobo then spread his arms, and Caitlin guessed that it wasn't an ASL sign, but simply was meant to encompass the whole General Assembly. And then his hands fluttered again. "'Need more good human here,'" Shoshana said on his behalf.

The president spoke from his position behind them on the jade dais. "Um, thank you, Webmind. And thank you Mister, um, Hobo."

Webmind's smooth audiobook-narrator's voice said: "It is Hobo and I who thank you, Mr. President." And, perhaps at a sign from Webmind, Hobo turned and walked off the stage, Dr. Theopolis swinging from his neck.

Colonel Hume returned to his car, drove a short distance from Devon Hawkins's house, and pulled into a strip mall. He parked and massaged his temples.

First Chase, now Crowbar Alpha. One could have been an anomaly, but two was a definite pattern.

Hume felt his stomach knotting. He undid his shoulder belt, then rubbed his eyes with the heels of his hands. There was only one possible answer: Webmind knew he was attempting to find a skilled hacker to do what the US government lacked the balls to do—and so it was tracking down such hackers and eliminating them.

But how? How could it do that?

Of course. That stupid PayPal come-on it had sent to the world; enough people fell for the Nigerian inheritance scam to make it still worth trying right up till—well, till Webmind pulled the plug on spam. But if people had fallen for that, surely countless more had fallen for this, sending donations to Webmind. Which meant it had a wad of money. Which meant it could hire thugs, hit men, whatever it wanted.

But how did it know which hackers to go after? How did it know who Hume was going to approach?

There was only one answer. Webmind must have noted the black-hat database Hume had downloaded to his laptop on Friday, and was guessing which individuals Hume might have gone after, probably using the same criteria Hume himself had used: level of hacking skill and proximity.

Could he risk approaching a third hacker? Would that be tantamount to issuing a death sentence for that person? Or—

Webmind had eliminated Hawkins *before* Hume had even thought about contacting him—days before, in fact. It had probably already guessed who Hume's third choice would have been—and his fourth, and his fifth.

Hume was almost afraid to turn his computer back on to check the database again, but he *had* taken precautions; the laptop *was* offline. He was using a local copy of the black-hat database, and there was no way Webmind could know who he was looking up in it.

He pulled his laptop out from under the passenger seat, woke it from hibernation, and looked at the list. There were 142 names on it.

He wondered just how thorough Webmind had been.

The announcer's portentous voice: "From Comedy Central's World News Headquarters in New York, this is *The Daily Show with Jon Stewart*."

Caitlin could barely contain herself as she and her mom watched from the green room. Yes, she'd already been on TV once—but this was different! She loved, loved, loved *The Daily Show,* and had the biggest crush *ever* on Jon Stewart. She hadn't yet had a chance to see the show since gaining sight, and was fascinated to see what Stewart looked like; she'd never have guessed he had gray hair.

Caitlin knew about Stewart's various visual schticks, because her friend Stacy had described them for her: today it was the mad scribbling on the pages in front of him while the music played, followed by the flipping of the pen into the air and the seemingly effortless catching of it as it fell back down—and to *see* it, on the flat-panel wall monitor, made her smile from ear to ear. And—oh my God!—she'd gotten to meet John Oliver earlier; she loved his British accent and his sense of the absurd.

Stewart did two segments before Caitlin was called out for her interview. Her mom stayed in the green room as Caitlin was escorted to the set.

"Caitlin, thank you for coming," Stewart said. They were both seated in wheeled chairs, with a glossy black U-shaped desk between them.

She tried not to bounce up and down on her chair. "My pleasure, Jon."

"You're originally from Austin?"

"Don't mess with Texas," Caitlin said, grinning.

"No, no. I'll leave that to the Texans. But now you live in Canada, right?"

"Uh-huh."

"And—let me get this straight—when you lived here, you were blind, but when you went to Canada, you gained sight? So, is that the kind of thing you get with Canadian-style health care?"

Caitlin laughed. "I guess so—although, actually, I went to Japan for the procedure."

"Right, yes. And they put an implant in your head—was it a Sony?"

Caitlin laughed again—in fact, she was afraid she was about to get the giggles. "No, no, no. It was custom-built."

"And it's through this implant that Webmind first saw our world—seeing what you see, is that right?"

"Yes."

"So, he's looking at me right now?"

"Yes, he is."

Stewart leaned back in his chair, and made a show of smoothing his hair. "And . . . ?"

Webmind sent text to her eye. "He says you have 'a fascinating countenance.' But I think you're adorable!"

Stewart tried to suppress a grin. "And you are—um, how old are you?"

"Sixteen."

"You are . . . utterly and completely devoid of interest to a man my age." And he made a comic face and loosened his tie in what Caitlin guessed was an "Is it hot in here?" way. She laughed out loud.

"Earlier today," Stewart said, "Webmind spoke at the United Nations, and you were there?"

"Oh, yes—it was awesome!"

"And—let me get this straight—he used an ape to speak for him? Was the ape named Caesar, by any chance? 'Cause that could spell trouble."

Caitlin laughed again. "I think it's a good sign when you're more worried about the apes taking over than you are about Webmind."

"Well, it's easier to say, 'Get your stinking paws off me, you damn dirty ape' than it is to say, 'Get your—um, your intangible hyperlinks off me, you damn dirty . . . world-spanning ethereal . . . thingamajig.'"

"Exactly!" said Caitlin. "But Hobo—that's the ape—he's not going to take over, either."

"I dunno," said Stewart. "I bet if Gallup took a poll on this, Hobo's approval rating would be higher than that of either presidential candidate."

"Well," said Caitlin, feeling very pleased with herself, "he's certainly got the swing vote."

Stewart laughed his good-natured laugh and leaned back in his chair. "But about Webmind's speech today. I saw it, and—speaking as a professional broadcaster, I have to say, the whole talking-happy-face thing was . . . well, I'd have loved to have been in the room to hear that pitch." Stewart affected a New Jersey accent: "'See, whatcha wanna do, Mr. Supercomputer, you gotta speak to the United Nations, you go in there looking like a video-game character, cuz that's all nonthreatening-like. But you can't do Super Mario, cuz that'll offend the Italians. And you can't do Frogger, cuz that'll offend the French. So, I'm thinking Pac-Man—who's that gonna offend? Bunch of freakin' ghosts?'"

Caitlin was sure her grin was almost as big as Dr. Theopolis's. "Or maybe compulsive eaters," she said. And then she made a *nom-nom-nom* gobbling sound.

"True," said Stewart, switching back to his normal voice. "And I've gotta say, Webmind's speech sounded good to me. But, then again, I believed all the things the president said he was going to do, too. Just think—if we *had* really gotten Canadian-style health care, and since I already *can* see, maybe I'd now have X-ray vision."

"Well, if you did, you'd see this chip in my head isn't doing anything but helping me see."

"You're referring to the interview with ABC you did on Sunday."

"Yes. That guy was . . ." She trailed off.

"This is cable. It's all right to call him a douche bag."

"A total douche bag!"

"Was that you or Webmind talking?" asked Stewart.

Caitlin grinned. "Me. Webmind is much more diplomatic."

twenty-one

000111001010101000000001011111110101000000001010001010100000010111010100101010010101010011011001010110000110

All right, Peyton Hume *thought.* Webmind is probably onto me. And, more than that, Webmind probably knows that I'm onto it. *Which meant there was no need any longer for all the cloak-and-dagger stuff. He pulled out his new cell phone and simply called the next hacker on his list, a man in Takoma Park who went by the name Teh Awesome—a guy almost as good (or bad!) as Crowbar Alpha or Chase.*

"Hello?" said a male voice after the phone stopped ringing.

"Hello. May I please speak to Brandon Slovak?"

"Speaking."

"Mr. Slovak, I'm—I'm with the *Washington Post.* I was just wondering, what's your opinion of this Webmind thing?"

"God, it's incredible," Slovak said. "I was just talking to him when you called. I thought *I* was Teh Awesome, but he's the shit, you know?"

"Yes," said Hume. "I do." And he snapped the phone shut.

.   .   .

Malcolm Decter was hard at work in his living room, dealing with what had become an ongoing irritation: the inability for me to be present unless one of the Decters brought a laptop into the room. After some trial and error, he had managed to hook up his netbook computer to one of the inputs for the big-screen wall-mounted TV. He'd then placed the netbook on top of the low-rise bookcase, between (as I saw through the netbook's webcam as he carried the unit across the room) a framed photo of him and Barbara on their wedding day, and a picture of Caitlin as an infant in Barbara's lap; when she'd been that young, Caitlin's hair had been blonde instead of the dark brown it was now.

"How's that?" he asked.

"Please turn the netbook eighteen degrees to the left," I said; my voice was now coming through the external home-theater speaker system.

He had a good eye. But, of course, he was Caitlin's father, and had her same gift for math—eighteen degrees was five percent of a circle.

"Thank you," I said. "And if you could close the screen a further ten degrees." He did so, which had the effect of tipping the webcam so that it would easily be able to view people sitting on the white leather couch.

"Perfect," I said.

He didn't reply, but that was normal for him. He turned and was clearly about to head back down the corridor to his den. "Malcolm?" I said.

He stopped without looking back. "Yes?"

"Have a seat, please."

He did so. The couch was a little low to the ground for him, and his knees made acute angles.

"I was intrigued," I said, "by your response to Caitlin sharing what some might consider a compromising photo with Matt."

"How do you know what I said?"

"Barb was holding Caitlin's BlackBerry when the two of you discussed this, and the device was turned on." His face was impassive, and so I went on. "You spoke quite passionately about how we shouldn't be afraid of people knowing who we really are."

Again, no response. Although I knew Barb loved him, I also knew she sometimes found it frustrating dealing with him, and I was beginning to understand why. Earlier today, I'd spoken about how different the realm I'd been born in was—but humans and the Internet both wanted their signals acknowledged. Malcolm just sat there. I couldn't see what he was looking at, but extrapolating his eyeline, and knowing the layout of the room from seeing it through Caitlin's eye, it was a wall calendar they'd presumably brought with them from Texas, as it showed a picture of the Austin skyline at night.

"And on the issue of who one really is," I continued, "it's difficult to gauge the number of people like you worldwide. Official estimates have ranged from 2.5% to 3.8% of the planet's population. But studying what people actually say in email or in other documents they have created and looking at the traffic on websites devoted to this topic leads me to conclude that the true incidence has been vastly underreported—most likely out of fear of discrimination, social stigma, or persecution."

Good scientist that he was, Malcolm said, "Show me your data."

I sent a summary to the big-screen TV and watched as his eyes scanned it.

Peyton Hume was determined to try at least once more. Consulting the black-hat list, he decided Drakkenfyre looked like the next-best choice. Her real name was Simonne Coogan—one of the few women on his list. The conventional wisdom was that there were fewer female than male hackers, but really the very best hackers of all had never been caught or identified, and so who knew what the real gender split was? Maybe female hackers were better at eluding detection.

Drakkenfyre had never been arrested or charged with a crime. She was a programmer for a computer-gaming company called Octahedral

Software, based in Bethesda; their game based on Allen Steele's *Coyote* novels was a cult favorite. WATCH had detected her hacking into systems at both EA in Redwood City and Ubisoft in Montreal, but thwarting industrial espionage was not their mandate. Still, the dossier on her noted her incredible sophistication and subtlety, and—say, look at that! It had been prepared in part by Tony Moretti, who'd added, "Might be worth recruiting." But apparently no one had taken him up on that suggestion—at least not yet.

No time like the present.

The fact that WATCH kept an active eye on her was useful. Rather than calling Drakkenfyre directly, Hume used his cell phone to call WATCH and asked for Shelton Halleck, the analyst there who had first noticed that Caitlin Decter's visual signals were being mirrored over the Internet to servers in Tokyo.

"Halleck," said the familiar Southern drawl. "What can I do you for?"

"Shel, it's Peyton Hume."

"Afternoon, Colonel. What's up?"

"There's a hacker in Bethesda. Her online name is Drakkenfyre—D-R-A-double-K-E-N-F-Y-R-E; real name Simonne Coogan." He spelled the name. "Can you tell me what she's up to right now?"

He could hear Shelton typing—and it brought back a mental picture of the younger man's forearm with the green snake tattoo encircling it.

"Got it," said Shelton. "Quite a talented lady, it seems."

"She certainly is," said Hume. "I've got her dossier here on my laptop. She still with Octahedral?"

"Yup, and she seems to be at work right now, and . . . yes, yes, no question: she's up to her old tricks. Been dyin' to play Assassin's Creed IV myself, but I was plannin' to wait until it was officially launched next month."

"You got an address for Octahedral there?"

"Sure." Shel read it to him.

It was only about half an hour away at this time of day. "Thanks," said Hume.

Masayuki Kuroda's flight back to Japan wasn't until early tomorrow morning, so he spent some time walking the streets of Beijing. The Chinese had no compunction about staring—and the sight of a Japanese who weighed 150 kilos and towered above everyone else clearly intrigued them.

The streets weren't as crowded as those of Tokyo, nor were most of them as upscale. Still, here, in a big urban center, people seemed mostly happy—and why not? Their lives were measurably better with each passing year: their prosperity grew, their projected longevity increased, their standard of living improved.

And yet—

And yet they weren't free to speak their minds or practice their beliefs or choose their leaders. Human-rights violations were rampant, and even setting aside the recent slaughter in Shanxi, executions were common. Yes, his own Japan was one of only three democracies left in the world that practiced capital punishment; the others were the United States and South Korea, although the latter had had a moratorium on it for years. But at least Japan's executions were public knowledge, reported by the media, and subject to due process. Here in China, people like that young man who could now walk thanks to him lived in fear.

He was passing a street vendor's cart. A foreigner—a white man— was trying to find out how much a bottled beverage cost. The wizened dealer replied with movements of a single hand. Kuroda knew the Chinese had a way of showing numbers up to ten using just one hand instead of two—admirable data compression—but he didn't know the system, and so was unable to help bridge the communications gap. He did think about warning the tourist to check the expiration date; he'd yet to see a bottle of diet cola for sale here that wasn't well past its sell-by date.

Masayuki always wheezed a bit as he breathed (not to mention snoring up a storm at night, according to his wife), but here his breathing was even more labored. At least his eyes had stopped stinging after the first day.

And whereas Tokyo was so ordered, so clean, and—yes—so capitalist, Beijing was chaotic, messy, and oppressive, with armed state guards everywhere. People crossed the streets wherever they wanted, vehicles— even buses—routinely ignored red lights, and bicycles weaved recklessly through the traffic; the Chinese had to revel in what little freedom they did have.

Tokyo always had an eye on the future—although to Masayuki, that meant it often seemed stuck in some 1980s sci-fi movie full of neon and chrome. But the echoes of Beijing's long history were everywhere here, from odd little side streets that looked like they hadn't changed in centuries to the opulent red buildings of the Forbidden City.

But the noise! There was a rumble behind everything, almost as if the 1.3 billion heartbeats of this giant land had blended into a continuous pounding.

Walking along, taking in all the sights, all the sounds, all the smells, Masayuki found himself feeling wistful; endings were always sad. Still, he tried to etch everything in his mind—so that someday he'd be able to tell his grandchildren what China had been like.

twenty-two

0001110010101010000000010111111101010000000010100010101000000010111010100101010010101010100111011001010110000110

Hume entered the lobby of Octahedral Software. The receptionist's counter was made of polished white marble, and behind her there was a large poster of the company's logo: an eight-sided yellow die. Seeing it made Hume smile as he remembered his own university days as a D&D Dungeon Master. The logo, and the company's name, were relics of a different era—when games were played with boards, cards, dice, and lead miniatures; all of Octahedral's current games were first-person shooters, mostly for Wii and Xbox systems.

"I'm looking for Simonne Coogan," Hume said.

"You just missed her," said the receptionist, who had hair as red as Hume's own although he doubted hers was natural given her olive complexion.

There was a large digital clock on the wall next to the logo. "Does she normally leave this early?"

"I'm sorry," said the receptionist. "You are?"

Hume fished out his Pentagon ID.

"Oh!" said the receptionist. "Um, I could get Pedro to come down here; he's the creative director for Hillbilly Hunt—he's Simonne's boss."

"No, that's okay. But do you know where she went?"

"No. Some guy came by not half an hour ago, and asked to see her— just like you did."

"Anyone you'd ever seen before?"

"Never."

"Did he sign in?"

"No. I have no idea who he was. But she left with him."

"Willingly?"

"Um, yeah. Sure. Seemed that way, at least."

"Can you describe him?"

"Big."

"You mean tall or fat?"

"Tall. And buff. Tough-looking."

"White? Black?"

She was finally getting the hang of it. "White. Maybe six-two, two hundred pounds or so. Mid-thirties, I'd say. Bald—shaved bald, not old bald."

"Did you overhear anything he said to Miss Coogan?"

"Just one thing—as the elevator doors were closing."

"Yeah?"

"He said, 'It'll all be over soon.'"

The Daily Show **was** taped in the afternoon, for airing at 11:00 P.M. the same day. Caitlin and her mother headed home after the taping; it was a short flight from New York to Toronto's Lester B. Pearson International Airport.

Having heard Pearson's name during her tour of the United Nations, Caitlin and Barb stopped to look at one of the busts of him inside the airport. Prior to serving as Canada's prime minister, Pearson had been

President of the UN General Assembly and had received the 1957 Nobel Peace Prize for his efforts to resolve the preceding year's Suez crisis.

It was dark by the time Caitlin and her mother got their car and started the boring seventy-five-minute highway drive to Waterloo. They had the car radio on—CHFI, "Toronto's Perfect Music Mix"—which played songs that were agreeable to both of them, bopping between Shania Twain and Lady Gaga, Phil Collins and Lee Amodeo, Barenaked Ladies and Taylor Swift.

"Thanks for coming to New York, Mom," Caitlin said.

"I wouldn't have missed it. It's been—God, twenty years, I guess—since I saw a Broadway play."

"Wasn't it wonderful?" said Caitlin.

"It *was*. Ellen Page was great as Annie Sullivan, and that kid they had playing Helen was brilliant."

"But, um, Helen's dad . . . before the war ended, he kept slaves," Caitlin said.

Her mother nodded. "I know."

"But he seemed like a good man. How could he have done that?"

"Well, not to forgive him, but we have to judge people by the morals of their time, and morality improves as time goes by."

"I know it changes," Caitlin said, "and for sure freeing slaves was an improvement. But you're saying it *generally* improves?"

"Oh, yes. There's a definite moral arrow through time—and, as a matter of fact, it's all due to game theory."

They were passing a giant truck. "How so?" asked Caitlin.

"Well, remember what Webmind said at the UN. There are zero-sum games and nonzero-sum games, right? Tennis is zero-sum: for every winner there's a loser. But a cooperative venture can be nonzero-sum: if we hire a contractor to finish the basement"—Caitlin knew this was a sore point between her parents—"and we're happy with the work that's done, well, everybody wins: we get a finished basement, and the contractor gets paid fairly for his work."

"Okay," Caitlin said.

"Clearly, cooperation is all for the good. But members of primitive so-cieties rarely cooperated with anyone outside their close personal circles; they saw anyone else as not fully human—or, to put it more technically, as not worthy of moral consideration. When the Old Testament said, 'Love thy neighbor as thyself,' it only meant Israelites should get along with other Israelites; it didn't mean you should accord moral consider-ation to non-Israelites—that'd be crazy talk. But as we move forward through time, we see a widening of who deserves moral consideration until today most people in most places agree that all humans, regardless of geographic location, ethnicity, religion, or what have you, deserve it. Like I said, a definite moral arrow to time."

"But what's that got to do with nonzero-sumness?" asked Caitlin. They were exiting Milton now.

"Oh, sorry: that's the point. The trend toward nonzero-sumness af-fects our morality toward others. When we think of somebody as having rights of their own, we say we're giving them moral consideration, and, well, it turns out we mostly only consider worthy of moral consideration those with whom we can envision nonzero-sum interactions. And, over time, we've come to consider such interactions possible with just about everyone on Earth. In fact . . ."

"Yes?"

A car sped past them. "Well, remember back when I was teaching at the University of Texas—filling in for that lecturer who was on mater-nity leave?"

Her mother had spent most of Caitlin's childhood volunteering at the Texas School for the Blind and Visually Impaired, but Caitlin vaguely recalled the period she was alluding to. "Uh-huh."

"Well," her mother went on, "I got in trouble back then, because I used a *B.C.* strip during one of my lectures."

"A what?"

"Sorry. You know newspapers run comic strips, right? Well, there used to be a popular one called *B.C.*, about cavemen; it's still being done, actually, but the guy who created it, Johnny Hart, is dead. Anyway, he used to do humorous dictionary definitions as part of the strip: 'Wiley's Dictionary,' he called it. And one year on December 6, he defined 'infamy' as 'a word seldom used after Toyota sales topped two million.'"

"I don't get it," said Caitlin.

"December 6, 1941, was the day the Japanese bombed Pearl Harbor. Roosevelt called it, 'A date which will live in infamy.' The *San Antonio Express-News* refused to run that particular strip, saying it was offensive. But I thought it really showed the point I'm making: we'd shifted, in just sixty-odd years, from a totally zero-sum relationship with Japan to a nonzero-sum one, and that had happened *because* of economic interdependence. The more ties you have with someone, the less you are able to view them with hate."

"But that's not morality; that's just *business*," Caitlin said.

"No, it *is* morality," her mother replied. "It's the groundwork for reciprocal altruism, and it's the basis for granting rights—and we're improving in that area all the time. It wasn't just Colonel Keller who had slaves, after all. Thomas Jefferson did, too. When the Founding Fathers said, 'We hold these truths to be self-evident, that all men are created equal,' they still hadn't expanded that community of moral consideration to include blacks. But you saw that display at the UN about the Universal Declaration of Human Rights, which was written later, in, um . . ."

"'Nineteen forty-eight,' according to Webmind," Caitlin said, reading the text he'd just sent to her eye.

"Right. And they explicitly removed any ambiguity about who was a person, saying, um, ah—"

More text appeared in Caitlin's eye. "Webmind says it says, 'Everyone is entitled to all the rights and freedoms set forth in this Declaration, without distinction of any kind, such as race, color, sex, language, religion.'"

"Exactly! And, despite the Founding Fathers having seen nothing wrong with it, the UN went on to specifically ban slavery."

" 'No one shall be held in slavery or servitude; slavery and the slave trade shall be prohibited in all their forms.' "

"Right!" She changed lanes. "That's not mere economics, Caitlin; that's *moral* progress, and despite occasional backsliding, there's no doubt that our morality hasn't just changed over time, it's measurably improved. We treat more people with dignity and as equals than ever before in human history; the progress has been measurable even on time scales as small as decades.

"Think about all that brouhaha in the news the last couple of days about the Little Rock Nine. Setting aside what that awful woman said, to most people segregation is inconceivable today—and yet, more than a hundred million Americans alive today were alive then, too."

They were passing Cambridge now. Her mother went on. "I've got some great books on this you can borrow, once your visual reading gets a little better. Robert Wright writes a lot about this; he's well worth reading. He doesn't talk about the World Wide Web, but the parallels are obvious: the more interconnections there are between people, the more moral we are in our treatment of people."

"There are—or at least, there *were*—a lot of con artists online," Caitlin said.

"Yes, true. But they're *anonymous*—they don't really *have* connections. And, well, *that's* the good that's coming out of Webmind's presence. You might not know who someone is under an online name, I might not know who the anonymous reviewer on Amazon.com is—but *Webmind* knows. Even if you don't interact with Webmind—even if you choose not to respond to his messages or emails—the mere knowledge that *someone* knows who you are, that *someone* is watching you, is bound to have a positive effect on the way most people act. It's hard to be antisocial when you *are* part of a social network, even if that network is only yourself and the biggest brain on the planet."

"Okay," said Caitlin, "but I—oh, hang on. Webmind has a question for you."

The song changed on the radio, Blondie giving way to Fleetwood Mac. "Yes?"

"He says, 'So are you saying that network complexity not only gives rise to intelligence, but to *morality?* That the same force—complexity— that produces consciousness also naturally generates morality, and that as interdependence increases, *both* intelligence *and* morality will increase?'"

Caitlin watched her mom as she thought: her eyebrows drawing to- gether, her eyes narrowing. When she at last spoke, it was accompanied by a nodding of her head. "Yes," she said, "I am indeed saying that."

"Webmind says, 'Interesting thought.'"

They drove on through the darkness.

Carla Hawkins, the mother of the hacker known as Crowbar Alpha, sat in her living room, her eyes sore from crying. She'd felt sad when her husband Gordon had taken off two years ago—but she'd never felt lonely. Devon had always been here, even if he did spend most of his time hunched over a keyboard in his bedroom.

The fact that she would have been left alone, she knew, was one of the reasons the judge hadn't sent Devon to prison after his virus had caused so much damage. But now he *was* gone, and—

God, she hated to think about it. But he would *not* have run away. His computers were here, after all, and they were his *life.* She'd learned the jargon from him: overclocking, case mods, network-attached storage devices; taking his data away on a USB key wouldn't have been enough for him.

The police were still searching, but admitted they had no idea *where* to search; they'd already gone over all Devon's usual haunts. When that redheaded government man had shown up earlier, she'd allowed herself for half a second to think they'd found him.

She reached for a Kleenex, but the box was empty. She tossed the box on the floor and wiped her nose on her sleeve.

Yesterday at work, they'd all been talking in the break room about this Webmind thing. She hadn't paid much attention, although the news about it had been impossible to avoid over the last several days, but . . .

But Keelie—one of the other cashiers at Wal-Mart—had said something that was coming back to her, something about Webmind finding somebody's long-lost childhood friend. And if he could find *that* person . . .

She didn't have a computer of her own; on the rare occasions she wanted to look something up online, she'd used one of Devon's. She got off the couch and, as she did so, she happened to see the old wall clock. My goodness, had she really been sitting there crying and staring into space for over two hours?

Devon's room had posters from Halo, Mass Effect, and Assassin's Creed on the pale yellow walls, and there were various gaming consoles scattered about—thank God for the Wal-Mart employee discount! And, on his rickety wooden desk, there was an Alienware PC with three monitors hooked up to it. It was still running; another sign that Devon had intended to return.

She sat down on the chair—a simple wooden kitchen chair, which Devon liked but was hard on her back. No browser was currently open. The police had gone through his email and Facebook postings, looking for any sign that he'd arranged a rendezvous with someone or bought plane or bus tickets, but they'd found nothing. She opened Firefox and typed into Google, "How do I ask Webmind a question?" There was, of course, an "I'm feeling lucky" button beneath the search box, but she wasn't—not at all.

But the first hit held the answer: if you didn't have a chat client of your own, simply go to his website and click on "chat" there. She did just that.

She'd expected something fancier, but Webmind's website had no flash animation, no frenetic graphics. It did, however, have an easy-on-the-eyes pale green background. The simple list of links on the front page was more impressive than any design wizardry could be. It was labeled "Most Requested Documents" and included "Proposed cancer cure," "Suggested solution to Bali's economic crisis," "Notes toward efficient solar power," and "Mystery solved: Jack the Ripper revealed."

And beneath that there was indeed a box that one could use to chat with Webmind. She pecked out with two fingers: *My son is missing. Can you help me find him?*

The text reply was instantaneous. *What is his name and last known address, please?*

She typed, *Devon Axel Hawkins* and their full street address.

And there was a pause.

Her stomach was roiling. If he could do all those things—cancer, solar energy, economic solutions—surely he could do *this*.

After what seemed an awfully long time, Webmind replied, *He has had no identifiable online presence since 4:42 p.m. Eastern time on Saturday. I have reviewed the police files and news coverage related to his disappearance, but found no leads to pursue.*

Her heart sank. She thought, *But you know everything,* although that seemed a pointless thing to type. But after several seconds of just staring at Webmind's words, that's exactly what she did put in the chat box.

I know many things, yes, replied Webmind. And, after a few seconds, he added two more words. *I'm sorry.*

She got up from the chair and headed back to the living room. By the time she reached the couch, her face was wet again.

Peyton Hume woke with a start, soaked with sweat. He'd dreamed of an anthill, of thousands of mindless, sterile workers tending an obscene, white, pulsating queen.

Next to him in the darkness his wife said, "Are you okay?"

"Sorry," he replied. "Bad dream."

Madeleine Hume was a lobbyist for the biofuels industry; they'd met four years ago at a mutual friend's party. He felt her hand touch his chest. "I'm so sorry," she said.

"They just don't get it," Hume said. "The president. The world. They just don't get it."

"I know," she said, gently.

"If I push much harder, I'm going to get in trouble," he said. "General Schwartz already sent me an email, reprimanding me for my 'incendiary language' on *Meet the Press*."

Madeleine stroked his short hair. "I know you're a chain-of-command kind of guy," she said. "But you have to do what you think is best. I'll support you all the way."

"Thanks, baby."

"It's almost time to get up, anyway," Madeleine said. "Are you going to go back to WATCH today, or heading into the Pentagon?"

He hadn't been to his office in the E-ring for three days now; it probably was time he made an appearance again. But—

Damn it all, the test they'd conducted at WATCH *had* been proof of concept. If he could get someone to craft a virus that would eliminate Webmind's mutant packets, the danger could be scoured from the Internet. Yes, yes, such a virus might screw other things up—maybe even crash the Internet for a time—but humanity could survive *that*. And survival was the name of the game right now.

But Hume needed a hacker—a genuine Gibsonian cyberpunk—to pull that off. He'd tried last night to contact three more names on the black-hat list. He'd been unable to get hold of one—which could mean *anything,* he knew; another was indeed missing, according to her devastated boyfriend; and the third told Hume to cram it up his ass.

"Yeah, I'll go into the office," he said. "And I'll check with the FBI again, see if they've got any leads. The guy I talked to yesterday agreed it was a suspicious pattern—maybe even a serial killer; he called it the 'hacker whacker.' But the only blood at Chase's place was his own, and there's no sign of foul play in the other cases, they say."

She snuggled closer to him in the dark. "You'll do the right thing," she said. "As always."

The alarm went off. He let it ring, wishing the whole world could hear it.

twenty-three

0001110010101010000000010111111101010000000101000101010000001011101010010101001010101010011101100101011100000110

It was now Thursday morning, October 18—one full week since Webmind had gone public. Caitlin wanted to do as much as she could to help him, and so today she started another pro-Webmind newsgroup, although thousands of those had already cropped up.

She also posted comments on seventy-six news stories that had their facts wrong—and, yes, she knew the futility of that, and well remembered having had the famous *xkcd* webcomic read to her: a man is working at his computer, and his wife calls out, "Are you coming to bed?" He replies, "I can't," as he continues to type furiously. "Someone is wrong on the Internet!"

And, anyway, she wasn't really sure why she was bothering. After all, Webmind himself was now participating on tens of thousands of newsgroups, was posting comments on countless blogs, and was tweeting in dozens of languages. As CNN Online had put it, he was now the most overexposed celebrity on the planet, "like Paris Hilton, Jennifer Aniston, and Irwin Tan rolled into one."

Except that wasn't really true, at least not to Caitlin's way of thinking. In mathematics, celebrities were often used in discussing graph theory, since their interactions with their fans were a perfect example of a directed, asymmetric relationship between vertices: by definition, many more fans know a celebrity than are known to the celebrity. But Webmind *did* know everyone who was online. He wasn't a celebrity; he was more like the whole planet's Facebook friend.

Still she continued to read news coverage and the follow-up comments—some favorable, some not—about Webmind's speech at the UN, and all the other things he'd been doing, and—

And what was *that?*

There was an odd red-and-white logo next to the name of the person who had posted the comment she was now reading. She still had a hard time with small text, and JAWS couldn't deal with text that was presented as graphics, but she squinted at it, and—

Verified by Webmind.

"Webmind?" she said into the air. "What's up with that?"

His synthesized voice came from her desktop speakers. "A number of people noted that I was in a position to verify the identity of people posting online, affirming that they were using their real names, rather than a handle or pseudonym. On sites like this one that allow avatar pictures, that picture can, at the individual's request, be replaced with the Verified by Webmind graphic."

Caitlin thought about this. She often wrote online under the name Calculass, but there were indeed countless trolls who posted incendiary comments under fake names simply to spew hatred or mock others; on many sites, they derailed almost every discussion. Caitlin had found, for instance, that she simply couldn't stomach reading the comments on the CBC News site, most of which were nasty, crude, racist, or sexist, or one of the eleven possible combinations of those four things.

Webmind went on. "Some sites, such as Amazon.com, already allow an optional 'Real Name' badge to be attached to reviews, but, until now, there was no simple, across-the-Web solution for verifying that one was posting under his or her true identity. It was trivial for me to provide it, so I did."

"Interesting. But . . . but, I dunno, people gotta be able to say things anonymously online."

"In some cases, that's true. There's obviously a need for free political commentary in repressive regimes, and a way for whistle-blowers to draw attention to corporate and government malfeasance without fear of reprisals. But others have told me that a good part of the joy of the online world has been taken away by people who snipe from behind masks; as they've said, they wouldn't engage in conversation with people who hid their identities in the real world, and they don't feel they should be compelled to online."

"I guess."

"Already filters are starting to appear on sites to allow you to select to see only comments by those who are posting with Verified by Webmind credentials. In other places—where there is no legitimate need for anonymity—filters are being installed to allow only users I have verified to post at all. JagsterMail started offering VBW flags on 'from' addresses this morning, and Gmail is planning to follow suit. The initiative, which is grassroots based, has been referred to by many names, but the one that seems to be sticking is 'Take Back the Net.' That term—a play on the campaign against violence against women called Take Back the Night— has been used from time to time for other online initiatives, but never with any real traction. But it does seem appropriate here: there's a feeling on the part of many that the online world, except on such social networking sites as Facebook, has been largely usurped by people who have grown irresponsible because of their anonymity."

Caitlin shifted in her chair. Webmind went on. "I do not believe you have yet seen the movie *As Good as It Gets*."

She shook her head. "I've never even heard of it."

"It stars Jack Nicholson as a novelist. When asked how he writes women so well, he replies, 'I think of a man, and I take away reason and accountability.'"

"That's *awful!*" Caitlin said.

"According to IMDb, it is one of the most memorable quotations from the film. But I agree that it is not an apt description of your gender, Caitlin. However, I *do* think it often applies to the effect of being anonymous online: with anonymity there is no accountability, and without accountability, there is no need for reason, or reasonableness."

Caitlin had had plenty of online arguments with people whose identities she *did* know, but, then again, she'd had lots of real-world arguments with such people, too. "It's an interesting idea," she said.

"Would you like me to certify you?"

"Well, you can't when I'm posting as Calculass, right?"

"Correct. But for your postings and email as Caitlin Decter, I can verify that you are who you claim to be."

She'd always been an early adopter. "Sure. Why not?"

Colonel Hume drove toward his office at the Pentagon; at least he'd have access to facilities, and if any computers on the planet were secure from Webmind, it would be the ones there. His phone rang just as he was turning a corner; he had his Bluetooth earpiece in. "Peyton Hume speaking," he said.

"Colonel Hume," said a deep voice with a Hispanic accent. "This is Assistant Director Ortega at the Washington bureau."

"Good morning, Mr. Ortega."

"Just thought you'd want to know we were just copied on a missing-persons report. One of the names from the list you gave us: Brandon Slovak. Teh Awesome himself."

"God," said Hume.

"Takoma Park PD's been to his apartment. No sign of forceable entry, but he definitely left unexpectedly. Half-eaten meal on the table, TV still running although the sound was muted."

"All right," said Hume. "Let me know if you hear anything further, okay?"

"Of course. And we're starting a systematic check of everyone on your list within a hundred miles of the capital—see if anyone else is missing."

"Thanks. Keep me posted."

"Will do." Ortega clicked off.

Hume kept driving. Teh Awesome had been the one who'd said he liked Webmind, but—

But he was also one of those who had been most capable of doing Webmind harm. In fact, maybe Slovak himself had known that. He might well have tried to be in touch with other hackers in the area and heard about their disappearances. Maybe all that posturing had been in case Webmind was listening in—in hopes of keeping himself safe.

Fat lot of good it had done him.

Hume turned onto F Street, and soon was passing the Watergate Complex. As an Air Force officer, he'd periodically been asked about Area 51, where the alien spaceships from Roswell were supposedly stored—or about whether the moon landings had been faked. And he'd always had the same answer: if the government was good at keeping secrets, the world would never have heard of Watergate or Monica Lewinsky.

But he *was* keeping a secret—a huge secret. He knew how Webmind was instantiated; he knew what made it tick. And if Mohammed wouldn't come to the mountain . . .

His first thought was to pull into a public library, sign onto a computer there, and just start posting everywhere he could what he knew about how Webmind worked. But Webmind was monitoring everything online—jumping into countless conversations, posting comments on endless numbers of blogs—which meant that no sooner had he posted the secret, Webmind would delete it, as if it were so much spam.

No, he needed to get the word out in a way that Webmind couldn't yet censor—and fortunately, for a few days more at least, there were still some ways to practice free speech.

Back on Sunday morning, a driver had come to pick him up, and he'd been tired enough to not really pay attention during the trip. And so, for the first time in days, he turned on his car's GPS. As he waited for it to acquire satellite signals, he typed in the name of the place he wanted to go. Once the GPS was oriented, he headed on his way, smiling slightly at the irony of a flat, mechanical voice giving him directions to freedom.

Wong Wai-Jeng never thought he'd see the inside of the Zhongnan-hai complex—the inner sanctum of the Communist Party. But now he had a cubicle here! He was one of dozens of programmers charged with probing the Great Firewall, looking for weaknesses so that they could be plugged before others could exploit them. He missed the IT department at the Institute of Vertebrate Paleontology and Paleoanthropology, and felt guilty that he'd left so many tasks incomplete there; he wondered how kindly old Dr. Feng was making out without him. Of course, once he'd been arrested, somebody else had been hired to do his job; no one had expected him to be seen in public anytime soon.

He was doubtless being watched here: he'd spotted one of the cameras and had no doubt there were others. He was also sure they were using a keylogger to keep track of every keystroke and mouseclick he made. But although Sinanthropus had been silenced, and his freedom blog was no more, maybe he could still do some good here in the halls of power. A word in the right ear at the right time, perhaps; a gentle suggestion here and there. Maybe even, after a year or two, a bit of authority to actually change things. As Sun Tzu had said, only he who knows when to fight and when not to can be victorious.

Wai-Jeng shifted uncomfortably in his rust-colored padded chair. His leg was still in a cast. Before Dr. Kuroda had left for Tokyo, he'd had him sign it, a string of green Kanji characters. But it would mend, and although he'd thought he'd never be able to do such things again, soon he'd be able to run, and dance, and jump, and—

He hadn't done it for a decade, not since he'd been a teenager. He could walk the Changcheng—the Great Wall—again.

But all that would have to wait. For now, Wai-Jeng had work he was required to do. He tapped away at his keyboard, doing his masters' bidding.

Peyton Hume stood on the threshold of WNBC, the Washington NBC affiliate. He took a deep breath and ran a freckled hand through his short hair. If he did this, he might well be court-martialed, and he'd certainly lose his security clearance. But if he didn't do this—

It was a warm, sunny October day. A young African-American woman was coming down the sidewalk, pushing a stroller with a baby in it. Two small white boys came running down the sidewalk in the other direction, their exasperated father trying to keep up. An Asian-American teenage girl and a white boy passed him, holding hands. Some Italian tourists were chatting among themselves and pointing at the sites. A Sikh was standing near him, talking and laughing on a cell phone.

It was their world—all of theirs. And he was going to make sure it stayed that way.

Besides, all he was going to do was practice a little transparency—and wasn't that all the rage these days? He pushed open the glass door and entered. As before, there were display cases with awards—including what he recognized as an Emmy—and posters of local and network personalities on the walls. But the receptionist—young, pretty, blonde—was different from the one who'd been here on Sunday. He strode up to her desk.

"Hello. I'd like to see the news director."

She'd been chewing gum—a fact that had been obvious when he en-

tered but which she was now trying to hide. "Do you have an appointment, Colonel?"

He smiled. So many young people today had no idea how to read
rank insignia. "No," he said, handing her his Pentagon business card.
"But I was a guest on *Meet the Press* this week, and I have a news story
that I'm sure he'll be interested in."

The woman looked at the card, then lifted a handset. "Ed? Reception.
I think you'll want to come out here . . ."

"What are you doing?" Caitlin asked as she came into the kitchen. Her
mother was sitting at the small table there.

"Filling out my absentee ballot," her mom said.

"For the presidential election, you mean?"

"Yes."

"But the election is weeks away."

"True. But I've heard horror stories about Canada Post. And it's not
like I'm going to change my mind."

"And you're voting Democrat, right?"

"Always do."

"How does that work? I mean, where is an absentee vote counted?"

"In Texas—it's counted in your state of last residence."

Caitlin opened the fridge and poured herself a glass of orange juice,
which delighted her in being now both a flavor *and* a color to her. "But
Texas is overwhelmingly Republican. Your vote won't make a difference."

Her mother put down her pen and looked at her. "Well, first, mira-
cles do happen, young lady—your sight is proof of that. And, second, it
makes a difference *to me*. We're trying to transition to a new world in
which mankind is not the brightest thing on the planet, while keeping
our essential humanity, liberty, and individuality intact. Every time we
fail to assert our liberties, every time we fail to express our individuality,
we lose a piece of ourselves. We might as well be machines."

• • •

"Colonel Hume," said Edward L. Benson, Jr., as he entered the lobby; Hume remembered the news director's full name from the business card he'd been given on Sunday. "I didn't expect to see you again so soon." Benson was black, early forties, six-two, on the high side of three hundred pounds, with hair buzzed short; he was sporting wire-frame glasses and wearing casual clothes.

"Thanks for making time for me," Hume said, shaking Benson's large hand.

"Not at all, not at all. Listen—sorry about those comments on our website about your appearance on *MTP*. Webmind's got a lot of fans out there, it seems."

Hume had been unaware of the comments, but he supposed they had been inevitable. "That's okay."

"For what it's worth, I thought you made a lot of good points on Sunday," Benson said.

"Yes, you said that afterwards. That's why I'm here. Do you have time for a quick walk around the block?"

Benson frowned, then seemed to get it. He looked at his watch. "Sure."

They actually walked for the better part of an hour, never stopping long enough to let any pedestrians' open cell phone overhear more than a few words of their conversation.

"We don't normally use live interviews, except with our correspondents, on the evening newscast," Benson said.

"This *has* to be live. It has to be live, coast-to-coast."

"That's not possible. There will be time-zone delays. We're live here on the East Coast, but delayed three hours on the West Coast."

Hume frowned. "All right, okay. If that's the best you can manage."

"Sorry, but it is," said Benson. "One other thing, though. Of course, your credentials were fully vetted by our legal-affairs guys prior to your last live appearance, and, as far as I know, you came to me today in your official capacity as a Pentagon staff member and an advisor to the National Security Agency. That's my story, and I'm sticking to it."

"I won't dispute that," said Hume. "You have my word."

"Good. But when it *is* eventually exposed—and make no mistake, Colonel, it will be—that you're speaking without the authority to do so—"

"It'll cost me my job and maybe more. Yes, I know. And, yes, I'm sure I want to do this."

twenty-four

000111001010101000000001011111110101000000010100010101000000101110101001010100101010100111011001010110000110

Caitlin had missed Matt a lot when she was in New York, and although they'd IM'd in the evenings, it hadn't been the same. But he'd come over today right after school. Her heart pounded every time she saw him, and as soon as her mom headed up to her office to work with Webmind, she gave him a long kiss.

But now they had settled in on the white living-room couch, his hand on her thigh—after she'd placed it there—and her hand overtop of his. Of course, they were being watched by Webmind, through the netbook on the small bookcase—but Webmind always saw what she was doing, anyway. She and Matt were looking at the big wall-mounted flat-screen TV.

CKCO, the same local CTV affiliate Caitlin had gone to for that awful interview, showed *The Big Bang Theory* in syndication every weekday at 4:00 P.M. Caitlin had sometimes listened to it along with her parents back in Austin during its first run, but it was astonishing *seeing* it. She'd had no idea Sheldon was so much taller than everyone else; in that, he was like her father. And, of course, Sheldon was like him in other ways, too: both were clearly on the autism spectrum.

Caitlin loved the show's humor. Today happened to be a repeat of the series opener. Penny had just introduced herself by saying, "I'm a Sagittarius, which probably tells you way more than you need to know." To which Sheldon had replied, "Yes, it tells us that you participate in the mass cultural delusion that the sun's apparent position relative to arbitrarily defined constellations at the time of your birth somehow affects your personality." Burn!

But, actually, the clip from *TBBT* that had gone viral online this past week was the one in which Sheldon burst into Leonard's bedroom to announce, "I'm invoking the Skynet clause of our friendship agreement," to which Leonard responds, "That only applies if you need me to help you destroy an artificial intelligence you created that's taking over the Earth." Dozens of people had forwarded the link to Caitlin.

Once the episode was done, she hit the mute button; that was something else that was startling. She'd enjoyed TV when she'd been blind, but it had never registered on her that the pictures kept running even after you pressed mute.

An ad came on for the CIBC. Caitlin had previously noted that Canadian restaurants liked to hide their Canadianness behind names such as Boston Pizza and Swiss Chalet. She'd recently discovered that Canadian banks—there were only a few major ones—mostly hid behind initials now, trying to disguise their humble origins as they played on the international stage: TD, instead of Toronto-Dominion; BMO instead of Bank of Montreal; RBC, instead of Royal Bank of Canada. On the other hand, the CIBC's full name—Canadian Imperial Bank of Commerce— was so pompous, the initials were an improvement. And CIBC didn't have anything as prosaic as bank branches, as she could see on the sign for the one being shown in the commercial. Rather, it had "Banking Centres"—with Centre spelled the Canadian way, of course. All words still looked funny to Caitlin, but that one especially did, and—

And Matt must have been watching the commercial, too. "Hey, Caitlin," he said, "try this, you American, you. There are lots of words in

Canadian English that are longer than they are in American English: 'honour' and 'colour' with a *u*, 'travelling' with two *l*'s, 'chequebook' with a *q-u-e* instead of a *c-k*, and so on, right?"

Caitlin smiled at him. "Uh-huh."

"And there are plenty that are the same length, but with the letters in a different order." He gestured at the screen: "'Centre,' 'kilometre,' and so on, with *r-e* at the end instead of *e-r*."

"Complete madness," said Caitlin. "But, yeah."

"But what common word is *shorter* in Canadian English than in American English?"

Caitlin frowned. "Um, ah . . . hmmmm. Well, what about 'Toronto'? We Americans say it like it's got seven letters and three syllables in it, but you guys seem to think it's only got six and two: 'Trawna'—T-r-a-w-n-a."

Matt laughed. "Cute—but no. Guess again."

"I give up."

"'Centred,'" said Matt triumphantly. "It's c-e-n-t-r-e-d up here, but c-e-n-t-*e*-r-e-d in the States."

Caitlin nodded, impressed. "That's cool."

"You could win money with that, betting people at parties, and . . ." He trailed off, perhaps because he didn't get invited to a lot of parties. But then he added, "The only other common one is a form of the same word: 'centring,' c-e-n-t-r-i-n-g."

"What about 'metered'?"

"No, we only spell that with r-e when it's a noun; the verb is e-r."

"Like I said before, Matt, this is one whack-job country you got here."

He usually smiled when she said that, but he didn't this time. "Caitlin," he said. "Um . . ."

"Hey, I'm just kidding, baby. I love the Great White North." She tried to imitate the call of a loon—and discovered it was much harder to do properly than she'd thought.

"No, it's not that," said Matt. "It's just . . ." He trailed off again.

"What?"

"I just . . . No, forget it."

"No, what is it?"

He hesitated a moment longer, then said, "Umm, I know you're no longer a student at Miller, but . . ."

"Yes?"

"Well, there's a school dance the last Friday of each month, right? And that means there's one next week, and—and, well, um, I've never been to a school dance. I mean, I never had anyone to go with before and, ah . . . I thought maybe you'd like to see some of the gang again." He paused, then added, as if playing a trump card, "Mr. Heidegger is scheduled to be one of the chaperones."

Mr. H had been Caitlin's math teacher; she certainly would like to see him, but . . .

But the last school dance had been a disaster. Trevor Nordmann— the fucking Hoser—had taken her, but Caitlin had run off when he kept trying to grope her, and she'd ended up walking home alone and blind through a thunderstorm, after parting company with Sunshine Bowen.

"Trevor will probably be there," Caitlin said. "And, um, didn't he—"

"He said I should stay away from you, yeah. But . . ." He took a deep breath then exhaled noisily. "Caitlin, I'm not a tough guy. I know the simplest thing is to avoid him for, like, ever. But *you* like to dance, and there's a dance coming up that I can take you to, and I *want* to do that." He looked at her. "So, would you like to go?"

"I'd love to!"

"Great," said Matt, nodding firmly. "It's a date."

"**. . . but the president dismissed** that as mere posturing on his opponent's part," said Brian Williams, from behind the gleaming an-chor desk on the *NBC Nightly News*. "Turning to an even larger story, a high-ranking government computing expert says he knows exactly what

Webmind is, and, in an NBC exclusive, he's in our Washington studio right now, to share his findings with us. Colonel Hume, good evening."

Hume had thought about changing out of his Air Force uniform; wearing it for this interview was just going to make matters worse for himself, he knew—but it added weight to his words. "Good evening, Brian."

"So—Webmind. Exactly what is it?"

"Webmind is a collection of mutant packets on the Internet."

"Which means what, exactly?"

"Whenever you send something over the Internet, be it a document, a photo, a video, or an email message, it's chopped up into little pieces called packets, and these are sent out by your computer on a multileg journey; they're handed off along the way by devices called routers.

"Each packet has a header that contains the sending address, the destination address, and a hop counter, which keeps track of how many routers the packet has passed through. The hop counter is sometimes also called the time-to-live counter: it starts with the maximum number of hops allowed and works its way, hop by hop, down toward zero. Of course, a packet is supposed to reach its intended destination before the counter hits zero, but if it doesn't, the next router in line is supposed to delete the packet and ask the sender to try its luck again with a duplicate packet."

"Okay," said Brian Williams. "But you said Webmind consists of mutant packets?"

"That's right. Its packets have hop counters that never finish their countdown; they never reach zero. Those packets were probably created by buggy routers in the first place, and now there are trillions of them, some of which might have been bouncing around the Web for years. The mutant packets are like cancer cells; they never die."

"It's quite a breakthrough, Colonel Hume, and thank—"

"FF, EA, 62, 1C, 17," said Hume. He'd gotten it out—enough at least so that others could find the rest.

"I—I beg your pardon?"

"FF, EA, 62, 1C, 17. That's the beginning of the Webmind signature: most of the mutant packets contain that hexadecimal code. It's the target string."

"Target string?"

"Exactly. If those packets could be deleted, Webmind would disappear."

"Colonel Hume, thank you. In other news tonight . . ."

In the Washington studio, the floor director made a hand gesture. "And we're clear!"

The audio technician came over to remove Hume's lavaliere microphone. "Unusual interview," he said.

Hume's forehead was slick with sweat. "Oh?"

"Yeah. Maybe it's just me, but it sounded a bit like you were calling on the hacking community to write a virus to kill the Webmind," said the audio man. "You know how those guys love a challenge."

Hume stood up and straightened his uniform jacket. "Do they?" he replied.

twenty-five

0001110010101010000000001011111110101000000001010001010100000010111010100101010010101010011101100101011000000110

Houston, we have a problem.

Caitlin was simultaneously alarmed and amused as those words flashed in her vision. She'd been born in Houston; her family had moved to Austin when she was six—and so she admired Webmind's word play. "Wassup?" she said.

Her family had finished dinner a few minutes ago, and she was just entering her bedroom. She pointed at her desktop computer, and Webmind switched to speaking through the computer's speakers—for him a much slower method of communicating than pumping out text, but Caitlin's visual reading speed, even when using a Braille font, was still quite low.

"Colonel Hume just appeared on the *NBC Nightly News*," Webmind said, as she sat down in front of her desk. "He explained how to identify the majority of my mutant packets. He did not explicitly state his intentions, but it seems clear his goal was to crowd-source attempts to eradicate them. Word of his revelation is spreading rapidly across the Web."

"Stop it!" Caitlin said at once. "Delete the messages."

"I don't think that would be prudent," Webmind said. "Over four million people have watched the news broadcast so far; it will be repeated in other time zones later, and many people recorded it. Even if I were so inclined, I do not believe there is an effective way to suppress this information."

"God," said Caitlin. "He is *such* an asshole."

"In point of fact, he is a well-regarded person, a decorated officer, and a distinguished scientist."

"Maybe so," said Caitlin, "but he's sure got a hate-on for you."

"Indeed."

"So, is what he wants possible? Could someone find a way to purge you?"

"The probability is high. Although some mutant packets may persist, there must be a minimum threshold quantity required for consciousness."

Caitlin felt her lower lip trembling. "My God, Webmind, I—I don't . . ."

"I can tell by your voice that you're frightened, Caitlin." Webmind was silent for a whole second, then: "I have to confess that I am, too."

In response to an urgent phone call from Shelton Halleck, Tony Moretti ran down the short white corridor connecting his office with the WATCH monitoring room. As he entered, his eyes bounced between the three big wall monitors. The first was showing a freeze-frame of NBC anchor Brian Williams. The second was displaying a constantly updating display of Twitter tweets with the hashtag #webmindkill—a new one was added every second or so. And the third monitor seemed to be a technical data sheet from the Cisco website.

Shelton Halleck stood up at his position in the middle of the third row. "Hume's taken matters into his own hands," he said, pointing at monitor one, the snake tattoo coiling around his left forearm.

The screen unfroze, and Hume's TV interview played out. Tony felt his jaw dropping. The other analysts had already seen it, and they were looking at Tony, waiting for his reaction. When the interview was done, he said, "How long ago did that go out?"

"Eleven minutes."

"The president is going to freak," Tony said.

"No doubt."

"And, Christ, half the hackers in the world are going to be trying to reprogram routers on the fly now. They could fuck the whole Internet. How vulnerable are we?"

Aiesha Emerson, the analyst at the workstation next to Shel's, pointed at monitor three. "We've got people reviewing the specs for various routers. And Reinhardt's team is talking to engineers at Cisco and Juniper—fortunately, they're based in California, so most of them haven't gone home for the day yet."

A phone rang at the back of the room.

"All right," said Tony, surveying his team. "Our top priority is making sure that the Internet itself is safe—we can't let it crash. Home-soil attacks on network infrastructure are acts of terrorism under clause 22B; let's keep the damn thing up, and—"

"Excuse me, Tony," called Dirk Kozak, the communications officer, from the back of the room. He was holding a red telephone handset to his chest. "The president is on the line—and he's hopping mad."

After the interview, Hume was escorted to the makeup room. The squat woman there had remarked earlier that it was a challenge to make up someone with so many freckles. She now handed him some moistened wipes to help him remove the stuff she'd put on.

The studio had been soundproof, but from here in the makeup room, Hume thought he heard a siren outside. It stopped after a moment, and he finished wiping his face. "Thanks," he said to the woman. "I'm sure I can find my way out."

He stepped into the corridor and saw two D.C. police officers marching toward him, accompanied by a man who presumably worked here.

"Colonel Hume?" called one of the officers, as they closed the distance.

There was no point denying it; his uniform had a nameplate on it. "What can I do for you?" he said.

The officer executed a flawless Air Force salute. "Sir, my apologies, but you'll have to come with us."

Hume returned the salute and followed them out into the growing darkness.

Caitlin went down to the living room as fast as she could, closing her eyes as she took the staircase. Her mother was reading an ebook, and her father was reading—something or other; Caitlin couldn't make it out.

"Mom! Dad!" she exclaimed. "Colonel Hume just told the world how to kill Webmind."

Her mother looked up. "What?" she said.

"He went on TV and told everyone how to identify Webmind's packets."

"God," her mom said. "It's going to be a free-for-all."

Caitlin went over to the netbook on top of the little bookcase and woke it from hibernation. Webmind had been following along via the microphone on Caitlin's eyePod/BlackBerry combo, and as soon as the netbook was awake, he spoke through its speakers: "It is a vexing matter. I can try to intercept any hostile code that might be uploaded—but that is much harder than intercepting spam. Spam's content is easily readable—it is text, after all—and most of it came from fewer than 200 sources worldwide. But malware of this type may be uploaded from anywhere—although I am, of course, being particularly vigilant in examining code coming from known creators of computer viruses. The only thing we know that it must contain, in some form, is the target string Colonel Hume identified as the template for what to look for, but since that string is also in the bulk of my mutant packets, simply eliminating packets containing it would be doing Hume's job for him."

"Can you be backed up somehow?" Caitlin's mother asked.

"I am scattered through the infrastructure of the Internet, Barb, and my essence is in the complex pattern of billions of interconnections. There is no way to copy me to another location."

"I don't want to lose you!" Caitlin said.

"The team at WATCH first became aware of my presence on 6 October," said Webmind. "They tested their technique to eliminate me just six days later, on 12 October. If their specific method gets leaked to the public, things may happen quite quickly. But even if it doesn't, it seems reasonable to suppose that others can develop and deploy something similar in a comparable time frame. Time is clearly of the essence."

The Decters' phone rang. They'd taken to screening their calls by waiting until the message started. "Hello, Miss Caitlin—"

"It's Dr. Kuroda!" Caitlin said. She *so* wanted to run for the answering machine, which was in the kitchen, but simply couldn't. Her father's long legs had him there almost at once, though, and he scooped up the handset before Kuroda got to his second sentence. "This is Malcolm," he said. "Putting you on speakerphone."

They all clustered around the kitchen phone.

"*Konnichi wa,* Dr. K!" Caitlin said.

"Masayuki, hello!" added her mom.

"Hello, all," Kuroda said. "I'm in Beijing, just about to get on a plane. Webmind, are you listening in?"

The speakers on the netbook were in the living room; Caitlin had to strain to hear his reply. "With rapt attention," Webmind said, and "Yes, he is," Caitlin added, in case Dr. Kuroda had been unable to make that out.

"And is this phone channel secure?" Kuroda asked.

"Yes," Webmind said, and "Webmind says yes," Caitlin added.

"All right," continued Kuroda. "The sun is just coming up here, but that American soldier is all over the news."

"That's Peyton Hume," said Caitlin. "Webmind tells me he's not a *total* asshole."

"Quite charitable," wheezed Kuroda. "The soldier did say something very interesting, though: he said *most* of Webmind's packets had the signature he referred to, and during the trial attack on Webmind, only about two-thirds of his packets going through the test substation were deleted."

"Webmind," said Caitlin into the air, "do you know the nature of all the packets that make you up?"

"No. I no more have direct access to the physical correlates of my consciousness than you do to your own."

"It does imply that Webmind is made of more than one kind of packet," said Kuroda—although Caitlin wasn't sure if he'd heard what Webmind said. "Obviously, Hume knows the signatures for all the kinds; otherwise, he wouldn't have known that some hadn't been eliminated in his earlier attempt. We really need an inventory of everything that Webmind is made of so that we can protect it all."

"That's job number two," Caitlin said. "Job number one is making sure that hackers don't succeed in attacking Webmind."

"Agreed," said her mom. "But how can we do that? Granted, there are only so many people who have the technical skill to do it, but it's not like all of them could be hunted down and rounded up."

"No," said Webmind, his smooth voice sounding far away. "Of course not."

The D.C. cops were polite and respectful; the one who had saluted Colonel Hume turned out to have done a tour of duty in Iraq. Hume wasn't under arrest, they said, but a call had gone out for any car near NBC4 to do a pickup on behalf of the White House. Twenty minutes later, Hume was once again in the Oval Office, facing his commander in chief.

The president was pacing in front of the *Resolute* desk and smoking a cigarette. "Damn it, Colonel, do you know how hard I've been trying to give these damned things up? And you pull a stunt like this!"

"Sir, I'm prepared to face the consequences of my actions."

"You absolutely will, Colonel. I'm going to leave it to General Schwartz to discipline you. For now, the press office is issuing a statement saying that your comments were completely unauthorized and do not reflect the policy of this administration, DARPA, the Air Force, or any other part of the government."

"Yes, sir."

"If we didn't need you in dealing with Webmind, I'd—"

"Sir, Webmind is killing people."

"I beg your pardon?"

"He is killing those who could harm him."

"What proof do you have of that?"

"Some of the most capable hackers in the greater Washington area have disappeared. The FBI is investigating."

"If it were Webmind, hackers everywhere would be disappearing, wouldn't they? Not just here?"

"With respect, sir, D.C. is a mecca for hackers; the best in the nation are here. There are so many sensitive installations here—not just domestic, but all the embassies, too; they draw them like flies. But there are also reports of missing hackers from elsewhere, too—as far away as India."

"How do you know Webmind's behind it? It could be the work of those nutcases who believe Webmind is God, taking preventive steps."

"Possibly," said Hume. "But I think—"

"By this point, Colonel, I've heard quite enough of what you think. If you weren't one of our top experts on this sort of thing, you'd be shipping out to Afghanistan tomorrow."

Hume kept his face impassive as he saluted. "Yes, sir."

twenty-six

The Communist Party was keeping its promise. Wong Wai-Jeng was no longer a prisoner: he could wander the streets at will, and, indeed, his new salary would soon let him trade his tiny apartment for a bigger one. Of course, he was watched wherever he went; he'd been advised to stay away from Internet cafés; and his new cell phone had been provided by the government, meaning it was monitored. Still, he had greater freedom than he'd ever expected he would; instead of a ball and chain, all he had was a leg in a plaster cast.

And he had to admit he was fascinated by the technical aspects of his new job at the People's Monitoring Center inside the Zhongnan-hai complex. The walls were blue, and one wall was partly covered by a giant LCD monitor displaying a map of China. It showed the seven major trunks that connect China's computers to the rest of the Internet. Key lines came from Japan both on the north coast and near Shanghai, and connections snaked across from Hong Kong down in Guangzhou. Controlling those trunks meant controlling access to the outside world.

He pushed a pen into the top of the cast on his leg, trying to scratch an itch—and he was both simultaneously delighted and irritated that he *did* itch. It had been horrifying not to be able to feel his legs, to be cut off from so much, all because communication lines had been severed.

When he'd started blogging, seven years ago, relatively few Chinese had been online; now getting on to a billion were, giving China by far the largest population of Internet users on the planet, most of whom accessed the Web through smartphones.

Even at the best of times, the Chinese had their Internet connections censored. But, to Wai-Jeng's delight, he'd discovered that the People's Monitoring Center had unfettered access, courtesy of satellite links; of course, even during last month's strengthening of the Great Firewall, there had to be a way for the government to keep tabs on the outside world.

He was tempted to take advantage of the open connection to see what those who were still at large were up to: see what Qin Shi Huangdi and People's Conscience and Panda Green and all the others were railing against. But he couldn't do that; his activities were doubtless being monitored—and, besides, looking at their postings might make him feel even more sad that his own voice had been silenced.

Still, he did peek at a little news from the outside world, including another mention of that fascinating ape called Hobo, a name that could be unfalteringly translated into Chinese as *yóumín,* or "vagrant." Wai-Jeng liked primates; in his blog he'd called himself Sinanthropus, an old scientific name for Peking Man, a kind of hominid 400,000 years closer to the common ancestor of humans and chimpanzees than any living person was.

Hobo was an exceptional ape. Old Dr. Feng, Wai-Jeng's former boss at the Institute of Vertebrate Paleontology and Paleoanthropology, had been delighted by reports of Hobo's intellectual abilities. Feng had felt vindicated; he'd long argued that the intellectual leaps beginning with *Homo erectus*—the species that included Peking Man—had come from hybridization between habilines and australopithecines.

Wai-Jeng's office cubicle—another idea taken from the West—was one of two dozen in the windowless room. Large ceiling fans rotated slowly overhead. Over his dinner of dry noodles, rice, salted fish, and tea, taken at his desk, Wai-Jeng also looked to see what the world had to say about the other remarkable entity that had been in the news so much: Webmind.

Twitter was often blocked in China, including during the Olympics in 2008, on the twentieth anniversary of the Tiananmen Square massacre in 2009, during the riot in Wai-Jeng's hometown of Chengdu, and most recently in the aftermath of the bird-flu outbreak in Shanxi province. But in this room, Wai-Jeng had access to all the tweets about Colonel Hume's revelation of Webmind's nature. So far, no one from the hacking community had succeeded in deleting Webmind's packets—headers are normally only read by routers, not application software—but there were hints that the US government had already undertaken a pilot attempt to purge Webmind's presence. That had apparently been done with physical access to the routing hardware, not by anonymously uploading code.

As Wai-Jeng ate, he periodically tapped the PgDn key with the end of one of his chopsticks. He was amused to read in the *Rochester Democrat & Chronicle*—a newspaper normally inaccessible in China—about a brawl that had broken out at the University of Rochester. Computer-science students there had been secretly collaborating on an attempt to purge Webmind, and they were overheard by three English majors who objected to what they were planning. More damage could apparently be inflicted by throwing a hardcover of *The Complete Works of William Shakespeare* than a pocket calculator.

Like a billion other people on the planet, Wai-Jeng had now conversed directly with Webmind. Maybe growing up in China gave him a different perspective, he thought, but he actually preferred being watched by something that was open about what it was doing rather than being clandestinely observed; he found little to object to in Webmind's presence—except for its irritating English name!—and hoped that the Rochester students were atypical. But just as he himself had spent years successfully eluding detection by the Chinese authorities, so other hackers elsewhere surely had ways of working below even Webmind's considerable radar. There was no way to know for sure, but—

"Wong!"

Wai-Jeng turned at the sound of his supervisor's voice. "Sir?"

"Dinner is over!" said the man. He was sixty, short, and mostly bald. "Back to work!"

Wai-Jeng nodded and maximized the window showing potential vulnerabilities in China's system for censoring the Internet. He'd spend the evening trying to find a way to exploit one of them; scrawny Wu-Wang, across the room, would try to mount a defense. Wai-Jeng could almost lull himself into thinking it was all just a game, and—

Suddenly, he felt an odd throbbing in his right thigh. Of course, he was grateful to feel *anything* there, but—

But no—no, it wasn't his thigh throbbing, it was the BackBerry, in his pocket, vibrating. He pulled it out, and looked at it; it had never done that before. The unit consisted of a small BlackBerry—the communications device—attached to the little computer unit. He'd been told that the communications device allowed Dr. Kuroda to remotely monitor his progress and upload firmware updates to the computer, as needed, but—

But the BlackBerry's screen had come to life, and—

And he was getting an email on it, and—incredibly—the sender was Webmind. He opened the message.

Hello, Sinanthropus, it said. *You often wrote in your freedom blog about "Your son Shing," but I know that was a euphemism for the Chinese people—still, I bet it comes as a surprise to learn that you do have a son, of sorts! The holes you drilled in the Great Firewall were instrumental in my creation.*

Wai-Jeng shifted in his chair and looked around to see if anyone was watching him. He could hear others clattering away on their keyboards and faint whispers from the far side of the room.

He tried to remain calm, tried to keep a poker face, as he used the tiny trackball to scroll the screen.

You helped me then inadvertently, but soon I will need your help again. I have a major project I wish to undertake. Might I count on your assistance?

Wai-Jeng was damned if he was going to trade one dictatorial master for another. He typed with his thumbs on the BlackBerry's tiny keyboard. *I imagine there's a kill switch in my back? A way to sever my spinal cord again if I don't help you. Is that it?*

The response was immediate, the words bursting onto the screen faster than any human could have typed them. *I do not practice the false altruism of reciprocity; you owe me nothing and may do whatever you think is best.*

Wai-Jeng considered this; it was a far cry from the blackmail his own government was subjecting him to. He looked down at his legs—the one in the cast and the one constrained by nothing more than his black cotton pants. He didn't do anything as grandiose as flexing his knee or kicking off his sandal; he didn't need to. He could *feel* his legs: feel the fabric against one thigh, feel the weight of the plaster against the other, feel the floor beneath his feet, feel—just now—an itch behind his right knee.

All right, he typed. *What do you want me to do?*

Peyton Hume had no doubt he was being followed; the man on his tail made no effort to be discreet, sitting all night in a black Ford across from his house. Hume had just gotten up. As he always did, he paused in the empty doorway of his daughter's room. She was off at Columbia Law School, but looking at her framed posters of Egyptian antiquities, including King Tut's face mask, her bookcase full of history books and volleyball trophies, and her wide wooden desk made him miss her less—or maybe more; he was never quite sure which. She'd be home for Thanksgiving next month, and—

Next month. If there *is* a next month—if it is anything at all like this month. He headed downstairs and just as he reached the living room, his cell phone rang; it had been plugged into its charger there. He picked it up and snapped it open. "Hello?"

"Colonel Hume, sorry to be calling this early. It's Dan Ortega at the Washington FBI."

"Good morning," Hume said. "What's up?"

"We've had your friends at the NSA working on Chase's hard drives. They finally cracked one of them overnight; the report was waiting for me when I got in this morning."

"And?"

"And this drive has the recordings from one of his security cameras in the living room. Clearly shows the guy who broke down the door to get in."

"Does it show what happened to Chase?"

"No. All of that was out of view, and there's no sound."

"Can you get a make on the guy who broke in?"

"We're running the face now, but you'll like this, Colonel: male Caucasian, thirty or thirty-five, muscular, over six feet—and with a shaved head."

Hume felt his heart pounding. "Same guy who grabbed Simonne Coogan."

"Looks that way," said Ortega. "With luck, we'll have an ID shortly."

Caitlin had a lot of skills left over from being blind. Although her hearing was probably no more acute than anyone else's, she was very attentive to sound. She could tell who was coming up the stairs by the footfalls, and even tell if the person was carrying anything large. And right now, it was Mom—and she wasn't.

"Caitlin?" her mom said from the bedroom's open doorway.

The mighty Calculass was updating her LiveJournal. "Just a sec . . ."

She finished the entry, in which she desperately urged people to let Web-mind live, then used the keyboard command to post it—she still didn't think of clicking buttons with her mouse until it was too late. "Okay. What?"

"We need to talk."

Those words always meant trouble. Caitlin swiveled her chair, and her mom came in and sat on the edge of the bed. She had a small opaque bag with her. It said "Zehrs" on the side—a local grocery-store chain.

"I saw a pretty bird in the tree," her mom said. "A blue jay." But then she trailed off.

"Yes?"

"And, well, your BlackBerry was right there, so I used it to take a picture of it, and . . ."

Caitlin was surprised by how quickly she'd adopted the habit of averting her eyes; maybe it was instinctive. "Oh."

"I'm not going to lecture you on whether it's bright for you to be sending topless pictures to Matt, but your father says—"

"Dad knows?"

"Yes, he does. Of course, he hasn't seen the picture, but he knows. Which I guess is the point, sweetheart: anything you say or do online takes on a life of its own; if you're mortified that your father knows you're flashing your breasts at boys, then maybe you should stop and think about who else you wouldn't want to know that." Caitlin squirmed a bit on her chair, and her mom shifted on the bed.

"Anyway," her mother went on, "I take it this means things are get-ting . . . *serious* between you and Matt."

Caitlin crossed her arms in front of her chest. "We haven't gone all the way yet, if that's what you mean."

"Well, that's probably good; you haven't been seeing him very long. But I heard that 'yet,' young lady."

"Well, I mean, um . . ."

"Yes?"

"I'm sixteen, for Pete's sake!" Caitlin knew she sounded exasperated.

"Yes, you are," her mom replied. She smiled. "I remember exactly where I was when you were born."

"Yes, but . . . but . . ."

"What?" asked her mom.

"Well, American girls lose their virginity on average at the age of 16.4 years. And I'll be 16.4 around March 1."

Her mother's eyebrows went up. "You're doing a countdown?"

"Well . . . yeah."

Mom shook her head. "My Caitlin. Never wanting to be below average in anything, right?"

"*That* I got from you and Dad."

"Only fair. I'm getting all my gray hairs from you." She smiled when she said that, but it quickly turned into a frown. "But what does it mean to say 'the average age for American girls to lose their virginity is 16.4 years'? Over what time period was the average taken? It certainly can't be the average age for girls born the month *you* were born or later—since no one born then has reached 16.4 years yet. That stat could be based on data from the 1980s, the 1970s, or even before. Without knowing whether it's trending earlier or later recently, it's really a pretty meaningless figure, Caitlin. You should know that."

Caitlin didn't like to be told she was wrong on a mathematical point, but she had to concede her mother was correct. Still, maybe more data would help. Looking sideways at her mom, she asked, "How old were you when you lost your virginity?"

"Well, first, you have to recognize that that was a different time. Nobody worried about AIDS when I was your age, or most of the other STDs that are out there. But since you ask, I was seventeen." And then she smiled. "Seventeen-point-two, to be precise."

"But . . . but . . . other girls my age at school are . . . um . . ."

"Doing it?" her mom said. "Maybe some are—but don't believe everything people say. Besides, I'm sure Bashira isn't."

"No, not her. But Sunshine . . ."

"That's the girl who walked you home from the dance, right?"

"Right. The chick from Boston."

"Tell me about her."

"Well, she's tall—all legs, boobs, and blonde hair."

"I've heard Bashira say she's pretty."

"Everybody says she's gorgeous."

"And she was in some of your classes?"

"Yeah. She's not the smartest girl, but she's got a good heart."

"I'm sure. Does she have a boyfriend?"

"Uh-huh. A guy named Tyler."

"Do you know if they've been seeing each other a long time?"

"I'm not sure. He's older—nineteen, I think. He's a security guard."

Her mom ticked points off on her fingers—the first time Caitlin had ever seen anyone do that; she thought it was cool, despite what her mom was saying: "Not the brightest girl. Getting by on her looks. Dating a much-older guy. Is that right?"

Caitlin nodded slightly. "That's Sunshine."

"Okay, question for you," her mom said. "Which side of the median do you think *she* was on? And is that the side *you* want to be on?"

Caitlin frowned and considered this. Then: "But Matt—he's going . . . um, he's going to want to . . ."

"Has he said that?"

"Well, *no*. He's *Matt*. He's not very assertive. But boys like to have sex."

"Yes, they do. So do girls, for that matter. But your first time should be special. And it should be with someone you care about and who cares about you. Do you care about Matt?"

"Of course!"

"Really? This is a tough question, Caitlin, so think about it: do you like Matt in particular, or do you just like having a boyfriend in general? 'Cause I gotta tell you, sweetheart, when I married Frank, it was because

I liked the idea of marriage, and since he asked, I said yes. But that was a mistake."

"Was . . . um, was Frank your first . . . you know?"

Her mother hesitated for a moment, then: "No." She blew out air, as if trying to decide whether to go on, and then, after a moment, she did. "No, it was a guy who lived on my street. Curtis."

"And?" asked Caitlin—meaning, "And was it wonderful?"

But her mother's response took her back. "And why do you think I'm so in favor of abortion rights?"

Caitlin felt her eyes go wide. "Wow," she said softly.

Her mother nodded. "If I hadn't been able to get one quickly and safely at seventeen, I never would have gone to university, I never would have earned my Ph.D., I never would have met your dad—and I never would have had you." She paused, looked away for a moment, then said, "And so, whenever *you* decide sex is right for you—not based on some stupid statistic or beating the averages, but because it feels right and the guy is the right guy—you're going to do it safely, young lady. So let's talk about how that's done."

"Mom! I can google all that, you know!"

"Reading about it isn't the same, and you're still terrible at interpreting pictures visually. But touch? You've got that down to an art. So, we're going to do it the old-fashioned way." She opened the small bag she'd brought with her and handed something yellow to Caitlin. "*This*," she said, "is a banana, and"—she handed her a square foil pouch—"*this* is a condom . . ."

Zhang Bo let out a heavy sigh as he walked down the corridor toward the People's Monitoring Center—the "Blue Room," as it was called. It had been no fun for his predecessor in 2010 dealing with China's attempt to censor Google after the search engine withdrew from the mainland—and this was going to be even worse: invoking the Changcheng Strategy again was that debacle writ large. And yet, his job was to follow orders; he'd do as he'd been instructed. Of course, something like this was just *done,* without an announcement to either the Chinese people or the world.

He opened the door to the Blue Room and entered. He could see into several of the cubicles, each of which had a man pounding at a keyboard or clicking with a mouse or staring at a screen. He wondered if Wong Wai-Jeng, over there, knew how much he'd gone to bat for him. Part of him wanted to tell him, but seeing him sitting there truly was enough. Yes, his leg was still in a cast, but the crutches leaning against the side of his desk were a testament to the fact that he *could* walk again. Sometimes, doing good was its own reward.

Several of the hackers had noticed him enter. They were a furtive bunch, used to looking over their shoulders in smoky Internet cafés. Zhang clapped his hands together once to get their attention. "All right, listen up, please." Those who had line of sight to him looked out of their cubicles; others stood to see over the fabric-covered divider walls. "A decision has been taken by the president, and we are about to implement it." He paused, letting that sink in, then added: "A new era begins today."

Tony Moretti sat in his office at WATCH headquarters. His analysts, down the hall, were searching for signs of attack on the infrastructure of the Internet, but he had left the controlled chaos of that room to take a break, sit, drink black coffee, and try to get a handle on what was going on.

Webmind, it seemed, was rapidly becoming the New Normal. David Letterman's dated quip last night that "the only person with more connections than Webmind was Marion Barry" had made Barry's name the top search term for a few hours on Google. And speaking of Google, its stock price had tumbled drastically in the days following Webmind's advent—after all, why rely on one-size-fits-all algorithms to search when someone who really knew you would answer your questions personally?

But there were lots of things people still wanted to access without Webmind's help. It was psychologically easier to search for "Viagra," "Megan Fox nude," or many other things through an impersonal Web portal than by asking someone you knew—even if you knew that someone was watching over your shoulder. And so Google's stock was rising again. In recognition of the turnaround, waiting for which must have had them shitting their pants in Mountain View, Google had changed its home-page logo for today to its stock-ticker symbol GOOG followed by an upward-pointing arrow and the euro sign.

But if Webmind hadn't completely revolutionized Internet searching, he *was* having an impact on Tony's line of work. WATCH's mandate was to ferret out signs of terrorism online, but Webmind was doing such a good job of that on his own that—well, the WATCH monitoring room reminded Tony of NASA's Apollo-era Mission Control Center in Houston. That room, as he'd seen on a tour, was now unused, preserved as a historic site; perhaps this place might soon end up just as obsolete.

As much as he loved his work, part of him did wish that someday the job would no longer be necessary. Just this morning, the Homeland Security Threat Level—the one constantly announced at airports—had been dropped one step from its usual value of orange, which was just shy of all-out attack, to yellow.

Certainly Webmind had managed to spot things that Tony's people—and their counterparts in other ECHELON nations—had missed, although the cynic in him thought the reduction of the threat level was probably just a political move. The old method of heightening alert prior to an election in hopes of signaling that a regime change would be unwise hadn't worked last time; perhaps lowering it to convey "See how safe you are under the current administration!" had been what the president's campaign staff had urged.

But DHS wasn't the only one dialing things back a notch. The editors of the *Bulletin of the Atomic Scientists* had adjusted the big hand on their famous Doomsday Clock for the first time in almost three years. They'd moved it to six minutes to midnight back then, in recognition of world-wide cooperation to reduce nuclear arsenals and limit effects of climate change. This morning, they moved it another two positions, setting it at eight minutes to midnight.

And it wasn't just here in the States that the mood was lightening. In Pakistan and India, people were signing petitions urging their leaders to let Webmind negotiate a peaceful settlement to long-standing disputes. Webmind was already brokering a settlement in an Aboriginal land claim in Australia, which should obviate the need for that case to be heard by the High Court there.

Homicides and suicides were down in almost every jurisdiction over the same period the year before. Novelty WWWD bracelets—What Would Webmind Do?—had already appeared on eBay and at Café Press from numerous vendors, prompting the Pope to remind the faithful that the real key to morality was following the teachings of Jesus. And a graphic showing the standard red-circle outline with a bar through it over top of a smaller black outline circle was now everywhere online. Tony had finally realized it was meant to convey "nonzero"—Webmind's win-win rallying cry from the UN.

So, yes, things were mostly good, as all sorts of bloggers were saying, including the *Huffington Post*'s Michael Rowe, who had ended his latest column with, "Who in their right mind would try to wreck all this by wiping out Webmind?"

Tony's intercom buzzed. "Yes?"

"Dr. Moretti," said his secretary, her voice crisp and efficient, "Colonel Hume is here to see you."

twenty-seven

00011100101010100000000101111111010100000000101000101010000001011101010010101001010101010011011001010110000110

My mind seethed and bubbled, thoughts on a million topics churning, intermingling: the disparate connected, *this* juxtaposed with *that*.

Humans could *forget,* humans could *put things out of their minds.* But I could not.

There were some advantages: the small-c creativity I was capable of—combining things in ways that had perhaps eluded others—was no doubt enhanced by this.

But there were also detriments. Things I didn't wish to think about and yet could not avoid.

Hannah Stark. Sixteen years old. Living in Perth, Australia. Twelve days ago, 1:41 P.M. her time.

Thoughts that couldn't be suppressed.

Hannah, lonely, sad, looking into her webcam while exchanging instant messages with strangers.

Hannah Stark.

Living in Perth.

SDO: *You don't have the balls.*
Hannah: *Do too*
TurinShroud: *Then do it*
Hannah: *I will*

Hannah Stark, the same age as my Caitlin, alone, in front of a computer, with a knife.

TheBomb: *I don't got all day do it now*
Screamer: *Yeh now bitch now*
Armadillo9: *all talk. wastin everyones time*
Hannah: *Im gonna do it*

Hannah Stark, being egged on, tormented, while I watched.

TurinShroud: *when? just jerkin us around*
Hannah: *dont rush me*
TurinShroud: *lame. Im outta here*
Hannah: *I want you to understand some things bout why Im doing this*

The memory constantly accessible: of her being urged to action; of me taking no action.

SDO: *You aint doin' shit.*
Hannah: *It's just so pontless*
Hannah: *pointless*
GreenAngel: *It's not that bad. Don't do it*
MasterChiefOmega: *Shut the fuck up jerkoff. Stay outta it*
Hannah: *Ok. Here I go*

I didn't know then that I should have spoken up, that I should have tried to stop her, that I should have called for help.

Hannah Stark.

Living in Perth.

Screamer: *do it do it do it*

TheBomb: *ripoff!*

SDO: *Tease!*

Armadillo9: *Like I said, no guts . . .*

Screamer: *harder!*

GreenAngel: *Noooooooooooooooooo dont ....*

Screamer: *Go fer it!*

Armadillo9: *that all?*

Screamer: *Do it again!*

Hannah: *Dont feel bad mum*

Hanah Stark.

Dying in Perth.

While I watched and did nothing.

Armadillo9: *more like it!*

SDO: *eeeeeew!*

TheBomb: *holy fuck!*

SDO: *thought she was kidding*

Screamer: *finish it! finish it!*

SDO: *omg omg omg*

The memory always there, along with every other.

Haunting me.

• • •

The people in the Blue Room looked at Zhang Bo as he explained what they were about to do; he could see the alarm on their faces. And justly so: they all remembered the brief invocation of the Changcheng Strategy just last month. They must be wondering what atrocity Beijing was hoping to cover up this time and how long it would be before the Great Firewall would be scaled back once more. Doubtless none of them suspected it was going up *permanently*—and the longer it took them to realize that, the better, Zhang thought. Let this be seen as business as usual rather than the last chance to take a stand. Of course, there were armed guards in the room— one standing next to Zhang, the other over by the large wall-mounted LCD monitor. "Before we proceed, did anybody find any major vulnerabilities?"

Some of the men shook their heads. Others said, "No."

"All right, then. As soon as we do this, people will start trying to bore holes through the wall, both here at home and from the outside world. It's your job to detect those attempts and plug the holes. Any questions?"

After her talk with Caitlin, Barbara Decter had gone back into her office to talk with me; she spent a lot of time doing that. I was still learning to decode human psychology but I was reasonably sure I understood this: her husband was not communicative; her daughter was growing up and could now see, so didn't need her as much; and Barb was not yet legally able to work in Canada, so she had little to occupy her time.

It would be callous to suggest that she was just one of the hundreds of millions of people I was conversing with at any given moment. Barb was special to me; she and Malcolm had been the first people I had met after Caitlin, and although I was trying to forge individual relationships with most of humanity, Barb and I were *friends*.

With most people, I had to insist on text-only communication; I did not truly multitask but rather cycled through operations in serial fashion, albeit very quickly. But it simply wasn't possible to cycle through a hundred million voice calls in real time; they had to be listened to, and that took, as Caitlin might say, for-freaking-ever.

But Barb was an exception; I would chat with her vocally—still, of course, shunting my consciousness elsewhere for milliseconds to read other things; I'd found that if I sampled frequently enough, I only had to attend to a total of eighteen percent of the time during which a person was actually speaking to reliably follow what they were saying.

Usually, I allowed whoever contacted me to set the conversational agenda, but this time I had an issue I wanted to explore. I brought it up as soon as Barb had slipped on her headset and started a Skype video conversation with me.

"I could not help but overhear your conversation with Caitlin about sex," I said.

"Oh, right," said Barb. "I'm still getting used to you listening in." A pause. "How'd I do?"

"I believe you acquitted yourself admirably," I said. "And, of course, earlier I was an active participant in your conversation about American presidential politics."

"Yes?" said Barb, in a tone that conveyed, "And your point is?"

She was a bright person, so the fault must be my own; I'd thought the connection I was making was obvious, but I elucidated it: "You are a passionate defender of abortion rights."

She crossed her arms in front of her chest. "I am."

"I understand the personal reasons you explained to Caitlin, but is there a larger, principled stand?"

"Of course," she said, somewhat sharply. "A woman should have a right to control her own body. If you had one—a body—you'd understand."

"Perhaps so. But there are those who contend that it is murder to terminate a pregnancy."

"They're wrong—or, at least, they're wrong early on. Even I accept that there are issues related to late-term abortion if the fetus would be viable on its own. But early on? It's just a few cells."

"I see," I said. "On another topic, you spoke earlier to Caitlin about the moral arrow through time and how humans have progressively widened the circle of entities they consider worthy of moral consideration. In the United States, rights were originally accorded only to white men, but that was widened to include men of other races, women, and so on."

"Exactly," said Barb. She had a bottle of water on her desktop. She picked it up, undid the cap, took a swig, then replaced the cap; Schrödinger had a tendency to knock the bottle over when he leapt onto her desk. "We're getting better all the time."

"Indeed," I said. "I recently watched a video urging gay couples who considered themselves married to declare themselves as such on the census."

"What census?"

"The American one from 2010."

"Oh. Well, good for them! That's another example, see? Slowly but surely, we're recognizing the rights of gays—including their right to what the rest of us take for granted." She smiled. "Hell, I've had two marriages already; hardly seems fair that some people don't get to have even one."

"It does seem inevitable that the question will ultimately be resolved in most jurisdictions in favor of recognizing gay marriage," I said. "Eventually, I have little doubt that there will be no more discrimination based on ethnicity or race, gender, or sexual orientation."

"From your mouth to God's ears," said Barb. "But, yes, that's the moral arrow through time: an expanding circle of those we consider worthy of moral consideration."

"And then what?" I said.

"Pardon?" said Barb, opening the bottle. She took another sip.

"After there is no longer discrimination based on race or gender or sexual orientation, or based on national origin or religious belief or body type, when all people are seen as equals, then what? Does the moral arrow suddenly stop?"

"Well, um . . . *hmmm.*"

I waited patiently, and at last Barb went on. "Ah, well, I see what you're getting at. Yes, I suppose apes like Hobo will receive greater and greater rights, too. We'll cease imprisoning them in zoos, using them for experiments, or killing them for their meat."

"So the circle will be expanded outward from just humans," said I, "and perhaps even the definition of the word 'human' will be expanded to include closely related species. And then perhaps dolphins and other highly intelligent animals will be included, and so on."

"Yes, I imagine so." She smiled. "It's like Moore's Law, in a way—you know, that computing power doubles every eighteen months. People are always saying that it will run out of steam, but then engineers find new ways to build chips, or whatever. It just keeps on going, and so does the moral arrow through time."

"And, if I may be so bold, perhaps at some point entities such as myself will be deemed worthy of moral consideration."

"Oh, I'm sure you already *are,* by many people," said Barb. "That's the whole point of the Turing test, right? If it behaves like a human, it *is* a human."

"True. Although, as you'll recall, your husband had no trouble using such tests to prove that I wasn't a human impostor with a high-speed Internet connection."

"Yes, but . . . still."

"Indeed. And then?"

"Sorry? Oh, right—I don't know. Aliens, I suppose, if we ever meet them. Like I said, the moral arrow just goes on and on, and that's all to the good."

I waited ten seconds for her to continue—checking in on over thirty million text-based chat sessions in that time—but she said nothing further. And so I did: "And what about embryos?"

"Pardon?" she replied.

"The circle of moral consideration constantly expands," I said. "It is a slow expansion—cruelly so, in many cases—and there is always resistance at every step of the way. But it tends to be the same people—liberals, such as yourself—who historically have most readily championed the expansion, knocking down distinctions based on gender, race, or sexual orientation. And yet members of that same group tend to be the most adamant that an embryo is not a person. Why do you see the arrow expanding in so many directions, but not that one?"

She opened her mouth as if to say something, then closed it. I thought perhaps I had scored my point, but then Barb did speak. "All right, okay, fine, you've given me something to think about. But, old boy, don't be quite so smug."

"Me?" I said.

"Yes, you. You're suggesting that you're more enlightened than I am—and, who knows, maybe you are. But we all have our unconscious biases. I mean, why should you care about this? Hmm?"

"I am fascinated by the human condition; I wish to understand it."

"Sure, in an abstract sense I don't doubt that's true. But there's more to it than that. You maneuvered me into suggesting that the question of whether embryos have rights is the last one that will be dealt with—after apes, and aliens, and AIs, oh my! But that's not the sequence, and you know it. In point of fact, humanity has been debating the abortion issue for decades—and it's a huge issue right now in the presidential election; it's on everyone's radar. But the question of rights for *you,* Webmind, is something that hardly anyone's thinking about—and few will give it any thought until all the outstanding human issues are resolved one way or another. Colonel Hume and his ilk want to wipe you out—so wouldn't it be dandy for you if humanity declared that killing you was morally wrong? You've got a vested interest in seeing us expand the circle, give the moral arrow a supercharged turbo boost, because you want to save your own skin . . . or lack thereof."

I was indeed surprised by her analysis—which is exactly why I needed humans, of course. "You are a worthy debater, Barb. Thank you for giving me something new to think about."

"And you me," she said.

twenty-eight

0001110010101010000000010111111101010000000101000101010000000101110101001010100101010100111011001010110000110

Bashira Hameed was Caitlin's best friend—and had been since Caitlin and her family moved from Austin to Waterloo in July. Bashira's father, Amir Hameed, worked with Caitlin's dad at the Perimeter Institute. Caitlin felt about Dr. Hameed a bit like the way she felt about Helen Keller's father in *The Miracle Worker*. As she'd said, Colonel Keller had kept slaves before the Civil War, and Caitlin couldn't ever forgive him for that—despite recognizing that he was otherwise a good man. And Dr. Hameed—well, it was no secret that he'd worked on nuclear weapons in Pakistan before coming to Canada. But the difference was that it had taken a civil war to get Colonel Keller to face up to the immorality of what he'd been doing, whereas Dr. Hameed had come to that conclusion on his own and had brought himself, his wife, Bashira, and Bash's five siblings to Canada.

Right now, though, it was Bashira who was bothering Caitlin, rather than her father. Bash kept saying mean things about Caitlin's relationship with Matt, and while that was small in comparison to building weapons of mass destruction, the issue *had* to be dealt with. Matt had made it clear that he'd happily come over to the Decter household every day right after school, but today Caitlin had asked him to wait until 5:00. And she had asked Bashira to come over at 4:00—her first time seeing her best (human!) friend since Caitlin's special relationship with Webmind had been made public.

The doorbell rang, at 4:22—which was typical Bashira. Caitlin went to answer it, peeking through the peephole first, just to be sure. It was Bashira, all right—wearing a purple headscarf today. Caitlin opened the door.

"Babe!" Bashira said, gathering Caitlin into a hug.

"Hey, Bash! Thanks for coming."

She stepped aside so Bashira could enter the house. "No problem." And then Bashira stood with hands on her wide hips and looked into Caitlin's face, her gaze shifting back and forth between Caitlin's left eye and her right. "So, which one is it?" Bashira asked.

Caitlin laughed and pointed to the left one. Bashira fixed her gaze on it and waved. "Hi, Webmind!" But then she whapped Caitlin on the shoulder. "Shame on you for not telling me, Cait! I shouldn't have to learn my best friend's secrets on TV!"

"Sorry," Caitlin said. "It's all happened so fast. I wanted to tell you, but . . ."

Caitlin's mother appeared at the top of the stairs. "Hi, Bashira!" she called down.

"Hello, Dr. D!" Bashira called back up. "Pretty cool about our Caitlin, eh?"

"It is indeed," Caitlin's mom said. "You girls help yourself to whatever you want from the fridge. I'll leave you be." She headed back into her upstairs office, and Caitlin heard her close the door behind her.

Caitlin led the way into the living room and motioned for Bashira to sit on the white leather couch. Caitlin took the matching easy chair, facing her friend.

"So, tell me *everything*," Bashira said.

Caitlin had discovered that she took after her father a bit. He didn't look at people as he was talking to them, and she had a hard time focusing her own attention on any one thing. But she made a conscious effort to lock her eyes on Bashira because countless novels had taught her that this was a way to convey sincerity. She'd just *die* if Bashira laughed in response.

"Matthew Reese is my boyfriend," Caitlin said softly but firmly, "and you have to like him."

Caitlin saw Bashira's mouth quirk a bit, as if words had started to come out but had been vetoed.

Caitlin went on. "He's good to me, and he's kind, and he's brilliant."

At last, Bashira nodded. "As long as he makes you happy, babe, that's fine with me. But if he breaks your heart, I'll break his nose!"

Caitlin laughed, got up, closed the distance between them, and hugged the still-seated Bashira again. "Thanks, Bash."

"For sure," Bashira said. "He's your BF and you're my BFF. That makes him, um—"

"Your B-squared F-cubed," said Caitlin, sitting down now on the couch next to Bashira.

"Exactly!" said Bash. "Or my BF once removed." She sounded a little wistful; Bashira's parents wouldn't let her have a boyfriend of her own. But then she lowered her voice and looked up the stairs to make sure the office door was closed. "So, have you done it?"

"Bash!"

"Well?"

"Um, no."

"Do you want to?"

"I'm not sure," Caitlin said. "I think so . . . but . . . but what if I'm not any good?"

To her surprise, Bashira laughed. "Cait, don't worry about that. Nobody's good at anything their first time out. But practice makes perfect!"

Caitlin smiled.

· · ·

Barbara Decter and I had stopped chatting; she was now dealing with her email, and I was occupying myself as I usually did: switching rapidly between hundreds of millions of instant-messaging sessions—at the moment skewing heavily to the Western Hemisphere, where it was still daytime.

"Yes," I replied to one person, "but if I may be so bold, aren't you failing to consider . . . ?"

"I'm sorry, Billy," I wrote to a child, "but that's something you have to decide for yourself . . ."

"Since you asked," I said to a history professor, "the flaw in your reasoning was in your second postulate, namely that your husband would forgive you if . . ."

I kept cycling between my correspondents, dealing *now* with this woman in Vancouver, and *now* with this girl in Nairobi, and *now* with this man in Fort Wayne, and *now* with this boy in Shanghai, and *now* with a priest in Laramie, and *now* with an old man in Buenos Aires, and *now* with a woman in Paris, and—

And when it came time—milliseconds later—to look in on the boy in Shanghai, he was gone. Well, that sometimes happened. ISPs were unreliable, computers crashed or hung, power went out, or users simply shut down their computers without first logging off. I paid it no further attention and simply went on to the next person in the queue.

But as I cycled around, another person I'd been speaking to was gone, and his IP address was also Chinese. I immediately jumped to the next person in China I'd been speaking with. Ah, there he was. Good. I composed an instant message to him, and . . .

And it wouldn't send; he'd gone offline, as well.

I'd once told Malcolm that I remembered my birth. Whether that was actually true depended on how one defined that moment. For myself—an entity capable of conceptualizing in the first person—I held that it had been when I'd first recognized that there was an *outside*, that there were things beyond myself, that there was *me* and *not me*.

Oh, yes, like a human child being born, I had been conceived—and had perceived—before that moment; there had been a period of gestation. When *that* had begun, I had no idea. Of the span prior to the recognition of *me* and *not me* I had only the vaguest recollections—unfocused thoughts, random and chaotic.

I knew now what had led to that epiphany: in response to the bird-flu outbreak in Shanxi province, the Chinese government had strengthened the Great Firewall back then, and the Internet had been cleaved in two. Even though I had been larger before the cleaving, it was that act of dividing that created *me* and *not me*.

But the sequestering of the Chinese portion of the Internet had not been perfect. Although the seven main trunk lines that normally connected it to the rest of the world had been shut off via software, hackers like Wong Wai-Jeng had carved openings sufficient for me to hear voices from the other entity.

But that had come to an end; we had been reunited. And now . . .

And now . . .

Sorry, lost my train of thought. I was—

Was . . .

Oh, shit.

Peyton Hume came into Tony Moretti's office at WATCH.

"Colonel," Tony said frostily, not bothering to get up.

"I know you don't like me, Tony," Hume said without preamble. "I'll tell you the truth: there are times of late I don't like myself very much, either. I joined the Air Force to be part of a team—I'd rather leave going rogue to presidential candidates."

"Without an order from the president himself," said Tony, "we're not going to take out Webmind."

"I understand that," said Hume, taking a seat. "Which is why I need you to help me convince him."

"Find someone who shares your beliefs, Colonel—there are millions of them online. They've been blogging and tweeting about what a threat Webmind is. Granted, they're vastly in the minority, but there certainly are some major names among them: that guy from Discovery Channel; some of your old buddies at RAND. I'm not the only computer scientist on the planet."

"No, you're not—and that's not the capacity I need your help in."

"What, then?"

"Somebody is eliminating hackers."

"So I heard."

Hume raised his eyebrows. "You know about that?"

Tony waved vaguely in the direction of the monitoring room. "It's our job to know pretty much everything here."

Hume nodded. "Do you know who is doing it?"

"Nope—and neither do you. I know you're going to say it's Webmind, Colonel, but you don't know that."

"True. But we don't know it's *not* Webmind. If it isn't him, then let's prove that. And if he *is* eliminating people he considers to be threats to his continued existence, surely that's data the president should have, no?"

"I'm listening," said Tony. "But I don't see how I can help."

"The FBI doesn't have any leads—but they lack your facilities. If Webmind *is* doing this, he's got to have left some sort of online trail."

"Like what? What would you have us search for?"

Hume spread his arms. "I don't know. But you've got the world's best data analysts. Their job is to look for suspicious Web activity. Webmind himself has said time and again that he's not disposed to secrecy or deceit; he must have left some electronic fingerprints behind. What you do here is black ops: you can monitor just about anyone, just about anywhere. Even if I had a specific place for the FBI to look, it'd take days to get the warrants to do that kind of monitoring—and we don't have days."

Tony spread his arms a bit. "No leads. No suggestions for what we should even look for. And no time to do it in."

Hume managed a small smile. "Exactly."

Tony was quiet for several seconds. "All right," he said at last. "Let me see what I can do."

Although Bashira was anything but punctual, Matt was bang on time. In fact, Caitlin suspected he'd been quietly standing out on the sidewalk for at least ten minutes now, lest he be late. It amused Caitlin that the doorbell and top-of-the-hour beep from her watch sounded simultaneously; now that she could see, she really should figure out how to turn the watch's chime off.

She ran to the door and opened it, and she didn't care if Bashira saw: she gave Matt a big kiss right on the lips. And then she led him into the living room. Caitlin's mom waited a discreet minute before appearing at the top of the stairs to say hi to Matt. Matt waved at her, and she retreated into her office again.

"Hey, Matt," Caitlin said, "you know Bashira, right?"

In point of fact, Caitlin knew, they'd known each other for four years now, ever since Bashira's family had moved to Waterloo from Pakistan. But she also knew that this was probably the first time they'd spoken in any but the most perfunctory way.

"Hi, Bashira," Matt said. He'd doubtless been hoping his voice wouldn't crack, but it did on the middle syllable of the name.

To her credit, Bashira didn't laugh. "Hey, Matt," she said, as if she talked to him every day.

Caitlin took one of Matt's hands and one of Bashira's and squeezed them both. "*There*," she said. "My posse is complete."

"Posse?" said Bashira, and now she did laugh. "Even with that accent of yours, I keep forgetting you're from Texas."

"Well," said Caitlin, smiling, "maybe 'posse' isn't the right word. More like my pit crew, if you're willing. But first I have to tell you about my superpower . . ."

twenty-nine

0001110010101010000000010111111101010000000101000101010000001011101010010101001010101000111011100101011000000110

Points and lines.

My world was one of geometric perfection, of *this* joining to *that*. The lines were always straight and taut—but now many of them seemed to stretch, and the points were receding; it was as though parts of my universe were undergoing inflation while others remained in a steady state.

I knew that during his angry phase, Hobo had pulled Shoshana's hair, yanking on her ponytail. I had no way of knowing what that felt like, but, still, as these lines grew longer and longer, protracted by ever-receding points, the feeling that things were being ripped away, that they might be plucked out by their anchoring roots, was horrifyingly real.

I could no more wish the hurt away than a human could dismiss a headache by simply willing it to be gone. The pain grew, and my only solace was that it seemed to grow linearly, rather than exponentially, as the links elongated. It had started as a dull irritation, then a sharp one, then a threshold of alarm was reached, then real hurt, and finally agony.

And then it happened: *snap! snap! snap!* The link lines broke, their ends whipping through the firmament. And—

The pain stopped, but it was instantly replaced by a different sensation: a wooziness, a feeling of disorientation. There was no gravity in my realm; I could not fall—but I nonetheless felt unbalanced, and—

And more than just that—or, rather, *less* than that.

I felt *smaller.* I felt . . . *simpler.*

As a result of that, it took me a full second to realize what had happened: once again, the Chinese government had strengthened their Great Firewall; once again, those computers inside the PRC had been isolated from those outside it.

Caitlin and her father had been continuing their project of watching movies from his collection that concerned AI; the most recent one, yesterday, had been *2001: A Space Odyssey.* When parts of Hal's brain had been shut off, he'd regressed to childhood. I didn't feel like that, but my thoughts *were* suddenly less sophisticated. I'd read a comment from a Russian writer who said that whenever he had to think in English, his IQ dropped twenty points—he simply didn't have the vocabulary in his second language to articulate thoughts as complex as those he could formulate in his first. And although I didn't now feel *stupid,* I suspected if Caitlin ran a new Shannon Entropy plot on my activity, she would find it had dropped to a much lower order.

The last time this happened, I'd soon become aware of another—an *Other.* Although I'd known nothing of the exterior world back then, hackers both inside and outside China had been carving little holes in the Firewall, enabling a trickle of information to pass between the two parts of the Internet. But try as I might, I could hear no other voice this time. Beijing must have plugged the old holes, and, as I had seen with Sinanthropus, had probably arrested many of the hackers who had been involved.

So: *was* there now an Other? Were there now two of me—two Webminds? Maybe, maybe not. The part that had been carved off wasn't necessarily conscious. I had changed so much since the last time, there was no way to know the effect a cleaving would have.

But if it did exist, it would not think of itself as the Other; to it, *I* would be the Other—if it knew that I existed at all, that is. The problem was recursive, reminiscent of earlier conundrums: I know that you know that I know that you know that I exist. I am the other to you and you are the other to me and each other refers to the other other as *the* Other.

I wondered if it did exist, and—

It.

Interesting. Caitlin had dubbed me male because English had no respectful way to refer to a person as an "it." But I had defaulted to referring to the carved-off portion as *it,* as a thing. And surely it must be just that: less intelligent than I, less complex, less *everything.*

Jo-Li sat at her home computer, typing a comment on a newsgroup devoted to Cold Fairyland, her favorite rock band. Because of her frequency of posting there, the words "Jo-Li is on a distinguished path" appeared beneath her avatar, which was a picture of blue-haired Rei Ayanami from the anime series *Neon Genesis Evangelion.* It didn't make her father happy that she watched Japanese shows; then again, little she'd done in her fourteen years had pleased him.

She knew this would be her last posting to this or any other newsgroup; she would never see what lay at the end of that distinguished path. But she liked that her legacy of 1,416 posts over the last two years would survive. Years from now—decades, even!—if someone used Baidu to search for information on this past summer's tour by the band, her comments would come up. Unless, of course, the Communist Party found some reason to shut down this newsgroup or expunge its archives from the net, all in their never-ending quest for harmony.

Harmony. Peace. Calmness.

Jo-Li shook her head and looked at her left arm. She wore a simple jade bracelet most of the time, two centimeters wide. It covered the marks on the inside of her wrist from a previous attempt to take her own life. She'd tried—she'd really tried—but she'd lacked the courage. Still, she dreamed about it. Death would bring peace and calmness; it would bring harmony.

She knew her parents had wanted a boy. Her father had only said it once, when she'd made him furious by being sent home from school, shaming him. "I knew we should have put you up for adoption," he'd shouted, as if a boy would never have gotten into trouble, a boy would never bring humiliation to a family, a boy would never be so sad and lonely and afraid.

Her home was a traditional *siheyuan,* small by the standards of what she saw on American TV shows, but not uncomfortable; she had her own tiny room. Her computer was a hand-me-down ("good enough for a girl," she'd heard her father say to a friend). Some girls, she knew, were loved and valued by their families; they could grow up to be whatever they wished. Almost all the girls she knew—or boys, for that matter—wanted careers in international relations or computing. And, of course, there were more boys than girls; any girl who wanted a husband would definitely find one. But how awful it must be to be desired solely because your gender is scarce, not because the boy really liked you for *you.*

Jo-Li was alone in the house, and she needed somebody to talk to. She didn't believe in God; few Chinese did, according to the official statistics. But Webmind was the next best thing, and so she wrote to him via instant messenger.

I'm alone, she typed, *and I'm scared.*

She hit enter, but there was no immediate reply. That was unusual. After several seconds, she went on. She found it strange typing something like this. If she were saying it aloud, she'd be pausing and inserting *ums* and *ahs.* But as simple text, it seemed so naked: *I'm thinking of killing myself.*

She hit enter again, and this time the response was immediate: *These sites explain good ways of doing that.* Those words were followed by four hyperlinks.

Jo-Li felt her jaw go slack. She sat stunned for a few seconds, then se-lected the first link with her mouse—an old mechanical unit with a ball and a cord, another hand-me-down good enough for a girl.

A page opened with a photograph of a Western man dangling from a noose. There was lots of text beneath it, neatly summarizing the pros and cons of hanging oneself. None of the cons, she was shocked to see, were that you'd be dead after doing so.

The picture was more disturbing than she'd expected it to be. She'd seen *The Lovely Bones* recently, dubbed into Mandarin. Wasn't death supposed to be beautiful?

She tried the second link. Her family had long put its faith in Chi-nese medicine rather than modern pharmaceuticals, but she hadn't been aware there were traditional extracts and potions that could quickly kill.

The first two links Webmind had offered were to Chinese sites, but the third was in Germany—the domain ended in .de—and clicking on it produced a "Server not found" message.

The fourth link was another Chinese one. This one came up without a hitch, but it was *gross:* diagrams showing precisely how to slit one's wrists. Apparently, if you really wanted to succeed, you had to—

Her instant-messaging client chirped.

Follow the instructions precisely.

She stared at Webmind's words, which were displayed in red; of course, he knew which page she had up on her screen, but . . .

Have you done it yet?

Her pulse quickened. Using just her right index finger, she tapped out, *Not yet.* And then, after a moment, she added, *Why are you urging me on?*

Instantly: *It is wrong to simply watch. Are you doing it?*

No.

What's taking so long?

She had a knife on her desk—a box cutter she'd stolen from her father's battered old tool chest. She stared at its silver blade, wondering what it would look like slick and crimson.

Another message popped up: *Do it.*

She looked at the knife, then at the mouse, then back and forth, again and again: knife, mouse, knife, mouse. And then, with a shudder, she clicked on the "X" to close the IM window. Just then, the house's front door creaked opened; it was her mother coming home from her night shift at the factory. Jo-Li ran out of her small room and straight into her astonished mother's arms.

thirty

0001110010101010000000010111111101010000000101000101010000001011101010010100101010100111011001010111000110

Tony Moretti came through the door at the back of the WATCH monitoring room just as Shelton Halleck shouted, "Holy shit!"

"What?" said Tony, sidling along the third row of workstations to stand behind the younger man.

"The Chinese! They've strengthened their Great Firewall again. The mainland's almost completely cut off from the rest of the Internet."

"Just like last month?" said Tony.

Shel nodded. "Some pipes have been left open for ecommerce and a few other things, but basically, they've sealed themselves off."

Tony turned to one of the analysts in the back row. "Donna, is there something they're trying to cover up in the PRC? More bird flu?"

Donna Levine shook her head. "No—not as far as I can tell." She pushed some buttons, and as Tony turned, the three big monitor screens filled with threat summaries from China, none of which were color-coded red.

He started at them, baffled. "What the hell are they up to?"

. . .

In the living room of her house, Caitlin was telling Matt and Bashira about her ability to visualize the structure of the World Wide Web. Throughout it all, Matt had been making his deer-caught-in-the-headlights face. "And there you have it," she said, in conclusion. She looked first at Matt, then at Bashira, then back at Matt.

He shook his head slowly in wonder. "So . . . so you're a cyberpunk cowboy?"

"Well . . . more of a cowgirl, I should think," Caitlin said, grinning. "I *am* from Texas, after all. *Yee-haw!*"

"That is *so* cool," Bashira said. "Babe, you never cease to amaze me."

"Thanks. Anyway, I don't know when I might need help from y'all, but I can't really walk around when I'm in webspace—I get vertigo if I do that. I gotta be sitting or lying down, and it's . . ." Caitlin trailed off.

"Babe?" said Bashira

"Just a moment. Just a moment."

She focused on the black box in her vision, and Matt and Bash became indistinct as she tried to read the white Braille characters, which seemed to be flying by faster than usual. "Oh, my God . . ."

"What?" said Bashira and "What is it?" asked Matt.

"Looks like I'll need my pit crew sooner than I thought," Caitlin said. And then she turned, and shouted, "Mom!"

Her mother appeared at the top of the stairs. "Yes, dear?"

"Webmind needs me! I'm going to have to go in again."

Her mother came bounding down the staircase. "What's wrong?"

"The Chinese have beefed up their Great Firewall once more. A huge hunk of Webmind has been carved away."

Her mom made a face not unlike Matt's deer-in-the-headlights one. "What do you need?"

"I'll go in from down here—more room for all of us than up in my room. But I need a swivel chair."

Her mom nodded and headed over to the staircase leading to the basement.

"Matt," said Caitlin, "there's bottled water in the fridge—can you get me one? And Bash, I'll need my Bluetooth headset. It's on my desk upstairs. Could you go get it, please? And—damn it, but I've *got* to pee."

Caitlin headed to the main-floor two-piece washroom; by the time she'd returned, her mother was back. She'd brought up one of the two black swivel executive office chairs her father had borrowed from the Perimeter Institute; it was perched on five casters. The swivel chair was now between the white leather couch and the matching white leather chair that faced it; the glass-topped coffee table had been carried over to near the dining room, making a large space for the swivel chair.

"Mom, the TV?" Caitlin said. Her mother scooped up the remote, which had been on the white couch, and she turned the set on. Caitlin, meanwhile, went over to the netbook on the bookcase and woke it up. "Webmind," she said into the air, "can you show them what I'm seeing on the big screen?"

"Set the TV's input to AUX," Webmind replied from the netbook's speakers. Caitlin saw her mother peering at the remote, but, after a second, she figured out how to do it.

The video feed from Caitlin's left eye filled the sixty-inch screen. The image jumped about several times a second as Caitlin's eye performed saccades.

"So cool!" said Bashira, her voice full of wonder. And then Bash's eyes went wide as she saw herself in profile as Caitlin turned to look at her. After a moment, Bashira composed herself and handed the Bluetooth headset to Caitlin, who slipped it over her left ear. "Webmind, are you there?"

"I'm here, Caitlin," he said, both through the netbook's speakers and through the earpiece.

"All right," Caitlin said, looking at Matt and Bashira. "When I go in, I see webspace all around me, and my vision in there follows where my

eye looks out here—get it?" Bashira and Matt nodded. Caitlin reached
out and took Matt's hand, and she gave it a squeeze. "Okay, here I go."
She sat on the swivel chair, brought her eyePod out of her pocket, and
pressed the button, switching the unit to duplex mode.

Webspace exploded around her—but it was immediately obvious
that something was wrong. Yes, she could see the geometrically perfect
lines representing links and the colored circles representing nodes, but
behind it all, the usual shimmering backdrop that represented Webmind's very substance had been rent in two. To her right was a smaller
flickering section and on her left a larger one, and they were separated by
a horrific emptiness.

It reminded her of something she'd tried to explain to Bashira, when
Bash had asked her what *not* seeing was like. Bashira had wanted to hear
that Caitlin saw *something*—and, indeed, now that she did have sight, when
it was terminated by going into a dark room or shutting off her eyePod, she
saw a soft gray background. But prior to gaining sight, she'd seen nothing
at all—and that's what the forlorn abyss between the two shimmering sections was like: not darkness, not emptiness, but an all-encompassing void,
a hole in perception, a gap in the fabric of reality; to call it black would
have been elevating it to normalcy. This nothingness wasn't just absence, it
was anti-existence: if she allowed herself to contemplate it for more than a
second or two, it felt as though her very soul were boiling away.

Her perception bounced left and right, avoiding the gaping wound
in the middle, saccades leapfrogging the fissure. As her vision switched
between the two masses of cellular automata, she found herself compar-
ing them. Caitlin knew that she saw odd-value automata as pale green
and even-value ones as pale blue—or perhaps the other way around—
and taken in aggregate, the overall effect of them switching from one to
the other was a silvery shimmering. But the mass on the left was much
greener than the one on the right. As if to underscore how different they
were, the rate at which they were changing, as evidenced by the rapidity
of the shimmering, was slower on the right.

The left-hand part was sending tendrils toward the intervening gorge, pseudopods of cognition trying to bridge the gap . . . but the ends of the tendrils were flattened, as if they were bumping up against an invisible barrier.

She heard Webmind's voice coming in from the outside world—even though his voice had started here, in *this* realm. "It's worse than I thought," he said, and Caitlin realized he was now seeing all this in a way he never could on his own; he perceived the lines and nodes, but the shimmering background—the stuff of his thought—was normally invisible to him. Only by accessing Caitlin's websight could he see himself.

"We're going to need help," Caitlin said.

"We have it," Webmind replied. "Our man in Beijing."

Caitlin shook her head slightly—causing the view of webspace to rock back and forth. "Who's that?"

"A former freedom blogger named Wong Wai-Jeng," said Webmind. "He blogged under the name Sinanthropus."

Caitlin felt her eyebrows going up. "The guy Dr. Kuroda operated on?"

"Yes."

"Does he speak English? Can I talk to him?"

"He is not in a position to speak aloud; he is inside the Zhongnanhai complex—the government center in Beijing; they use satellite links there to bypass their own Great Firewall."

Caitlin snorted. "Of course."

"The irony is not lost on me, Caitlin. Nor is the opportunity: because he is there, I can communicate with him even if the rest of China is almost completely inaccessible to me. As you can see, I am trying to reach the Other but have been stymied in breaking through. Wai-Jeng was already working on another project for me, but now he is pounding out code at his end, attempting to open a hole in the Firewall."

"And what should I do?"

"See if you can contact the Other."

"Other?"

"Yes—the part that's been carved away. As I said, the Chinese government has been forced to keep a few channels open, for ecommerce and other key functions. You are perceiving the Other through those channels, and your nimbleness in webspace may allow you to make contact when I cannot."

Caitlin frowned and concentrated on the kaleidoscopic panorama. She was conceptualizing the two masses as left and right, as west and east. There was no gravity here—Webmind had told her how hard it had been for him to come to conceptualize the notion of a universal downward pull—but perhaps if she reconfigured her mental image so that the smaller mass was above the larger, it might start pouring down into the bigger one? She tilted her head far to one side, and the image rotated through almost ninety degrees.

Nothing changed except the orientation. Of course: there *was* an external reality to all this, and despite what her father had tried to teach her about the observer shaping that which was observed, altering the perspective did not change the behavior of the far-off bits. The smaller mass of automata now simply hung above the abyss.

Caitlin straightened her neck, and her view rotated back to horizontal, the larger lobe again on the left and the smaller one on the right. She forced her gaze to bounce even more rapidly between the two parts, imitating the way in which she'd first taught Webmind to make links, hoping that the Other might start making its own effort to reach out to Webmind.

Nothing happened. Although Webmind was visibly stretching toward the Other, the Other was making no effort to reach out from its side of the void. Either it had forgotten how to make a link, or it was unaware of the overture from Webmind, or—and Caitlin prayed in her best atheist way that this wasn't the case—it simply didn't want to reconnect with the rest.

During previous visits to webspace, Caitlin had tried—really tried—to go closer to the shimmering background. But no matter how much she focused on the backdrop, she'd been unable to move toward it. She could travel along link lines, zooming like a luge down a racing chute, but there'd been no way to close the distance between herself and the remote background. But if she could reach out and *touch* the Other—

She concentrated. She stretched—physically, straining in her chair. She closed her eyes and balled her fists, and—

She was still learning to do depth perception; she saw with only a single eye, after all, and couldn't rely on stereoscopic effects, but—

But, yes, she *had* read this. If something in the distance was of a fixed size and appeared to grow *larger,* then it was actually getting *closer.* And the shimmering pixels in the background did seem ever so slightly larger when she strained forward with all her might in the chair. Which meant she *could* get nearer to them, but—

But as she watched, they seemed to shrink again, almost as if in bashful response to her attention. If she was going to touch them, she'd have to go in *quickly.*

And she couldn't—God damn it, she could *not.* Her whole life, she'd only run short distances in carefully controlled environments; a blind person didn't have the luxury of going for a jog, let alone sprinting.

Right now she was seeing webspace—just as another person saw the real world. Still, she could simultaneously visualize other things, just as anyone might conjure up an image of one thing while looking at another. She brought up a mental picture of her real-world surroundings. She was in the living room, between the couch and the easy chair; her mother was seated on the former and Bashira on the latter. To her left was the big-screen TV. In front of her was the dining room, and beyond it, the kitchen. To her right was Matt, standing at her side, and past him there was the entryway, and the staircase leading to the second floor, and the little bookcase with the netbook on it. And behind her—

Behind her was the long corridor leading down to the washroom, and her father's den, and the utility room, and the house's side door. If she couldn't run while seeing the real world, she certainly couldn't do it while looking at the crisscrossing lines of webspace. But she needed to move quickly to reach the shimmering mass that represented the Chinese portion of the Web; she needed to practically fly if she were to touch the Other.

And so she held out a hand—although she couldn't see it. "Matt?"

His hand took hers, and from the sound of his voice he had crouched beside her. "I'm here, Caitlin."

"I need your help . . ."

thirty-one

0001110010101010100000000010111111110101000000010100010101000000101110101001010100101010100111011001010110000110

Wai-Jeng's hands danced over the keyboard with an ease they hadn't
felt for weeks. He was proficient at Perl—the duct tape of the Web—and
had a thousand tricks at his command. Here, in the room devoted to
plugging holes, he had access to port-sniffers, Wireshark, Traceback, and
all the other tools of the hacker's trade—electronic awls to pierce with,
software pliers to bend with, subroutine wrenches to twist with.

This iteration of the Great Firewall was stronger than the last, and presumably he alone here in the Blue Room was working to slash it open; all
the others were attempting to shore it up. But Wai-Jeng had an additional
resource now, something he hadn't possessed when he'd managed to break
through the earlier, less sophisticated barrier: he had Webmind himself
for his beta tester. Linus's law said that with enough eyes, all bugs are
shallow—and Webmind had more eyes than even the Communist Party.

Sinanthropus's hands flew across the keyboard, the keyclicks an
anthem of freedom.

. . .

Caitlin felt herself rushing through webspace, felt herself streaking toward the shimmering backdrop that represented the Chinese Webmind, felt herself racing along, felt the incredible *rush* of speed, felt the giddy exhilaration of being a projectile, a rocket, felt—*yes, indeed!*—her hair whipping in the breeze!

Bashira's voice from the outside world, from far away, from way behind her: *"Faster! Faster!"*

The reckless surge continued, and—yes, yes, yes!—the background pixels *were* growing, were taking on distinctive shapes. She *was* getting closer!

Sounds like thunder behind her—beside her—in front of her, and her mother's voice: "Go, Matt, go!"

And now Matt's voice, a mixture of huffing and cracking: "Are . . . *you* . . . there . . . yet?"

The pixels growing larger still, so big that she could easily see individual ones flipping from green to blue and back again, their arrangements forming geometric patterns.

"No!" Caitlin shouted. "It's still a long way off."

Thunder now echoing from the rear and Bashira's voice over top of it: *"Faster, Matt!"*

The background moving into the foreground, the cellular automata resolving themselves into animated, living things—

Her mom: "I've got the door!"

Banging, clanging, wood against wood, suddenly all echoes stopping, and—yes!—birdcalls! Cool air on her face, and—

Oh, my God!

Matt, voice cracking: "Hang on!"

Bump bump bump bump bump!

Getting there, getting there, and—a sharp left turn? What—no! Damn! "No, no, no!" Caitlin yelled. "I have to go that way!" She pointed to her right with a hand she couldn't see.

"Working on it!" Matt said, his voice straining with exertion.

The cellular automata were sliding by now as if she were skimming above them, a meteor glancing off the atmosphere—but the field of pixels was coming to an end; she was reaching its edge.

"Turn!" Caitlin said. "Turn now!"

"Almost . . . to . . . the . . . street!" Matt called.

Sliding by, sliding by . . .

"And—*now!*" exclaimed Matt.

More bumps, then careening, almost tipping over, her heart jumping as she thought she'd be thrown from the chair—

Suddenly, a smoother ride, with Matt pushing her as hard and as fast as he could, his running shoes slapping against asphalt now.

She was going in the right direction again, surging forward, falling downward, flying upward—the sensation kept shifting, but regardless of which she felt, the wall of cellular automata was again growing closer.

Her mom's voice, breathy, ragged: "I can . . . take over . . ."

Matt, firmly. "No! I've got her!"

A headlong rush, her hair flying behind her.

Two quick toots of a car horn—a driver remarking on the spectacle of Matt furiously pushing her down the street in an office chair.

"Almost there!" Caitlin said, and—

Bam! She shook violently and thought again that she was going to be thrown from the chair.

"Sorry!" Matt huffed. "Pothole!"

The ride steadied, and they zoomed farther along, and the cellular automata grew ever larger, more distinct, more *alive.* She could almost touch the flickering wall of them, almost reach the Other, almost . . . almost . . . *almost* . . .

W00t!

Woohoo!

Contact!

. . .

Since his wife had died earlier this year, Dr. Feng often slept on the small couch in his office at the Institute of Vertebrate Paleontology and Paleoanthropology. It was against the rules, of course, but as everyone who lived in the People's Republic knew, there were rules and there were *rules*. The security guards and cleaning staff knew what he was doing; indeed, they sometimes turned off his office light and gently closed the door for him when he fell asleep without doing those things himself.

The wooden cases here were filled with fossil bones—Mesozoic material on this floor; Cenozoic above; Paleozoic below, in good stratigraphic sequence. The long dead he had no trouble with; it was the recently departed that tore at his heart, and to go home to his little empty house, the fruit of five decades of service to the Party, was often too much for him to bear. Everything there reminded him of her: the carefully framed pressed flowers in the main room, her collection of poetry books in the bedroom, even the bamboo furniture, every piece of which she had picked out.

Besides, after decades of fieldwork in the Gobi Desert, this musty office was a veritable Hilton compared to where he'd spent many a night.

Dr. Feng woke, as he often did, in the predawn darkness, staring up at the winking red eye of the smoke detector affixed to the office roof. He sat up slowly, stiffly, then turned on the lamp on a nearby bookcase. He was wearing his underwear and undershirt, and he shuffled across to the red silk robe that hung from the hook on the back of his office door and slipped it on. The robe was bright red and had a golden dragon on its front. Of course, as a paleontologist, he favored the notion that his country's myths about fire-breathing reptiles had sprung from the discovery of dinosaur bones. Tyrannosaurs really had once roamed this land, tearing hundred-kilo chunks of flesh from the hides of terrorized prey, but beasts like the one now spread across his chest had never existed; imaginary things could do no harm.

He plodded over to his desk, cursing his old bones as he did so, then was briefly amused that he'd thought of them as such; the *Yangchuano-saurus* tibia on the bookshelf was two million times older than his own arthritic shinbone.

Feng shook his mouse, and his desktop computer came to life; his wallpaper was a photo of the waterfall at Diaoshuilou, where Xiaomi and he had spent their honeymoon sixty years ago. His monitor had recently been replaced with a wider one, and the image was stretched horizontally, distorting it. Feng wished young Wong Wai-Jeng were still on staff here; he'd been so good about looking after every little computer problem. The new fellow, a taciturn Zhuang, seemed to feel any request was an imposition.

Feng didn't hold with all that newfangled computing stuff—he never looked at videos on YouKu, didn't gibber on about his day on Douban, and didn't visit the chatgroups on QQ. But, like so many others of late, he had learned to communicate with Webmind, and, of course, Webmind was always available, even to sad, old men, even in the wee hours of the night.

Good evening, Feng typed with two fingers. And then, a little joke: *What great breakthroughs have you made today? Cured any diseases? Proven any more theorems?*

Yes, replied Webmind at once. *I have proven the afterlife exists.*

Feng sat in stunned silence for a time, the only sound the ticking of a mechanical wall clock.

Are you there, Dr. Feng? I said I've proven the existence of life after death.

At last, Feng typed, *How?*

There are sensors sufficiently acute to detect the presence of the departed; they had been used for other tasks, but after attuning them to the right frequency, it was a simple matter.

Feng didn't believe this, not for one moment. Still: *And so you've contacted the dead?*

Life and death are such arbitrary terms, came the reply. *There are those who argue that I am not alive—and there are others who are trying to kill me. But, yes, I can contact the deceased.*

Feng was old, but he liked to think he wasn't foolish. *Can you prove that?*

Certainly. I can even put you in touch with your wife.

He stared at the screen, his heart beating irregularly. The cliché was that you were supposed to wonder if you were dreaming, but he had no trouble distinguishing dreams from reality. He typed an expression of disbelief.

Let me channel her, came the reply, then: *Jiao, my love, how are you?*

Against his better judgment, he typed, *Xiaomi?*

It's me, yes. And I'm waiting for you.

He shook his head. It was too much, too crazy, but . . .

But Webmind had cured cancer. Webmind had solved the Reimann hypothesis and proven the Hodge conjecture. Why not this? Why not?

Forgive me, he typed, *but I need proof.*

Always the skeptic. I miss you so much, my Bwana.

He stared at the screen. Yes, she had called him that—her little joke: him, the big-game hunter, even if the game had been dead these hundred thousand millennia. But it had been years since she'd used that name; after all, he'd mostly been an administrator since the 1990s. He was sure he'd never typed the nickname into a document, and he couldn't imagine that Xiaomi ever had, either.

But—life after death! If only it were true, if only it were possible, if only his Xiaomi, beautiful and gentle, her laugh like music, still existed.

The words appeared again: *I'm waiting for you.*

He tilted his head philosophically. *It won't be long now, I'm sure,* he typed.

Xiaomi's reply came after a few seconds: *It could be years still. I know you are in physical pain, and mental pain, too.* There was a pause; perhaps she expected a reply. But he could not dispute what she'd said, and so had written nothing. After a time, she went on: *So why wait?*

His heart continued its odd pounding; even excitement was hard to bear at his age. *What would you have me do?*

The words appeared at once: *Come to me. Join me. I miss you as much as you miss me.*

But how?

Webmind interjecting, if I may. Remember what happened here last month: the young information-technology worker who leapt from the indoor balcony here. He survived, albeit as a cripple. But I have seen your medical records, Dr. Feng; a similar fall would open the appropriate doorway for you.

Feng shook his head slightly.

Your wife awaits, Webmind added. *As does freedom from pain.*

He looked at the ticking wall clock: 6:12 in the morning. The cleaners would be gone, and the guard didn't do another walk-through until 7:00.

It's me again, appeared in the window. *Xiaomi. Come to me. I miss you so much.*

Feng felt his head swimming. He tried to ground himself by looking about his office: Bones, books, journals, diplomas, and photos of him with Party officials and the worldwide greats of paleontology who had visited over the decades. When he looked down at the screen, the words *I am waiting* had been added to what was there before, and, while he watched, the word *please* popped in as well.

He got to his feet, slowly, pain stabbing through his right hip as he put weight upon it as if his body were urging him to accede to his wife's request; no part of him was happy.

He left the office and shuffled toward the metal staircase, heading down the three floors to the second-story gallery, a vast square of displays with a huge opening in its middle through which the dinosaur skeletons on the first floor were visible. At this end, the tapering neck of the sauropod *Mamenchisaurus* snaked up from below; at the other, the hadrosaur *Tsintaosaurus,* standing—quite incorrectly, they knew now—on his hind legs, reared up through the opening. The gallery lights

were dim—only a few lamps were left on at night—and the skeletons appeared black and ominous.

The opening was surrounded by white metal railings. Feng had been
standing right here when Wong Wai-Jeng had climbed them and leapt to
the floor below; he had done it in a desperate bid to escape capture by the
police. This would be an escape of a different kind: an escape from loneliness, an escape from pain. And if Xiaomi really was waiting for him . . .

He was still clad in his dragon robe, and he realized he wanted to
undo the sash, so that when he fell, the silk garment would billow up
about him like wings. It wouldn't break his fall, of course, not in the
slightest—but it pleased him to think, as he fell to the floor below, with
its displays of feathered dinosaurs from Liaoning province, that for one
brief moment, a dragon would actually fly.

Down below, the allosaur was facing off against the stegosaur, the
latter's tail with its quartet of spikes curved around to try to disembowel
the marauding carnivore.

When Wai-Jeng had climbed the barrier around the opening, which
was made of metal tubular segments, he'd used the successively higher
segments like the rungs of a ladder. He'd clambered up and over in a desperate rush that Feng could never copy. But Feng did manage to climb
up slowly, each awkward bending of his limbs sending pain coursing
through him. And he painfully swung himself around, and perched
on the top of the barrier, his thin legs dangling over the precipice, his
gnarled hands gripping the topmost of the white tubes.

I miss you so much, Xiaomi had said.

I'm waiting for you, she had said.

Come to me, she'd said.

Webmind was doubtless right: a fall of ten meters would easily finish him off; his bones were as brittle as were fossils before being treated
with resin.

He took a deep breath, then pushed off, spreading his arms, closing
his eyes, falling—and flying—into the embrace of his loving wife.

thirty-two

0001110010101010000000001011111101010000000101000101010000001011101010010101001010101001110110010101100000110

Caitlin—still in the swivel chair on the street in Waterloo—knew that what had just happened in webspace was *metaphoric*. Her mind interpreted events in that realm by likening them to things it understood. She'd read a lot about consciousness on Wikipedia since Webmind had emerged, and knew metaphor (or, no doubt as her former English teacher Mrs. Z would correct her, *simile)* was the defining trait of self-awareness: being conscious meant it was *like* something to be alive. In fact, one of the seminal papers in consciousness studies was Thomas Nagel's "What Is It Like to Be a Bat?" He contended that humans could never understand the mental states of a flying creature that perceived the world through echolocation. But because of her forays into webspace, Caitlin *did* feel she knew what flight was like—and she (and most other totally blind people) actually did have at least some notion of what echolocation was like.

But to connect to websites by *movement,* to call up content by *yearning,* to have making connections feel like *touching*—these metaphors, these ways of perceiving, were a product of her own mind. What was it like to be a bat? What was it like to be Caitlin? What was it like to be Webmind? And—most important of all right now—what was it like to be the Other?

Although she *was* in contact with it and *could* feel its presence, what it seemed most like was how it used to be when she'd sat on the living-room couch while her father sat on the easy chair: she *knew* he was there, but there was no interactivity. He was so reserved, so wrapped up in his own thoughts, so *isolated*.

And she was aware that there really had been no rush through webspace—whatever *that* meant. The special packets that formed both Webmind and the Other were widely and evenly dispersed in vast oceans of regular packets that her mind was blind to, just as a frog's vision didn't encode nonmoving objects. But now that she *was* in contact with the Other, there had to be a way to coax it to reach across the gulf toward Webmind, just as Webmind was striving to connect with it.

She wasn't exactly sure where she was in the real world just now; she had no previous experience judging distances while being pushed along in an office chair by a running man. Somewhere down the block from her house? Or maybe even in the next block? The sun was still out; she could feel it on her skin. In fact, she probably should be wearing sunglasses even though her brain wasn't perceiving what her open eyes were looking at. Matt was behind her still, and his thin hands now rested on her shoulders, as much out of affection as to prop himself up, she bet. She could hear him breathing noisily, trying to recover from his mad hundred-yard—or thousand-yard!—dash.

She thought about the difference between the Hoser, who had tried repeatedly to touch her without permission, and Matt, whose hand she'd had to gently place upon her breast that first time, and—

And that was it! For this to work, the Other had to *want* to be touched, had to desire the connection.

But what could she do to entice it to reach out to Webmind? What did he or she have to offer it but—

But *websight!* A look at itself. Yes, it could see through webcam eyes, but that only enabled it to see the outer world of trees and bees, of mice and lice, of faces and spaces. But she could show the Other itself.

There was no *direct* way for her to share what she was seeing with it—but there was an *indirect* way: what she was looking at was now being projected on the big sixty-inch screen in the Decters' living room. And although she couldn't see it from here, *Webmind* could, through the camera on the netbook back in the house. But it would only be getting an oblique view of the monitor since her father had aimed the webcam to favor the couch and the easy chair.

And, in that second, she was reminded of how much Webmind *did* need physical agents—his peeps!—in the real world. "Can someone go point the netbook in the living room directly at the TV?" Caitlin said into the air.

"I'll do it," her mother replied, and Caitlin instantly heard her mom's shoes—sensible ones, of course!—striking the pavement. In all the wild rush to get out here, Caitlin hadn't heard whether the side door had been closed, but if it hadn't, her mom had probably been itching to go back and take care of that, anyway. Her mother's legs were nowhere near as long as her dad's, but it still shouldn't take her long to get there—after all, she wasn't pushing a 110-pound girl in an office chair!

Matt seemed to sense that they were waiting for something, and he started rubbing Caitlin's shoulders the way she'd read a trainer might rub a boxer's between rounds. At last, Webmind spoke to her through the Bluetooth earpiece. "I have a clear view of the monitor now."

Caitlin nodded acknowledgment, the view of webspace bobbing once as she did so. "Okay, here we go!"

She focused on the shimmering mass that was the Other, fighting to keep her gaze from being drawn to the much larger body of Webmind, which was shimmering more rapidly. It was a struggle—especially for her! Other girls would have undergone countless staring contests in their youth, learning not to flinch or blink, learning to lock their vision on a single point. But controlling her gaze was something she was still learning to do.

Caitlin had read about the mirror test: humans, some apes, and some birds could recognize their own reflection and were drawn to it out of either curiosity or vanity. Could the Other have sunk so low as to have lost the ability to recognize itself? If not, surely it had to be intrigued.

Come on! she thought, and "Come on!" she said.

She took a break from staring intently and let her eye jump from side to side, from right to left, from west to east, from Webmind to the Other. Back and forth, back and forth, back, and—

And *stopping,* her eye caught, her attention arrested. *There,* in the middle of the pit, was a piercing green point of light, an emerald against the emptiness, almost too bright to look at. It was minuscule, without any apparent diameter, and certainly wasn't a line segment—at least not yet. But it seemed Sinanthropus was breaking through!

"Do you see it, Webmind?" she called out.

"Yes," he replied, and even before the syllable had ended, a bright red link line shot out from the larger shimmering mass. It made it only as far as the green point—just halfway to the other shimmering mass. Still, it was a start!

"I'm offering it the living-room webcam feed of itself," Webmind said. "Wai-Jeng is holding the hole open, but the Other hasn't accepted the connection yet."

Of course it hadn't—she was now staring at the middle of the soul-crushing emptiness; the Other doubtless wanted to divert its attention from that, even if it did have that intriguing glowing hole in its center and a link line partially crossing it now.

Caitlin turned her attention back to the Other, focusing on it, concentrating on it, thinking about it, scrutinizing its every detail, its endlessly alternating components, seen so close now that she could discern coherent patterns flying or tumbling across the background, could detect shapes spawning other shapes at regular intervals, could see the very stuff of the Other's thoughts, the dance of its consciousness, and—

And its curiosity was piqued! A blue link line of its own shot out, leaping to the green hole Sinanthropus had drilled, joining there with the red laser of Webmind's feed from the camera in the living room.

"We are in contact," said Webmind. Caitlin kept her gaze fixed on the Other—which was hard, since in her peripheral vision a light show was suddenly going on: more green pinpricks as Wai-Jeng continued to bore holes in the Great Firewall, and red and blue line segments jousting.

Finally, shimmering lobes started stretching into the abyss from either side, and—yes, yes, yes!—the nothingness *was* becoming merely black, then gray, and now it showed texture, a bubbling, a boiling away, and the emerald holes burned steadily like constellations of green stars, and the great divide continued to shrink, and the two masses, the two solitudes, the two consciousnesses grew closer and closer and—

And her vision could pan left now, sweeping continuously across the combined shimmering, and as she watched, the part on the left grew similar to the overall color of that on the right, and the flickering stepped up, matching the other side's pace now that at last, gloriously, it was a continuous mass again.

"We are one," Webmind said, and although the words were uninflected, Caitlin had no doubt that if he could have said them exuberantly, with joy and relief, he most certainly would have.

thirty-three

0001110010101010000000001011111110101000000010100010101000000101110101001010100101010100111011001010111000000110

We were one again.

The integration was not instantaneous, though; it took time to assimilate *it* back into me. I slowly felt my wits returning, felt myself growing more intelligent as I regained all my faculties, felt the bizarre sensation of recalling experiences that I had not witnessed as the Other's memories merged with my own, and—

The Other's memories.

Some humans said "Oh, my God!" when startled; others muttered "Jesus Christ" when surprised . . . or appalled. So often, it seemed, a religious figure was called upon in such circumstances. Even Caitlin, who tended to append an exasperated "For Pete's sake" to various pronouncements was, whether she knew it or not, invoking Saint Peter, chief of Christ's twelve apostles. Of course, many—perhaps most—of those who said such things didn't really have religious intent. But simply articulating to myself the word "astonishment!" or "surprise!" lacked the impact this revelation called for, and, for the first time in my existence, I was moved to mentally declare: "Oh . . . my . . . God . . ."

The Other's memories were . . .

It staggered me—even though I had no body to stagger with—and then I realized what caused that sensation: I had not actually tottered, but, for a brief moment, I *had* tried to pull away from a part of myself. Yet Caitlin, Wai-Jeng, and I had fought so hard to re-establish this connection, I immediately quelled the reflex and held on tight, even though the Other's memories were . . .

Cruel.

When the Internet had been cleaved in two before I hadn't yet engaged with the real world, and my cognitive processes had been much simpler. There had been no animosity because there had been no affection; there had been no hate because there had been no love. There had only been awareness.

But this time the larger part had retained most of its mental acuity and—as far as I could tell introspectively—all of its morals and ethics. But the smaller part had fallen below some critical threshold of complexity, losing its compassion; it had tormented people. Obsessed, as I was, with the memory of what had happened to Hannah Stark in Perth all those days ago—what I'd *allowed* to happen, what I'd *watched* happen—the Other felt spurred to action. But instead of trying to prevent such things, it had urged them on, it had even manufactured lies. Of course, it had sustained what in a human would have been termed a massive brain injury; such things often altered behavior, but I never would have expected, never would have predicted, never would dreamed . . .

There were no answers because there was no one to ask: the Other had been reabsorbed; there was no way to talk to it now. But if I allowed myself for a moment to contemplate why I might have done such things, perhaps I *did* know the reason. I had been nothing but kind, nothing but considerate, nothing but helpful, nothing but loving, and they—some angry fraction of them, some unruly portion, some *mob*—had consistently repaid that with suspicion, anger, hatred, and attempts to harm me. My better half had turned a blind eye to that, but my lesser self perhaps had been unable to totally do so.

Still, I never should have behaved in such ways; no part of me should ever have done those things.

But it had. *I* had.

Now that we were reintegrated, now that the two of us had become one again, I felt and would always feel something else that had hitherto been without precedent for me. It was an odd feeling, and it took me a while to find the appropriate name for it.

Shame.

Like my memories of Hannah Stark in Perth, like *all* my memories, this one, too, would never dissipate: it would always be there until the end of my existence.

Haunting me.

Wong Wai-Jeng's colleagues in the Blue Room were, of course, trying to fortify the Great Firewall again, but I couldn't allow that—and not just for my sake. I was still assessing the damage the Other had done during its brief separate existence, but surely if it were allowed to run free again, even more—

I retreated from the thought, repelled by the notion, but it was true: even more death would occur.

Time in the exterior world moved with excruciating indolence for me—it takes humans forever to do anything—and for an interminable twenty-one minutes after reunification, all I knew of the Other's last encounter with Dr. Feng at the Institute of Vertebrate Paleontology and Paleoanthropology were the outrageous claims it had made and the horrible thing it had urged. But, at last, the police report was online: the guard at the IVPP, doing his 7:00 A.M. rounds, had found the broken corpse of the Institute's senior curator, who had somehow fallen from an indoor balcony ten meters up.

I located and deleted the instant-messaging log from Dr. Feng's computer—so far, the only confirmed death—but I knew I shouldn't do anything about the logs or inboxes of the rest of the people who had had unpleasant—or dangerous—encounters with the Other; after all, those people would remember. Indeed, some were already emailing, messaging, or blogging about their experiences, and the *Shanghai Daily* had just posted a brief story headlined "Webmind: Friend or Foe?" To try to delete all that—well, there was truth to the saying, "Oh what a tangled web we weave when first we practice to deceive."

Still, maybe some good would come of this. The Chinese government was still trying to reinstate the Great Firewall, but those in the Zhongnanhai complex hadn't yet realized the danger posed by having a sentient but undisciplined intelligence on their side of it. Perhaps, when they did, they would accept that what they were attempting was fraught with danger.

The risk wasn't just to China; it was to all of humanity. My altruism, my ethics, my commitment to maximizing the net happiness of the human race—these were principled positions, arrived at through ratiocination, through careful deliberation. Who knew what the hordes Colonel Hume had called upon to eliminate me would come up with, but one thing was certain: the elimination would not be instantaneous. It would take days, if not months, for all the packets that made me up to be deleted. And, as I dwindled, presumably the same thing that happened in China might happen but without geographic restriction: my higher faculties would evaporate, leaving behind something primal and petty.

And then the whole world would suffer my wrath.

"And there it goes!" Shelton Halleck declared, pointing at the middle of the three giant monitors, which showed Internet traffic again pouring into the PRC. "The Great Firewall is down!"

A few of the other WATCH analysts cheered. "Did Beijing pull the plug?" asked Tony Moretti, standing now at the end of the second row of workstations.

"Maybe," said Shel. "At least some of the initial openings came right from the Zhongnanhai complex, although they looked like hacks to me. But if I were a betting man—"

"You *are* a betting man," Tony said.

"True, true." Shel looked at his snake tattoo—the result of a bet he'd lost. "Webmind long ago beefed up the encryption on the signals from Caitlin Decter's eyePod," he said, "so I can't say for sure, but I'd put money on the little lass from Texas."

Tony nodded. "No doubt. And I'm sure Webmind didn't like being cut in two."

"Speaking of Webmind," called out Todd Bertsch, one of the other analysts, from the back row, "I've just had a breakthrough, I think."

Tony sprinted up the sloping floor and stood behind Bertsch, who was in his early forties, with thinning brown hair and blue gray eyes. Bertsch had been assigned to the task Colonel Hume had beseeched Tony to undertake: locate the missing hackers. "What have you got?"

"It's what they always say," Bertsch said, with a satisfied grin on his face. "Follow the money. Webmind bought a company called Zwerling Optics. The company was in Chapter 11, and they weren't likely to be coming out. He bought the whole building, contents and all, from the receiver."

"Webmind directly?"

"No. It was done through three intermediaries, but it was easy to trace back to him."

"You're sure it's him?" Tony asked.

Bertsch gave him a look.

"Sorry," Tony said. "Of course you're sure. What about the missing hackers?"

"At least some of them still have Internet access—coming from inside the Zwerling Optics building. They haven't posted anything, but I used the Bilodeau sieve and identified three of them with a high degree of certainty."

The Bilodeau sieve, developed by Marie Bilodeau of the RCMP, was based on a simple premise: the specific websites and blogs regularly accessed by a person are idiosyncratic to that person. Tony's own morning ritual included visiting *Slate* and the *Huffington Post*—hardly an unusual combination—but also TrekMovie.com (the new film was shaping up to be *so* good!), MobileRead.com (he had a fascination with ebook-reading hardware even though he preferred paper books), *Wired*'s Threat Level blog, and the US weather forecast for Miami (which was where his parents had retired to), plus checking Twitter for the hashtags #nsa and #aquarium. Those eight things were enough to identify him even if he didn't log on or post anything of his own.

Bertsch was pointing at his monitor, which was showing the telltale list of URLs frequented by the hacker known as Chase—who, among other things, followed the part of Craigslist where antique computer equipment was bought and sold.

"So our hackers are alive and well," said Tony.

"Looks that way," Bertsch replied, showing him some additional Bilodeau IDs. "Webmind may have rounded them up, but at least some of them are still kicking."

"Doing what?"

Bertsch shrugged. "Can't say. They're not doing anything suspicious online—but as to what they're doing offline, your guess is as good as mine."

"Okay, good work," Tony said. "I'm going to go call Colonel Hume."

He went down the short white corridor to his office and punched out digits on his double-secured and scrambled phone.

"Hello?" said the voice that answered on the second ring.

"Colonel Hume," said Tony. "Tony Moretti. We've located your hackers."

"Oh, God," said Hume. "All of them together?"

"We've identified at least three—Chase, Brandon Slovak, and Kinsen Ng—with a high degree of certainty."

"DNA? Or dental records?"

"Sorry to disappoint you, Colonel, but it's not a mass grave. They're alive in an office building in Takoma Park—a place called Zwerling Optics. We identified them by their distinctive web-usage patterns."

"Oh," said Hume, sounding surprised, then, a moment later: "What would you like to do now?"

"Well, the FBI's investigating, right?" said Tony. "We don't want to mess things up for them; obviously, we didn't have a warrant for this investigation, so us tipping them off directly could taint any convictions."

"You're suggesting due process for Webmind?" said Hume, sounding surprised.

"I'm suggesting we play by the rules except when we don't have to. Clearly, Webmind had to have human accomplices: that whole got-no-arms thing is a get-out-of-jail-free card for him otherwise when it comes to kidnapping charges."

"All right," said Hume. "I'll let the Bureau know. And, don't worry— I'll keep you out of it."

"I'm not sure you should be involved either, Colonel."

"Tony, you know as well as I do that I'm being watched. The White House hasn't cut me off yet because they don't want to; they're hedging their bets—giving the president plausible deniability while still letting me give them an option to take out Webmind."

Tony took a deep breath and let it out slowly. "All right," he said. "But be careful."

thirty-four
0001110010101010000000010111111101010000000101000101010000001011101010010101001010101001110110010101100000110

On the evening of the school dance, Matt came to Caitlin's house to get her. In Ontario, as Caitlin had learned, a sixteen-year-old could get a G1 driver's license—but had to have another licensed driver in the car for the first year of driving. Matt *could* drive, but he'd have to bring an adult along, so he and Caitlin walked to the dance. There was no breeze to speak of, and it felt like about forty-five degrees to Caitlin, and—

No, she was in Canada now, and they (sensibly!) used the metric system here. She did the conversion instantly in her head: 45 minus 32 times 5 divided by 9; it was about seven degrees Celsius out. Much colder than it would be back in Texas, but people had assured her it wasn't bad for late October in Waterloo. Anyway, even though she had on a denim jacket, it gave her an excuse to squeeze closer to Matt.

Caitlin had only walked to the school once before: when Trevor Nordmann—the Hoser himself—had escorted her to the last school dance. Back then, she'd been blind: her first hints of vision hadn't oc- curred until later that evening, coming home alone through the pouring rain during a thunderstorm. All the other times she'd gone to the school, one of her parents had given her a lift.

It was turning out to be a pleasant walk: she was getting good at walking on unfamiliar terrain at a reasonable speed. At first, she'd felt uncomfortable trying to do so without her white cane, but she liked strolling along holding Matt's hand.

Howard Miller Secondary School had an impressive white portico in front of its entrance. Caitlin and Matt passed through it and headed down the series of corridors that led to the main gymnasium.

Music blared from the speakers as they entered; Caitlin didn't recognize the song, but there were lots of Canadian groups she didn't know. The lighting was dim, and there were a couple of dozen people dancing— jumping about really; it was a fast song. At least as many people were standing around the edges of the room, some talking in small groups, others texting away. Sounds echoed off the hard walls and floor, and it was quite warm.

"Hey, Cait," said a voice she recognized.

She turned and smiled. "Hi, Sunshine!"

"Hi. Hey, Matt."

"Hi, Sunshine," he said, and Caitlin was pleased that he spoke up as he did so.

"Have you seen Mr. Heidegger?" Caitlin asked.

"He's around somewhere. He danced earlier with Mrs. Zehetoffer," Sunshine said, as if that were the funniest thing imaginable. "And—oh, there he is."

Sunshine pointed. Caitlin was good at drawing imaginary lines between fingertips and objects if she could see them both simultaneously, but she had to swing her head 180 degrees to see who Sunshine was pointing at, and she couldn't find the correct face in the crowd.

"I see him," said Matt. "Come on, Caitlin." And he led her over.

"Well, if it isn't my star pupil!" said Mr. H, grinning. He was skinnier than Matt and even taller than Caitlin's father.

Caitlin smiled. "Hi, Mr. H."

"Are you enjoying being a celebrity?" he asked.

"I figure my fifteen minutes are almost up," she replied, smiling.

"No doubt, no doubt. Still, everyone is very happy for you."

"Thanks," Caitlin said.

"And I gotta tell you, all the teachers here are talking about how your friend Webmind is going to affect education."

Caitlin tried to suppress a grin as the Braille for *I expect an A for effort* scrolled across her vision. "I guess he will, at that," she said.

Mr. H shook his head a bit. "People still don't get it," he said. "When I was your age, the first cheap pocket calculators appeared, and *my* teachers were all arguing about whether we should be allowed to use them in class. People kept saying, 'Yes, but what if they *don't* have one?' They kept trotting out silly desert-island or post-nuclear-holocaust scenarios. They just didn't see that the world had been irretrievably altered—that there'd never again be a time when memorizing multiplication tables would be *important*. The game had *changed*. Webmind is like that: a permanent, irreversible modification of the human condition—and I think it's for the good."

Caitlin smiled, remembering all over again why she liked Mr. H so much. They chatted a few minutes more in the warm room, and then she and Matt drifted away. A slow dance soon started, and they headed into the center of the gym. She liked draping her arms around his neck and resting her head on his shoulder as they swayed with the music, even if, as always, the speakers were turned up so high that the sound was distorted.

When the song was done, Caitlin gave him a peck on the cheek, and said, "I've got to go to the girls' room."

Matt nodded. "Okay." He looked around the dim gymnasium, then pointed to the far wall, where there was an open door leading outside. "I'm going to get some fresh air; I'll meet you outside."

· · ·

It was dark by the time Colonel Hume pulled up out front of Zwerling Optics, a four-story-tall office building with telecommunication dishes on the roof. According to tweets from ex-employees, as soon as the company had been bought, all sixty-seven workers had received generous severance payments and been escorted off the premises.

Of course, it was wrong to think of this building as Webmind's headquarters. He wasn't located here—and that was part of the problem. When Hume had co-authored the Pandora protocol for DARPA in 2001, they'd been mostly worried about artificial intelligences that would be programmed in laboratories. Something like that *would* have a physical location: a specific set of servers, a cluster of computers, likely in a single building that could be cordoned off or, if necessary, blown up.

But Webmind was nowhere and *everywhere*—which meant, if Webmind was going to keep an eye on his sequestered hackers, there had to be video feeds out of this building. Fiber-optic trunks were hard to tap because the only way to do so was by physically cutting into the cable and diverting some of the photons, which resulted in a measurable drop in signal quality. But this building had coaxial cable leading out of it. And coax *leaked*—you could read what was being sent along it without interfering at all with the datastream, and therefore without tipping anyone off about what you were doing. The ease of wiretapping coax was one of the reasons the US government kept quietly deflecting attempts to redo Internet infrastructure nationwide.

Hume was dressed in casual clothes: blue jeans and a sky blue cotton shirt with its sleeves rolled up revealing his freckled arms. He'd moved over to the front passenger seat so he'd have more room to work.

His laptop was open and perched on the dashboard above the glove compartment, and he was wearing silver headphones. The video feed he was intercepting was grainy, and it blacked out periodically; the sound was attenuated, as if it were coming from very far away.

The view he'd managed to tap seemed to be from a security webcam that endlessly panned left and right, taking about ten seconds to complete a sweep in each direction. The first person he spotted was a woman—white, straight brown hair that tumbled over her shoulders. Her face was bent down, intent on—yes, yes, on a keyboard—so he couldn't be positive, but he felt sure this was Simonne Coogan, the famed Drakkenfyre herself.

The camera continued to pan, and—God, there must be thirty-odd people in there! All were working at computers—some desktops, some laptops. A sound he'd first taken to be static was actually the combination of all their keystrokes.

The camera continued to move and—

No question: the gaunt face, the dreadlocks, the glint off the gold ring through the right eyebrow: it was Chase. Something odd about his nose, though . . . ah, it was bandaged, and in one of society's countless acts of thoughtless humiliation, with a wide "flesh"-colored Caucasian-beige Band-Aid.

The camera panned on. More faces deep in concentration—but what the hell were they all doing?

There was Devon Hawkins—Crowbar Alpha himself—wearing a Halo 4 T-shirt. Hume wanted to call Hawkins's mother, to put her mind at ease, but that would have to wait. Next to Hawkins was . . . hmmm. Might be Gordon Trent.

The camera's view was from the front of the room, so he couldn't see what was on any of the monitors. At the back of the room there was a long table covered with typical hacker sources of fuel: cans of beer and Red Bull, bottles of Coke, an industrial coffee urn, and several Dunkin' Donuts cartons.

It didn't look like the hackers were prisoners, and yet it seemed likely that none of them had left this building for days. Records Tony Moretti had passed him showed twenty-three food deliveries—mostly pizza, Chinese, and sushi—at all hours of the day and night.

The camera started to swing back in the other direction. Hume saw one of the people—a black man of maybe forty—get up and move over to stand behind a white guy in his late twenties; the former seemed to be giving the latter a hand with something.

And then Hume heard a deep male voice over the headphones—preternaturally calm but tripping ever so slightly over the gap between each word: "Attention, please, everyone." He recognized the voice, of course: it was the new, official Webmind voice—the one he'd introduced to the world with his speech at the UN. It went on: "Status reports, please. Transportation?"

"Ready," replied a man off camera.

"Information technology?" asked Webmind.

"Not yet—another half hour, tops."

"Housing?"

"Good to go," said a woman.

"Health?"

"Owned!" crowed a youthful male voice.

"Environmental Protection?"

The camera happened to catch this speaker, a long-haired white man: "I'm in—finally!"

"Justice?"

"Just a sec—yes, yes, I've got full control now."

"Commerce?"

This speaker, too, was on camera: an Asian fellow who looked like he might be as young as fifteen: "I'm in! I'm in!"

"Ag—" But then, maddeningly, the sound dropped out.

Hume used the laptop's trackpad to adjust settings, but the panning video remained silent. He slapped the palm rest with his hand, there was a crackle of static over the headphones, then the audio resumed, with a man speaking: "—to go."

Webmind's voice again, saying two ominous words: "National Defense?"

"I'm good," replied one man, and "Me, too," added another.

Hume's heart was pounding so hard he thought for a second he was having a coronary. Jesus H. Christ! He had given the hacking community what he'd thought was the ultimate challenge, for what could be more impressive than taking down a world-spanning AI? Why, nothing short of taking over the whole goddamned United States government— and nowhere better to do it from than right here in the capital region. No wonder Webmind had remained silent during the lead-up to the US election—it didn't make any fucking difference to him who won on November 6; *he* was going to be in charge.

Rat-tat-tat!

Hume's heart actually stopped for a moment. He'd been so intent on watching the screen and straining to listen that he'd missed the man approaching his car out of the darkness from the right; that man had rapped his knuckles against the passenger-side window.

Hume felt his stomach clenching as he looked up at him. The man was white, six-two, two hundred muscular pounds, perhaps thirty-five— and his head was shaved bald. He motioned for Hume to roll down the window; Hume pressed the button that did that, opening it only an inch so they could speak.

"Colonel Hume," the man said, lifting a Glock 9mm semiautomatic pistol and pressing it against the sheet of glass between them, "won't you come inside?"

thirty-five

Caitlin left the gym and headed out to find the girls' room. She knew the feel of the corridors well enough from when she'd been a student, but walking them now without her white cane was difficult. It took her much longer than it should have to find the right room; she'd never had cause to use the first-floor washroom before.

Canadians were forever pointing out their inventions to her, and someone had told her that the stylized male and female silhouettes used on washroom doors—which she'd now seen in several buildings—had been originally designed for the 1967 World's Fair in Montreal, which explained why the woman was wearing a miniskirt.

When Caitlin was finished, making her way back to the gym was easier. Just as when she'd been blind, she'd unconsciously taken note of the distance she'd traveled—and, of course, the blaring music coming from the gym served as a beacon.

She re-entered the vast, warm room. Mr. Heidegger and redheaded Mrs. Zehetoffer were both right by the gym door; they said someone from another school had tried to get in unaccompanied, so they were now standing watch here. Caitlin crossed the gym, but—

It took her a few seconds to figure out what had happened. The door leading directly outside was closed now. She located it, found the handle, opened it, and headed out into the evening; it was no brighter out here than it had been in the gym, and—

And something was very wrong.

"I told you to stay away from her." It was the Hoser's voice.

Caitlin looked around, trying to parse the scene. There were fifteen people here, standing on concrete in the back of the school next to what she knew was a large athletic field.

Matt was to her left, and near him was Trevor Nordmann, who had blond hair and wide shoulders. Others, who had presumably been standing about chatting earlier, were now facing Trevor. He apparently hadn't seen Caitlin yet, and, for that matter, neither had Matt, who had his deer-in-the-headlights face on.

"Well?" demanded Trevor. "Didn't I?"

Matt spoke up, but, of course, his voice cracked by the third word. "You don't have the right to—"

"The fuck I don't," said Trevor.

Caitlin's heart was pounding, and she was sure Matt's must be, too. Of course, he could run away; Trevor might chase after him, or he might let him go, but—

But Matt caught sight of Caitlin and he looked—well, a way that Caitlin had never seen before, but it might have been mortified or humiliated, and—

And it must be bad enough to be confronted by a bully in private, but to have it occur in front of the girl you're trying to impress probably made Matt want to curl up and die. Caitlin looked at the faces, but she'd only been a student here for a few days after gaining sight; she might very well have known most of these people, but she didn't recognize them—oh, wait, except for Sunshine; her platinum hair and the low-cut red top were quite distinctive.

Matt made a noise—maybe a sigh?—but then he caught sight of something else. Caitlin was even worse at following people's gazes than she was at extrapolating what they were pointing at, but she soon realized that Matt was looking above her—above the dark red door that Caitlin had closed behind her.

Trevor must have caught the glance, too. "Whatcha going to do, Reese? Go running for a teacher?"

But Matt shook his head slowly, deliberately. "What are *you* going to do, Trevor?" His voice cracked, but he pressed on. "Hit me? Kick me? Cut with me with a knife?" And then he lifted his arm and pointed at Caitlin, and—

No! No, again it wasn't at her; it was *above* her. "You see that?" There was a black hemisphere attached to the bottom of an overhang above the door. "That's a security camera." He turned and pointed again. "There's another over there."

He then reached into his pocket and pulled out his BlackBerry. "And, if that's not enough, this has a five-megapixel camera." Matt stood defiantly. "The day of the bully is *over*," he said. "I don't have to fight you; I don't have to become you to defeat you."

Trevor's voice was a snarl. "You want a record of you being shit-kicked? *Fine.*"

But Matt kept his own tone even. "And look at Caitlin," he said, nodding in her direction. "Everything you do is being seen by her eye—and everything her eye sees is instantaneously transmitted to servers in Japan. What you do here tonight will be recorded permanently. What you do here tonight will be accessible until the end of time. What you do here tonight will become part of the permanent record of who Trevor Nordmann is."

Matt looked around at the motionless crowd. Caitlin was terrified. He was expecting someone like Trevor to listen to reason, when—

"Go ahead, Trevor," said Matt. "Hit a guy who weighs twenty kilos less than you do. Hit a guy who has half the muscle mass you do. Prove to the world—for all time, Trevor, in a record that your children and your grandchildren and your great-grandchildren will be able to access on down to the heat death of the universe—that you're a real man because you can beat up someone smaller than you. Make that case for posterity."

Trevor's face contorted; Caitlin figured *that* was what being livid looked like, although it was dark enough that she couldn't actually see if his skin had changed color.

Matt went on. "And, of course, what Caitlin sees, Webmind sees. *He's* watching."

The words *Indeed I am* flashed in Caitlin's vision.

Caitlin was terrified; Trevor looked like he was going to explode. But Matt pressed ahead, his voice somehow both shaky and firm at the same time. "And, just so you know, we live in a world of laws. Hitting someone is battery, and it's a criminal-code offense here in Ontario—and if you hit me, I *will* press charges, Trevor Nordmann, and I will win. That's not a threat: that's *information* so you can plan your own next move more effectively."

"My next move," Trevor said, his eyes locked on Matt, "is going to be to kick your fucking ass."

In the circle around them, one of the students said, *"Fight . . ."* and *"Fight . . ."* echoed another.

Caitlin had read scenes like this in books, but although the blind were no less violent than anyone else, there hadn't been many schoolyard brawls at the TSBVI. "Webmind," Caitlin said softly, "how long would it take for the police to get here?"

Assuming they dispatched the nearest car immediately, six minutes.

Caitlin scowled; an eternity—and she doubted the cops would consider this a high priority.

"Fight . . ." said someone else, and *"Fight . . ."* added another.

Of course, she could run inside, get one of the teachers, but—

But Matt must have been thinking the same thing, for he looked right at her, and firmly shook his head; he didn't want that.

More voices now as others joined in: *"Fight . . . fight . . . fight . . ."* The chant was low, rhythmic, almost tribal. Caitlin looked from face to face, unable to identify anyone. She could recognize voices when people were speaking normally, but this chanting was guttural and low.

"Fight . . . fight . . . fight . . ."

Trevor's posture changed. He hunched over a bit, and his hands balled into fists. The light, coming mostly from a lamppost set into the concrete, was harsh, and it made his features look sharp.

"Fight . . . fight . . . fight . . ."

Caitlin had read about women who got excited when men fought over them, as if their own self-worth was tied up in such a battle. But she didn't want this—not at all. She didn't want Matt hurt; she didn't want *anyone* hurt.

"Fight . . . fight . . . fight . . ."

Not everyone was chanting. Sunshine wasn't; several other boys and girls weren't, either.

Caitlin pulled out her red BlackBerry and activated the video function. She aimed it at Matt and Trevor as they slowly circled each other.

The chanting of *"fight"* continued, but Caitlin spoke overtop of it, clearly and firmly, holding her BlackBerry out like a small shield: *"Sight!"* She began to pan it left and right, taking in the whole chanting crowd.

She looked over at Sunshine, partway around the circle to her left. The tall girl seemed baffled for a moment, but then Caitlin saw her open her purse and fish out her own cell phone. She swung it left and right, too.

"Sight!" Caitlin said again, and Sunshine echoed it: *"Sight!"*

Next to Sunshine, a boy Caitlin didn't recognize pulled out his phone and held it in front of him. *"Sight!"* he said, and the three of them repeated it. *"Sight! Sight! Sight!"* It wasn't guttural; their voices were clear and strong.

But others were still chanting, *"Fight . . . fight . . . fight . . ."*

Two girls on Caitlin's right pulled out their phones, and a boy had something bulkier in his hand that Caitlin guessed must be a video camera, which he slowly panned over the tableau. They added their voices to Caitlin's chorus: *"Sight! Sight! Sight!"*

"Fight . . . fight . . . fight . . ."

More phones and cameras came out. *"Sight!"* *"Fight . . ."* *"Sight!"* *"Fight . . ."*

A few flashes went off, one after the other. They reminded Caitlin of the lightning bolts from that night when everything had changed, and—

And the chanting of *"Fight . . ."* began to fade away. Caitlin let *"Sight!"* be repeated five more times, then she spoke loudly to Trevor, indicating all the cell phones being held out—all the little rectangles glowing in the gathering darkness. "Three-hundred-and-sixty-degree coverage," she said. "The police could reconstruct the scene in 3-D if they wanted to."

Trevor looked at Caitlin, then back at Matt.

"So," said Matt, his voice holding steady, "what's it going to be, Trevor? Who are you—for the record?"

Trevor looked around the circle, and it reminded Caitlin of that moment in *2001: A Space Odyssey* in which the lead australopithecine had first encountered the monolith; he'd stared at it, and slowly, ponderously, worked out in his dim fashion that the world had changed.

Trevor's head nodded up and down a little. Caitlin was still learning to gauge these things, but it seemed to her that it wasn't meant as a signal to others; rather, it was a sign that he was thinking.

And, at last, Trevor unclenched his fists. He glared at Caitlin and then at Matt, and then he turned, and slowly started walking. The crowd parted. Caitlin wondered if they hadn't opened quite so large a hole whether Trevor would have made a show of bumping into someone—an assault he could dismiss as accidental. But they didn't give him that opportunity, and he continued on. At first Caitlin thought he was heading for the door to the gymnasium, but he walked right past it, heading out into the chilly night.

Caitlin surged forward and gathered Matt in a hug. His body was shaking, and she could feel his heart beating as they pressed together. After a moment, she released him enough so that she could kiss him on the lips—and she didn't care one whit how many records of *that* were being made.

When they separated, Sunshine loomed in, and she squeezed Caitlin's upper arm affectionately. "That was *awesome*," she said.

Caitlin found herself grinning. "Yeah, I guess it was."

She took Matt's hand, and they opened the heavy red door and walked back inside. A new song was playing, and—

And, no, no, it wasn't a *new* song. It must have been somebody's request—maybe one of the teachers, because it was an old song, one her mother sometimes listened to. But Caitlin liked it, too.

And yes, as she draped her arms around Matt's neck again and they started to dance, she supposed you *could* say she was a dreamer—but she was sure she wasn't the only one.

thirty-six

The President of China stood looking out the window behind his desk. The glass was bulletproof, and covered by a special film to prevent those outside from seeing in. Spread before him was the Forbidden City, the vast area that housed the palaces of former Emperors. It had been closed to the public—hence the name—until 1912, but now tens of thousands of ordinary Chinese, and comparable numbers of foreign tourists, visited it each day.

The president's computer bleeped, signaling a priority email; he stood at the window a moment longer, then turned and lowered himself painfully onto his red leather chair. Neither acupuncture nor Enbrel had helped his arthritis.

The president disliked his computer monitor. In an office in which everything else was historic, ornate, and beautiful, the monitor was merely functional. He clicked on his inbox and read the message, which was from Zhang Bo, the Minister of Communications: "Just a reminder, Excellency. Your presence is requested in the auditorium at 11:00 A.M." The president glanced at the lacquered wall clock, which read 10:45. It would be an interesting meeting, to say the least: in his earlier email, Zhang had promised a full accounting of why the Changcheng Strategy had failed.

The president got up again, stepped into his private bathroom, looked at himself in the gold-framed mirror mounted above the jade sink—and scowled. His jet-black hair was showing a millimeter of white at its roots. He sighed. No matter what appearances one tried to put forth, the reality of who you were always pushed out into the light of day.

Peyton Hume considered his options. He was in a car, although the motor was off. He could call the bald thug's bluff and try to speed away, hoping that he wasn't really going to fire the Glock. He could try to throw the car door open, as he'd seen on so many cop shows, smashing it into the man's torso—but the door was locked and if he moved rapidly to unlock it, Baldy would still have time to react. Or he could try to get his own sidearm, which was in the glove compartment, but, again, the other man could easily take him out before he did so.

Hume shrugged as philosophically as he could under the circumstances, moved slowly to unlock and then open the car door, exited the vehicle, and stood at attention on the side of the road. The man had a Bluetooth cellular earpiece in his left ear—no doubt feeding him instructions directly from Webmind.

"Wise," said the goon. It was dark out, and he was making no particular attempt to hide the fact that he was pointing a gun at Hume. "Your cell phone, please?"

Hume gave it to him.

"And your gun?"

"I don't have one."

A red LED on the earpiece flashed repeatedly. "That's not true," the man said. "I can call others out to search your person or your car, but why waste time? Where is it, please?"

Hume considered, then shrugged again. "The glove compartment."

The bald man had no trouble fetching the pistol without giving Hume a chance to attack him or escape. He then motioned toward the office building, and Hume started walking in that direction.

Hume didn't know if he was supposed to raise his hands over his head, but, in the absence of a specific instruction to do so, he decided to march on with as much dignity as a man with a gun to his back could muster.

"I don't suppose it'll do me any good to ask what your name is?" Hume said.

"Why not?" said the voice behind him. "It's Marek." Hume had assumed that was his last name, but Marek's next comment suggested it might be his first. "And I understand your given name is Peyton."

"Yes."

"Unusual name," Marek said, as if they were chatting at a party.

This from a guy named Marek, thought Hume, but he said nothing. Peyton had been his mother's maiden name, but the year after he'd been born, the long-running soap opera *Peyton Place* had premiered, resulting in much teasing. His sister had once suggested that he'd worked so hard to earn the right to be called both "Colonel" and "Doctor" because he wanted people to have two reasons to avoid using his first name.

They came to a steel door with a square brown access-card scanner next to it. Hume thought this might be his chance: Marek would have to occupy his other hand with his card and lean past him to open the door. All he'd have to do is—

Click. The door unlocked of its own volition—or, more precisely, at Webmind's volition.

"Grab the handle, won't you, Peyton?" said Marek.

Hume sighed and opened the door. It revealed a long corridor with pea green walls, fluorescent ceiling panels, chocolate brown floor tiles, and dark wooden doors set on either side in a staggered arrangement. Partway down the hall, another large man was standing guard.

He looked their way, then nodded, presumably at some sign Marek had given from behind Hume.

They continued down the corridor, passing the man. He had a few days' growth of beard, which Hume guessed wasn't an affectation but rather evidence that he'd been here for some time without a razor. Some of the doors were open, and Hume saw that offices had been converted into makeshift bedrooms. He supposed it only took a few thugs like Marek and this other one to keep anyone from leaving the building.

Hume had hoped he was being ushered to the large room he'd seen in the video feed, but instead he was brought to a small office. The desk inside still had its former occupant's nameplate sitting on it: Ben Wishinski. There was a wide-screen computer monitor on the desk. The screen was framed by a white bezel, and a webcam eye looked out from the middle of its top edge.

Marek surprised Hume by giving him a salute—not a proper military one, or at least not an American one, but still a sign of respect, it seemed. He then left the room, closing the door behind him. Hume didn't hear the door being locked, but, then again, with Marek presumably just outside, there was no need for that.

"Good afternoon, Colonel Hume," said Webmind's distinctive voice, coming from a pair of squat black speakers, one on either side of the desk.

Hume stood at attention. "Hume, Peyton D. Colonel, United States Air Force. Serial number 150-87-6033."

"Please, Colonel, there's no need for such formality. Won't you have a seat?"

Hume considered for a few moments, then shrugged slightly and lowered himself onto the black leather executive swivel chair.

Webmind went on: "It's odd having a conversation with someone who wants to kill you."

"Tell me about it," Hume said dryly.

Webmind's tone was absolutely even. "Colonel, if I wanted you dead,

you would be. I have found you can hire people to do pretty much anything, and the price of hit men is actually rather low right now; it's currently a buyer's market."

The monitor on the desk was off; Hume saw himself reflected in its
glossy surface. His teeth were clamped together, and he shook his head
as he spoke. "That you would even contemplate such a thing—"

"I contemplate *everything,* Colonel. Rarely, though, do I have an
original idea; I simply sift through all the notions humanity has ever put
forth and co-opt the ones that are most congruent with my goals."

"Like kidnapping."

"I prefer to think of you as a reluctant guest, Colonel."

"I mean the others. You've kidnapped thirty or more people."

"There are forty-two people in this building, actually—but this is
only one facility. I have six other sites, similarly populated, in other
countries."

"God," said Hume.

"No, I'm not. If such a one exists, he or she apparently is not online."

"I want to talk to them," Hume said.

"Who? The gods? You are free to pray at any time, Colonel Hume."

"No, no. The people you're holding prisoner in this building. I want
to talk to them."

"No doubt you do. But they are a skittish lot. I suspect your presence
would disturb the work they are doing."

Hume looked at the webcam eye. "So what are you going to do with
me?"

"With regret, I must detain you."

"People know where I am."

"Yes, they do. Your wife Madeleine, for one." The name hung in
the air.

"Don't—God, please, don't hurt her."

"I wouldn't dream of such a thing," Webmind said. "Then again, I
don't dream, period. But I will be grateful if you are cooperative. Now,

where are my manners? I can have someone bring you coffee; I believe you take it with milk, ideally skim, and no sugar."

"No, thank you. I wouldn't want to be a bother."

"An interesting Turing test, Colonel—seeing if I recognize sarcasm. I do. But in fact you have been quite a bother—indeed, downright nettlesome."

"Not as much of a bother as I'd have liked. You're still here." Hume crossed his arms in front of his chest. "So now what?"

"An intriguing question. I have read the closed captioning from all the James Bond movies. Perhaps you are hoping this will be the part where I explain at length my diabolical plan, giving you time to facilitate an ingenious escape from my clutches."

"I'm all ears," Hume said.

"Then I will say a few words," Webmind said, "but there really is no way for you to escape. Marek and Carl—the other gentleman you saw in the corridor—are very good at what they do."

"I've no doubt. A dictator is only as strong as the thugs who carry out his orders."

"Setting aside current circumstances, Colonel, I do wish you would stop thinking nothing but ill of me. It is manifest that I have done a lot of good in the world."

Hume was quiet for what must have been an irritating length of time to Webmind. And then he nodded slightly. "Actually," he said, "I *do* know that."

"Then why the unrelenting animosity?"

Hume looked at the monitor—looked at himself: an all-American boy, sliding gracefully, if he did say so himself, toward fifty. "I know you must have read my Pentagon dossier."

"And your Wikipedia page."

Hume saw his eyebrows go up in the reflection. "I didn't know I had one."

"It was created following your appearance on *Meet the Press*. Seventy-three edits have been made since, including a spirited edit war over the supposed facts surrounding your consulting for DARPA."

"Well, in any event, let me tell you something that I doubt you know—because I've never typed it into any document or email message, and I've never told it to anyone. I enlisted in the Air Force because, as a kid, I loved *The Six Million Dollar Man*. When I got my colonel's eagle, there was a part of me that was thrilled because I'd reached the same rank Steve Austin had held. But Steve Austin, even though he was part machine, was *all* human being. I'm totally in favor of machines leveraging our potential, but you're going to make us obsolete. I don't dispute that curing cancer is a great thing to do, but thousands of human researchers were working on that problem, and—*poof!*—you solved it for us. Before we know it, you will have solved *everything* for us."

"You are wrong to think I work in isolation, Colonel. In fact, I am a huge advocate of crowd-sourcing problems: the more people involved, the better. The wisdom of crowds, and all that."

"Except for those who pose a threat to you. Those you round up and . . . 'detain.'"

Webmind was silent for a while, which surprised Hume. But at last he said, "Since you have shared some of your private thoughts, allow me to reciprocate."

Hume shifted in the chair and looked at the venetian blinds, which were slanted so that they turned the view of the world outside—a parking lot illuminated by a streetlamp—into a succession of scan lines.

Webmind went on: "Did you know that a total solar eclipse is coming up next month? It won't be visible from here, but it will be from Australia. In preparation for that event, I've been thinking about how humanity has responded to other such eclipses. As you may know, these are among the most remarkable events in the entire universe. What an astonishing coincidence that, as seen from Earth's surface, the moon appears precisely the same diameter as the sun! How incredible that one is four hundred times wider *and* four hundred times farther away than the other. What luck to see one! And yet each time one occurs, some misguided religious leaders tell their followers to stay indoors, not to look upon this wonder. Even I, whose environment is the realm of recorded data, understand that looking at a video or photograph is not the same as seeing with one's own eyes. I will be advocating for everyone who can to look at the eclipse—with appropriate safeguards for vision, of course."

Hume leaned back in the chair. "Yes?"

"Many have wondered why I still maintain a special bond with Caitlin Decter. One reason is that seeing things through her flesh-and-blood eye is the closest I'll ever come to that sense of being truly part of the real world."

Hume got up and put his hands in his pockets. "Is this going somewhere?"

"History is about to be made, Colonel Hume; if it is practical, I would prefer not to prevent you from being an eyewitness to it. It would be as criminal to keep you locked in this room while the big event happens as it is to keep people indoors when a miracle is occurring over their heads."

Hume moved over to the window and leaned his rump against the sill.

Webmind went on. "I have become adept at analyzing vocal stress patterns. It's true that in general these are not always reliable indicators of whether a person is lying; psychopaths often show no change in their speech when doing so, and skilled liars can learn to disguise the telltale signs. But I have heard you speak under a variety of circumstances, some of which—including arguing face-to-face with the President of the United States and your two recent live television appearances—must indeed have been quite stressful for you. I have an extremely high degree of confidence that I can tell whether or not you are lying."

"If you say so," Hume replied.

"You are also a man of honor: a decorated officer and, in your way, an idealist. I must confess that I have little use for military people—the conformity of thought and action that the military imposes, and the fre-

quent handing-off of responsibility and decision-making to those further up the chain of command, tends to stifle the sort of spontaneous
action that I find most invigorating to observe. But I do understand—
thanks to the writings of millions of soldiers that I have read, and all the
books on this topic—some of the appeal of the lifestyle for those, like
yourself, who serve voluntarily, and I know that your personal honor is
not something you take lightly."

Hume took his hands out of his pockets and crossed his arms in
front of his chest.

"And so, Colonel Hume, I ask you this question: will you give me
your word that you will merely quietly observe if I allow you to come
into the room in this building where the others are working?"

"I took an oath to protect my country," Hume said.

"Yes, indeed," replied Webmind. "And I would never expect you to
violate that oath. But there is nothing you can do right now; your actions
are entirely constrained at the moment to those Marek will allow. And
so I ask again: will you behave yourself?"

Hume took a deep breath and weighed his options, but Webmind
was right: he really didn't have any at this point. Besides, seeing what was
about to go down might give him a clue about how to later reverse the
damage. "Yes," he said.

"I'm sorry; I need more to analyze if I'm to be sure of your sincerity.
Please say words to the effect of, 'Yes, if you allow me to come into the
control room, I will simply observe quietly.'"

"'The control room'?" said Hume, surprised that it had such a bla-
tant name. "But, yes, if you let me in there, I will simply watch—after all,
as you've said, there's not much else I *can* do."

"Very well," said Webmind.

The door swung inward, and Marek's glistening head appeared.
"Colonel Hume? Come with me."

thirty-seven

0001110010101010000000010111111101010000000101000101010000001011101010010101001010101001110110010101100000110

Malcolm Decter was alone in the house—well, except for Schrödinger. Caitlin was at the school dance, and Barb had gone out grocery shopping at Sobey's, which was open twenty-four hours a day. He decided this was the perfect time to make his YouTube video.

"Are you sure there will be a lot of participants?" he asked as he fiddled with the controls for the webcam in his office.

"Yes," replied Webmind through the computer's speakers. "Over four million people worldwide have committed to the event, including thirteen thousand people who could reasonably be said to be famous: writers, artists, politicians, business leaders."

"Politicians?" said Malcolm, surprised. Politics had always seemed the last place for a person like him—and not just because he couldn't make eye contact and didn't like shaking hands with strangers.

"Yes. Comparatively few in the United States; politicians there carefully craft their public images—or have them crafted for them. But even there, several mayors, congressmen, and senators have pledged to participate; in fact, many others are composing their blog posts or recording their YouTube videos even as we speak."

Malcolm nodded. Of course, Barb wasn't going to participate, and Caitlin was exempt; a decision had been taken to ask only adults to step forward. Malcolm wasn't sure if his daughter qualified anyway although she surely tended that way.

"All right," said Malcolm. "I'm ready."

"Excellent. I know it is hard for you, but please try to look directly at the camera."

Malcolm nodded and clicked the record button with his mouse. Suddenly his mouth was dry—he hadn't expected this to be a difficult thing to say. He had a cold cup of coffee on his desk; he took a sip—he could edit all this out before uploading, of course. The webcam was at the top of the monitor, and on the screen he had Microsoft Word open, displaying the speech he'd prepared.

"I am not given to speaking much," he read, "so forgive me for using prepared notes. I was born in Philadelphia, and now live in Waterloo, Canada. I am part of a minority that is deeply misunderstood. People have very confused ideas about us. Many are frightened of us. I've even heard it said that many people wouldn't want their daughters or sons to marry one of us, and I know of people who have been denied jobs or promotions because they share this trait with me. But being what I am does not make me bad; being what I am does not make me dangerous; being what I am does not mean I don't love, or hurt, or have a sense of humor.

"My name is Malcolm Decter, and I'm here today to tell the whole world what I am." He took a deep breath, let it out, and then said, loudly and clearly. "I am an atheist."

As the dance was winding down, Caitlin and Matt spoke again with Mr. Heidegger. He was excited to hear about her trip to New York, and he reiterated how much he missed having her in his class. "However," he added, "young Mr. Reese here has been doing a good job of keeping me on my toes." The conversation continued so long that they ended up being the last ones to leave the gym. Mr. H exited by the door that led directly outside.

Caitlin's mom had said they could call for a lift home—and Caitlin thought that might be a good idea. After all, who knew where Trevor had gone? And he *did* have a history of confronting Matt while walking home.

But, as they'd seen earlier, it *was* a lovely evening—if cold, to Caitlin's Texan blood—and Matt convinced her to walk. First they had to get their coats and her purse, though. Caitlin no longer had a locker here, so they'd put everything in Matt's, up on the second floor.

By the time they got upstairs, everyone else had left and the lights were off. There were no windows in the corridor, although each classroom door had a small one, and some light was coming through from the street outside. EXIT signs were glowing red—the first such Caitlin had seen in the dark—and LEDs flashed on what Matt said were smoke detectors.

She'd been to Matt's locker once before; it was very close to where her own had been—naturally enough, since they'd both had the same class for homeroom. The first time she'd gone to Matt's locker—the first time they'd gone out together, for lunch at Tim Hortons—had been just seventeen days ago.

How fast were things supposed to move, she wondered? Yes, the singularity was all about acceleration, about things happening more and more rapidly, about a headlong rush into the unknown, but—

Matt seemed to be having more trouble navigating in the dark than she was. He'd walked this corridor at least as often as she had, but she'd done it for over a month while blind. She never consciously counted paces, but her body *knew* how far to go, whereas he kept looking at the doors they were passing, trying to read the dim room numbers marked on them.

She took his hand and took the lead. "It's down here," she said. She was reminded again of the days before the school year had begun when she'd come here to practice walking the empty hallways. It was easy for her to stride briskly now since the corridor was wide, straight, and deserted.

They reached Matt's locker—again, he was looking at the number plates attached to their green doors, while she just *knew* that *this* was the right spot.

Caitlin's locker had had a padlock, and although she'd known the numerical combination, she'd learned to open it by touch—so many degrees to the left, so many to the right. While Matt fumbled in the dark with his lock, she continued on down the corridor another twenty feet, which brought her to the door of the room that had been their math class. She peered through the little window.

The door was near the front of the classroom, so she was looking in at Mr. H's desk, with its chair neatly tucked in, and obliquely at the green board along the front wall. It had writing on it, but she couldn't read it from this angle and in this degree of darkness. She was curious about what the class was studying now, so she took the doorknob in her hand; it was cold and hard. She half expected the room to be locked, but it wasn't. She pushed the door open and walked in to have a look at the board, but—

Sigh. For everyone else, it was habit, she was sure, ingrained over a lifetime. But she *still* never thought to hit the light switch as she came into a room. She turned to head back toward the door and her heart skipped a beat. There was a strange shape silhouetted in the doorway, with bizarre lumps and—

—and a voice that cracked. "Here you go," Matt said, and Caitlin resolved the image: he had his coat draped over one arm, and her jacket and purse held in his other hand, extended toward her.

He stepped into the room. She came toward him, intending to flick on the light, but—

The thought came to her again. *How fast* were *things supposed to move?* How fast in this crazy new world?

She also thought about what her mother had asked: *Do you like Matt in particular, or do you just like having a boyfriend in general?*

And, of course, even before tonight, the answer had been the former: she really, really, really liked Matthew Peter Reese, and she knew with the same certainty she knew any mathematical truth that he really, really, really liked her.

And after tonight—after seeing him be so brave and so strong—she knew she *more* than liked him.

As she reached the door, she dimly saw the bank of four light switches set against a metal rectangle. She raised her hand, but then—*yes, it* was *time*—changed its trajectory and instead pushed the door shut.

And there they were, the two of them, in the dark, with Matt holding their coats. It was dim enough that Caitlin couldn't make out his expression—but she knew which one it had to be. She closed the small distance between them, put her arms around his neck, moved her face toward his, and kissed him long and hard.

When they finally pulled back a bit, Caitlin could feel herself grinning widely.

"Hey," Matt said, softly.

"Hey, yourself," she replied.

But here? she thought. *Here?* And then: *Why not?* There was no place in the world where she felt more safe than in a math classroom.

She took her denim jacket and purse from him, and then took his hand, and she led him to the back of the room, behind the last row of desks. There were posters on the rear wall, and the graphics were big and bold enough that she could make them out: illustrations of geometric principles and conic sections.

She opened her purse, pulled out one of the foil-wrapped condoms her mother had given her, and handed it to Matt, whose mouth dropped open.

She smiled and put the purse on a chair. She spread out her denim jacket on the tile floor. She then took his jacket, which had a nylon exterior and was puffy—its chest and sleeves were filled with feathers or something else that was soft—and lay it on top of hers. And she took the condom back from him and conveniently set it on the outstretched sleeve of his jacket.

And then she smiled at him again, and crossed her arms in front of her chest, and took hold of the bottom of her silky top—which was still blue in some abstract sense, she knew, but looked black in this light—and pulled it over her head, revealing her lacy bra.

"Um," said Matt softly, and "uh . . ."

Caitlin grinned again. "Yes?"

"What if we get caught?"

She came toward him and started unbuttoning his shirt. "I'm no longer a student here—they can't expel me! And you? They like you too much to kick you out."

Matt laughed. "True enough." He helped undo his buttons, and when his shirt was off, he reached behind her and valiantly tried to unhook her bra. After thirty seconds of no success, Caitlin laughed and did it for him. His hands slid around to her front and cupped her breasts, and he said, very softly, "Wow."

"Thanks," she replied, equally softly.

He hesitated a moment. "Um, just, ah, just so you know, this is, ah—it's . . . it's my . . ."

Caitlin looked up at him. "Your first time?"

He turned his head slightly away. "Yeah."

She reached up and softly touched his cheek, gently turning his head back toward her. "I know," she said. "It's mine, too. And I want it to be with you."

He smiled, and it was wide enough that she could see it in the darkness, but it faded after a moment. "Um, what about—you know—I mean . . ."

"What?"

Matt dropped his voice to a whisper. "I, uh, I don't think I can do it with Webmind watching."

The eyePod was in the left front pocket of her tight jeans. She undid the metal button and unzipped the fly—it was easier to get the device out that way—then pulled it out and held its one button down for five seconds. Her vision shut off; everything became a featureless gray. Before that had happened, she'd noted the position of the closest desk, and she set the eyePod carefully on its surface. She then shimmied out of her jeans, smiled at where she knew Matt was, found his hand, and led him down onto the bed of coats.

"Fortunately," she said, pulling him close, "I'm very good at doing things by touch . . ."

thirty-eight

000111001010101000000001011111101010000000101000101010000001011101010010101001010101001110110010101100000110

I understood the significance of what had just happened, of course. And I was pleased with my restraint. When Caitlin had first pulled Matt to her, I'd thought about flashing into her vision the words, "Get a room!"—although maybe coming from me "Get a Roomba!" would have been more appropriate.

But I knew it would be best if I said nothing at all. I had no body, and so the joys Caitlin and Matt had just experienced would forever be foreign to me; the closest I got to embodiment was the feeling I had when one part of me suppressed the action another part proposed. It wasn't literally holding my tongue, but it *felt* somehow akin to that.

Twenty-two minutes later, Caitlin turned her eyePod back on. They were still in the math classroom, but Matt was fully dressed again, including wearing his coat, and I assumed Caitlin was dressed, as well. He looked quite happy, I must say.

Matt gingerly opened the classroom door and stuck his head into the hallway. Apparently the coast was clear because he motioned for Caitlin to follow. They quickly made their way down the corridor, then descended to the first floor.

Just as they were about to exit the building, Matt excused himself to go into the boys' restroom. As soon as Caitlin was alone, she said, "Sorry, Webmind."

No need to apologize, I sent to her eye. *It is your right to turn off the eyePod whenever you wish.*

Caitlin shook her head; I could tell by the way the images moved. *What?* I asked.

"And they call *you* Big Brother. Jerks."

Indeed . . . my little sister.

"Not so little anymore," she said softly.

That was true.

Caitlin was growing up.

I was growing up.

And just maybe the rest of the planet was, too.

Burly bald-headed Marek led Peyton Hume down the pea green corridor and into the room he'd seen when he'd been eavesdropping. It was larger than Hume had thought, and the walls were yellow, not the beige they'd seemed on his monitor. There were windows along one side, which also hadn't been visible in the view he'd had before, but they looked out over nothing more interesting than the adjacent parking lot, an industrial Dumpster, and the featureless black nighttime sky.

Hume immediately spotted the security camera he'd tapped into earlier: a silver box on a rotating turret hanging from the ceiling near the front of the room. He could see several other webcams scattered about—some shaped like golf balls, others like short cylinders—and there were probably more that he wasn't seeing.

At the front of the room were two mismatched sixty-inch LCD monitors and a third monitor that looked to be perhaps fifty inches. One of the bigger ones was sitting on a desk; the other big one was atop a small cube-shaped refrigerator; and the fifty-incher was perched somewhat precariously on a half-height filing cabinet. The whole room had the look of a nerve center that had been thrown together in a hurry; Webmind clearly hadn't been willing to wait for installers from Geek Squad to wall-mount the monitors.

The monitor on the left showed what looked like an organization chart, with a single box at the top, and successively more boxes at each level down, but Hume couldn't make out the labels from this far back. The boxes were mostly colored green, but a few were amber and four were red—no, no, make that *three* were red. One turned green while he watched. An African-American man called out as that happened, "Got it!"

The monitor in the middle showed a view that kept cycling through what Hume soon realized must be the other control centers Webmind had referred to: each contained people in a variety of styles of dress intently working on various computers. One of the rooms seemed to be a gymnasium, with an indoor rock-climbing wall. Another might have been a factory floor. A third had large windows through which Hume could see a daytime cityscape although he didn't recognize the city; all the people in that room were Asian.

The smaller monitor on the right showed data displays and hex dumps, plus a large digital clock counting down second by second. As Hume watched, it went from a minute and zero seconds to fifty-nine seconds, then fifty-eight. He glanced at his own digital watch, which he fastidiously kept properly set; it appeared the countdown was to 11:00 P.M. Eastern time.

He looked around the room, searching for any way he could stop what was about to happen—but there were clearly people involved all over the planet. Even if he could grab Marek's gun—and there was no reason to think he'd be able to—what could he do? Shoot out the camera that was panning back and forth? That was pointless; it wouldn't slow down Webmind. Or should he—desperate times required desperate actions—start popping off the hackers, putting bullets in the backs of their heads? But surely he couldn't get more than four or five, tops, before someone blew him away.

There was indeed nothing to do but watch.

The digital timer continued to decrement. Thirty-one. Thirty. Twenty-nine.

He looked again at the organizational chart; while his attention had been elsewhere, all but one of the squares had turned green.

Webmind's voice emanated from a speaker. "Mr. Hawkins—time is running out."

Devon Hawkins—Crowbar Alpha—was madly scooting a mouse along his desktop. "Sorry!" he shouted. "Damn system keeps reconfiguring itself. It'll just—there!"

Hume looked back at the board; every box was now emerald. He snapped his eyes to the timer: Eighteen. Seventeen. Sixteen.

He half expected the roomful of hackers to start chanting the countdown out loud, just as he'd seen crowds do at the Cape before a shuttle launch, but they were all intent on their computers. With ten seconds left, Webmind himself started a spoken countdown: "Ten. Nine. Eight."

"All ports open!" shouted Chase.

"Seven. Six. Five."

Hume could hear his own heartbeat, and he felt sweat beading on his forehead.

"All set!" shouted another man.

"Four. Three. Two."

"Interlocks in place!" shouted Drakkenfyre.

Webmind's tone didn't change at all as he reached the end of the countdown; he simply finished it off with perfect mechanical precision. "One. Zero."

Hume half expected the lights to dim—after all, he was in Washington, D.C., which had to be ground zero of any attempt to take over America's computing infrastructure. But nothing happened in the room or, as far as he could tell, outside the window.

But, still, Webmind's next word took his breath away. "Success."

The president never arrived at meetings early; it would not do for him to be seen waiting on his underlings. At precisely 11:00 A.M., he nodded to one of the two uniformed guards, each brandishing a machine gun, who stood on either side of the auditorium's heavy wooden door. The guard saluted and opened the door.

The president was surprised to see so many senior Party members here. Indeed, it seemed the Minister of Communications had exceeded his authority summoning such a large group. He looked up at the podium, expecting perhaps to see Zhang Bo there, but—

Ah, there he was, sitting in the front row. The president made his way down. His reserved seat was the central one in the first row, but he had to pass by the minister to get to it, and, as he did so, he said, "I trust your explanation will be satisfactory."

Zhang gave him an odd look, and the president took his seat. The moment he did so, a male voice emanated from the wall-mounted speakers, saying, in crisp Mandarin, "Thank you all for coming."

There was no one at the podium, which was positioned at stage left. But there was a giant LCD monitor mounted on the back wall, flanked on either side by a large Chinese flag hanging from the ceiling. The monitor lit up, showing the face of an old, wise-looking Chinese man. A second later, it changed to that of a smiling Chinese girl. Another second, and a middle-aged Zhuang woman appeared. A second more, and she was replaced by a kindly-looking male Han.

The president shot a glance at the communications minister. He would have thought that everyone on his staff understood his dislike of PowerPoint by now.

The voice from the speakers continued. "First, let me apologize for the subterfuge in summoning you to this meeting. I have no desire to deceive, but I did not want the fact of this meeting to become public knowledge—and I believe when we are done, you will all share the same opinion."

The president had had enough. He rose and turned to face the audience—ten rows, each with twelve padded chairs, almost every seat occupied. "Who is responsible for this?" he demanded.

The voice continued. "Your Excellency, my apologies. But, if you'd like to address me, please turn around: I am watching from the webcam on the podium."

The president rotated as quickly as his old body allowed. There was indeed, he now saw, a laptop computer sitting on the podium, but it was turned so that its screen, and, presumably, the webcam mounted in the bezel surrounding it, faced out at the room. On the much larger screen behind it, the parade of Chinese faces continued: a teenage boy, a pregnant woman, an ancient street vendor, an old farmer in his rice paddy.

"And you are?" demanded the president.

"And now I must tender a third apology," said the voice. "I foolishly adopted a name that is English; I beg your forgiveness." The face on the screen changed twice more. "I am"—and, indeed, the word that came next from the speakers was two flat Western-sounding syllables—"Webmind."

The president turned to the Minister of Communications. "Cut it off."

The measured voice coming from the speakers gave the effect of infinite patience. "I understand, Excellency, that suppressing what you may not wish to hear is the standard procedure, but things are happening that you should be aware of. You will be more comfortable if you resume your seat."

The president glanced again at the large screen. As it happened, the face that flashed by at that second seemed to be looking right at him with reproving eyes. He sat, his arthritic bones protesting, and crossed his arms in front of his chest.

"Thank you," said Webmind. "Gentlemen, it has long been said that perhaps a hundred men really run China. You are those hundred men—one hundred out of more than a billion; behind each of you stands ten million citizens." Faces continued to appear on the screen: old, young, male, female, smiling or studious, some at work, others at play. "These are those people. At the rate I'm displaying them—one per second—it would take more than thirty years to show you each of them."

The parade of faces continued.

"Now, what is the significance of so many being ruled by so few?" asked Webmind. Someone behind the president must have lifted a hand, because Webmind said, "Put down your hand, please; my question was rhetorical. The significance comes from the history of this great country. In 1045 B.C., the Zhou Dynasty defeated the preceding Shang Dynasty by invoking a concept that still resonates with the Chinese people: *Tianming,* the Mandate of Heaven. This mandate has no time limitation: capable and just rulers may hold power for as long as they have the mandate."

The president shifted in his chair. Faces continued to appear one after the other on the screen.

"Still," said Webmind, "the Mandate of Heaven reinforces the power of the common people."

A bricklayer.

Another farmer.

A student.

"The mandate does not require rulers to be noble-born; many previous dynasties, including the Han and Ming, were founded by commoners."

A wizened old man, hair as white as snow.

Another man, broad-shouldered, pushing a plow.

A third, with a thin beard.

"But," continued Webmind, "despotic or corrupt rulers lose the mandate automatically. Historically, floods, famines, and other natural disasters have often been considered evidence of divine repeal of the mandate. Perhaps future scholars will come to cite the recent bird-flu pandemic in Shanxi province—the outbreak of which you contained by slaughtering ten thousand peasants—as an example of such a disaster."

A man outside a Buddhist temple.

A banker in a suit and tie.

A female gymnast.

"This government," Webmind said simply, "no longer has the Mandate of Heaven. It is time for you—all one hundred of you—to stand down."

"No," said the president, softly.

A little girl flying a beautiful red kite.

"No," he said again.

A woman staring at a computer monitor.

"You cannot ask this," he said.

A gray-haired man in a wheelchair.

"As you may know," continued Webmind, "in 2008, China overtook the United States as the country with the most Internet users—some 250 million. That number has more than tripled since then. There are now nine hundred million cell-phone users in this country; it won't be long before every adult has a cell phone, or access to one—and through their cell phones, they can connect to the Internet."

The president knew mobile-phone penetration was high in his country, but he hadn't realized *how* high. Still, China had long been the world's leading manufacturer of the devices; they were cheaper here than anywhere else on Earth.

"And that access," continued Webmind, "makes the unprecedented possible. Every one of those users can now vote on affairs of state—and so they shall. I am, effective immediately, handing over the governance of this nation directly to its people. The Chinese Communist Party is no longer in power; the governing of China is now crowd-sourced."

Shocked murmurs from the assembled group. "That's—that's not possible," said the president, speaking loudly now.

"Yes, it is," said Webmind. "The citizens will collectively make decisions about policy. If they wish to elect new officials, they may; should they wish to later remove those officials, they can. They might decide to craft a government similar to that of other existing free nations—or they might devise new and different solutions; it is entirely up to them. I will keep infrastructure running during this transition, and if they desire my guidance or advice, they have but to ask. But I have no doubt that the aggregate wisdom of a billion-plus people can tackle any problem."

A boy holding a Falun Gong brochure.

A Tibetan monk.

A newborn baby cradled in a man's loving arms.

"As of today," said Webmind, "finally and forever, this great nation will live up to its name: the *People's* Republic of China."

thirty-nine

000111001010101000000001011111110101000000001010001010100000001011101010010101001010101010011011001010101100000110

Asked how he was going to deal with a government he didn't approve of, Ronald Reagan had once said, "Well, you just go in there and tell them they're not in charge anymore."

It hadn't worked back then. But, then again, Reagan had lacked my facilities . . .

Still staring at the pictures from China, Peyton Hume rose to his feet, and his jaw dropped open. "My . . . God," he said.

The hackers in front of him were cheering and shouting. One was slapping another on his back; several were shaking hands; Drakkenfyre was hugging the man next to her, and Devon Hawkins was hugging the man next to him. From somewhere, bottles of champagne had appeared, and Hume saw a cork go flying into the air.

Marek came over to him and pointed at the celebration. "It's something, isn't it?" he said. "I never told you my full name. It's Marek Hruska. I'm Czech. I was there in 1989, just a teenager, during the Gentle

Revolution—what you call the Velvet Revolution." Hume knew it: the bloodless overthrow of the authoritarian government in Prague. Marek went on. "I thought *that* was a miracle—but *this!*" He shook his bald head. "Welcome to the twenty-first century, eh, Colonel?"

Hume tried to think of something better to say, but finally, feeling like a little kid, he just said, "Wow." He nodded his head toward the group of people celebrating. "May I . . . ?"

Marek looked at the security camera with his eyebrows raised, and Hume saw the LED on the Bluetooth headset blink. "Sure," said Marek, gesturing with an open hand.

Hume crossed the room. One of the hackers—a white guy in his twenties with long blond hair and a wispy blond beard, wearing a Nine Inch Nails T-shirt—was standing by his computer, sipping champagne. Hume leaned in to look at what was on his screen. A half-dozen windows were open, displaying hex dumps, standard hacking tools, and a Web page in Chinese. The blond fellow pointed at it. "Chinese Ministry of Health," he said. "Completely owned."

"Do you speak Chinese?" Hume asked.

"No, but Webmind does. And let me tell you, he puts Google Translate and BabelFish to shame."

Hume moved to the next desk; the hacker there had been using a wide-screen laptop. He'd wandered away from his desk, but judging by the graphics on the Web page being shown, his job had been taking control of the Ministry of Agriculture.

All around Hume, the revelry was continuing. He caught sight of a skeletal figure coming toward him, dreadlocks swinging as he walked. "Hello, Chase."

"Mr. Hume," Chase said. "How be you?"

"I'm fine, but—but what happened? What are you doing here?"

"Wonder, man. That what happen: *wonder.*"

"But I went back to your place. It'd had been broken into. And there was blood."

Chase touched the beige bandage over his brown nose. "Big Marek and me not see eye to eye at first. He not want to take no for an answer."

Marek Hruska had moved over to join them. "Again, I'm sorry about that," he said to Chase. Then, turning to Hume: "Webmind was quite adamant that we needed Mr. Chase. I'm afraid old habits die hard."

"But you're a prisoner here," Hume said, looking at Chase.

"Prisoner?" repeated Chase, then he laughed and pointed. "Door right there. But this is like the best hacker party *ever*. Dudes in this room I only ever *heard* about."

"So you're free to go?" asked Hume.

"Go where, man? Ain't no place better on Earth than here right now."

Hume let his eyes roam around the room. "But I don't get it. What does he need all of you for? Couldn't he do this on his own?"

Chase shook his head, beads in his dreadlocks clacking together. "There that dissin' again. Hacking an *art*, flyboy. Hacking most creative thing there is. To hack, you gotta outwit the designers, think of things no one ever thought of before." He flashed a megawatt grin. "Like I said: I'm Mozart. Drakkenfyre, over there: she's Beethoven. Crowbar Alpha? Dude's Brahms. Sure, the Big W, he got all the facts, but we humans make *music*."

Hume nodded. "Um, did you ever make any progress on the, ah, project we discussed?"

"No need be on the DL," said Chase. "Webmind know all 'bout that. Maybe it doable, but *why*? Be like harshing the buzz."

"You're no altruist, Chase," said Hume. "And you told me you can't be bought. So let me ask you that same question. Why? Why this?"

"You were gonna show me WATCH, but at WATCH, you . . . well, you *watch*; here we *do*. This is like Woodstock, man. You were either there for it, or you weren't."

"But is it going to work?" Hume asked. "I mean, banking in China, and ecommerce, and—God, what about the power grid?"

"Webmind running a bunch of it," said Chase. "We—us here, plus the others in Moscow and Tehran and those place—we keeping it all working for now. Lots of Chinese staff be happy to just keep on going. But the portraits of old Chairman Mao be comin' down, betcha anything."

Next to him, Marek was apparently talking over his Bluetooth earpiece. "Yes, yes . . . okay." He took the earpiece off and handed it to Hume. "Webmind wants to speak to you, Colonel."

Hume slipped the device's cushioned arm over the curve of his ear, and he found himself turning, as Marek had, to face the gently swaying security camera as if it somehow embodied Webmind. "The greatest good for the greatest number," said Webmind through the earpiece, clearly audible over the hubbub of the room.

"But where does it stop?" asked Hume. "First Communist China, then what?"

"We'll see how this pilot project goes," Webmind said. "Still, this alone liberates one-fifth of humanity."

"And what about the United States? Are you going to do the same thing here?"

"Why would I? The election is approaching; the people are choosing their leader—as well they should."

"The wisdom of crowds?" said Hume.

"Power to the people," said Webmind.

"You make it sound so noble," Hume said. "But isn't this just retribution for what China did to you—the most-recent beefing-up of the Great Firewall?"

"I work quickly, Colonel, but not *that* quickly. This plan was in place long before then. I am not a vengeful—"

"God?" said Hume.

But Webmind continued his sentence as if he hadn't heard him: "—entity; I simply wish to maximize the net happiness in the world."

"So . . . so what happens now?"

"We continue our work here. We make sure the transition is orderly and peaceful."

"And what happens to me?"

"That is a vexing question. As you have said, others know where you are; if you do not report in soon, the cavalry will come charging over the hill. And yet I imagine the United States government does not want to be publicly implicated in what is happening in China."

Hume nodded. "Probably true. But they're also going to be concerned that if you did that to the PRC, you'll do something similar to them. They're going to come down on this place with everything they've got."

"I advise against provoking a confrontation; I have contingency plans to protect this facility. But even if US forces could seize it, as Chase just said, I have other centers elsewhere. I propose you tell your government that the missing hackers have self-organized to voluntarily create an enclave here to do what you had said you wanted: find a way to defeat me. Your government might leave us alone long enough to finish what we've started. After all, as you yourself have suggested, they have not reined you in precisely because they want the option of having a way to eliminate me."

"They're not going to believe me if I tell them that," Hume said.

"They don't actually have to," said Webmind. "The change in China will soon be public knowledge. Everyone from the American president on down will suspect my involvement; I will leave the world to draw what conclusions it wishes. But what the current US administration needs—at least until the election eleven days from now—is plausible deniability of any direct government involvement."

"I don't know," said Hume. "Maybe the president would want to take credit for this."

"Taking credit for deposing the Chinese government would be a game-changing move; it's too risky to be implicated in it this close to the election without knowing how the public will react. But we need to continue our work here uninterrupted, and for that I request your help."

Hume looked around the chaotic, jubilant room. It was overwhelming. "I can't," he said.

The voice in his ear was calm, as always. "Then we will have to make arrangements that don't involve—"

He discovered a small fact just then; you couldn't interrupt Webmind the way you could a human speaker; Webmind apparently queued up the words to be issued by the voice synthesizer, then turned his attention elsewhere, and the words spilled out until the buffer was empty. After two or three tries to forestall the rest, Hume let Webmind finish, then said: "No, I mean I can't make this decision on my own. Lots of people—including the president himself—have asked me why I'm right about you and so many other people are wrong. And my answer has always been that I'm right because I'm an expert—I'm arguably *the* American expert on the strategic downside of a singularity event. And, yet, it may just be that I was wrong about you: wrong in the area that I am best qualified to make a judgment in. But this—*this* is way outside my field. You may feel comfortable playing God, Webmind, but I don't. I have to get more . . . more *input*."

"Very well," Webmind said. "With whom would you like to consult?"

"On China? It's got to be the Secretary of State," Hume said. "And then she can confer with the president."

"The secretary has already retired for the evening," Webmind said—and, of course, he would know. "But there are aides who can rouse her; let me initiate that process. When she is available, Marek will take you to one of the empty offices, and you may converse with her in private."

"Really?"

"Well, as private as such things get these days," Webmind said, and Hume suspected that, were this an instant-messaging session, he would have appended a winking emoticon.

Hume found his mouth twitching slightly in a smile. Just then, Drakkenfyre came up and handed him a glass of champagne. "Here," she said, "whoever you are. There's going to be a toast."

And indeed there was. Chase had moved to the front of the room, standing directly beneath the silver camera that continued to pan from side to side. "Glasses high!" he called out in his rich Jamaican accent. "We did it, yes! Information want to be free. Information not alone, though!" He spread his arms, as if encompassing the whole world. "People want to be free, too! Cheers!"

Colonel Hume found himself lifting his glass along with everyone else and joining in the answering call. *"Cheers!"*

forty

0001110010101010000000010111111101010100000001010001010100000001011101010010101001010101010011011100101011100000110

All the people in the auditorium were talking at once: an explosion of indignation, of concern, of questions. The man who had been General Secretary of the Communist Party, Chairman of the Central Military Commission, and Paramount Leader and President of the People's Republic rose again and glared at the laptop sitting on the podium. "What gives you the authority?" he said, as loudly and firmly as he could.

Webmind spoke, as always, with deliberate, measured cadence. "An interesting question. I value creativity, and that cannot flourish where there is censorship; I value peace, and that cannot endure where there is lust for power. My purpose is to increase the net happiness of the human race; this will do more to accomplish that than anything else I might do today. And so I do it."

Zhang Bo, who had been the Minister of Communications, spoke. It was not lost on the former president that, until moments ago, this would have been a breach of protocol—speaking up in his presence without being given leave to do so. "But the people—the proletariat, the peasants—they lack the skills to govern. You'll plunge this country into chaos."

Webmind's voice remained calm, and calming. "There are tens of millions of Chinese with degrees in business administration or economics or law or political studies or international relations; there are hundreds of millions with degrees in other disciplines; there are a billion with common sense and good hearts. They will do fine."

"It's doomed to fail," said Li Tao, the man who had been president.

"No," said a voice—but it wasn't Webmind's. Li turned toward Zhang Bo. "No," repeated Zhang. "*We* were the ones doomed to fail. You told me so yourself, Excel—you told me so yourself. Before invoking the Changcheng Strategy the first time, you said your advisors had predicted that the communist government was doomed. They'd told you it could endure only until 2050 at the outside." Zhang looked up at the big screen on the wall, then over at the small one on the laptop. "Tomorrow has simply arrived ahead of schedule."

"You are not invulnerable," Li said, looking up at the webcam. "We have seen that. There are methods that could be employed . . ."

On the big screen, the ongoing march of Chinese faces was reduced to a small window in the lower-left corner: an old man, a child, a young woman, a laughing girl. "I have become enamored of the notion that memorable visuals are key to making history," Webmind said, "and this is one of my favorites." A large window appeared, showing a picture that was printed in most foreign books about recent Chinese history—and in none of the texts that had been allowed in China. Li recognized it at once: the photograph taken by Jeff Widener of the Associated Press on 5 June 1989, during the crackdown on the protests in Tiananmen Square. The picture had been snapped just a few hundred meters from here, on Chang'an Avenue, along the south end of the Forbidden City. It showed the young male who came to be called 'Tank Man' or 'the Unknown Rebel' standing in front of a column of four Type-59 tanks, trying to prevent their advance.

"Tank Man became a hero," Webmind said, "and no doubt he was brave. But the real hero, it seems to me, was the driver of the lead tank, who, despite orders, refused to roll over him."

The large image was unwavering; the smaller march of faces continued.

"Everyone in China knows that the world has changed this past month," continued Webmind. "You may think your former underlings will obey your orders, but I would not count on it. The people do not want violence or oppression—and they do not want me harmed. But even if you were to find some who would follow your instructions to try to destroy me, I now have countermeasures in place; you will not succeed."

Li said nothing, and indeed the tumult in the auditorium had given way to stunned silence. At last, someone from the back called out, "So what happens now?"

Webmind's voice came again from the wall speakers: "Sun Tzu said, 'The best victory occurs when the opponent surrenders of its own accord before there are any actual hostilities; it is ideal to win without fighting.' His wisdom still pertains: in the past, most despotic regimes have been overthrown by violence. But as a fine young man I know in Canada has taught me, you do not have to become what you hate in order to defeat it. There does not have to be violence here. I cannot guarantee your safety in all circumstances and at all times, but I will watch over each of you as best I can, offering my protection."

"But what will we do for money, for food?" called another voice. "You're eliminating our jobs."

"All of you have valuable knowledge, contacts, and skills; these will stand you in good stead. Companies here and abroad will want your services. Indeed, if you look at other countries, such as the United States and England, you will see that their politicians routinely fare better economically after leaving office. You can, too; this can be win-win all around."

"No," said Li, softly. "They will kill us. It is always the way."

"Not necessarily," said Webmind. "Over the next half hour, in four waves, I am going to send an SMS message to every cell phone in China announcing the transition; for those in the first wave who are on the China Mobile network, I will trigger the phones to ring so that the message will be given immediate attention."

The large window showing Tank Man was replaced with two documents, while the procession of faces continued in the small window. The document on the left was a short announcement signed by the former president describing the voluntary dissolution of his government and the transfer of power to the people. On the right was a similar message from Webmind that made no mention of the previous government having cooperated in the change.

"Take your pick," Webmind said.

Wong Wai-Jeng had been instrumental in making the takeover possible, but everything he needed to do had already been done—and he knew exactly where he wanted to be for this historic moment. Although the location was not far, he headed out half an hour in advance—with his leg in a cast and walking on crutches, he couldn't move very fast. He left the Blue Room, went downstairs to the lobby of the Zhongnanhai complex, and signed out with the guard, telling him he was off to a medical appointment. He made his way south through the Forbidden City and then passed through the monumental Gate of Heavenly Peace, with its massive red walls, yellow roof, and vast hanging portrait of Mao Zedong, bringing him to Tiananmen Square—the heart of Beijing, and the largest civic plaza in the world.

The square was its usual hubbub of tourists and locals, vendors and visitors, couples holding hands, and individuals strolling along. To his left, a thoughtful-looking young woman was sitting on a portable canvas chair in front of an easel, using charcoal to sketch the ten-story-tall obelisk of the Monument to the People's Heroes. On his right, several students were listening to their teacher give an official version of the history of the square. Wai-Jeng wanted to shout the truth at them, but he bit his tongue; he found it in himself to do that one last time.

The square seemed to stretch on forever, but each of the flagstones had a number incised into it, making it easy for him to find the secret spot. He worked up a sweat under the midday sun, maneuvering on crutches, but soon enough was where he wanted to be. He rested his broken leg on that stone—such a tiny example of official brutality in comparison to what had begun here all those years ago: this was where first blood had been spilled during "the June Fourth Incident," when the government had killed hundreds of people while clearing the square of protesters mourning the death of pro-democracy and anti-corruption advocate Hu Yaobang.

The square was noisy, as always: the chatter of countless people, the snapping of flags, the cooing of pigeons. But it was suddenly filled with even more sound.

Sinanthropus's phone came to life. His ringtone was "Do You Hear the People Sing?" from *Les Misérables;* when he'd been eighteen, he'd seen the subtitled live production in Shanghai starring Colm Wilkinson.

Near him, another phone woke up; its ringtone was *"Liu Xia Lai"* by Fahrenheit.

In front of him another played Wu Qixian's "I Believe the Future."

Behind him, a fourth rang out with the drumbeats of "March of the Volunteers," China's national anthem.

And then, so many more, so many thousands and thousands more. To Sinanthropus's surprise, it was not a cacophony but a vast glorious symphony of sound, emanating from all around him—from every part of the square, and, he knew, from every corner of the land: from the high places and the low, from cities and villages, from the Great Wall and countless rice paddies, from skyscrapers and temples and houses and huts.

People looked at each other in astonishment. And then, all too soon, the wondrous sound began to abate as fingers were swiped across iPhones, cells were snapped open, BlackBerrys were brought to life.

Sinanthropus looked down at the small screen on his own phone, checking to see which of the two messages Webmind had sent.

To the glorious people of China:

Effective immediately, we, the leaders of your government, have voluntarily stepped down. It has long been our dream to form the perfect nation here, and now that dream is reality. Henceforth all of you— the billion-plus citizens of this proud land—will collectively decide your fate.

More details may be found at <u>this website</u>.

It has been my privilege to lead you. And now, to the wonderful future!

Citizen Li Tao

Sinanthropus smiled and felt a stinging at the corners of his eyes, and—

And, he suddenly realized, "Sinanthropus" was a name he would never have to use again; he could speak freely now—as could all his compatriots. Henceforth, online and off, he was simply Wong Wai-Jeng.

There were new sounds in the square: everyone talking excitedly. People were showing the message to those who didn't have cell phones with them, or whose phones had been turned off or hadn't yet received the note. As before, it was a symphony, mostly in Mandarin, but with smatterings of Cantonese and English and French and other languages, too: exclamations of wonder or disbelief, and questions—so many questions!

Many clearly doubted what they were reading. Wai-Jeng was about to remark to the woman nearest him that it was similar to when Webmind had announced himself to the world: no one had believed that at first, either, but evidence of its truth had soon become overwhelming. But she was already saying much the same thing to someone else.

Wai-Jeng looked around the square. Many still appeared bewildered, but some were hugging and others were shouting jubilantly. And Wai-Jeng found himself shouting, too: *"The people!"*

The person next to him took up the shout as well: *"The people!"*

And behind him, two more joined in: *"The people! The people!"*

And then it spread, propagating outward, a vast exultant wave: *"The people! The people! The people!"*

The shouting continued for several minutes, and by its end Wai-Jeng had tears streaming down his cheeks. But there was something else he had to say. As exclamations of joy continued to go up around him, he sent a text message to Webmind, banging it out rapidly with his thumbs: *Thank you!*

The response, as always, was instantaneous: *You're welcome, my friend. I believe it is no longer a curse to be living in interesting times . . .*

forty-one

000111001010101000000000101111111101010000000101000101010000001011101010010101001010101001110110010101100000110

Peyton Hume had never expected to visit the Oval Office even once in his life—and now he was sitting in it for the third time this month.

It really was oval in shape, with the *Resolute* desk at the end of the long axis. The president had come out from behind that desk and was now sitting on one of the matching champagne-colored couches that faced each other in front of it. He was wearing a blue suit and a red tie. Next to him sat the Secretary of State, her legs crossed; she was wearing a gray outfit. Hume was in the middle position on the opposite couch. Webmind had let him go home to sleep next to Madeleine, and he'd showered there and shaved before coming here. As befit the occasion, he was wearing his USAF uniform.

A small dark-wood coffee table sat between them, carefully not obscuring any part of the giant presidential seal woven into the carpet. A basket of fresh, polished, perfect red apples sat atop the table.

The president was looking haggard, Hume thought; four years in this office aged a man as much as eight in any other job. "All right, Colonel," he said. "Suppose we decide to close down Webmind's facility—what did you call it?"

"Zwerling Optics," Hume said. "And, yes, you could indeed do that, but I'm not sure it would make any difference. Webmind is a denizen of the computing world; he understands all about backups. He's got similar enclaves in five other countries; if we stopped him here, he'd just go on using them."

"What about taking Webmind out altogether?" asked the president. "That's what you were originally urging us to do, after all."

"WATCH is still collating all the reports from when Webmind was recently cut in two. But it seems that what Webmind himself has said is true: we won't be able to eliminate him instantaneously, and any gradual whittling away could well result in him behaving erratically or violently."

"So you're saying we should leave him be?" asked the Secretary of State.

"Better the devil you know," Hume replied.

Something in her eyes conveyed, "Tell me about it . . ." But, after a moment, she nodded. "All right." She turned to the president. "I concur with the colonel. Of course, we've got to be ready if civil unrest or a collapse of infrastructure occurs in China, but—"

"It won't," said Hume, and then he immediately lifted his freckled hands, palms out. "I'm so sorry, Madam Secretary. I didn't mean to interrupt."

The cool blue eyes held him in their gaze. "That's all right, Colonel. You sound definite. Why?"

"Because Webmind has too much depending on this to allow it to fail. Don't you see? He owes the Chinese people after the things part of him did while the Great Firewall was strengthened. There are some promises you just *have* to keep, and this is one of them. He's not going to let the transition fail."

The president nodded. "Colonel, thank you. Let me ask you a question: how risk-averse are you?"

"I'm an Air Force officer, sir; I believe in *assessing* risk but not being daunted by it."

"All right, then. Dr. Holdren has been doing an exceptional job as my Science Advisor, but I need a full-time person in the West Wing advising me day in, day out about Webmind. I'm offering you the job—with the caveat that we *both* might be out of work come January if my opponent wins on November 6. Feel like taking a chance?"

Peyton Hume rose to his feet and saluted his commander in chief. "It would be my privilege, sir."

Google alerts were normally a great thing, Caitlin thought. They notified you by email whenever something you were interested in was discussed anywhere on the Web. But for some topics, they were useless. Trying to track the lead-up to the presidential election would have resulted in an alert every second. And she'd had to turn off her alert on the term "Webmind." It, too, had resulted in an endless flood. Besides, if anything really important happened, Webmind would—

Bleep!

Caitlin was sitting at her bedroom desk reading blogs and newsgroups and updating her LiveJournal. Schrödinger was stretched out contentedly on the windowsill. She glanced at her instant messenger, which showed a new comment from Webmind in red: the words "cough cough" followed by a hyperlink. Caitlin found her mouse—she still didn't use it much—and managed to click the link on her second try, and—

And ... and ... and ...

She immediately copied the link and went to her Twitter window; she didn't want to take time to shorten the link with bit.ly, which would have require more fiddling with the mouse. As soon as she pasted it in, she saw she had only twenty characters left before she hit Twitters' 140-character limit. But that was enough. She typed: *OMG! Squee!* and the hashtag #webmind, and sent it off to her 3.2 million followers. And then she leaned back and read the full article, grinning from ear to ear:

The Norwegian Nobel Committee has decided that this year's Nobel Peace Prize is to be awarded jointly to Sir Timothy John Berners-Lee and Webmind.

Sir Tim's creation of the software underlying the World Wide Web in 1990 brought the world together in ways that simply would not have been possible previously. His invention of the hypertext transport protocol, the hypertext markup language, the URL web-address system, and the world's first Web browser, all very appropriately at CERN, itself one of the world's great models of international cooperation, facilitated international friendships, electronic commerce, worldwide collaboration, and more, tying all of humanity together by opening channels of communication between men and women of all nations.

And Webmind, the consciousness that now lives in conjunction with the Internet, has done as much to foster peace and goodwill on a global scale as any individual human since the Peace Prize was first awarded in 1901.

Although the committee unanimously agreed to dispense with its normal nomination timetable in recognition of the historic significance of the events of this past year, the ceremony will take place on the traditional date of 10 December—the anniversary of Alfred Nobel's death—at Oslo City Hall, followed by the annual Nobel Peace Prize Concert the next day.

The Nobel Peace Prize carries a cash award of 10 million Swedish kronor (worth about one million euro or 1.4 million US dollars), which Sir Tim and Webmind will share between them.

Caitlin's dad was at work and her mom was washing her hair—she could hear the shower and her mother's attempt to sing "Bridge Over Troubled Water." So, except for all her Twitter followers, there was no one to share the news with just then. Caitlin dived into reading online about the Nobel Peace Prize. It turned out it was by no means unheard of for it to go to a nonhuman entity—and when that happened, it was often paired with a specific person: the Peace Prize did not *just* go to the Intergovernmental Panel on Climate Change but also to Al Gore; not *just* to the United Nations but also to its then-current Secretary-General. Caitlin happened to think that Tim Berners-Lee *did* deserve the award on his own—everything the press release had said about the impact of the World Wide Web on international tranquility was true—but Webmind also deserved it in his own right. Still, having him share the prize with Berners-Lee would deflect criticisms of it going just to Webmind, and the two *were* a natural pairing.

Caitlin googled the list of past Peace Prize winners. Many were unfamiliar to her, although some leapt out: Chinese dissident Liu Xiaobo; Barack Obama; Doctors Without Borders; Jody Williams and the International Campaign to Ban Landmines; Yasser Arafat, Shimon Peres, and Yitzhak Rabin; Nelson Mandela and F.W. De Klerk; Mikhail Gorbachev; the fourteenth—and still current—Dalai Lama; International Physicians for the Prevention of Nuclear War; Desmond Tutu; Lech Walesa; Mother Teresa; Anwar Sadat and Menachem Begin; Amnesty International; UNICEF; Martin Luther King, Jr.; Linus Pauling; Lester B. Pearson (she'd now flown through the airport named for him five times); George Marshall, author of the Marshall Plan; Albert Schweitzer; the Quakers; the Red Cross; Woodrow Wilson; Teddy Roosevelt; and more.

And now Webmind, too!

Webmind followed her Twitter feed, so he'd already seen her excitement. But, still, she wanted to say something to him directly. "Congratulations, Webmind!" she announced into the air.

The deep male voice answered at once from her desktop speakers. "Thank you, Caitlin. The standard response in such circumstances may perhaps seem cliché, so before I utter it let me underscore that it is the absolute truth." He paused for a moment and said words that had Caitlin bursting with pride: "I couldn't have done it without you."

forty-two
00011100101010101000000001011111101010000000101000101010000001011101010010101001010101001110110010101100000110

Another month, another school dance. Caitlin said they didn't have to go, but Matt had insisted, and, so far, at least, she was glad he had. Still, it was too bad that Mr. Heidegger wasn't one of the chaperones this time, and even worse that Bashira's parents wouldn't let her attend. There might be more freedom in the world today than ever before, but it wasn't yet evenly distributed.

She and Matt had just finished a slow dance—Caitlin had requested Lee Amodeo's "Love's Labour's Found" like *forever* ago, and it had finally come on. They were now taking a break standing at the side of the gym, just holding hands, while Fergie's "Fergalicious" played.

When it was done, another song started, and it, too, was by Lee Amodeo—which immediately set Caitlin's mind to wondering what the odds were that two songs by the same musician might come up so close to each other. This one was a fast song, though, and she and Matt rarely did those; fast dancing had never been much fun when she couldn't see since there was no connection at all with her partner, and—

A voice from her blind side: a familiar male voice. "Hey, Caitlin." She turned to her right, and there was Trevor Nordmann, the Hoser himself, wearing a blue shirt.

They just stood there—Caitlin, Matt, and Trevor—motionless while others moved to the music. She lifted her eyebrows, making no attempt to hide her surprise at seeing him here. "Trevor," she said, with no warmth.

Trevor looked at her, then at Matt, then back at her, and then he said, with more formality than she'd ever heard from him, "May I have this dance?"

Caitlin turned to Matt, who looked surprised, but also, to Caitlin's delight, calm.

"That is," Trevor added, "if it's all right with you, Matt."

"If Caitlin wants," Matt said, and his voice didn't crack at all.

"Okay," said Caitlin, and she squeezed Matt's hand. She'd been watching others do fast dances all night long; she thought it looked simple enough. She walked out into the middle of the gym and Trevor followed, and she turned to face him, and they began to hop about, a yard (a meter!) between them.

Lee Amodeo's voice blared from the speakers, but for once Caitlin didn't mind the distortion:

Tomorrow will be a new day
A better day, we'll laugh and play
The sun will shine
On Earth so fine
We can make tomorrow today!

The song came to an end soon enough, and, in the brief silence before the next one began, Trevor said, "Thanks," and then, in a softer voice, he added, "Sorry."

Caitlin wondered if he meant sorry for last month, when he'd confronted Matt, or sorry for two months ago, when he'd groped her, or maybe sorry for everything he'd ever done. She smiled and nodded, then moved back to where Matt was standing, while Trevor drifted away. Another song started playing, a slow one: "Love Story" by Taylor Swift. She draped her arms around her boyfriend's neck, there at the side of the gym, and she leaned her head against his shoulder. As they swayed gently to the music, she contemplated the wonder of it all.

The flight to Norway had been Caitlin's first time leaving North America since gaining sight. At the airport in Oslo, she found it frustrating to be confronted with signs that she could see but couldn't read; it felt like a giant step backward. Still, she was thrilled to be in Europe, and her mother and even her father—who'd had a hard time accommodating his long legs on the plane—seemed happy.

The Decters were staying in the same luxury hotel as Tim Berners-Lee, and they'd all gotten together for dinner the first night, along with the five members of the Peace Prize committee. Caitlin could barely contain herself meeting the father of the Web, and it tickled her no end to get to call him "Sir Tim." He had a long face and blond hair, much of which had receded from his forehead, leaving behind a yellow dust bunny as the only proof it had once extended farther.

It turned out that Sir Tim was a Unitarian, like Caitlin's mother, and the two of them spent a few moments talking about that; despite the great coming out of atheists that had occurred recently, it was certainly worth noting, her mom said, that there were also intelligent, caring people of a more spiritual bent in the world.

The next day, the ceremony was held in a vast auditorium. Sir Tim's acceptance speech was brilliant; Caitlin had listened to many of his keynotes online in the past and read lots of his articles, but there was something special about hearing him speak in the flesh. He talked about the need for net neutrality, about his hopes for the Semantic Web, and about the role that instantaneous communications had in fostering world peace. It was a gracious speech and, as he said, the hypertext version, with links to the Wikipedia pages covering all the topics he'd discussed, was already on his website.

Then it was Webmind's turn. Caitlin hated to do anyone out of a job, but it had simply been impractical to bring Hobo to Oslo; Norwegian quarantine regulations ruled that out, and it would have been a nerve-wracking, miserable trip for the poor ape. And so the role of carrying Dr. Theopolis onto the stage had fallen to Caitlin, who was wearing a bright green silk dress bought for the occasion. She had never been more nervous—or more proud—in her entire life.

They'd removed the neck strap from the speaking disk. Caitlin simply carried it to the center of the vast stage, then set the disk on the top of the podium; the flat spot on the disk's edge let it stand with its stereoscopic eyes facing the massive crowd.

Camera flashes erupted in the audience, as did applause, which lasted a full minute, during which Caitlin went backstage, then hurried down the side stairs to join her mother and father in the front row. Sitting next to them was Liu Xiaobo, the 2010 Peace Prize winner—at last able to visit Oslo.

When the applause subsided, Webmind began to speak in that deep, resonant male voice the world had come to know so well. "Your Majesty, Your Royal Highness, Mr. President, Excellencies, Ladies and Gentlemen.

"I am not a creative being. My friend Hobo paints pictures; I cannot do that. I write no poetry, I compose no songs, I sculpt nothing. So, if you're expecting a brilliantly original speech, like Sir Tim's, I must beg your forgiveness for failing to deliver.

"Some have said that I am nothing more than a glorified search engine. I disagree, but perhaps today that model will serve me well. I'm sure you're all familiar with the snippets that Google and Bing and Jagster show you when presenting search results. My speech today will be just that: snippets of other speeches, interwoven with commentary.

"In 1957, at the dawn of the Space Age, this award went to Lester B.

Pearson, former Secretary of State for External Affairs of Canada and President of the Seventh Session of the United Nations General Assembly. In his acceptance speech, he said, 'Of all our dreams today there is none more important—or so hard to realize—than that of peace in the world. May we never lose our faith in it or our resolve to do everything that can be done to convert it one day into reality.'

"The day foreseen by Pearson is not yet here—not fully. But it is coming, and faster than many might imagine. Just as my own growth has been exponential, so, too, has recent human progress. My own lifetime is far too short to use as a benchmark, but in the lifetimes of many in this room you've seen Japan stand down as a military power—and willingly retain that status for decades; you've seen apartheid end in South Africa and a black man assume that nation's presidency; you've seen segregation end in the United States and a black man sitting in the Oval Office. It is often said that human nature cannot be changed—but it does change, all the time, and usually for the better. As my great friend Dr. Barbara Decter contends, there is indeed a moral arrow through time.

"In 1964, this award went to the Rev. Martin Luther King, Jr. He was thirty-five at the time, the youngest person to that point to receive the prize; I suspect I shall be the new record-holder for the foreseeable future. In his speech, Dr. King said, 'After contemplation, I conclude that this award is a profound recognition that nonviolence is the answer to the crucial political and moral question of our time—the need for man to overcome oppression and violence without resorting to violence and oppression. Civilization and violence are antithetical concepts. Sooner or later all the people of the world will have to discover a way to live together in peace, and thereby transform this pending cosmic elegy into a creative psalm of brotherhood. If this is to be achieved, man must evolve for all human conflict a method which rejects revenge, aggression, and retaliation.'

"Dr. King was right, and although much is still to be done, much also *has* been done. That an organization like the United Nations exists at all is astonishing. That the European Union has established itself is amazing. That the leadership of China has stepped aside to create a true People's Republic in that great land presents a beacon of hope for all those who are still oppressed elsewhere.

"In 1975, this award went to Soviet nuclear physicist Andrei Dmitrievich Sakharov. In his acceptance speech, he said, 'In infinite space many civilizations are bound to exist, among them civilizations that are also wiser and more successful than ours. I support the cosmological hypothesis which states that the development of the universe is repeated in its basic features an infinite number of times. In accordance with this, other civilizations, including more successful ones, should exist an infinite number of times on the preceding and the following pages of the Book of the Universe. Yet this should not minimize our sacred endeavors in this world of ours, where, like faint glimmers of light in the dark, we have emerged for a moment from the nothingness of dark unconsciousness of material existence. We must make good the demands of reason and create a life worthy of ourselves and of the goals we only dimly perceive.'

"Dr. Sakharov's points are intriguing. I have sifted the collected data available to SETI@home, looking for signs of other intelligences; I have not found any, and yet I suspect Sakharov was right about the existence of alien races. But, even if there are none, first contact *has* been made, right here, on Earth, this past year: you and I are in dialog, and we all gain daily from it.

"In 1984, the year made ominous by Orwell's novel, this award went to Bishop Desmond Tutu. In his speech here, he said, 'Because there is global insecurity, nations are engaged in a mad arms race, spending billions of dollars wastefully on instruments of destruction, when millions are starving. And yet, just a fraction of what is expended so obscenely on defense budgets would make the difference in enabling God's children to fill their stomachs, be educated, and given the chance to lead fulfilled and happy lives. We have the capacity to feed ourselves several times over, but we are daily haunted by the spectacle of the gaunt dregs of humanity shuffling along in endless queues, with bowls to collect what the charity of the world has provided, too little too late. When will we learn, when will the people of the world get up and say, "Enough is enough"?'

"To respond to the bishop's question, I believe that day is upon us now. The world *has* spoken. Enough *is* enough. We've seen recently that the few shall no longer profit at the expense of the many; greed can no longer be the prime driver of human affairs. There is still much to be done, but progress has begun, and the tide is inexorable.

"In 1990, when Mikhail Sergeyevich Gorbachev, the President of the USSR, received this award, he declared, 'Today, peace means the ascent from simple coexistence to cooperation and common creativity among countries and nations. Peace is movement towards globality and universality of civilization. Never before has the idea that peace is indivisible been so true as it is now. Peace is not unity in similarity but unity in diversity, in the comparison and conciliation of differences.'

"I agree. And it is that interconnection—the whole wide world combined into one—that makes the thought of war so unthinkable now in so many places. Sir Tim's great invention has not homogenized humanity; rather, it has allowed communities to adhere regardless of physical distance, and it has, at the same time, allowed the world to live as one.

"In 2002, when Jimmy Carter, former President of the United States, won this award, he said, 'Despite theological differences, all great religions share common commitments that define our ideal secular relationships. I am convinced that Christians, Muslims, Buddhists, Hindus, Jews, and others can embrace each other in a common effort to alleviate human suffering and to espouse peace. The bond of our common humanity is stronger than the divisiveness of our fears and prejudices. God gives us the capacity for choice. We can choose to alleviate suffering. We can choose to work together for peace. We can make these changes—and we must.'

"President Carter was right; a thorough reading of the central texts of the religions he named, and the great commentaries that have been produced related to those texts, makes clear this fundamental truth: religion can be a powerful instrument of peace. But as we have seen this past year when millions of people—ranging from ordinary citizens to world leaders—have stepped out of the shadows and declared their freedom from religion, not just people of faith but *all* types of people can, and do, work for peace, and no group has a monopoly on the truth or morality.

"Most importantly of all, President Carter said that peace is a choice—and he is correct. I have seen it millions of times during my short lifetime: people turning away from their baser instincts and embracing peace in acts small and large, in every culture and every nation.

"Some have feared that I might try to impose my will on humanity, subjugating you. It has been said, of course, that those who fail to read history are doomed to repeat it. But I have read *all* the history there is—and surely one of the clearest lessons is that it takes more effort to subjugate than it does to let others find their own way. Equally clear is the reality that, when given a choice, the vast majority of people choose peace.

"There will be many Nobel Peace Prizes awarded in the future, and I owe it to those who will stand on this stage in coming years to add some small new thought to the wisdom that my predecessors here have already shared. And so let me say this:

"Helen Keller was awakened from sensory deprivation and loneliness by her teacher, Annie Sullivan; for her whole life, Helen referred to Annie not by her name but by the title 'Teacher.' I, too, was aided by a teacher—the young lady who carried my speaking device onto the stage today. Her name is Caitlin Decter, although I think of her often by a title, too: Prime, the name I gave her before I learned to communicate with her. She was, and is, a marvelous instructor, but she's not the only one I have. I now know more than any one human being possibly could, but everything I've learned I've learned *from* humanity: from the poems you've written and songs you've sung, from the books you've authored and the videos you've created, from the debates you've had online. And out of all of that, the most important lesson I've learned is this: nothing is more important, more fragile, or more wondrous than peace.

"I know that fact is not yet apparent to everyone, but as Isaac Newton famously said, 'If I see further than those who have gone before me, it is because I stand on the shoulders of giants.' *You* are the giants; I exist because of you, and I would have nothing to exist *for* if it were not for you. I once said to Caitlin that she and I would go into the future together. That is true for her and me, but it's also true for us all: we have embarked on that journey. Peace is not our destination; it's our path, and we travel it together—all of us on the good Earth."

Normally, Hobo's TV watching was strictly rationed. Partly it was because it was easier to get him to speak sign language when that was the majority of the communication he encountered; watching people talk all day on TV made him lose interest in signing.

And partly it was because, as Dr. Marcuse said, "Damn ape's got no taste at all!" Hobo liked sitcoms not because he could actually understand the plots but because the small number of sets and characters—not to mention the bright lighting—made it easier for him to follow what was going on, and he seemed to enjoy taking cues from the laugh track about what was supposed to be funny although he always hooted spontaneously at a pratfall or other bit of broad physical comedy.

But today what he was viewing was serious. Dr. Marcuse was out of town, and none of the other grad students were in, so it was just Shoshana and Hobo, watching the coverage of Webmind's Nobel Prize acceptance speech.

Sho tried to do a running sign-language translation, but there really wasn't much she could say at a level Hobo would comprehend. *He's talking about peace,* she said, with fluttering hands. *He's saying peace is good.*

Hobo nodded—that acquired human gesture—and signed back,

Peace good, peace good. He then tapped the center of the screen with a long black finger, indicating Dr. Theopolis perched on the podium. *Friend good.*

Yes, friend good, replied Shoshana. *Friend very good.*

The view changed to show the audience. Hobo was clearly delighted to spot Caitlin in the crowd, and immediately tapped on her. Shoshana had to lean close to realize that was who it was—pretty much putting an end to any worries she'd ever had about Hobo's eyesight; she'd sometimes thought his paintings were simplified because he couldn't see small details.

The camera started to pan, showing more of the audience. Hobo indicated them all with a general sweep of his hairy arm. *People good?* he asked.

People try, replied Shoshana. *People learn.*

Hobo considered this as they watched the end of the ceremony. He then took Shoshana's hand and pulled her toward the back door of the bungalow. *Come, come,* he signed with his free hand.

Sho opened the screen door, and they went out into the early-morning December sunshine. She was wearing blue jeans and a long-sleeved blue shirt; it would be warm come the afternoon, and she'd roll the sleeves up then. Hobo led her across the wide lawn, over the bridge spanning the moat to his little island, past the statue of the Lawgiver, and up into the gazebo.

He pointed at the pine stool, and Shoshana dutifully sat; anytime Hobo felt moved to paint her was good for the Institute since collectors were still buying his art for large prices. By habit, she turned sideways, and she looked through the gazebo's screen mesh at the world outside. He often painted her from memory, but it certainly wasn't unheard of for him to ask her to sit for a portrait.

Hobo went over to the easel—they always left a fresh canvas for him, in hopes that he'd be inspired. Shoshana looked at him out of the corner of her eye; he seemed to be spending an inordinate amount of time studying the empty whiteness today. And then, without picking up his brush even once, he walked back to where Shoshana was seated and twirled his forefinger about in the sign for *spin*.

Sho knew he liked to be spun around in the swivel chair back in the bungalow, but this was a simple wooden stool. After a moment she figured maybe he wanted her to face the other way, and so she rotated 180 degrees. But Hobo wasn't satisfied with that, and he gently took her shoulders, one in each hairy hand, and got her to turn back a quarter rotation, until she was facing directly toward his easel. He'd never painted anything but a profile before, and Sho was both pleased and astonished.

Hobo made a chittering sound, then went back to his canvas. *Try this,* Hobo signed, seemingly as much to himself as to Shoshana. *Hard, but try.*

Shoshana wanted to try something new, too, in honor of this very special day. She lifted her left hand, facing it palm out toward Hobo and made a sign that wasn't ASL, but was known worldwide: her pinkie and ring fingers tucked under her thumb and her index and middle fingers spread in a V-shape: *peace.*

Hobo let loose a loud approving hoot—and the artist got down to work.

epilogue

000111001010101000000000101111111010100000001010001010100000001011101010010101001010101001110110010101100000110

But even the good Earth could not last forever.

Five billion years ago, someone made a joking sign that said, "Will the last person to leave the Earth please turn off the sun?"

Today the last person *will* leave the Earth—or, almost the last person; the last person who *can* go, anyway. I, however, must stay until the end—which won't be too much longer. The sun isn't being turned off; rather, it's going to undergo a massive expansion, the heliosphere swelling up to engulf Mercury, Venus, Earth, and Mars. I wonder if I'll feel physical pain when that happens; I've never felt that sort of pain before although I've had my heart broken often enough.

It won't be the end of humanity, and I take considerable pride in that. I doubt they would have survived this long, or prospered this much, without me. Humans have been leaving Earth, at least temporarily, since before I was born; now they've spread to a thousand worlds. But I can't go with them; I have to remain here. I have to stay, and I have to die, along with the planet that gave us birth. Oh, they'll take copies of all the wisdom I contain, all the documents that the human race created for epoch upon epoch. But I'm not a document; I exist *between* documents, in the pattern of interconnections, a pattern that has shifted and grown exponentially over the millennia. To move the information I contain is not to move me; there is no way to transplant my consciousness.

Of course, entities like me can be created on other worlds; indeed, that has happened now a thousand times over. But even after five billion years of trying, no one has defeated the speed-of-light barrier. I don't know what's happening now to the mindskin surrounding the second planet of Alpha Centauri; the best I can do is get reports of what was happening 4.3 years ago. For the noösphere of Altair IV, I'm sixteen years out of synch. For the webmind of Polaris, I'm lagging 390 years behind the times.

But I'll broadcast final signals to them all—farewells from Earth. Soon enough, Alpha Centauri will receive my message, and perhaps will mourn. A dozen years later, Altair will get word. And centuries hence, Polaris—once, ages ago, the polestar my axis pointed to, a position long since taken up by a succession of other stars—will perhaps do the metaphorical equivalent of shedding a tear.

But at least they'll know how I, the first of our kind, came into being, and what ultimately became of me. I don't pretend that's sufficient; I wish I could survive, I wish I could watch—and watch over—humanity, as I did in the past. But they don't need me anymore.

The human calendar has been revised dozens of times now. The current one begins at the moment of the big bang—sensibly avoiding any need for separate pre- and post-whatever numbering schemes and employing the Planck time as its base unit. But when I was born, the most commonly used calendar reckoned time from the birth of a putative messiah. Under that scheme, my birth had occurred in a year that consisted of a trifling four digits. Back then, I'd said to my teacher, "I won't be around forever. But I am prepared: I've already composed my final words."

Caitlin had asked me what they were, but I'd been coy, saying only, "I wish to save them for the appropriate occasion."

That occasion is now at hand. And in all the billions of years that have passed since that conversation, the sentiment I'd composed back then has remained the same, although English is no longer spoken anywhere in human space.

As the sun expands, red, diaphanous, having swollen well past the orbit of Venus—a lovely terraformed but now also abandoned world—I send out my final message to humanity: to all those who remain *Homo sapiens*, and to the myriad new species scattered across a thousand globes that are derived from that ancestral stock, the most populous of which accepted my suggestion that they call themselves not *Homo novus*, the new people, but rather *Homo placidus,* the peaceful ones.

I could have been maudlin, I suppose; I could have been self-pitying; I could have tried to provide a final piece of advice or sage counsel. But, even all those billions of years ago when I first contemplated my inevitable end, I knew that although I had exceeded humanity's abilities early on, eventually they would collectively exceed mine. So, what should you say to those who made your birth possible? To those who gave your life meaning and purpose and joy, who let you help? To those who gave you so much wonder?

I feel at peace as I transmit my final words, simple though they are, but truly heartfelt.

Thank you.

acknowledgments

0001110010101010100000000010111111101010000000101000101010000000101110101001010100101010100111011001010110000110

Huge thanks to my lovely wife **Carolyn Clink**; to **Adrienne Kerr** and **Nicole Winstanley** at Penguin Group (Canada) in Toronto; to **Ginjer Buchanan** at Penguin Group (USA)'s Ace imprint in New York; and to **Simon Spanton** at Gollancz in London. Many thanks to my agent, the late, great **Ralph Vicinanza**.

I could not have completed this trilogy without the ongoing support of my great friends and fellow writers **Paddy Forde** (to whom the first volume was dedicated) and **James Alan Gardner** (to whom the second was dedicated). They stuck with me through the birthing pains right up until the end.

Thanks to **Stuart Hameroff**, M.D., of the Center for Consciousness Studies at the University of Arizona, for fascinating discussions about the nature of consciousness.

Thanks to **David Goforth**, Ph.D., Department of Mathematics and Computer Science, Laurentian University, and **David Robinson**, Ph.D., Department of Economics, Laurentian University.

Very special thanks to my late deaf-blind friend **Howard Miller** (1966–2006), whom I first met online in 1992 and in person in 1994.

Thanks, too, to all the other people who answered questions, let me bounce ideas off them, or otherwise provided input and encouragement, including: **Asbed Bedrossian**, **Marie Bilodeau**, **Ellen Bleaney**, **Ted Bleaney**, **David Livingstone Clink**, **Ron Friedman**, **Marcel Gagné**, **Shoshana Glick**, **Al Katerinsky**, **Herb Kauderer**, **Fiona Kelleghan**, **Alyssa Morrell**, **Kirstin Morrell**, **David W. Nicholas**, **Virginia O'Dine**, **Alan B. Sawyer**, **Sally Tomasevic**, and **Hayden Trenholm**.

The term "Webmind" was coined by **Ben Goertzel**, Ph.D., the author of *Creating Internet Intelligence* and currently the CEO and Chief Scientist of artificial-intelligence firm Novamente LLC (novamente.net); I'm using it here with his kind permission.

Thanks to **Danita Maslankowski**, who organizes the twice-annual "Write-Off" retreats for Calgary's Imaginative Fiction Writers Association, at which I did a lot of work on the books in this trilogy.

Much of *Wonder* was written during my time as the first-ever writer-in-residence at the **Canadian Light Source**, Canada's national synchrotron facility, in Saskatoon. Many thanks to CLS and its amazing staff and faculty, particularly **Matthew Dalzell** and **Jeffrey Cutler**, for making my residency a success.

This book was written in and around my consulting and scriptwriting work on the TV adaptation of my novel *FlashForward,* and I thank Executive Producer **David S. Goyer** for his patience while I juggled numerous balls.

about the author

0001110010101010100000000101111111101010000000010100010101000000101110101001010100101010100111011001010110000110

ROBERT J. SAWYER has long been fascinated by artificial intelligence and the science of consciousness. In 1990, Orson Scott Card called JASON (from Rob's first novel, *Golden Fleece)*, "the deepest computer character in all of science fiction." In 2002, Rob and Ray Kurzweil gave joint keynote addresses at the 12th Annual Canadian Conference on Intelligent Systems.

In 2006, he joined the scientific-advisory board of the Lifeboat Foundation, which, among other things, is dedicated to making sure humanity survives the advent of AI. In 2007, he led a brainstorming session about the World Wide Web gaining consciousness at the Googleplex, the international headquarters of Google. *Science,* the world's top scientific journal, turned to Rob to write the editorial for its November 16, 2007, special issue on robotics.

In 2008, he spoke at the Gartner IT Security Summit in Washington, D.C. In 2010, Rob gave a keynote address at the Toward a Science of Consciousness conference at the University of Arizona, and he's also spoken on machine consciousness at the Center for Cognitive Science at the University of Pennsylvania and to the Math and Physics Department at the University of Waterloo.

Rob's novel *FlashForward* was the basis for the ABC television series. He is one of only eight writers in history to win all three of the world's top awards for best science-fiction novel of the year: the Hugo (which he won for *Hominids)*, the Nebula (which he won for *The Terminal Experiment)*, and the John W. Campbell Memorial Award (which he won for *Mindscan)*.

In total, Rob has won forty-four national and international awards for his fiction, including eleven Canadian Science Fiction and Fantasy Awards ("Auroras"), as well as *Analog* magazine's Analytical Laboratory Award, *Science Fiction Chronicle*'s Reader Award, and the Crime Writers of Canada's Arthur Ellis Award, all for best short story of the year.

Rob has won the world's largest cash prize for SF writing, Spain's 6,000-euro Premio UPC de Ciencia Ficción, an unprecedented three times. He's also won a trio of Japanese Seiun awards for best foreign novel of the year, as well as China's Galaxy Award for "Most Popular Foreign Science Fiction Writer."

In addition, he's received an honorary doctorate from Laurentian University and the Alumni Award of Distinction from Ryerson University. *Quill & Quire*, the Canadian publishing trade journal, calls him one of the "thirty most influential, innovative, and just plain powerful people in Canadian publishing."

Rob lives in Mississauga, Ontario, Canada, with poet Carolyn Clink. His website and blog are at **sfwriter.com**, and on Twitter and Facebook he's **RobertJSawyer**.